PraiS

★"A droll ... ...ders
breathless ... with laughter and anticipation."
—*Kirkus Reviews*, starred review

"Owen learns a lot about how to be a true friend and what
courage really is in this fast-paced, action-packed tale."
—*School Library Journal*

"A creative and adventurous romp, which will
especially please the fans of Riley's earlier series."
—*School Library Connection*

Praise for *THE STOLEN CHAPTERS*

"A fictional character's megalomaniacal scheme to insert
himself into every novel ever written precipitates a merry chase
through meta-realms in this brain-cracking sequel."
—*Kirkus Reviews*

"The twists and turns in this volume
are sure to keep readers coming back for more."
—*Booklist*

Praise for *SECRET ORIGINS*

"A literary hall of mirrors, with plenty of thrills
and laughs to keep 'nonfictionals' in the game."
—*Kirkus Reviews*

"Sure to entertain."
—*Booklist*

STORY THIEVES

WORLDS APART

JAMES RILEY

ALADDIN

NEW YORK LONDON TORONTO SYDNEY NEW DELHI

ALADDIN

An imprint of Simon & Schuster Children's Publishing Division
1230 Avenue of the Americas, New York, New York 10020
First Aladdin paperback edition March 2019
Text copyright © 2018 by James Riley
Cover illustration copyright © 2018 by Vivienne To
Also available in an Aladdin hardcover edition.
All rights reserved, including the right of reproduction in whole or in part in any form.
ALADDIN and related logo are registered trademarks of Simon & Schuster, Inc.
For information about special discounts for bulk purchases, please contact Simon & Schuster Special Sales at 1-866-506-1949 or business@simonandschuster.com.
The Simon & Schuster Speakers Bureau can bring authors to your live event.
For more information or to book an event contact the Simon & Schuster Speakers Bureau at 1-866-248-3049 or visit our website at www.simonspeakers.com.
Cover designed by Laura Lyn DiSiena
Interior designed by Tom Daly
The text of this book was set in Adobe Garamond.
Manufactured in the United States of America 0720 OFF
2 4 6 8 10 9 7 5 3
The Library of Congress has cataloged the hardcover edition as follows:
Names: Riley, James, 1977- author.
Title: Worlds apart / by James Riley.
Description: First Simon Pulse hardcover edition. | New York : Simon Pulse, 2018. |
Series: Story thieves ; [5]
Identifiers: LCCN 2017049435 (print) | LCCN 2017060324 (eBook) |
ISBN 9781481485760 (eBook) | ISBN 9781481485746 (hc)
Subjects: | CYAC: Books and reading—Fiction. | Characters in literature—Fiction. |
Adventure and adventurers—Fiction. | Magic—Fiction. | Imagination—Fiction. |
BISAC: JUVENILE FICTION / Action & Adventure / General. | JUVENILE FICTION /
Social Issues / Friendship. | JUVENILE FICTION / Humorous Stories. |
Classification: LCC PZ7.1.R55 (eBook) | LCC PZ7.1.R55 Wor 2018 (print) |
DDC [Fic]—dc23
LC record available at https://lccn.loc.gov/2017049435
ISBN 9781481485753 (pbk)

This one's for Liesa. It's not hyperbole to say she's the greatest editor—NAY, human being!—of our time.

CHAPTER 1

Owen sat patiently while the doctor rummaged through some files in a folder. Eventually the doctor pulled out a picture of a dog—a spotted dalmatian—and showed it to him. "Now close your eyes and try to picture this dog in your head," he instructed Owen.

Owen nodded. But once his eyes closed, he frowned, realizing he couldn't bring an image of the dog into his mind. It was like there was a complete blank. He could remember words describing the dog, like "dalmatian," "spotted," "tail," and "paws," but for whatever reason, he couldn't build an image using those words. He opened his eyes again, a bit confused, and stared harder at the photo. This shouldn't be that difficult. He could see it clearly, right there in front of him. This wasn't complicated.

Owen shut his eyes again, knowing he could do this . . . and came up blank.

"I can't picture it," he said, wondering why he didn't feel more frustrated.

"The technical term for what's happening to you is aphantasia," the doctor said. "You've lost the ability to visualize anything in your head. Basically, your imagination doesn't exist anymore. But don't let it worry you. I can't imagine it'll affect your life too much."

"That's odd," Owen's mother said, raising one eyebrow. "He's always had an active imagination. But ever since he disappeared for a few days and then turned up in London, he's been acting different."

"It's not just him," the doctor said. "I've seen it in people all over town, from kids to adults to the elderly. It happened to me, even." He showed Owen's mother the picture. "Most likely you, too."

As his mom went through the same test, Owen stared off into space, feeling strangely calm. Losing his imagination seemed like it *should* worry him. But it didn't really feel that bad, like the doctor said. So he couldn't picture a dog in his head. It wasn't like *that* came up too often. And really, what was he using his imagination for anyway? Wasting time in school? Making up things that didn't exist? Nothing important, in other words.

"I can't picture it either, you're right," his mother said, opening her eyes. "So is there a cure?"

"Cure?" the doctor said, blinking in confusion. "Of course not. This is just how things are now. I can't imagine us ever coming up with a fix."

"Well, as long as it's healthy and normal," his mother said, smiling at the doctor. "If Owen's okay, we should be going. My shift starts soon at the library."

The doctor wrinkled his nose. "Does anyone even come in anymore?"

"No, but we're bringing in more nonfiction," his mother said. "That's all anyone's been checking out lately anyway."

On the way to the library, Owen went over the assignments he would have turned in that day in school. Everything seemed correct to him, but he went over them a second time, just to be sure. Math was a subject to be taken very seriously, according to adults, and he trusted their judgment.

They arrived at the library a few minutes after Owen started his math assignment over, so he sadly placed his papers in the textbook, marking his spot. "Why don't you get your London punishment out of the way first?" his mother said. "That way you can enjoy your schoolwork as a reward."

That seemed logical. After Owen had spent a few days away from home, first in Jupiter City and then trapped with Kara Dox in a time prison, his mother had gone a bit insane, contacting every police station and hospital within four states. But as soon as Owen called her from London, she immediately calmed down and arranged for him to fly back.

He hadn't expected that, honestly, but now knowing that she had no imagination helped explain things: She literally couldn't imagine him ever returning while he was missing, so had completely lost it. But now that he was back, she couldn't picture him leaving again, so his punishment was more about the principle.

She did ask where he'd been, though, and he obviously told the truth: He'd been helping Bethany, who was half-fictional, find her missing father in a superhero comic, only to be thrown into a *Pick the Plot* book by a fictional man named Nobody, who had then separated the fictional and nonfictional worlds and sent Owen and Bethany back to the nonfictional world through the last open portal between their worlds, the one that led to Neverland. And since that portal connected to London, that's where they emerged.

She seemed a bit confused by some of the explanation,

but couldn't imagine any other way he could have gotten to London, so accepted his story. Logic dictated that he should be punished for his actions, so in spite of not being able to picture him ever repeating his crimes, she and Bethany's mother had agreed on a punishment: Bethany and Owen would help Owen's mother in her library every night for a year.

That didn't seem that bad to Owen, since that's what he did most nights anyway. And now he had an excuse to hang out with Bethany every evening, doing homework or quizzing each other on facts they could memorize. All in all, it was a pretty pleasant punishment.

What wasn't pleasant, though, was having to deal with the books at the library. As his mother had said, almost no one came in anymore, so Owen and Bethany ended up spending most of their time clearing fiction books off the shelves to make room for more nonfiction.

Not that Owen could blame them: Though he'd once spent most of his time reading, now whenever Owen tried to read his old favorite books, he couldn't picture the stories in his head. Without an imagination, he was just reading words, not seeing any characters or situations.

But like the doctor had said, was that really a bad thing?

Now he had so much more time for the nonfictional world, and for performing tasks that he was given to the best of his abilities. What better way to get ahead in life than that? Owen couldn't imagine anything.

And making room for nonfictional books in the library was easy enough. Spike, his fictional cat, sat in the empty spaces in the bookshelves, periodically jumping up to a higher one just to get a better look. Every so often Spike would meow, and Owen would pet him, which always made him miss his fictional friends for some reason, and he'd wonder what they were doing and where they were now. Were they fighting back against Nobody still? Or had they given up, since things weren't really that bad with the worlds separated?

Weirdly, he only seemed to think about them while petting Spike. That made sense, though, since Spike was fictional himself, and logically he'd remind Owen of other fictionals.

"Hey," said a voice from behind him as Owen scratched Spike's head. He turned around to find Bethany standing there with a worried look on her face as all thoughts of his fictional friends seemed to drain from his mind. "Are you okay? I felt so bad that you missed school today!"

"I'm fine," Owen said, shrugging. "Apparently something's

going around. I'll be there tomorrow and can catch up on anything I missed."

Bethany's face lit up as she dropped a bag of textbooks into his lap. "Oh, don't worry! I brought you everything we went over today. I can help you catch up right now." She beamed at him.

He returned her smile. "You're way too nice to me, you know that?"

"There's no such thing," she said, patting him on the shoulder. "You're my best friend. I'm just looking out for you. Besides, after everything the fictional me put you through, I owe you for years."

Owen nodded, not wanting to argue the point again. Ever since they'd returned, Bethany had decided that her fictional self had been the part of her that had caused all of her problems, from jumping her father into a book in the first place, to getting them kidnapped by Fowen—Owen's fictional self—to losing Owen to Nobody in Jupiter City. Owen didn't really see how that made sense, but arguing with her about it didn't seem to help, so he'd just let it go.

"That wasn't your fault, you know," he said. "I could have said no each time."

"I shouldn't have put you in that position. If I just hadn't given in to my fictional half over and over, none of it would have happened. It makes me so *angry* . . . !" She paused and took a deep breath, then slowly let it out. "Sorry, I need to stop blaming her. Every time I do, I try to remember Gwen, EarthGirl. *She* never thought one bad thing about me, no matter how many mistakes I made. Thinking of her helps remind me not to judge myself so harshly."

"She was pretty great," Owen agreed. "You know who I miss the most?"

Bethany shrugged. "I can't even imagine."

Owen started to say a name, then stopped. "It doesn't really matter. We should get back to work. Mom wants us to finish the kids' section tonight before we study. " He nodded at the books piled behind him. "Do you want to start at the back of the alphabet, and I'll take the front?"

"Hold up just a moment there, you two," said a deep, booming voice. A man easily seven feet tall strode over to them carrying a box full of books. The man's muscles bulged out of his tailored black suit, and he walked strangely, stopping every few feet to strike a pose. He also wore sunglasses inside, which seemed a bit odd to Owen, given that the lights in the library weren't that bright.

The man's sudden appearance sent Spike scrambling to hide elsewhere in the library, which wasn't unusual. The man watched him go with a strange look on his face. "Cute cat," he said, turning back to Owen.

"Can I help you?" Owen asked him.

"There was no one at the counter, so I came back here," the man said, dropping the box at Owen's feet. He glanced around and made a disgusted face. "Wow, you've really let this place go, haven't you? Yikes."

Bethany gave Owen a confused look that told him she had no idea who the man was either. "Did you want to . . . donate these books?" she asked.

"That's what I like about you, Bethany," the man said, grinning at her. "You always cut to the chase. Yes, that's exactly what I want to do. It's all Kiel Gnomenfoot books, straight from Jonathan Porterhouse." The man took a book out of the box and handed it to Owen. "The author said he was tired of having them around. Something about them being really badly written, and the main character is obnoxious and really terrible at magic and deserved to lose?"

Owen and Bethany shared another odd look. "You can definitely donate the books," Owen said to the man, "but we'll probably just end up adding them to our book sale. Not many people are checking these books out anymore."

"Oh, I have a feeling these copies will *jump* off the shelves . . . eventually," the man said, then winked in an exaggerated way. "Just give them time. Now, I really should be going. Have another old friend to see, a long way from here. I'll tell her you both said hi. In the meantime, give that copy a close look, Owen. You'll definitely find it interesting reading!" He waved and strode back toward the front of the library as Owen and Bethany just stared at each other.

"How did he know our names?" Bethany asked.

"And who could be an old friend of his that we would know?"

Bethany glanced at the book Owen was holding. "Are you going to look at that one, like he said to?"

Owen looked down at the cover, then brought it in close to his face, not sure what else to do. It was *Kiel Gnomenfoot and the Infinite Reality*, the fourth book, where Kiel and Charm tracked down one of the keys to the Source of Magic through parallel universes. He shrugged. "It looks like any other book."

Bethany took it out of his hands to drop it in the box. "His voice sounded a little familiar, but I've never seen his face. Maybe he's someone we met in a book or something?"

Owen shook his head. "That's impossible. No one can travel between this world and the fictional one anymore."

She sighed happily. "I know, I'm the least worried I've been in my life. Without my fictional self, I don't break rules or jump into books. My mom knows everything about me, and . . ." She trailed off, looking away. "I know I don't have Dad still, and that makes me sad. But you said he was okay when you last saw him, and I can't imagine anything happened to him after that, not since Nobody got his way. What would be the point of fighting anymore?" She brightened up a bit. "So really, everything worked out okay in the end, and now we're safe from my fictional self and her craziness. And there's no way that's going to change!"

Owen opened his mouth to agree, only to pause as the air between them began to spark, little electric fireworks exploding out of nowhere. Owen backed away in surprise, just as a person appeared out of thin air and crashed into Bethany. They both hit the floor hard, but the newcomer was the first one to stand, and Owen's eyes widened as he found himself staring at someone he never expected to see again.

"*Owen!*" Kara Dox shouted, hugging him tightly. Instantly, a thousand questions filled his mind and a torrent of emotions flooded over him. "I made it, finally! You wouldn't believe what I've gone through to get here!" She pulled away and took hold of his hand. "You need to come with me right away. I've seen your future, Owen. If we don't reconnect your world with the fictional one, you're going to *die!*"

CHAPTER 2

"Evening fell silently upon Jupiter City," Bethany whispered, crouching in the rafters of the warehouse as three big men wearing frog masks carried large boxes toward a loading dock. "But when evening falls, twilight *rises*."

"What are you *doing*?" Kid Twilight hissed from her right.

"Being awesome?" she said, making sure her Twilight Girl mask was secure on her face. It'd be pretty embarrassing if it fell off while she was kicking criminal butt in a few minutes. "Why, what are *you* doing?"

"*Not* narrating our every move," he said.

"Enough, both of you," Doc Twilight said to Bethany's left. "Twilight Girl, this is your graduation. You've only been training for a few months now, but you've reached the point where I think you're ready for the real thing. How are you feeling?"

"Evil will come to fear my name," Bethany growled as intimidatingly as she could.

Kid Twilight rolled his eyes, but her father frowned. "I know you're up for this, but I just want to say one last time, if you're not absolutely positive you want to be a superhero, that's completely okay. Your mother wouldn't exactly be thrilled if she saw what I'm letting you do." His face seemed to fall when he mentioned her mom, just like it always did.

"She wouldn't understand," Bethany said, trying not to sound annoyed about having the same argument again. "She's nonfictional and doesn't get what it's like for us, just like the old, horrible, boring Bethany didn't."

Kid Twilight nodded in agreement, but Doc looked concerned. "Who you were was *wonderful.* Just like who you are now. But don't forget that the goal here is to bring you back together when we reunite the worlds. I only agreed to train you to eventually take down Nobody, once we find a way to track him down."

"Sure, sure," she said absently. "And if that takes a while, then we'll just have to punch some justice to keep ourselves busy!"

Secretly, she'd been dreading the moment they'd find Nobody. Yes, he deserved justice, so when they tracked him down, she'd fight as hard as anyone to beat him. But right now, the worlds being separated was *amazing*. She didn't have to listen to all the guilt trips from her nonfictional self, worrying about every single little thing. For once she was free to take risks and enjoy herself. And because of that, and having her father around, this had been the greatest few months of her life.

"Don't forget, getting you back home safely to your mother is the most important goal here, Twilight Girl," her father said. "And that means you're going to be . . . what?"

She grinned at him and pulled three Twilight throwing stars from her belt. "*Stealthy*. I've got this, don't worry! I'll be totally safe. Now let's go beat up some bad guys!"

With that, she pulled out her Twilight launcher with her other hand, shot it at another rafter, and swung away.

"Sidekicks are the *worst*," Kid Twilight said, and followed quickly behind.

Doc Twilight dropped his head into his hands, then shot his launcher out as well.

The men wearing frog masks on the warehouse floor all had strange ray guns strapped to their backs, but their hands were full of boxes. Bethany let go of the launcher and dropped lightly to the floor, her cape settling around her. "It's moving day, punks," she growled at the criminals. "And guess who didn't order enough pizza for everyone!"

"What?" one of the men said, turning around with the box still in his hands. "'It's moving day'? What does that even mean . . . whoa, it's Kid Twilight!" He dropped the box and reached for his ray gun, then let out a shout as a Twilight throwing star struck his hand.

"It's Twilight *Girl*," Bethany said, launching another throwing star at a second criminal before sweeping the leg of a third leg, knocking him to the ground. "Kid Twilight's the one who's missing all the fun!"

Behind her she heard Kid Twilight growl in frustration. "*I* was waiting until we fully assessed the situation, *Twilight Girl*. Being stealthy? You've heard of it?"

"Sometimes *action* is required," Bethany said, and pulled her telescoping staff from her back, shaking it to expand it to full size. She shoved one end of the staff into the stomach of the first criminal she took down, then leaned on it, giving him her most intimidating look. "Now, let's just be clear on the name, okay?" she growled. "I don't want you giving Kid Twilight the credit when you're telling the other guys in jail how I beat you up."

The man groaned in pain. "No, I got it!" he said quickly, the staff digging in. "Twilight Girl, your name is Twilight Girl! I get it. I won't make that mistake again!"

"*Or* the mistake of breaking the law?" Doc Twilight asked, landing in the middle of the room. He gave Bethany a disapproving look. "That would be the most important lesson to teach criminals, wouldn't it, Twilight Girl?"

She grinned, then planted the other end of her staff on the ground and pushed off of it to kick the second criminal in the face, just as he tried to attack her. "We can agree to disagree."

Kid Twilight shook his head but picked up one of the other men on the ground by his shirt. "Where did you get these weapons? I've never seen anything like these in Jupiter City."

The man just laughed. "You're not getting anything out of me, Kid. You haven't seen what these things can do. And there are more where they come from. There's a pipeline into the city—"

A beam of light shot out from the doorway to the warehouse, striking the criminal in the leg. The man screamed in surprise, and Kid Twilight quickly pulled him behind some of the boxes, out of range of whatever had fired.

But other than the shock of it, the criminal didn't seem hurt at all. What had he been hit with? And who had fired at him?

"Twilight Girl, get under cover!" Doc Twilight shouted, leaping away as another ray shot directly at him. He pushed her behind another set of boxes and moved to follow, only for a third ray to hit him in the chest, knocking him to the ground.

Instantly, Bethany's entire body went cold, and all the fun of her first superhero patrol disappeared.

"Doc!" Kid Twilight yelled, moving to the hero's side, but a beam struck him next, and he collapsed as well.

"NO!" Bethany shouted, throwing her Twilight stars in the direction the beams had come from as she leaped toward her father. She heard the throwing stars hit, and someone groan. Whoever it was stumbled into the dim warehouse lights, and she gasped.

A man wearing a full-body toad costume (now with three Twilight stars embedded in each of his rubber costume biceps) bounced into view, staring at her through the mouth of the toad. "You're new," the costumed villain said. "Nice to see the Twilight family adding some *tadpoles*."

"What did you do to them?" Bethany shouted, pulling more Twilight throwing stars from her belt as she quickly looked between her father and the froggish figure. Her dad (and less importantly, Kid Twilight) *looked* unharmed, but that didn't mean anything in a world full of comic book weapons.

The villain smiled. "Let's just say that I . . . expanded their horizons." He lifted the gun and aimed it at Bethany. "Now, Twilight Tadpole, it's time for you to join your fellow heroes. With Doc Twilight out of the way, there'll be no one to stop the Toad Prince from taking over Jupiter City, once and for all!"

In spite of the situation, Bethany couldn't help but pause at this. "The *Toad* Prince?" she said. "Shouldn't it be the Frog—"

"No, it shouldn't!" the Toad Prince shouted. "Why does everyone ask that? Stop questioning me, lady!" He angrily pulled the trigger, and a beam of light shot out at her.

Without pausing to think, Bethany transformed herself into a tiny rubber ball and fell to the floor as the ray passed over her. She hit the ground hard, bouncing off at an angle.

"What?" the Toad Prince shouted, aiming the gun around the room. "Where did you go?"

She bounced again, closing in on him. Then, as she soared in an arc toward the villain, she morphed back into her normal superhero self in midair, slamming feet-first into the Toad Prince and knocking the ray gun from his hands. She drove her staff against his stomach hard enough to hold him in place, then yanked his mask off, revealing a man covered in warts. "What did you *do* to them?!"

The Toad Prince croaked in pain, then slowly smiled. "You'll find out soon enough! I've *finally* beaten Doc Twilight! After all this time, he and his sidekick—"

Bethany growled and hit him in the head with her staff, then turned back to check on her father. Doc was slowly pushing to his feet, though he didn't look very steady. Kid Twilight seemed to be more dazed and was barely sitting up.

Inwardly, she cursed herself for being too slow. Why had she waited so long to attack in the first place? She didn't have to listen to her cowardly nonfictional side anymore, after all. Not taking action was what had caused all of her problems before!

"What was that?" Doc Twilight asked, running his hands over his chest, as if looking for a wound. "I don't feel hurt, but something's definitely . . . different?"

Bethany ran to his side and carefully helped him stand, lending him her shoulder to help support him. "We need to get you to a hospital, or to the Lawful Legion," she said. "They'll be able to figure out what those ray guns do."

Beside her, she heard Kid Twilight gasp, and turned to find him staring at the criminal the Toad Prince had hit first with his ray. The man was still lying on the ground, only now his entire body was convulsing violently. Suddenly a flash of light exploded out of him, blinding them. It took a moment for Bethany's vision to clear, but when it did, she found that the criminal's clothing and frog mask had morphed into what looked like a man-sized peach costume.

"The Peach Pit will choke your justice, Doc Twilight!" the man shouted, rolling around as if he was trying to get to his feet, but having no luck. "As soon as I get up, there will be a reckoning!" He rolled over onto his face and groaned. "Um, can I get a little help over here?"

"The Peach Pit?" Kid Twilight said. "Have you heard of him, Doc?"

Bethany's father shook his head, looking worried. "Sounds like one of the Fruit of the Loons—"

"They would be so lucky!" the Peach Pit shouted, only to start shaking again. Another flash of light, and now he wore an ambulance driver's uniform instead of a supervillain costume. Without missing a beat, the man leaped to his feet, assessing the scene before him. "We've got men down in the Miracle Mile warehouses," he said into a radio on his shoulder, then rushed toward one of the other criminals. "Looks like three males, two unconscious, all three wounded via superhero." He bent over to check on the nearest henchman, who stared up at him in confusion. "Might be some blunt force trauma to the head. Standard Twilight actions, it seems."

"What is happening to him?" Bethany whispered to her father.

"I don't know, but we need to get to the Lawful Legion right away," he whispered. "Whatever this is, we'll need their help to figure it out." He clicked his Twilight communicator. "Legion transport, I have four to teleport to headquarters." He paused, then looked worried. "Legion transport? Is anyone there?"

The paramedic put his fingers on the downed henchman's wrist, looking at his watch like he was taking a pulse, then began to shake again. Another burst of light, and now he wore a brown furry costume and moved incredibly slowly.

"The . . . Sloth . . . will . . . ," he said, pausing with every word, only for the light to flash again. Bethany turned away as the brightness burst from the man faster now, and she heard him begin to scream. Squinting against the blinding light, she could just make out his silhouette as it grew larger or smaller, thinner or fatter, costumed or in normal clothes. Finally, the light explosions grew too frequent to watch, and Bethany covered her eyes with her arm as she heard him let out an awful scream.

All at once everything went silent and the light disappeared. Bethany dropped her arm, only to find the man was gone. She scanned the entire warehouse, but there was no sign of him. It was as if he never existed.

"Behold the power of possibility!" the Toad Prince shouted from the ground. "The man from another world was right. It truly is the most powerful weapon of them all!"

CHAPTER 3

"Kara?" Owen said, his mind racing with questions, thoughts, and emotions as she held his hand. How could she be here? What had happened to her since Nobody had sent her back to her world? What had happened to her future selves, and the Time Security Agency? Why had she come?

And most importantly, *how* had she made it to the nonfictional world? It shouldn't be possible, but here she was, standing right in front of him.

"Who else would it be?" Kara said, and pointed at the bracelet on her wrist. "I got ahold of a more advanced time bracelet, one that can track people down by their chronal signatures, and I used it to find you. Only to get over to *your* world, I had to go back in time first, to the beginnings of my universe, when our worlds were the same. Remember when we discovered that, back when we were escaping the time prison?"

Owen blinked in surprise. They'd discovered what, now? He did have a vague half memory of going backward in time after the time prison, and something about magicians . . . wait, there'd been magicians in this world, the nonfictional world! Those magicians had used magic to create a new universe, a place where magic could safely exist, after being attacked by the nonbelievers.

But wait. He *also* had a foggy memory of traveling *forward* in time and meeting his future self in a world taken over by the Countess. How could that be? He and Kara obviously didn't go to *both* the past and the future. Was this something to do with the readers, back in the *Pick the Plot* book? Did he have memories from all the choices? That seemed impossible. But Kara was immune to paradoxes, so—

"Are you okay?" Kara said, dropping his hand to take a step back. "You seem completely lost in thought."

As she let go of him, his questions all shut down and he shrugged. "Sorry, I got distracted for some reason. I sort of remember what you were talking about, but it doesn't really matter. What are you doing here?"

She gave him an odd look. "What do you mean? I came to

find you and make sure you were okay! You were going after Nobody, and I couldn't just abandon you, not after he stuck me back in my reality halfway through everything. I figured that if he returned me to my world, he might do the same for you." Her forehead wrinkled. "But once I got to your universe and traveled forward to your time, something . . . *interfered* with my time bracelet, almost like a tractor beam, pulling me toward it in time." She shook her head. "It brought me to a point five years from now and almost trapped me there. I had to overload the time bracelet just to escape—"

"Owen, who's your friend?" Bethany asked, smiling politely and extending her hand.

"I'm *so* sorry, that was rude of me," Kara said, shaking Bethany's hand. "I'm Kara Dox. Owen and I are good friends."

Bethany raised an eyebrow. "Oh, really? He didn't mention you. How do you two know each other?"

Kara glanced at Owen, looking a bit hurt, but quickly turned back to Bethany. "I'm sure you two have been too busy to talk much. But he told me all about you, Bethany. I recognized you immediately from his description." She leaned in closer to whisper. "And don't worry, I know that you're half-fictional, so you don't have to hide it."

Bethany raised a hand to stop her, shaking her head. "Not anymore, actually. When Nobody separated our worlds, he split me in two." She shrugged, still smiling. "Now there's a fictional me and a regular, rule-abiding, nonfictional me. It actually makes a lot more sense this way."

This seemed to confuse Kara even more. "Makes . . . sense? But you're not yourself anymore! We have to fix that. And we can! You should both come with me, and—"

"Wait, hold on," Bethany said, her smile fading. "We're done with all that sort of thing. Owen and I are both safer this way, now that life is back to normal, without any fictional craziness. The last time we went into the fictional world, I almost got lost forever as a beam of light, and Owen got trapped behind the scenes of a comic book. What if we'd never come back?" She shook her head. "We can't just leave and run off on some adventure or another. There are consequences if something happens to us."

"We're really okay, Kara," Owen said. "Thank you for coming all this way, but you didn't need to. We're—"

Kara stared at him for a moment, then grabbed his arm. Instantly, the flood of questions hit his mind, and he couldn't figure out which to ask first. "What did you mean, I'm going to die if we don't reconnect the worlds, Kara? You mean like from natural causes when I'm really old, the normal way?"

Kara released his arm, and the questions stopped. "Actually, it doesn't matter," he told her. "But thank you for—"

"It's your heart," she said, touching his arm again. "Something happens to it, I'm not sure what. But I've seen you, Owen, five years from now. When I got pulled into your future by whatever was guiding me, my time bracelet still tracked you down—the seventeen-year-old version of you. And that you was lying in a hospital bed barely alive, Owen! I didn't have much time before a doctor came and called security on me, but the older version of you told me he needs to talk to you, so you can make things right. He said your heart wasn't working anymore, your robotic heart. And that's impossible, because it can't break down, right?"

Owen blinked, trying to keep up with her whole story. His heart? The one that he'd gotten from Charm, that Dr. Verity had inserted in him, way back when he'd first jumped into a Kiel Gnomenfoot book with Bethany? He put a hand on his chest and felt the regular thumping. "I . . . I don't know," he said. Logic said that a robotic heart would probably outlast a human one. But logic didn't really take into account a half-robotic girl building that heart in a fantasy world either.

"There's more," Kara said, holding his arm tightly now. "That future was nothing like what you've told me about your world. You have to see it, or you'll never believe it. Come back with me and talk to your future self. He knows how to change things, to reconnect the worlds. He told me!" She moved her hand down to his and squeezed it supportively. "And when we do that, *you* should be okay too, most importantly."

Owen looked away, his mind racing with questions and ideas in a way that he hadn't dealt with in months. Could Kara be right, that five years from now he'd be dying? But how could his robotic heart stop working? And how would reconnecting the worlds fix it? That didn't make any sense. His heart might have been made in the fictional world, but it still worked here, in the nonfictional one.

He turned back toward Kara, pulling his hand from hers. Instantly, things fell into a logical order in his mind. Fact: His heart was working perfectly now, and he couldn't imagine that changing. Therefore Kara had to be mistaken. Fact: Seeing the future would just lead to insanity and less ordinary advancement in life.

Plus, what could *he* possibly do to reconnect the worlds?

He couldn't beat Nobody, that was clear, not after losing twice now. After all, he was just a nonfictional kid, which wasn't any use against someone who could rewrite themselves to be whatever they wanted.

"I think I should just stay here, Kara," Owen said quietly, not looking at her. "Yes, Nobody separated our worlds and split Bethany in half. And I remember thinking that'd be bad at the time, but actually, things just seem *easier* now. Less of a headache all around, you know?" He gave her an apologetic look. "I'm fine too. So is my heart. Nothing's going to happen to it."

Kara just stared at him. "I didn't believe your future self about this at first. He warned me you'd lost your imagination, and only contact with something fictional would bring it back. But this is so crazy to actually watch it happen!" She took his hand again, which started another round of questions popping up in his head. His imagination could come back . . . just by touching something fictional? And she'd known this? More importantly, his future self knew it too? What was going *on* here?

"It all makes sense, Owen," Kara continued. "You lost your imagination when the worlds split. Remember what we learned, back in the past? The fictional world's magic came from *non-*

30

fictional people, remember? That's what the magicians used to create the fictional universe. But they left you nonfictional people a connection to that magic, your imagination. And now that the worlds are split, you've lost that connection!"

"But my heart came from the fictional world," Owen said. "If touching something fictional brings back my imagination, why doesn't that count?"

"If I had to guess, it has to do with what's happening to it in your future," Kara told him. "All the more reason to come with me and find out!"

Bethany stepped between them, looking uncomfortable as she separated them. "Kara, maybe you should go. Owen's mom might hear you, and then we'd get in trouble. After Nobody sent us back here, we landed in London, and that didn't go over well with our moms. We've been grounded ever since, and if they found out we'd been talking to a fictional person?" She laughed nervously. "We'd be in *huge* trouble."

Kara gave her a long look. "Really? Huge trouble? Like what? What do you think they might do to you? Let's think of some punishments for a second."

Bethany paused, then shrugged. "I'm sure they'd come up with something."

"What about throwing you into a lake of lava?" Kara asked, looking quickly between them. "Feeding you to land sharks? How about dressing you up like bananas and making you fight crime?"

Owen snorted. "Those things aren't real. But she's right, Kara. We're going to get in trouble. You probably should just go back to the fictional world. I'll be fine." He patted her arm, just to reassure her of that.

As he touched her, a tiny little voice inside of him screamed, *You won't be fine, she just told you that! Go with her to the future to see what she's talking about!* But as soon as he pulled his hand away, the voice quieted, so he ignored it. Whatever did happen to him in the future, it was logical that doctors and technology of that time could fix it. And who cared if being near her restarted his imagination a bit? What use was it anyway?

Kara turned to him and grabbed him by the shoulders, setting off the yelling in his mind again. "Don't you see what you're missing, Owen?" she said. "You just said *'Those things aren't real,'* but you've spent your entire life loving made-up stories and people." She rolled her eyes. "Not that they *were* made-up, but you know what I mean. Listen to yourself! You can't just think not having an imagination is okay. Your whole world lost their creativity, their curiosity, everything that lets people dream up new inventions, new technology, medicine, *everything*."

Bethany started to look panicked as Kara's voice grew louder, her hands still locked on Owen's shoulders. "Not to mention that our imagination is what keeps us from killing one another, since we can picture what it's like to be someone else!" she said. "You wouldn't think that's such a big deal, but I've seen what happens to your world in just five years without it, Owen. Come with me if you think not having an imagination is okay!"

She's right, the voice in his head told him. *You don't dream anymore, either during the day or at night. You can't read books or even things you yourself wrote. Remember that story you wrote about Bethany's father as the King of All Stories? You couldn't have done that now! And you barely even care what happened to your fictional friends, now that they're gone. This isn't you!*

"Things have changed, yes," he said, taking a step back from her and pushing her hands off of him. Instantly, the inner voice quieted again. "But that doesn't mean they're worse. They're just . . . different."

"They're better," Bethany said, looking pretty anxious now. "Seriously, Owen, your mom will hear her, and we'll get in *so* much trouble. They won't let us study together—"

"Studying?!" Kara said, her voice rising even louder. "That's what you're worried about? Owen's going to *die* if we don't fix things!"

"Owen? Bethany?" his mom called out from the front desk of the library. "Is there someone else back there with you?"

"Yes, Ms. Conners!" Bethany yelled back, then winced, giving Kara an apologetic look. "Sorry, I couldn't think of anything else to tell her. Lying's gotten a lot harder since we got back."

"I didn't see anyone go back there," his mother shouted, and Owen could hear her making her way back to them. "Who is it?"

Something smacked down on Owen's hand, and suddenly the voice in his head grew so loud he couldn't ignore it. "You're coming with me," Kara said to him as she closed her time bracelet around his wrist. "Bethany can study here all she wants, but I'm going to save your life and get you back to normal, Owen, no matter what!"

"What are you doing?" he shouted at her, trying to pull the bracelet off. But it sparked as he touched it, and he quickly pulled his hand away. "Where are we going? Kara, what is—"

"We'll get to all of that later," Kara said, grabbing his other hand. "Right now, Nobody messed up your entire world, and I'm going to prove it to you!"

"Kara," he said, "Nobody didn't do *anything* to me. He just sent me back, and now—"

And now you don't ask questions. Now you don't wonder about things, daydream about them being different. Now you have no curiosity, no creativity, no imagination. And what are you without those things? Ordinary, yes. But are you yourself?

"Owen?" his mother said, stepping into the children's section. "Who *is* this? What's that thing on your wrist?"

Kara smacked the bracelet, and the library and Owen's mom and Bethany and everything around them changed before his eyes, replaced by . . . something very different.

A huge crowd of people, all cheering. And a bonfire at least twice as tall as Owen.

A bonfire of *books*.

And all around it, soldiers in all-black uniforms with black reflective helmets watched the crowd, holding scary-looking futuristic ray gun rifles.

"See?" Kara shouted, pointing at the bonfire. "*Now* tell me that Nobody didn't change anything. This is your future, Owen! Look at what's coming if we don't fix this!"

CHAPTER 4

Bethany stared in horror at her father and his sidekick. Neither of them had started shifting into different versions of themselves yet, like the Toad Prince's henchman had. But it'd only be a matter of time. She had to do something, *quick*.

"We're getting you both to the Lawful Legion headquarters!" she shouted, then threw her arms around them as she used her superpower to morph into a Twilight plane. As her two superhero partners dropped into bucket seats in her cockpit, she clicked seatbelts over them, set her engines blazing, and took off straight through the roof of the warehouse, sending debris exploding out to the empty street below. As soon as she was clear of the building, she kicked her engines into overdrive, tearing across Jupiter City so quickly that they reached the Legion headquarters in a matter of seconds.

Unfortunately, her sensors picked up a flash of light from

the cockpit, and she knew that even seconds might not be fast enough.

The Legion's headquarters blipped on her radar, and she tipped her nose down toward it. Instead of coming in for a gentle landing, though, she plowed through the recently rebuilt glass wall of the Legion's headquarters and skidded to a stop in the same hall where she, Charm, and Gwen had fought the Lawful Legion when the superheroes had been under the Dark's mental hold.

Weirdly, the hall was empty. Where were the heroes chatting with one another, ready for the next mission? Where was Athena, dispensing wisdom to the younger heroes? Or Captain Sunshine, his smile as bright as the star that gave him his powers?

Morphing back to normal, she released Doc and Kid Twilight from her arms and stood back to see what she was dealing with. Doc Twilight now wore a Captain Sunshine costume, while Kid Twilight still had the Twilight symbol but now looked younger . . . and angrier somehow.

"Don't worry," she said, glancing around at the empty hall nervously. "I'm going to find the Legion, and we're going to fix you two!"

"The Legion?" Doc Twilight said, floating up from the

ground to grin widely at her. "Why, I'm the *chairman* of the Lawful Legion! What can I do for you, young lady?"

"Who are you two jerks?" Kid Twilight said, glaring at them. "Where's my dad, Doc Twilight?"

Bethany froze at this, and just stared. His . . . dad? Was he serious?

It didn't matter. Whatever Kid Twilight had turned into, it'd only last a few moments before he continued evolving until he disappeared completely. She didn't have time to waste.

"Be right back!" she shouted, then took off running. Bursting through the double doors behind the strangely empty receptionist desk, she passed into the Lawful Legion's inner sanctum, expecting to find at least some of the team. But even here, where a superhero was *always* on watch, the headquarters was empty.

Instead, walls were broken, the floor was scorched in several places, and Athena's staff hung embedded in the ceiling in the middle of the communications room.

"Hello? I need help!" she shouted, but no one responded. The Lawful Legion must have been attacked too, but by who? If it was the Toad Prince or someone with the same sort of weapons, then had the heroes already disappeared? If that was the case, was Twilight Girl going to end up the last hero in all of Jupiter City?

A thrill of excitement passed through her at that idea, but she shook it off. Not now. She could save the city all by herself *after* she'd fixed her father. And, well, Kid Twilight, too, if she had time.

She ran from room to room, doing a quick scan of each. There had to be something in the Legion headquarters that could help. Some kind of alien technology or mystical artifact, maybe? Or even—

Something caught her eye as she passed the door to the medical bay, and her mouth dropped open. Inside the mostly destroyed medical unit, there were foot-tall letters burned into the wall.

LAST ONE LEFT, the letters said. *COULDN'T SAVE THEM. GOING AFTER THE SOURCE OF THE RAY GUNS.*

So it *had* been the Toad Prince, or someone like him. And Captain Sunshine must have left this message using his sun vision, which both gave her hope and disappointed her. With the Captain still around, she had no doubt they'd fix everything. But she wouldn't be able to save Jupiter City all by herself, either. Lame.

Now she'd need to track down Captain Sunshine and see what he'd found. She started to leave the med bay but skidded to a stop as she noticed something way in the back of the room.

One of the stasis chambers had survived the destruction.

Her eyes widened, and she took off at a run back to the hall where she'd left her father and Kid Twilight. The stasis chambers had been designed to freeze the occupant in time, meaning they wouldn't age or even experience time passing at all, no matter what happened outside the chamber. The Lawful Legion had used a whole collection of them to travel into the future once, but thankfully, they'd negated that whole time line during the battle, or they'd still be occupying the stasis chambers now. Or so Bethany thought. Time travel was annoying.

Yes, there was only one stasis chamber that hadn't been destroyed now, but it was probably big enough to fit two people. Even if it wasn't comfortable, Bethany would stuff them both in there. Then she'd turn it on and freeze Doc and Kid Twilight in time, so they wouldn't get any worse while she found a cure for . . . well, whatever was wrong with them! She grinned widely, proud of herself for saving her father, and looking forward to holding this over Kid Twilight's head forever.

Bethany hit the central hall of the headquarters, then slid to a stop, her blood going cold as a very familiar wall of darkness enveloped her. She leaped backward out of it, her eyes wide, and quickly rubbed her arms, trying to restore their warmth. No. *No!* Not again! He couldn't have come back. She'd destroyed his powers—this wasn't possible!

And then a figure emerged from the darkness, a figure draped in shadows with red, pulsing eyes, and all thoughts of saving her father went out the window.

The Dark stared down at her with hatred, holding an unconscious Kid Twilight in his hands, though the boy now wore a lab coat and held a telescope, apparently just an astronomer now like his parents had been.

"You thought you could defeat *me*?" the Dark asked, throwing Kid Twilight to the ground at her feet. "The more light you shine, the more shadows appear, you foolish girl!"

"This can't be happening," Bethany whispered, shaking her head. "You're not the Dark anymore. I saved you!"

Her father laughed evilly, then launched a wave of shadows to strike out at her. She leaped away a moment before they slammed into the floor she'd been standing on, crushing it to pieces. *Whoa.* That was a new power. Maybe this wasn't the same Dark she'd faced before?

On the ground, Kid Twilight's unconscious body flashed brightly as he changed, and the Dark reeled back as if in pain. Bethany used that to her advantage, grabbing Kid Twilight (now wearing Twilight scuba gear and holding a harpoon) and pulling him back into the inner sanctum.

Groaning at his weight, she used her powers to give herself superstrength, and picked him up. That helped. Now it felt like he weighed nothing at all! She tossed him over her shoulder and ran him back to the medical area, where she unceremoniously pushed him into the stasis chamber.

One down, one to go.

"I will destroy all the light in this city!" the Dark shouted, crashing into the med lab like a wave of blackness. More shadows came screaming at her, and she dodged, leaving them to tear up the wall behind her, destroying Captain Sunshine's message. That gave her an idea, and she quickly used her power to give herself sunbeam eyes, just like Captain Sunshine.

"I'm sorry about this!" she yelled as she turned her new eye powers on her father. He shrieked in pain as the sun rays hit, and seemed to withdraw for a moment, only to grab at her again with an incredibly long arm.

She started to leap out of his way, but then realized she was standing right in front of the stasis chamber. If she dodged, he'd destroy the one chance she had to save them both.

Instead of escaping, Bethany gave herself the rest of Captain Sunshine's powers and grabbed the Dark's arm with her own sunlight-infused hands. Her father screamed, but she could feel the cold of his shadows seeping up through her fingers. She gritted her teeth at the deathly cold, but yanked on his arm, spinning him around toward the stasis chamber.

The Dark crashed into Kid Twilight inside it, still screaming something about defeating all of Jupiter City, but she slammed the chamber closed before he could move, then quickly punched the on button. Instantly, both her father and his sidekick froze in place, and Bethany collapsed to the floor, frantically rubbing her hands together just to keep them from going numb.

When she could almost feel her fingers again, she used her powers to turn herself back into regular Twilight Girl, before pausing to consider if she should at least keep the superstrength. That could have some advantages, after all. Maybe she could—

Wait a second. Superstrength? Sunbeam eyes? Captain Sunshine's powers? How had she done any of that?

It hadn't even occurred to her in the middle of the fight—she'd just . . . acted. But her superpowers had never been able to change her body that way before. In the past, she'd just been able to transform into inanimate objects. What was going on? Were her powers getting stronger? She flexed and considered herself in the glass wall of the med lab. Maybe she had just gotten better at using them? Either way, it was clear she was becoming more awesome. She grinned widely, then caught sight of her father in the stasis chamber and instantly lost all her excitement. Now wasn't the time, not for figuring out superpowers or celebrating a temporary win.

She walked over to the glass stasis chamber for a moment, staring at her father. "I'm going to fix this," she whispered, reaching out and touching the glass. "I don't care what it takes. I didn't find you just to lose you again. I know I'm not always perfect, and training me wasn't the easiest thing, but I can do this. I can be the hero you want me to be, both for you *and* Jupiter City."

Her father just stared out of the stasis pod with his red, hateful eyes, and she dropped her head, not able to look at him. This wasn't *fair*. She'd gotten so little time with him, and already he'd been taken away from her? If she'd only done more to find him over the past few years, hadn't let her nonfictional self hold them back with all those guilt-stricken, rule-following hang-ups, Bethany probably could have brought him back home years ago, and none of this would have happened.

"I'm not going to let anything hold me back now, Dad," she said. "Whoever did this is going to pay for taking you from me. You'll see. Twilight *will* fall on Jupiter City's criminals. And you'll be there to see it, I promise."

Realizing her vision was getting a bit watery, she turned, then with one last glance back at her father, she left, ready to punch some justice *hard*.

CHAPTER 5

The heat from the bonfire radiated over Owen, making the scene before him feel more like a fever dream than real life. As people threw more books on the fire, others cheered, and the soldiers with black helmets kept an eye on the crowd, their hands on their laser rifles.

And all of this was happening in what used to be the parking lot of his mother's library.

The library itself looked like it'd been set on fire, with scorch marks covering the few walls that still stood. The glass sliding doors had been shattered, and what was left of the library inside seemed to have been looted, as the building was completely empty now.

"Burn them!" someone shouted from behind Owen, making him jump. He turned to find a mother holding a baby close to her chest, screaming and waving her free hand in the air. "Don't let any more of those things get out!"

"What is going on here?" Owen whispered to Kara, who hadn't let go of his hand. She just shook her head sadly, her eyes on the crowd and the soldiers. Either she didn't know or this wasn't the place to talk about it.

How could this be happening, just five years from the present? It wasn't possible. Somehow, Kara must have taken them to another time, or another reality even. Could that be it? Had they traveled to the fictional world, and this was a dystopian future story?

His eyes drifted back to the bonfire, and he swallowed a wave of revulsion at the sight. Even if he had no interest in reading books anymore, burning them still felt like an obscene act.

A boy a few years younger than Owen walked toward the fire carrying what looked like an entire set of the Kiel Gnomenfoot books. He handed the stack to one of the black-helmeted soldiers, who seemed to tense up. The soldier carefully opened each book one by one, shook it, then threw it onto the fire. As he did, the other helmeted people tracked each copy with their weapons, as if the books themselves were dangerous. Finally, *Kiel Gnomenfoot and the Source of Magic* hit the bonfire, and the group of soldiers all relaxed a bit.

The disgust he'd felt before hit Owen a thousand times worse now. Those were the stories of his *friends*. Part of it was Owen's story too! To just set them on fire—

Kara grabbed his arm. "We should get out of here," she said, and slowly pulled him away. As she did, though, a thought occurred to him. If those are Kiel Gnomenfoot books, then how could this place be fictional? Kiel Gnomenfoot books would only exist in the nonfictional world.

Owen's entire body went cold, and he stopped in place, in spite of Kara's insistence. This had to be the nonfictional world! But that meant everything here was actually *happening*. He looked around in horror at the soldiers, the book bonfire, the cheering people, and wished he were wrong. This was *real*? This was the future he had to look forward to, just a few years away? But how? What could possibly have happened to turn these people into a mob?

"We really need to go," Kara whispered to him. "I think they're watching us." She nodded subtly toward the black helmets, and Owen followed her gaze. Two of the uniformed soldiers were staring in their general direction, though it was impossible to know exactly what they were looking at, since the helmets covered their faces completely.

"We haven't done anything wrong," Owen told her, but he had to admit he could feel their eyes on him too, and a slow chill went down his spine. "Let's get back home. I don't want to stay here a minute longer than we have to."

"You need to talk to your future self still, but it wouldn't hurt to have things ready to go, just in case," she said, reaching for his arm with the bracelet while watching the black helmets. She pulled his arm closer, then gently touched the time machine.

Sparks exploded off of the bracelet at her touch, and people nearby yelped and shouted out in surprise. Instantly, three of the black helmets started moving toward them in unison, almost robotic in their strides.

"Uh-oh," Kara said, yanking Owen harder toward the sidewalk leading away from the library parking lot. "We need to *go*."

"You two, stop," said a weirdly monotone yet human voice from behind them. "What is that device on your wrist, citizen?"

"Just a bracelet, um, sir?" Kara said, not looking back as she sped up their pace to just short of a run.

Two more black helmets cut them off from the sides, blocking their escape. "That looks like something from a science fiction book," one of them said, her voice also weirdly emotionless.

"Oh, it's nothing like that," Kara said quickly. "Completely normal. But we really do need to be getting home—"

"Let me see the bracelet, citizen," said the first black helmet, reaching his hand out for Owen's wrist.

"Get us out of here," Kara whispered to him. "Use your time powers!"

Time powers? Owen's eyes widened in shock, having completely forgotten about his powers in the months since Nobody had separated the worlds. There were so many moments he could have used them, too! He would have never been late to school or the library even once. Not to mention he could have had all kinds of fun adventures with them, walking across lakes without falling in, or watching movies on fast-forward. So many possibilities!

Kara stepped on his foot, jolting him back to attention. Right, his powers! As the soldier's hand grew closer, Owen concentrated, speeding time up for himself and Kara, who still held on to him. His heart began to beat faster and faster, and the black helmet reaching for him slowed almost to a stop, as did the others. Letting out a deep breath, Owen nodded at Kara, and they quickly passed beyond the soldiers, being careful not to touch any of them so Owen's power wouldn't kick-start their time too.

But as they reached the street, a strange pressure started growing on Owen's chest, and it grew harder and more painful with every step. He gasped and almost buckled at the knees, the pain was so intense.

"Are you okay?" Kara said, staring at him. "You just went completely pale."

"It feels like there's an anvil sitting on my chest," Owen said, gritting his teeth. Sweat broke out on his forehead, and for some reason, his left arm hurt. Then another sharp pain struck him like a lightning bolt in his chest, and he collapsed toward the ground as Kara struggled to hold him up.

"Owen!" she shouted as he hit the ground. Lights exploded in front of his eyes and the pain grew, radiating out through his body. "You have to stop using your powers!"

Through a cloud of agony, Owen realized she was right and immediately released his hold on time. As he did, the pressure on his chest slowly eased, letting him breathe again, while the sharp, lightning pains seemed less intense too, though they didn't stop completely.

"Where did they go?" one of the black helmets said behind them, and Owen realized they hadn't gotten far enough away. Right now, they were half-hidden in the darkness between streetlamps, but it wouldn't be long before the soldiers spotted them.

"I've got you," Kara said, and dug her shoulder in under Owen's arm, then half carried him behind some parked cars, where she lowered them both to the street.

"Find them," one of the black helmets said, and Owen heard several pairs of footsteps coming their way, each boot hitting the ground at the exact same time.

Kara moved to cover Owen with her body, hiding him behind the car as the black helmets strode past in unison. Their precise marching seemed as odd as everything else in the future, but Owen couldn't make his brain work properly to figure out why, not with the pressure on his chest still making it difficult to breathe, too.

What had caused the pain? He'd used his time powers before and hadn't ever had a problem with his heart. It was robotic, after all, and should have been able to handle this and more. Kara had said his older self was in the hospital for heart problems in the future. Was using his powers what caused his heart to stop working?

Even worse, had he just skipped the breakdown of his heart ahead five years by using his powers *now*?

As the black helmets moved past them and down the street, Kara moved off of him and wiped his sweating face with concern. "Are you okay?" she asked. "Can you walk? We need to get you to the hospital right now."

He grimaced. "I'll be okay. It's a lot better now that I'm not using the powers. I don't need to go to the hospital."

"Uh, you almost just died in the middle of the street, so yes, you do," she said. "You need a doctor. Maybe they can test your heart now and see what's going on before it breaks down completely." The thought seemed to cheer her up a bit. "Maybe this will even help save you in the future! Either way, your future self will know more about this, and everything. Come on."

She helped Owen to his feet, and put her shoulder back under his. As she did, he looked back at the library parking lot, where the crowd still cheered for the burning books and the black-helmeted guards watched over everyone, searching for anything out of the ordinary.

Kara was right. This wasn't a future he could let happen. Whatever it took, even if he did end up with a broken heart, Owen *had* to fix this. If that took reuniting the fictional and nonfictional worlds, then they'd just have to do that, and face Nobody—

Another chill went down Owen's spine at the thought of the faceless man. Twice Nobody had beaten him, each time without even trying.

After a third time, Nobody might be less forgiving, and not stop at pulling just Bethany in two.

CHAPTER 6

Bethany grimaced as she picked up Captain Sunshine's cape and communicator from the sidewalk in front of the Tip-Top Toys warehouse, right below a giant jack-in-the-box clown. The clown hung down from the factory sign in an amazingly creepy way. Its eyes seemed to follow her no matter where she went, which wasn't exactly comforting.

Even weirder, something about this place seemed familiar, like she'd been here before. But that couldn't be . . . they'd never been to these warehouses during her training, or when she, Charm, and Gwen had explored Jupiter City looking for her father, either.

Still, Captain Sunshine must have come here looking for the source of the ray gun weapons, so she'd need to investigate no matter how creepy the factory looked. After all, every sign now pointed to her being Jupiter City's only superhero, with the

Captain gone. She bit her lip to keep from smiling with excitement. Twilights didn't smile. They grimaced, with a little snark, and that was it. Even when they were about to save the entire city *single-handedly*.

"You're going to be proud of me, Dad," she whispered, touching the Twilight symbol on her chest. "I promise I'll use all the training you gave me. I'll be the stealthiest hero *ever*."

She shot her Twilight launcher out, then soared up to the second floor of Tip-Top Toys, where she slipped in through a broken window, careful not to disturb anything as she entered. The silence in the warehouse was so complete that even the slightest tinkle of broken glass could potentially give her away, and her father would have been so disappointed at such a rookie mistake.

Not willing to risk a light, she slowly moved across metal beams above what looked like an abandoned factory floor. Several assembly lines appeared to be broken down, with headless teddy bears and such lying all over the place. She shivered at the sight, not liking how this entire place just reeked of horror movie. This was *one* bad thing about being the last superhero . . . it could get a little creepy by yourself at times.

As she drew closer to the far side of the factory floor, she started hearing voices echoing up from the next room. Moving as silently as she could, she slid through a broken air vent, then slowly crept out onto the rafters above a well-lit room. Below her, several men carried boxes full of the same ray guns the Toad Prince had shot at them, but these men all walked on metal stilts and wore long robes with little windows drawn in vertical lines on them. The men were carrying the boxes into the warehouse from a glowing blue portal on one of the walls, and Bethany stared at it oddly. Why did that seem so familiar too?

"So these ray guns will make even the most powerful superhero disappear, just like Captain Sunshine?" asked an extraordinarily tall man in steel girder armor, a villain Bethany recognized from her father's files as the Skyscraper.

A heavily muscled man wearing a black suit and sunglasses grinned up at him. "Not exactly. The ray is pure possibility, and when you hit someone with it, they end up cycling through anything and everything they ever might have become, depending on each and every choice they made. And in this city especially, let's just say there are a *lot* of alternate time lines. Eventually all of those infinite possibilities become too much for them, and they become pure potential, disappearing into—"

"I don't care where they go," the Skyscraper said, examining the weapon. "As long as they work, I'm good." He slowly grinned, then aimed the ray gun at the man in the suit. "Still, it never hurts to have a second test. And your asking price *is* pretty criminal, after all."

The man in the sunglasses shook his head. "C'mon, big man. You really think I'm going to let you hit me with my own possibilities?"

The Skyscraper shrugged. "I don't see what's going to stop me."

The man in the sunglasses turned and looked straight up at Bethany. "Hey, Twilight Girl? That's your cue!"

Bethany quickly flattened herself against the rafter, but it was already too late. "We've got company!" one of the henchmen shouted, grabbing a possibility ray gun.

"Get her, whoever she is!" another said.

"He already said I'm Twilight Girl!" Bethany shouted in annoyance, and dove out into the air, shooting her Twilight launcher as she fell, then swinging directly into the steel girders of the Skyscraper.

The impact sent pain radiating through her feet, but she hit hard enough to send the Skyscraper off-balance, windmilling his arms for a moment before toppling to the ground with a crash. "Get her!" he screamed, struggling against the weight of the enormous steel armor covering his body. "And someone *help me up*!"

The Skyscraper's minions turned their ray guns on her, and she immediately dodged, remembering how fast the beams had been when they'd struck her father and Kid Twilight. Trying to keep them guessing, she leaped at the first henchman, then abruptly turned in midjump toward the second one and transformed into a locomotive, which struck the ground full steam ahead. She plowed into the second henchman, slamming him into the far wall hard enough to embed his stilts in the mortar.

"Whoa!" the first henchman shouted as she changed back to her regular self. "We've got a shape-shifter!"

"No, you've got a world of pain, *punk*," Bethany growled, and took out his ray gun with some Twilight throwing stars. A possibility beam struck the wall behind her, and it began to warp and change from brick to sand, collapsing the roof above it. Bethany winced, realizing she needed to finish this quickly.

Looking over the last few henchmen, she grabbed her Twilight launcher and shot it toward the Skyscraper, where it thunked hard into his armor.

"Ouch, hey!" he shouted, but she ignored him and used her

powers to give herself superstrength again. As the ceiling above them started to creak and groan, she yanked on her launcher's cable and swung the Skyscraper around in a circle. His steel girder armor plowed into two more of his henchmen, knocking them out and sending their possibility guns flying.

"I'd hoped Doc and his sidekick would be here too, Twilight Girl," the man in the sunglasses said. "Kinda disappointed I didn't get to see Doc in action. But I guess we can't have everything." He waved at her, then walked over to the portal in the wall.

"Don't move!" she shouted, but one of the rafters above her shrieked loudly and fell, and she had to push the henchmen out of the way. Using her superstrength, she picked up the Skyscraper and tossed him through the now-missing wall, followed by his henchmen, making sure they were all safe before the entire building collapsed.

"I actually thought you'd get here a lot earlier," the man in the sunglasses said, one foot already through the portal. He paused there for a moment and grinned at her. "But maybe I gave you too much credit. After all, you're only half the girl you used to be, huh?"

The shock of that hit Bethany like a fist, and she almost

stopped in midrun, in spite of the collapsing warehouse. "How . . . how did you *know* that?" she said.

The man just shrugged. "You'll have to catch me if you want to find out, *Bethany*."

And with that, he leaped through the portal.

As he did, the blue fire began to slowly swirl around, growing smaller the faster it went. Bethany screamed in frustration and lunged forward, kicking off with enough force to propel her through the ever-shrinking portal as everything erupted into chaos behind her.

The blue fire was so close that it singed her as she passed, but she made it, hitting the ground hard on the other side, just as the portal winked out behind her. She quickly jumped to her feet and pulled out more Twilight throwing stars, ready to face the man with the sunglasses . . .

Only, the man was nowhere to be seen. He'd completely disappeared.

She swore softly in anger and looked around, trying to find where he could be hiding, but stopped as she realized something odd: She recognized this place. It looked nothing like it had the last time she'd been here, what with the translucent ground below her feet cracked and shattered and the once-beautiful science fiction buildings now half-destroyed, but even through all the destruction, she knew where she was, and it *wasn't* Jupiter City.

"Quanterium?" she said softly. "What is going *on* here?!"

"That's my question," said a voice from behind her.

She whirled around to find herself face to eyeless face with a featureless man, his arms crossed over his chest.

"I do believe you've left your own story," Nobody said, slowly growing in size before her. "You've broken the one rule I gave you, Bethany. And we can't have *that*."

CHAPTER 7

"his isn't good," Kara said, fiddling with the time bracelet she'd taken from Owen's wrist. Owen's heart seemed to have somewhat recovered, and he was breathing much better now as they hid in some bushes outside of the massive town hospital. But now that the bracelet was off his wrist, his imagination had disappeared again, and he wondered what the whole point of this was. "I think we might be in trouble."

"Because of the mobs burning books or the time bracelet?" he asked.

"Both, but right now, this is our bigger problem," she said, holding up the bracelet. "Whatever's pulling time travelers to this date seems to be draining its energy somehow. I barely had enough power to leave last time, but it should have recharged by now." She furrowed her brow as she pushed a few buttons on the bracelet. "Usually it draws on energy from the fourth dimension for power, but for some reason, that seems to be blocked." She gave him a worried look. "As it is, I'm not sure we'd have the power to get you home."

Owen's eyes widened, and his heart began racing from anxiety instead of his time powers. "Are you kidding? There's got to be a way to fix it, right? Let's forget about this hospital thing and concentrate on recharging it!"

She just stared at him for a moment, looking confused. "Have you noticed how much more . . . concerned with your own self you get without your imagination?"

Owen paused, having no idea what she was talking about. "No? Isn't it logical to care about your own safety?"

"Logical, maybe," Kara said, looking back at the bracelet. "But not really you. Still, I think I might know a way to charge it in the hospital. I might be able to rig something up using those paddles they use to restart people's hearts. We could probably jolt the battery enough with one of those to power us through whatever's keeping us here and get you back to your normal time."

Owen's panic lessened slightly, but didn't go away. Finding defibrillator paddles in a hospital would mean breaking all kinds of rules. Yes, that was a lot better than being trapped in the future, but it could still lead to tons of trouble. "You know, that thing would be a lot easier to use if you could just plug it into a wall socket or something."

"There won't be a fourth-dimension adapter made for, like, fifteen years," she said, shaking her head. "But this should work. I've jolted other bracelets before, and it's been fine." She frowned. "At least, when they didn't blow up."

Owen sighed, ready to go back to his nice, normal time line, where there weren't soldiers burning books. Bethany had been right about Kara. All of this fictional nonsense just caused trouble. After all, what did it matter that the future was terrible to someone living in their proper time, back in the present? The future didn't even really *exist*, not back then.

"So this is the only way?" Owen asked. "Because I have no idea how we'll even get into the hospital. If I tell them who I am, they'll want to know why I'm out of my hospital bed." He paused. "That, and five years younger."

Kara shrugged, still staring at the bracelet. "Oh, we'll just make up a story. You can be your own little brother, maybe. We came to see your older brother who's a patient here. I'll be your friend from school or a cousin or something."

Owen cringed, hating the idea of not telling the truth. Making up a story to get them inside just seemed wrong. Surely explaining the situation to the hospital staff would result in everyone coming to an agreement and acting in an efficient and logical manner? But Kara was the one with the imagination, so maybe she saw problems with that plan that he couldn't. "Okay, but then we go straight to the paddles. No stops."

"No stops," Kara said, nodding. "Other than visiting your older self." Before he could object, she stood up and grabbed his hand. At her touch, his concerns about jumping back to his own time vanished, replaced by worries for the future. Yes, he had to get home, but not just to get away from all of this. He had to keep this future from ever happening!

Kara pulled him out of the bushes and led him toward the hospital doors, which parted as they drew close. They entered into a waiting area, where a woman in scrubs was working on a tablet at a large desk. There were a few people waiting in seats, but none seemed to be injured, which made sense, since this wasn't the emergency room, just the lobby for the regular hospital.

"Hello!" Kara said to the woman at the desk, dropping Owen's hand as they reached her. "We're here to see Owen Conners."

"Visiting hours are over in ten minutes," the woman said without looking up. She pointed at a sign on the wall that listed visiting hours from eleven a.m. to eight p.m. "You should come back tomorrow."

Well, that was that. "Okay, thanks," Owen said, and turned to go.

"Oh, we won't take long," Kara said, pulling him back. "This is Owen's brother. Don't you let family in after visiting hours?"

The woman looked up from her tablet. "Do you have identification?"

Kara just stared at her. "What, like a driver's license? We're both twelve."

The woman's eyes narrowed. "No, I mean your PFFIA identification cards. You're telling me you got this far from your home without being stopped by the PFFIA?"

With Kara's hand holding him in place, Owen's mind filled with questions. What was the PFFIA? Were those the black-helmeted soldiers? And what identification cards? Why was the future so paranoid? Was Kara right, that a lack of imagination really did make people more selfish?

"Oh, of course they talked to us," she said, waving her hand absently. "But they kept our IDs. Said we'd get them back when we left the hospital. You know how the PPTIZ is."

"The PFFIA," the woman said, looking more suspicious.

"That's the one," Kara said quickly. "So ten minutes?"

The woman rolled her eyes, but nodded. "Without your identification, I *should* call the PFFIA right now. But that'd mean I'd get questioned too, and then I'd be late getting home. And I shouldn't suffer just because you two can't keep your IDs." She glanced over at them as she tapped her tablet, and stickers printed out with VISITOR on them. She handed two of them to Kara and sighed. "Can't imagine that two kids could get into much trouble anyway."

"Nope, we're definitely rule abiders," Kara told her as she slapped one of the stickers on Owen's chest, then put the other on her shirt. "What room was Owen Conners in again?"

"Four eighteen. Take the elevator up. Family or not, if I don't see you back down here in ten minutes, I *am* calling the PFFIA."

"Thanks, you're really sweet," Kara said, then threw Owen a *what was that?* look as she walked them past the desk to a bank of elevators. One of the elevators was open and waiting, so they stepped inside, and Kara pushed the button for the fourth floor. The doors closed, and she let out a huge breath.

"What was *her* problem? Your older brother is sick!"

Owen just stared at her. "He's not actually my older brother."

"But *she* didn't know that. What is it with people in this time line? It's like they don't care at all about anyone. Where's the sympathy? Do they not have working hearts?" As soon as the words left her mouth, she seemed to realize what she said and turned bright red. "Oh, *wow*, I'm sorry. That's not how I meant it."

"Don't worry about it," Owen said. "But don't forget, we're here to recharge the time bracelet. Nothing else matters."

"Right," Kara said. "Nothing else except talking to your older self."

The elevator door opened, and Kara again grabbed Owen's hand, filling his mind with questions he had for his older self as she walked him toward room 418. A clock on the hallway wall said it was 7:55, meaning they only had five minutes now, but that should be enough time to get some information and charge the bracelet, hopefully.

Room 418's door was closed, so Kara gently knocked. "Owen?" she whispered, pushing it open and walking inside, leaving Owen in the hallway. The room was dim, lit only by multicolored lights on various monitoring machines, all attached to a body on the bed. Owen couldn't really see his future self very well, but that didn't really matter to him anyway. The practical thing to do was find the shock paddles before visiting hours were over.

"Owen, can you hear me?" Kara said, approaching the bed. She touched a button next to it, and a small reading lamp turned on, aimed right at Owen's older self. Owen turned away as the light illuminated the other version of him.

"I think he might be sedated," Kara said, sniffing like she was sad or something as she reached out and took his older self's hand. "See these stitches on his chest? They must have done at least a couple of operations on him. I don't know why they didn't do a transplant."

"Uh-huh," Owen said, looking over the machinery. They'd probably keep the—what was it called . . . crash cart?—somewhere near the bed, in case his older self's heart stopped. And there it was, just across the bed from Kara.

He quickly circled around and grabbed the paddles, then looked up at the clock. Still two minutes to go. They'd done it, all without getting involved in too many broken rules.

He pushed the power button on the crash cart, and the machine began to warm up.

"Hand me the bracelet," Owen said, reaching out to Kara over his older self.

"Owen, *look* at him," Kara said, wiping something off her face. Was she crying? "*This is you*. Your body, yourself. You're *dying*, Owen. We need to save you, both of you!"

"That's what the doctors are for," he said, shaking his head. "We don't have time to worry about that now. Give me the bracelet, and I'll power it up."

She stared at him sadly. "Look at yourself. *This* is why your future is the way it is. Everyone here is like you right now. All they care about is themselves, and none can imagine themselves as anyone else. You've lost all your sympathy, Owen! You weren't like this when your older self fought the Countess's daughter, remember?"

He frowned, again only half remembering that. "I was different then."

"Yes, you were," she said, sounding angry now.

Owen groaned in frustration. They were running out of time! "If I look at him, will you give me the bracelet?" he shouted finally. She took a step back in surprise at his irritation, but nodded. "Okay then! I'll *look*."

He quickly glanced down at his older self.

Future Owen looked barely alive. His skin was pale and sweaty, and his cheekbones jutted out like he hadn't eaten in days. Wires ran over his body, attached by little white pads every few inches on his chest.

A strange cold feeling filled Owen's stomach, and he shut his eyes for a moment, letting the image of his older self disappear in his mind. Such unpleasantness didn't really matter, after all. He was going to go back to his own time, and none of this would matter anymore. Finally, he looked back up to Kara. "There. Happy? Bracelet please."

He grabbed it out of her hand before she could object. "Owen, *look* at what Nobody has done to you!" Kara said. "We need to—"

Not waiting for her to finish, Owen dropped the bracelet on the ground, then grabbed the now-charged paddles and stuck them against the bracelet.

"Wait!" Kara shouted, running around to his side of the bed. But he didn't. This had gone on long enough, and it was way past time he went home and forgot all about this future.

If he didn't have an imagination, then at least he wouldn't have to constantly remember terrible things.

"Clear!" Owen shouted, just in case that was necessary, then hit the button on the paddles. A huge jolt of electricity pulsed through the bracelet, sending sparks exploding in every direction. The bracelet immediately began to smoke, and Owen pulled the paddles off in surprise, jumping to his feet.

"*No!*" Kara said, reaching for it, then yanking her hand away as it sparked again. "Why did you *do* that?"

"We have to get home!" Owen shouted at her. "I don't care what happens to me in the future. We can't stay here any longer!"

"We needed a way to not overload the bracelet first!" Kara said, looking furious. "You can't just pump that much electricity into it all at once. The circuitry is probably fried now!"

"What?!" Owen shouted. "Why didn't you say so? Now we really *are* stuck here!"

"I said I had to rig something up!" she shouted, then bit her lip and shook her head. "Doesn't matter, it's done," she said, picking up the bracelet with some gauze. "It's my fault. I should have explained it better, since you don't have . . . forget it. I'm going to go find a way to fix this. Just . . . just stay here, Owen. Maybe try to remember who you used to be while I'm gone."

Owen winced at that. "I'll stay. But don't get caught out there, or we'll never get home."

She looked at him sadly, then quietly slipped out the door without another word, closing it behind her.

"Is she gone?" said a gravelly voice from behind him. Owen's eyes widened, and he turned to find his older self staring at him with dark, sunken eyes. "Sorry, I had to wait until we were alone. If she knew what I was about to say, her antiparadox thing would probably mess it all up. We've got a lot to talk about, and it won't be long before the PFFIA catches you both." He slowly cracked a smile. "Anyway, how are you enjoying the future?"

CHAPTER 8

Nobody's body grew to double Bethany's size, towering over her as he reached out to grab her. Her heart began racing, and in spite of it all, she couldn't help but grin. *Nobody.* Here.

This was the man who had taken her father from her. This was the man who'd kidnapped Owen, who'd imprisoned them in Jupiter City, not letting her see Gwen or Kiel or anyone. This was the man who'd ripped her in half and separated her from her mother and her best friend.

And now, here he was, right when she really, *really* wanted to punch someone.

"Rules are for nonfictionals!" she shouted, and morphed into a cannon. She shot a cannonball straight into his chest, which seemed to stretch like a rubber band, then flung the cannonball right back at her. She dodged it by shrinking into a toy car, then turned back into herself, flinging Twilight throwing stars at him as she moved.

"This rule is the only one that mattered," Nobody said, his giant arms following her as she went. "I warned your father not to let you leave Jupiter City, or I would be less merciful with the freedom I allowed you."

"Freedom?" Bethany yelled as his arm stretched toward her. "To stay locked in one world? That's not freedom, that's a prison!" She morphed into a rocket and started to take off, only for him to yank her back down to the ground, crashing her hard against the already broken ground. The hit sent her reeling, and she transformed back into her human shape unconsciously.

"You have no idea what a true prison is like," Nobody told her, his fingers stretching around her now, then closing around each other. Everything went dark for a moment as his hands merged into each other, then light spilled in once more as his skin turned translucent, and she found herself in a sort of glass cylinder. "Why did you leave your world, fictional Bethany?"

She struck the sides of her prison, but the glass didn't even crack. "Someone brought some sort of ray guns to Jupiter City, and I chased him here. But you must know that, considering it had to be you!" She morphed herself into a ray of light, then passed through the glass prison, being careful to instantly turn back as soon as she had. The last thing she needed was to lose herself in a light beam again.

"You're sadly misinformed," Nobody told her. "But I quickly tire of this. I have important things to do right now, and you're interfering with them. Will you return to Jupiter City, and assure me that you will stay there until I say otherwise? Or will I be forced to deal with you even sooner than I originally intended?"

"Just try it!" she shouted, morphing her hands into spinning drills. "My dad's in danger, and there's no way I'm leaving here without finding a way to cure him!"

Nobody paused at this. "I was not aware of this. What has happened to Christian?"

She snorted and dove forward, driving her drills toward his legs. Nobody just opened holes in his limbs right around her attacks, then closed himself around her arms, trapping her. "You're lying," Bethany growled. "You did this on purpose with your possibility ray guns!"

"Ah," Nobody said, and released her. She started to morph

again, but his finger touched her head, and abruptly she froze in place, unable to move. "I see now. Don't worry, I have only temporarily rewritten you. You'll regain control of yourself once I return you to Jupiter City."

She just stared at him, paralyzed, while internally she screamed in frustration. How could he have defeated her so easily? He'd *rewritten* her? What did that even mean?

Nobody shrank back to his normal size and picked her up with one hand, while the other ripped a page open in midair. On the other side, she could see the Twilight cave beneath Jupiter Hill Observatory, her father's secret headquarters. She tried to struggle, but nothing worked, like her mind had completely lost all connection to her body.

"I never intended for Christian to be affected by this," Nobody told her, moving her around to face his eyeless eyes. "I wanted you to have as much time with him as possible, as a sort of gift to you. We are not enemies, Bethany Sanderson. And I would give you all the happiness in my power—that didn't interfere with my plans. So for your father, I apologize, and forgive this transgression of my rule. You did only what you had to do to save him."

He passed her through the ripped page and set her down on

the floor of the Twilight cave. As she touched it, she began to feel tingling erupting through her body, like every arm and leg had fallen asleep and was waking up at the same time.

"I need . . . to save him," she said, her mouth barely working.

Nobody just looked at her for a moment, then shook his head. "I'm afraid that's impossible, Bethany. His fate will be the same as all fictionals. I do apologize that you haven't had more time with him now. But rest assured that what is happening to him will ultimately lead to more freedom than you could ever imagine: the freedom of pure possibility."

She groaned as her body slowly started listening to her brain, and she pushed her hands beneath her to try to rise to her feet. "I . . . I *will* save him," she said. "And I'll . . . I'll stop you. Count on it."

Nobody just shook his head sadly. "No, you won't. Even if you learned to rewrite yourself, you'd never be able to hold yourself together. Enjoy what time you have left, fictional Bethany. And take a lesson from your nonfictional self and obey my rules. Otherwise, you'll join your father in his fate sooner rather than later."

He reached up to close the page, and Bethany roared in anger, trying to move quickly enough to stop him.

"Shh," a voice whispered in her ear, and something fluttered over her, like a cloth. A shimmering field filled her vision, and someone helped her up. "Don't say anything. I've got this."

Bethany's eyes widened as someone practically pushed them both through the gap in Nobody's page, just before it disappeared completely, and she found herself standing once more in front of the featureless man. She tried to bring her hands up to defend herself, knowing he wouldn't tolerate her breaking the rules a second time . . .

But Nobody didn't even notice her. Instead, he turned around and opened a page leading to what looked like a castle made out of storybooks. He stepped through, and the page closed behind him, leaving Bethany and whoever had just carried her through alone in Quanterium.

She pushed whoever it was away from her, and the shimmering cloth fell off of her. She readied herself for another fight, even if she could barely stand on her own. But no one was there, and she looked around anxiously. "Who's there?" she shouted. "What do you want?"

"A hug hello wouldn't be out of the question," a familiar voice said, and the air in front of her wavered as a cloth dropped to the ground between them, revealing a boy wearing black clothes and a black cape.

Kiel Gnomenfoot winked at her, then seemed to pause for a moment before his eyes rolled back into his head, and he collapsed to the ground.

CHAPTER 9

*O*wen slowly walked over to his older self, not sure how to respond. "Enjoying the future? Are you joking, because—"

"Um, obviously yes," his future self said, rolling his eyes. "I forgot how big a pain I am without any imagination."

Owen snorted. "Yeah, well, I didn't ask to come here. But what did you mean, the PFFIA is going to capture us? If that's true, I need to get Kara and leave—"

Future Owen shook his head, wincing in pain at even that amount of movement. "No, it's already done. It happened to me, and it'll happen to you. But that's not what we need to talk about—"

Owen held up a hand to stop him. "*Nothing's* already done. I can get out now, before they arrive."

His older self glared at him. "Are you really arguing with

me? I lived this already, I know what happens. And if I say you get captured, then you get captured. It needs to happen, to restore your imagination and get you to the fictional world. And when you get there, you're going to have to do what Kara's been telling you. You're going to have to face Nobody. If you don't reunite the worlds, *this* is what happens to us." He gestured at himself. "And we get off lightly. Our friends have it even worse."

Owen stared at him for a moment, not able to picture what his older self was saying, but knowing that he wanted no part of this. "I'm not going back there. There's nothing I can do against him. We've already tried that, remember? Twice."

His future self nodded slowly, then looked away. "Twice for you, three times for me, and more times than I can count overall. When *I* was here in your place, I talked to an Owen five years in my future, and he had talked to an Owen five years in his future. All of us told the next Owen what we tried to do to defeat Nobody, because nothing worked. But you, my friend, are going to break the chain."

Owen's eyes glazed over. "None of that makes any sense."

"Not right now, it won't," his older self said. "But you'll figure it out eventually. Anyway, I need to tell you what happened with my attempt." He cringed. "It went about as badly as it possibly could have. Me, Kara, Kiel, Charm . . . we all went to rescue Bethany. Nobody is going to take both versions of her *here*, into this story." He reached over to a nearby table and tapped some papers. "Remember this? We wrote it before going into Jupiter City for the first time."

Owen stepped closer to the table, picked up the papers, and flipped through them. He saw mentions of bookwyrms and an Outliner and a bunch of other things that made no sense to him now, but they *were* familiar. "This is the story I wrote about Bethany's dad being the evil King of All Stories," he whispered. "Like fan fiction. It was *so* bad. But then Nobody appeared in it and told me to stop writing, because I was influencing the fictional characters in it."

Older Owen coughed. "That's the one. You're going to really regret writing it too. *That's* where Nobody's going to take her. You'll have to fight your way to the Storybook Castle at the end of the story, but one by one, you'll lose your friends along the way, until finally it's just you against Nobody. And that's a fight that no Owen Conners has ever won yet." He narrowed his eyes and stared at Owen. "Not until *you*."

None of this made sense to Owen. As far as he was concerned, his older self was just spouting gibberish. "So if all of this is going to happen the same way every time, then I'm going to lose too. What's the point of even trying?"

"That's what I'm here to tell you, you unimaginative idiot," his older self said. "I hope I wasn't this much of a jerk to *my* older self. You have to think of a *new* way to fight him, something that none of the rest of us Owens have ever tried." He paused, taking a deep breath. "I tried to use my time powers against him, even knowing he could duplicate them. But because of that, none of the other Owens had ever tried it, so I figured, why not? But my heart couldn't take it, and it basically just gave out. I was *useless*."

He looked away, and Owen thought he could see a bit of color coming back into the boy's cheeks. "After I collapsed, Nobody sent me back here to get better. It wasn't out of kindness, but as one last punishment. He knew they could have fixed my heart there, in the fictional world. Instead, he wanted me to experience the future of our world firsthand."

His older self went quiet for a moment, and Owen dropped his head into his hands, not able to wrap his head around any of this. "You said none of the others used their time powers. But without those, we're completely normal. How could they possibly have tried to beat him without using powers?"

"The version of Owen I met here had gone in with magical spells," his older self said, struggling to talk now. The machines around him began to beep quietly, and Owen glanced at them nervously, hoping they weren't setting off any alarms with the nurses or doctors. "The Owen before *him* had all kinds of science fiction weapons. Owens have tried everything we could think of, from giving ourselves new superpowers to bringing in allies from around the fictional world, even once creating another Nobody to fight the first one. But nothing has worked. It always ends with us alone against Nobody, and no matter how powerful we are, he wins." Another wave of pain hit, and he clutched his chest.

"How many of us have tried this?" Owen asked quietly.

His older self shook his head. "It doesn't matter."

"How many?"

"Thousands, okay?" his older self shouted, and the machines' beeping grew more insistent. "Maybe there's no way to beat him, I don't know! But I do know that you have to *try*, or the world ends up like this, and we can't let that happen. Have you seen what they're doing outside? It's disgusting!"

"What happens if we *don't* get captured now?" Owen asked

quietly. "What happens if I just go home and ignore all of this?"

"You don't have a choice," his older self said, glaring at him. "You *always* go back to the fictional world. You'll want to, once you get your imagination back. Trust me."

"But what if I don't? What if I decide that someone else should handle this, since . . . well, since we know I *can't*? Since every time I've tried in thousands of different time lines or whatever, I lose? What happens if I just decide to not play the game?"

"It's not a game, and you don't have a choice!" Owen's older self said again.

"How can you know that?" Owen shouted.

"Because all of us asked this *exact same thing*, and we all went anyway!" His older self's face contorted with pain, and he gasped as he fell back against the bed. "We were all . . . selfish. Comes from having no . . . imagination. Our fictional heart is too worn down from using our time powers to give us the connection we'd need. Kara's right. Kara's always right about us. You can't imagine yourself in someone . . . else's shoes. But doesn't matter. I have . . . to tell you . . . there's one other thing—"

The door to the room crashed open and Kara leaped inside, then slammed the door behind her. "They're coming, Owen!" she said. "A doctor and a nurse. The lady downstairs told them we never came out and to call security. But I think your older self's monitors are setting off alarms too. We have to get out now!"

Owen looked from her to the door, then back at his older self, who was waving a hand for Owen to come closer. He wanted to run out the door, *knew* it was the right choice, but instead moved in and took his other self's hand. "What?" he hissed urgently. "What's the last thing?"

"You . . . you need to . . . tell her," his older self said, then winced, grabbing his chest. "You need to tell her the truth!"

"Her? You mean Kara? Or Bethany?" Owen said. Someone started to open the door, but Kara threw her weight against it, slamming it shut again. She gave him an anxious look and motioned for him to hurry.

"No," his older self said, his eyes drooping as the machines beeped louder and louder. "You know who I mean. You need . . . to tell her it was *you* . . . the whole time. Not him. Not *Kiel*. It was you."

And then the hand in Owen's drooped, and he gently laid it on the bed.

The door burst open, knocking Kara against the wall, and a woman in a long white coat came running in. "We're losing him!" she shouted as a nurse passed her, going for the paddles on the ground. The doctor turned to glare at Owen, who leaped out of the way. "Did you kids use the crash cart?" she said, glaring at him accusingly. "That is not a toy!"

Then she stopped, seeing Kara for the first time.

"You're the girl from earlier!" she said. "The one who disappeared right in front of me. You're one of *them*, aren't you! Don't you move, security's already on its way." She quickly punched a button behind her on the wall, and a whooping alarm sounded through the building.

Footsteps pounded down the hall toward them, and Owen just stared at Kara, not sure what to do. He couldn't use his time powers, not with his heart so weak. But if he didn't, they were going to get caught, just like his older self had said!

Kara looked around desperately, like she was searching for a weapon, but the doctor grabbed her from behind, locking her arms tightly around Kara's. "Oh no you don't," the doctor said. "You're not going anywhere this time. The PFFIA is going to question you and find out how you pulled that little trick!"

The footsteps were getting closer.

"Owen, run!" Kara screamed. "Save yourself!"

He stared at her, wondering if he could. His older self's

words raced through his head. *You won't have a choice.* But the footsteps outside were probably still far enough away that he could outrun whoever it was.

If he could get away, he could keep from getting captured, maybe not have to go back to the fictional world and not lose to Nobody again. And then he wouldn't have to end up in this hospital bed, dying in front of his past self.

It was the logical thing to do.

But something bothered him, way down deep, like a memory that didn't feel real . . . a feeling he'd had, when Kara was touching his hand. Every time they touched, his imagination came back and logic went out the window. Each time, instead of doing the practical, safe thing, he wanted to do what he thought was *right*, even if it ended up hurting him.

What if *that* was who he really was, and all he needed was to get his imagination back to see it? There wasn't any way to know for sure, so logically, he should escape while he could. That was the only thing that made any sense.

"We surrender," Owen said, raising his hands, fighting every urge in his brain screaming at him to run.

"No!" Kara shouted, but security guards quickly filled the room, grabbing her from the doctor.

"This one needs to be tested," the woman said as the guards took Kara. "She disappeared on me a few hours ago, right into thin air. She might be one of *them*." Then she pointed at Owen. "That one, I don't know. Give him to the PFFIA too, so it can question him. See what they both know about that bracelet she's got. It looks far too made-up to be real."

As the guards grabbed Owen's arms, the doctor's words echoed in Owen's brain. The bracelet looked too *made-up* to be real? What did *that* mean?

Then the guards pulled some sort of black cloth over Owen's head, and everything went dark.

CHAPTER 10

"Kiel!" Bethany shouted, leaping toward him and cradling his head in her arms. "Are you okay?"

The former boy magician slowly opened his eyes. "Oh, hey, Beth," he said, looking around. "Did I miss something? Have you always worn a cape?" He smiled. "I like the mask, very mysterious."

She glared at him. "You just collapsed after using some kind of invisibility cloak to keep Nobody from noticing me. Where did you . . . how did . . . what *happened* to you?"

Kiel tried to sit up, only for his eyes to go wide, and he fell back to the ground. "I seem to be a bit dizzy," he told her. "I'm not sure when the last time I had any food or water was. You don't happen to have any, do you?"

Bethany looked around, then saw something promising. "Stay here," she told him, and gently laid him back on the ground.

"Sounds good," he told her. "Wow, Charm really let this place get run down. We should ask her about that."

Bethany draped the invisible cloth over Kiel to hide him, marking the spot carefully in her mind so she could find him again, then pulled out three Twilight throwing stars and silently made her way toward a broken fountain down the street she'd appeared on. Kiel was right . . . something insane had happened to Quanterium. Buildings all around Bethany were destroyed, but each in a different way. Some looked like they'd collapsed into perfect spheres of their material, while others hung in midair, every component of the house floating just millimeters from the rest, like someone had pulled it all apart. One seemed to be swirling around like it was trapped in a whirlpool, but that couldn't be possible.

It wasn't just the buildings, either. The street she stood on warped into a loop a hundred or so yards in front of her, before rising straight up into the air as far as she could see. The once-great city square, where a Kiel Gnomenfoot statue would at some point be built, was now jiggling in the breeze as if it were made of some sort of gelatin.

And maybe worst of all, just a few blocks away from her, a wall of white nothingness cut through the city, a wall that was slowly, ever so slowly, *moving*. As she watched, a building right at the edge began to dissipate as the wall touched it, disappearing into nothingness, just like she'd seen the Toad Prince's henchman do.

What had happened here? Nobody seemed to be saying that what was happening to her father would be happening everywhere. Had whatever it was already started here? What had he said . . . the freedom of possibility? Was that what the all of nothingness was?

But why hadn't he known what she was talking about, when she mentioned the man bringing possibility ray guns into Jupiter City?

She reached the broken fountain safely and found robotic fish slowly swimming upside down in it. Hopefully that was a result of whatever happened here, and not a sign that the water wasn't good. She used her powers to morph her hand into a large jug, then filled it with water and brought it back to the spot she'd left Kiel. After a few moments, she located the invisibility cloth and pulled it off.

"That's new," Kiel said, staring at the jug at the end of her arm. "Have you always been able to do that?"

"Not exactly," she said, grinning in spite of herself. She

brought the jug to his mouth, and he slowly drank as she looked him over. Wherever he'd come from, he'd been through something awful. His clothes were ripped in places, and his skin was much paler than usual.

He drank as much as he could, then leaned back, his eyes on her. "I seem to have missed a few things while I've been out. Want to catch me up? What happened to Quanterium?"

"Um, this planet is from *your* story, not mine," she said. "Where have *you* been? How did you get here? Did you know Nobody—"

He held up a hand. "I followed him here, through one of his ripped pages. It was the first time he left that castle he lives in for the last few days. He captured me, Beth. Months ago now. I was supposed to meet you after a year, when I was exploring Magisteria to try to figure out what my purpose was, now that the war was over. Remember how I gave up magic?" He wiggled his fingers at her. "Haven't used it since. But every so often, a magic item here or there is still pretty useful."

"Nobody *kidnapped* you?" Bethany said, both her anger at the man and her horror for Kiel threatening to overwhelm her.

"He claimed to know you and said I couldn't be allowed to help you, not if the fictional world was going to survive," Kiel said. "Then he reached out, and . . ." A cloud passed over his face, and he looked past Bethany, not focusing on anything. "I couldn't see what he did, but I ended up in the middle of nothing. There wasn't anything there, just . . . white. Like that wall of nothingness in the sky behind you. Time didn't move, or so it seemed. I never got hungry or thirsty, at least not while I was in there. I couldn't move, but I could still think and talk." His voice grew softer. "I screamed for help, begged to be released, but no one ever responded. I don't know how long I was even there. . . ."

"How did you escape?" Bethany whispered.

"I didn't," Kiel said, shaking his head. "Someone freed me. I never found out who. I came out of the nothingness and found myself in a castle made of books. Whoever it was that helped me escape left me the invisibility quilt over there, and a few other choice items, along with a note. It said I should wait for Nobody to open a doorway to another story, then follow him. That was the only way I'd ever get out. So I waited, watching Nobody from under the quilt, for what must have been days. Just as I started thinking he was never going to leave, out of nowhere, he ripped open a page and traveled here. I followed him, only to find you fighting him."

He grinned. "Wish I could have been more of a help with that."

Bethany wiped her hand over her eyes, not sure what to say. "I can't believe he's had you this whole time," she whispered. "If I'd known . . ."

He shrugged. "You couldn't have. And besides, I found out a few things while waiting there. That white wave of nothingness out there? That's the pure possibility he's talking about. And it's happening in every fictional world. Well, all but one." He frowned. "Jupiter City was supposed to be last, he said. I didn't know what he meant by that until I heard him talking to you."

"What does it do?" she asked, staring up at the possibility above them.

"I don't really get the science," Kiel said. "Not that I really get *any* science. But Nobody talked like it'd take in the entire fictional universe, and we'd all become just pure possibility. He thought that would mean the universe could start fresh, without any interference from nonfictional people." He wrinkled his nose. "Sounded a lot like the Magister, honestly."

"Did he mention he separated the worlds?" she asked. "Not just them, but me, too. Now I'm solely fictional, and my annoying, horrible nonfictional self is probably reciting rules to Owen right now on their world."

Kiel stared at her, his mouth dropping open. "You're kidding. Are you okay? Beth, that's terrible!"

She laughed at the worry in his eyes. "It's not, really! I kind of love it, actually. I mean, I'm sure we'll have to go back eventually. . . ." She rolled her eyes. "But for now, it's the best. I'm not always worrying about pointless things, and I get to see my dad. . . ." She trailed off, remembering the state she'd left her father in. The memory hit her like a brick, and she sat back on the ground. How could she let herself get so distracted? She had to focus here! Her father was in danger!

"You found your father?" Kiel said. "That's great! Where was he?"

"Well, Nobody had him, too," Bethany said quickly. "But he's in danger of turning into this possibility stuff too, if I don't figure out a way to stop it. I tracked a guy here from Jupiter City, someone with weapons that did this to people," she said, pointing at the possibility wave in the sky. "And my dad got hit by one. He's okay for now, but I need to find that guy and figure out a way to reverse it."

"Right," Kiel said, slowly pushing himself up to a sitting position. "I'm ready. We'll save your dad, the entire fictional universe, and reunite you with your nonfictional self. Shouldn't be long now that I'm back to set things right." He grinned, then almost fell back over as a wave of dizziness hit again.

"Slow down," she told him. "I can carry you using my super-powers. But we need to find the man I chased here. Nobody didn't sound like he knew what the guy was doing, so maybe we can use that. But first we need to find him. He came through a portal here only a few seconds before me, but once I got here, he was gone."

"Maybe he had an invisibility quilt," Kiel said, picking his up.

"If he does, we're never going to find him without help," she said, helping him to his feet. "Let's try to find some Quante-rians, or at least a building that's still standing. Maybe we can contact Charm somehow and she can help!"

Kiel winced at that. "She's not exactly my biggest fan right now. I might have missed a few scheduled meet-ups."

"Oh, that's okay, she thinks you're Owen anyway," Bethany told him.

Kiel blinked. "I'm sorry, she thinks I'm *who*?"

CHAPTER 11

The first thing Owen saw when he pulled the hood off his head was a poster of one of the black-helmeted soldiers standing with his arms around a smiling family. Below them were the words, *If you see something impossible, alert the PFFIA!* A little boy in the picture was giving the black helmet a thumbs-up.

Owen groaned, and his muscles screamed as he tried to move. After security had put a hood on him, someone had handcuffed his hands behind him and thrown him into some kind of vehicle, where he'd lain facedown for a few minutes before it had stopped. Then they'd dragged him out again and set him to walking, letting him trip over and over, completely blind.

He'd ended up in an unfamiliar building, riding up in an elevator, then pushed into a room, where he landed on a bed. The handcuffs were removed, the door closed, and for a moment, everything had gone silent. Owen waited for three long, deep breaths before pulling the hood off, but he found himself alone.

Where was he? He rubbed his forehead, trying to clear the fog in his head. The room had just one door and no windows, the bed he sat on, a few posters, a toilet, and a sink.

Was this some kind of jail cell?

He winced, this time not from the pain in his muscles. The first time he'd been locked up, it'd taken Moira, a criminal genius, to rescue him and Kiel. Then he'd managed to escape from a time prison, but that took the help of fictional readers. This time, no one would be coming to rescue him. Only two people even knew where he was in this future: One was in a hospital unconscious, and the other was as trapped as he was.

You don't have a choice, his older self had said. *You need to be captured.* But that wasn't true! He could have done something, anything to try to escape, or at least to fight off the security guards in the hospital.

But no, instead he had to decide to go off on some crazy adventure, trying to save the future and regain his imagination. What had he been thinking? This was the nonfictional world, and things didn't work that way here. Why hadn't he listened to his logic?

After all, what could a normal person even do against something like this? Black-helmeted soldiers and weird propaganda posters from insane government agencies asking you to look out for anything impossible?

Not knowing what else to do, Owen glanced at the next poster. *Books are dangerous,* it said. *Burn all copies today to keep us safe!* Another smiling family and black helmet, this time in front of a burning book bonfire.

He turned away, sickened. What had happened here in the future? Why were *books* considered so dangerous? Without an imagination, no one could even read them.

The door opened abruptly, and Owen jumped in surprise as a black helmet entered the room. "Come with me," the man said in that monotone voice they all used. Owen nodded, unable to think of anything else to do, and followed the soldier outside.

His room turned out to be at the end of a long hallway filled with doors. Next to a bank of elevators, a sign claimed this was floor nineteen of the PFFIA, whatever that was. Was it some new police force in the future? Something like the CIA or FBI? Or just a place for black-helmeted soldiers to imprison anyone who did something even slightly suspicious?

The man in the black helmet stopped in front of a door with

a sign that said INTERROGATION ROOM 84, and Owen winced. *That* didn't sound promising. Not that he or Kara had really done anything wrong, beyond Kara making up a story about their identities back in the hospital. Did that really deserve an interrogation?

The man opened the door and gestured for Owen to enter, so he did. The black helmet didn't follow, though, and instead closed the door behind Owen. A lock clicked, and Owen took a seat at a small table in the middle of the room, directly in front of a glass wall. It was hard to tell if the wall was a mirror or window, given how dark the room was. The only light in the room shone down directly into Owen's eyes, now that he was seated.

He looked around for a moment, wondering if he was just supposed to start talking. "Hello?" he whispered, but no one responded. Finally, he started to stand back up, only for an image to appear on the glass in front of him.

It was his older self, lying in a hospital bed connected to tubes.

Owen frowned, not sure what was going on. Maybe this *was* about lying to the hospital staff? He slowly stood and began to move around the table to get closer to the image to see better.

"SIT DOWN OR YOU WILL BE TASERED," said a loud, emotionless voice over a speaker from somewhere above him. "DO NOT TOUCH THE *WALL OF TRUTH*."

Owen immediately jumped back into his seat, his eyes wide. "Who *are* you?" he asked softly.

"DO NOT ASK QUESTIONS. ANSWER THEM ONLY."

Owen swallowed hard, then nodded, waiting for the next question.

The voice, though, went silent.

On the wall before him, a doctor entered the hospital room (oh, this was a *video*, not a photo) and checked the machines, then frowned, shaking her head, and left.

Another few seconds went by, and then Kara appeared out of thin air in the hospital room.

What? Owen jumped to his feet, both worried and excited that she had escaped. But why had she gone back—

"SIT DOWN."

Owen took his seat again as Kara looked around, almost as if she were surprised. "Owen?" she said, her voice coming over the same speaker above him. "Owen, are you okay? What happened to you? Did Nobody do this?"

Nobody? Why would she . . . wait, this wasn't happening

live, was it? This was Kara *before* she'd come back to the past. This was when she learned that future Owen's heart wasn't working.

"Owen?" she said, touching his cheek, then looked at the machines. "Oh *no*, Owen, your heartbeat. It's barely *there*. Owen? What happened here?"

Owen's older self whispered something to her, too quiet for the video to pick up. She leaned in and listened to him for a moment, her face running through multiple emotions as he spoke. Abruptly, older Owen gasped in pain, and alarms began sounding on the machines.

The doctor appeared back on-screen, looking surprised. "Who are you? What are you doing here?" the woman demanded, and Kara backed away.

"I'm his friend, and I was worried—"

"His heart just stopped," the doctor said, pushing past Kara. "Get out of here. I need to try to start it again!"

Kara stepped out of the image, but he could still hear her voice. "Owen! It's going to be okay! I'll do what you said, and—"

"Get out of here!" the doctor repeated, and brought some paddles to Owen's chest. "Clear!" She hit the button, and future

Owen's body jumped. A second time, and the alarms stopped as the machines showed a steady, if weak, heartbeat.

"Is he okay?" Owen could hear Kara ask from off-screen.

"You're not supposed to be here," the doctor told her. "I'm going to have to take you to security. Come here and—"

And then she stopped, glancing around. "Where did she go? Security! We've got an intruder in here. I need—"

The image disappeared.

"WE'VE TESTED YOUR DNA," the voice over the speakers said. "YOU MATCH THAT OF OWEN CONNERS, THE TEENAGER CURRENTLY IN THAT VERY SAME HOSPITAL BED RIGHT NOW. THAT VIDEO WAS TAKEN THREE HOURS AGO. YOU THEREFORE *CANNOT* BE HIM. HOW DID YOU CHANGE OFFICIAL PFFIA RECORDS?"

Uh-oh. "I didn't change the records," Owen said quietly. "They must be wrong somehow."

"WHO WAS THAT GIRL? WE HAVE NO RECORDS FOR HER, AND NO EXPLANATION AS TO HOW SHE APPEARED AND DISAPPEARED IN THE HOSPITAL ROOM."

Owen bit his lip. He couldn't tell the truth, that she was

fictional and had traveled in time. That wasn't exactly the kind of thing a nonfictional person would believe. But how could he lie? He literally couldn't think of anything except the truth!

Ugh. Now would be a *really* good time for his imagination to start working again.

He fell back on Kara's story. "She's a friend of mine," he said slowly, concentrating on each word to make sure he didn't mess it up. "And a friend of my brother. That was him on-screen, my older brother Owen. That must be why our records were mixed up. She was going to check on him—"

"YOU ARE LYING."

Owen shook his head. "This is the truth!" he shouted, though it felt painful to even say. "You have to listen to me, that's my brother, and—"

"YOUR VITAL SIGNS SHOW THAT YOU ARE LYING. YOU WILL HAVE ONE MORE CHANCE TO TRUTH-FULLY ANSWER THE QUESTION. IF NOT, YOU WILL BE SENT TO REPROGRAMMING."

Owen sighed. "I can't . . . I don't know how—"

An image flashed on-screen again, this time showing the broken time bracelet.

"WHAT IS THIS DEVICE, AND WHAT DOES IT DO?"

Owen dropped his head, out of stories, out of lies. If they knew when he wasn't telling the truth, then it didn't matter anyway. "It's a time bracelet, okay?" he whispered. "It lets people travel in time."

There. Let his vital signs show that he wasn't making this up, and see what they did with *that*.

The voice was silent for a moment. "INSTRUMENTS SHOW YOU ARE TELLING THE TRUTH. THEREFORE, IT IS CLEAR THAT YOU HAVE HAD ILLEGAL CONTACT WITH FICTIONAL ENTITIES, SOMETHING THE PROTECTION FROM FICTIONAL INVADERS AGENCY CANNOT TOLERATE. YOU WILL NOW BE SENT TO TESTING TO DETERMINE IF YOU ARE FICTIONAL YOURSELF, OR MERELY A TRAITOR TO YOUR WORLD."

Owen blinked several times. Um . . . *what*, now? The protection from fictional who?

And he was going to be tested to see if he was *fictional*? How did they even know that fictional people were real to begin with?!

"I'm not fictional!" Owen shouted up at the speaker as two black helmets burst into the room, grabbing both his arms.

"I'm *nonfictional*! This is my world! I didn't do anything wrong! Let me *go*—"

But they didn't listen. Instead, one of the black helmets pulled out a small black box and stuck it into Owen's arm. Electricity zapped through him, and he fell to the ground, muscles twitching uncontrollably. Another hood came out, and again, the world fell into darkness.

CHAPTER 12

"Wow, a lot really *has* happened," Kiel said as Bethany drove him around the destroyed streets of Quanterium in car form, his invisibility quilt draped over her to keep hidden. She'd morphed into an electric car too, in an effort to keep her noise to a minimum, but there was only so much her superpowers could do about that. "So what did you say your superhero name was again?"

"Twilight Girl," Bethany growled through the car's radio.

Kiel snorted. "Twilight Girl? Really?"

"You're saying it wrong. *Twilight Girl*," she growled.

"Ah, I get it now," Kiel said. "And that explains the purple cape, because that's the color of the setting sun?" He reached around and pulled his black cape forward. "I mean, purple's okay, but isn't black much cooler?"

"It runs in the family, so don't push it," Bethany said, avoiding an enormous hole that seemed to go down several thousand feet right in the middle of the road.

"And Owen's a superhero now too?"

"My dad says so," Bethany told him. "I'm just glad he's not trapped anymore. At least he's safe in the nonfictional world. What could go wrong there?"

"Let's hope he isn't bored, at least," Kiel said, patting her dashboard. "Have I mentioned how incredible your power is?"

Her hood grew warm, which she took for blushing. "Only a few hundred times. Are you seeing anything? We're supposed to be watching for Quanterians and my suspect."

"The whole city is empty," Kiel said, looking out through the shimmering invisibility quilt as they drove by houses, stores, and government buildings, all destroyed in weird and terrifying manners. On one block, a localized black hole seemed to have eaten half of the houses. And on the next, a backward fire rebuilt a few homes in slow motion, unburning remnants of the buildings as it rose into the air. "Wait," Kiel said, slamming on Bethany's brakes, which was rude. "There. The Quanterian Center for Scientific Studies. It looks like it's intact, not all weird like the rest of the city."

Bethany shoved her brake pedal back toward him, throwing

his foot backward and off of her. "*I'm* the one driving here," she said, then slowly turned in the direction he pointed. The enormous complex that was the Center for Scientific Studies didn't look damaged, which made sense. Since Quanterians practically worshipped science, these buildings were probably better protected than the rest of the city, especially considering the experiments that happened within.

"If there's a working computer, I might be able to log into the Nalwork," Kiel said. "I guessed Charm's password a while back. If we can access the system, we can search the city for your guy and see if anyone else is around. At the very least, maybe there's a record of what happened here."

Bethany parked in front of the center's stairs and let Kiel out before morphing back into her human self. "The Nalwork?"

"Yeah, basically like your Internet in the nonfictional world, just with more virtual reality," Kiel told her, walking slowly up the stairs. She moved to support him, and together they made better time. "But we won't need to get into that, not for a few searches like this."

There wasn't any electricity running through the building's walls like there used to be, which didn't bode well for the lights inside. As they approached the massive unbroken entrance doors, Bethany grabbed her Twilight flashlight from her utility belt, turned it on, and quietly pushed the door on the right open.

Just like the outside, the interior of the science center seemed to have escaped any surreal changes. A tall, beautiful lobby opened into massive hallways that led off in various directions in a sort of half circle radiating out from the entrance. Down each hallway, she could just make out doors on either side, which she knew led to various types of laboratories.

"All the labs are open to the public," Kiel whispered. "That's why they all have windows, so you can walk by, see something you like, and jump into an experiment. Charm and I once tried forming a miniature galaxy while in disguise, but they kicked us out when I innocently suggested that the new species that showed up worship us."

Bethany grinned, then quickly fixed her Twilight glare back in place. Her father was in danger, and this was no time for jokes!

Bethany led Kiel down the central hallway, her eyes constantly moving, looking for any signs of life or at least a working computer. Each laboratory they passed seemed to have been abandoned in a hurry. While not as chaotic as the destruction outside, the labs still had overturned chairs, and desks covered with broken glass and cracked tablet screens. Three different labs were filled with some sort of gas, which was a good reminder that the labs were all airtight, thankfully, as there was no telling what those gases might do, or how poisonous they were.

Just as they were about to give up, Bethany spotted a soft light at the end of the hall, which turned out to be a small computer still running, probably on an internal battery. "Will this work?" she asked Kiel, carefully watching the door just in case anyone had heard their entrance.

"Let's try it," he said, and began typing on the computer. "Any guesses as to what Charm's password is? It's something that reminded her of why she was fighting."

"Is it 'Kiel Gnomenfoot'?" Bethany asked, pushing him gently on the shoulder.

Kiel snorted. "Unfortunately, no. It's the date of the accident that took her parents' lives." He typed it in, and the screen changed briefly, though Bethany couldn't read it from a distance. "Looks like the Nalwork is down for the most part, which makes sense. We won't be able to search the city, unfortunately." He paused, the screen flashing as he went from page to page. "There is something here, though, in the science center files. Something sent to Charm's personal account. It showed up as a notification as soon as I logged in."

"What, like a file or something?"

"Looks like a couple of videos," Kiel said, and pushed a button.

The computer beeped, and a video projection appeared in the air right above it, showing Charm holding a familiar-looking ray gun.

"Hello. Hi. This is a message for, um, whoever finds this." She sighed, looking deeply disgusted. "Wow, I hate doing these. But whatever. There's a very real chance that I'm not going to make it back from where I'm going, so it's good to have a record."

She held up the ray gun, showing it to the camera.

"This is the Prospect Enhancer, as my scientists called it. But to me, it's just a possibility ray gun." She brought it back and put her finger on the trigger. "I built it to use against a faceless mound of waste named *Nobody*."

CHAPTER 13

Owen's muscles eventually stopped twitching from the Taser, but since his face was covered by a hood again, everything still felt incredibly disorienting and surreal. Without being able to see, and with sounds muffled by the cloth, it was almost like this was some kind of dream . . . or it would have been, if he weren't getting pushed and pulled everywhere, tripping and smashing against the ground every few feet without any way to catch himself.

Finally getting shoved into a seat felt like a kindness, though he landed on his handcuffed hands and had to maneuver himself off of them. The floor beneath him started rumbling, followed by a jerking and a sense of motion, so apparently they were moving him again.

Wherever they were going, it didn't take more than ten or fifteen minutes to reach. Moments after the sense of motion stopped, rough hands yanked him to his feet, tore off his hood, and tossed him into the air.

The rush of air on his face energized him enough to at least try to get his feet under him as he flew, then hit the ground hard enough to send a shock wave up through his legs. The force of his stop knocked him off-balance, and he fell back against a large, black shuttle he'd apparently been riding in.

A large black shuttle that now *hovered* behind him.

Owen slowly stepped away from it, staring in shock at the vehicle as it floated a few feet off the ground. This was five years in the future, and they already had flying cars? When had *that* happened?

A second hooded figure appeared in the shuttle doorway, and Owen moved out of the way, not wanting to get hit. Someone yanked that person's hood off as well, revealing Kara looking confused and disoriented.

"Wait!" Owen shouted, but he was too late; the guard tossed her from the shuttle as well. Owen leaped forward to try to reach her, and she crashed into him hard, her momentum sending them both to the ground.

"Owen!" she said, rolling off of him and struggling to her

knees, her hands cuffed behind her back too. "Are you okay? Where are we?"

"No idea," he grunted, catching his breath after getting her shoulder in his gut. He nodded at the hovering shuttle as he rolled to his knees too. "Are you seeing this, or is it just me? It's floating, right?"

She nodded. "Is that unusual? We are in your future."

"Well, we weren't anywhere close to it in my time," he said. "But we also didn't have soldiers burning books, either."

"Get up," a black-helmeted soldier said, yanking Owen painfully to his feet, then undoing his cuffs. Kara followed a moment later, but as she rubbed her wrists, she glanced past Owen and stiffened at the sight of something.

"What is *that*?" she asked softly.

Owen sighed, really not wanting to see whatever horrible thing was there. Knowing he'd regret it, he slowly turned around.

Thousands of black helmets were lined up in rows, like an army preparing for battle. Each held one of the laser rifles Owen had seen at the book burning, along with other science fiction–looking weapons. Men and women in white lab coats holding computer tablets made their way between the ranks of black helmets to travel back and forth between various tentlike buildings.

But none of that was what had surprised Kara. Behind the army of black helmets was something oddly familiar: a giant black tower rising into the sky, one that Owen had first seen in the pages of a Kiel Gnomenfoot book.

The Magister's tower.

For a moment everything started to make sense. Whatever he'd thought before, this *had* to be the fictional world! That's why his interrogators had asked him if he was fictional. Sure, it didn't explain why they burned books or how everything had turned into a crazy fascist society, but maybe this was what happened when Quanterium invaded Magisteria. And if Quanterium *had* invaded, that definitely explained the technology and robotlike soldiers.

"Did they build that thing in the middle of some guy's yard?" Kara asked, pointing past the tower, and her words gave Owen a cold chill.

He looked to where she was pointing and found another familiar sight: Jonathan Porterhouse's mansion.

All of the hope running through him at the discovery of the tower crashed to the ground, dead. This *wasn't* the fictional world. This was the version of the tower that the Magister had built on Jonathan Porterhouse's property after escaping from his books into the real world, back when Owen and Bethany had first met. The Magister had built it as an exact replica of the one in the books, and he had been using it to unleash fictional monsters on the nonfictional world.

After Bethany defeated him, she and Owen had eventually convinced Mr. Porterhouse to tell people it was built for the Kiel Gnomenfoot movies, something he'd resisted making previously. But after his characters popped out of their books and threatened his life, suddenly Jonathan Porterhouse worried a lot less about keeping his stories pure, and he let the movie studio run wild.

Last Owen had heard, actually, the studio wanted to open the tower for tours. Only rumor had it that the first production assistants to explore the tower had run for their lives, screaming. Knowing what kind of things might be in there, Owen wasn't really surprised. And that was even after Kiel had sealed the doors leading to *truly* frightening things.

But what was this army of black helmets doing here? Why were they mobilizing on Jonathan Porterhouse's property? Plus, everything nearby glowed with a weird blue light, almost like it was covered by a force field or something. The various hovering shuttles passed through it okay, but the trees growing close to it had branches sheared off right where they touched the light.

Owen rubbed his forehead, feeling an enormous headache coming on. Flying cars were one thing, but force fields were *definitely* not coming in five years. What had happened in that time?

"Into the Determination Center," one of the black helmets said, shoving Owen forward. Kara followed just behind, and a group of the black helmets escorted them to one of the tent buildings close to the Magister's tower.

As they got closer, Owen noticed that the tower door was guarded by a smaller gate of shimmering blue light, as well as four of the black-helmeted soldiers. But why guard the tower? Nothing in there could get out, not after Kiel had locked it down. Maybe someone had broken into the sealed-off areas and released some sort of magic? Was that how they'd managed to build all of this new technology?

But none of it seemed *magical* so much as science fiction-ish. Of the two planets from the Kiel Gnomenfoot books, it definitely felt more like Quanterian tech, honestly.

"In here," a black helmet said, pushing Owen toward a door

that slid open as he neared. Owen started to object, a bit tired of all the shoving, but one look at his own reflection in the cold glass of the man's helmet made him turn quickly around and walk inside.

The Determination Center was filled with men and women in lab coats, all with various intimidating-looking instruments in their hands. As he entered, every one of them turned to stare. The nearest one roughly pulled Owen over, then ran a long, silver stick in front of him from head to toe. It lit up slightly around his chest, but otherwise had no reaction, and the woman frowned.

"Getting a slight reading around the heart," she said, then nodded to the next scientist. This one grabbed his arm and immediately stuck him with a needle, hard enough to make him shout out in surprise and pain.

"Oh, it's going to get worse than this," the man said, sneering at him as he pulled blood out of Owen. "And you deserve it. Welcome to the real world, fictional *scum*. And don't bother with the refugee story. We all know the *real* reason you're here is because you hate our reality."

"Fictional *what*, now?" Owen said. "I'm not . . . what refugee story—"

But before he could finish, another scientist pushed a screen in front of him and stared at it, frowning. "We've got a prototypical Homo sapiens," the man said, like he was checking off a list. "No extraneous extremities, no obvious mutation or genetic manipulation like some of the others. No signs of alien or mythological background. Could be fantasy related? Psionics also a possibility. Confirming some kind of technology in the heart region, could be fictional."

"I'm *nonfictional*," Owen shouted, wishing he was close enough to Kara to get at least a little bit of imagination back. He really needed an idea of how to get out of here! But before he could move, a loud beeping behind him made all the scientists look up.

The woman with the silver stick at the door had just run it over Kara, and the stick was going off like the most horrible alarm clock ever, bright lights flashing in time with the horrible noise.

"She's one of them!" the woman yelled. "Get her out of here immediately. Freeze her with the rest!"

"One of who?" Kara asked, but the scientists just stared at her in disgust. Two of the black helmets burst in from outside and grabbed her arms. "*Hey*, let go!"

"No!" Owen shouted, and leaped toward her, pushing the screen in front of him out of the way as he tried to climb over instruments and people to help her. A scientist grabbed him by his shirt, but Owen whirled around and kicked the man as hard as he could, and the scientist released his grip.

"Owen!" Kara shouted from just outside the door as black helmets flooded in, their laser rifles all buzzing as they aimed at Owen. He froze and put his hands into the air, unsure what else he could do.

He gritted his teeth in anger as he heard Kara scream again, farther away this time. He tried wracking his brain for ideas, something that might help him escape the tent and free her from the guards, but his mind just went blank. Argh, why did he have to be so *useless* without his imagination?

The black helmets slowly dropped their weapons and left the tent as the scientists turned back to Owen. "Test that one's genetics," the woman with the silver stick said, pointing it at him. "He's probably cloaking his fictional makeup somehow."

"I'm not fictional!" Owen shouted. "I'm Owen Conners, from—"

"We know who you are, Mr. Conners," said a woman toward the back of the building. She gestured, and a screen appeared out of nowhere in midair, showing the older version of Owen in the hospital. "However, the real Owen Conners is currently lying in a bed ten miles away. So tell us exactly how you're standing here, five years younger?"

"I'm not his fictional twin, if that's what you're saying!" he shouted. Two scientists grabbed him, and he struggled against them, but one stuck another needle into his arm, this time injecting something, and the world turned all woozy.

"How do you even *know* about the fictional world?" Owen asked, glaring at the weirdly blobby things standing all around him.

"You claim to be nonfictional, but you've never heard of the invasion by the fictionals?" one of the blobs said. "It happened here in your own hometown! Next time come up with a better story."

Owen started to say something snarky in reply, but he couldn't get past what the blob had said. An invasion by *fictionals*?

And then the room spun violently, and Owen collapsed to the floor, unconscious.

CHAPTER 14

T hat's the weapon that the man in the suit gave to our super-villains!" Bethany shouted, pointing at Charm's ray gun.

Kiel paused the video and looked at Bethany. "So she built it? But how did that man get it, then? And how does she know Nobody too? He really gets around, huh?"

Bethany frowned as Kiel's fists opened and closed nervously. Was he just joking to cover his fear? "She must have faced him after I saved my father. I missed a lot of it, since I was a light ray at the time."

Kiel just stared at her for a moment, then shrugged. "I think you left that part of the story out, but sure, okay. Anyway, why would she create something that could make people disappear?"

"Maybe she'll explain," Bethany said, nodding at the video. Kiel reached out and hit the button, starting it again.

"I've had my scientists working on this ever since that

Nobody guy beat me up and sent me back here," Charm said, staring at the ray gun. "Whoever he is, he can change himself into anything or anyone he wants. So if I'm going to destroy him, and I *am*, I needed some powers. And a friend of mine gave me a good idea on just how to do that."

She spread her fingers, and diagrams appeared on the screen, diagrams that Bethany recognized. They were the plans Charm had developed when working on Owen's superhero power ideas. As Charm zoomed in, Bethany gasped, realizing these plans in particular were for *her* powers.

"I gave my friend the power to turn into anything inanimate, by rewriting her DNA," Charm said, then waved her hand at the camera. "Don't bother with science questions, it shouldn't have worked. Different reality, different rules. But back here in the real world of Quanterium, I figured that could be a good starting point, only we'd have to take it to another level entirely, enabling whoever had the power to change into anything they wanted. So we developed the possibility ray gun for just that reason. To give me the same abilities as this Nobody idiot."

"Whoa!" Bethany shouted, grabbing Kiel and turning him toward her. "Are you kidding me? She didn't build these as weapons. She made them to use on *herself*!"

Charm paused for a moment and seemed to collect herself. "I . . . I lost some friends, fighting him," she said slowly, her voice getting quieter. "I mean, I know this thing is dangerous. I'm probably smarter than anyone else on this planet."

"She's not bragging, she really is," Kiel whispered.

"She's not acting like it!" Bethany said.

"But he hurt my friends," Charm whispered, looking off camera. "Bethany's already gone, but to find her, I'm going to need to take him down first. And then I have to find out what happened to Nice Flying Girl and Annoying Cape Kid. But above all"—she stopped again and swallowed hard—"I need to find Kiel."

"Me?" Kiel said.

"She means Owen, I think," Bethany said quietly.

"I know he's in some ridiculous disguise," Charm continued. "But I'm going to find him and bring him home. And considering he shouldn't have disappeared from the powers I gave him, I'm betting Nobody had something to do with that, too." She banged her robotic arm down on the table in front of her angrily, breaking the table in half.

"Wow, she really cares for him," Kiel said.

"I'll come back when we're ready to test," Charm said, then switched off the camera.

"Is that it?" Bethany said as the video disappeared.

"Two more files," Kiel said. "This one's the next day."

The video appeared in midair once more, this time showing the view from behind some goggles.

"Experiment Alpha, mark," Charm's voice came from off camera, and the goggles shifted to show the possibility ray gun in her hand. "Testing Prospect Enhancer on Science Police robot." The goggles shifted again as the ray gun warmed up, then focused in on an inanimate robot.

"Uh-oh," Kiel said.

"Everyone hold on to your behinds," Charm shouted. "Here we go!"

A beam launched out from her possibility ray gun, striking the robot directly in the chest. At first, just like with Bethany's father back in Jupiter City, nothing happened, and Charm began to swear loudly and angrily. But then the robot flashed with light, and where a Science Police robot had stood, there was now a boxy red-and-blue robot at least three times the size.

"Greetings, humans," the robot said. "I am Idealistic Peak, leader of the Noblots. How did I come to be here?"

"That's . . . odd," Charm said. "It doesn't seem very controlled. Maybe—"

The robot flashed again, then appeared back in its normal size, only much less intimidating. "Oh, dear," it said. "I do hope I am not interrupting anything. Should I show myself out?"

"Okay, not good," Charm said. "Shut it down. Shut it all down!"

The flashes of light appeared faster and faster, and the goggles turned away as Charm growled in pain, until the light grew continuous, then disappeared completely, along with the robot.

"Yikes," she said. "Okay, this doesn't work at all. We'll need to start over completely—"

"On the contrary," said another voice, and the goggles turned toward it, only to stop on a faceless humanoid creature.

"You!" Charm shouted.

"Yes, me," Nobody said, reaching out and taking the weapon. "And as I was about to say, I think this weapon works just *perfectly*."

And then the video ended.

Neither Bethany nor Kiel said anything for a moment. Finally, Kiel reached out and started the third video.

Charm appeared on-screen, now looking like she'd been through a war. Her robotic arm hung loosely from her shoulder, and she seemed to be trying to fix it with her other hand, even as she addressed the camera.

"I don't know if anyone will ever get this," she said. "But if anyone's watching, Nobody did this. He destroyed Quanterium." She nodded off-screen, and the camera turned to show a very similar sight to what Bethany had found when she arrived. "He took all of our Prospect Enhancers, and the research, then blew up most of them in the middle of the city. I think we're going to lose the entire planet, if not more."

Bethany shook her head in silence. Nobody . . . had done all of this? Was it all like Kiel had said, to restart the fictional world by turning it back into pure possibility? Even if that was the case, these were people's lives! Even if they still somehow existed, this was beyond cruel and terrible.

"I'm going to save my people," Charm said, slapping a panel closed on her robotic arm. The arm leaped to life, and she grabbed one of the possibility ray guns. "We don't have many options left, so I'm going to the one place where I know I can find help." She sighed, long and deep. "I really, really hate to do this. But as it is, I think only the Magister might be able to help."

"What?!" Bethany and Kiel shouted at the same time.

Her father had told her the Magister had escaped from the

textbook she'd left him in, showing up with Nobody when he'd split her in two. But now he was back in his original story?

"So that's where I'm headed with my people, to see him and beg for his help. If I don't make it back—and Kiel, you're the one watching this . . ." She paused, then looked at the screen with red, wet eyes. "I lost my family, I lost my people, and I've lost my planet. I'm not losing you, too. Wherever you are, I will *find* you. I promise."

And then the video went dark.

Kiel was silent as Bethany stared at him. "The Magister is back?" she said quietly. "If that's true, he must still be working with Nobody, and probably helped destroy this whole planet!"

Kiel nodded, then sighed. "There's no help for it. We've got no choice."

"What do you mean?"

"I mean, we're going to have to go have a little talk with my former teacher," Kiel said. "And if he harmed one wire in Charm's head, I'll make him wish he'd never been written."

Bethany grinned evilly. "I'm on board. Let's—"

She stopped in midsentence as something metallic clanked outside in the entrance hall. They both went silent, listening carefully as the clang repeated, then again. Kiel's eyes widened, and he pulled Bethany farther back into the lab, behind some tables.

"Do you think that's a Quanterian?" she whispered.

He shook his head. "I recognize that sound. Those are Science Police robots. And we're in trouble."

CHAPTER 15

Owen awoke to two black helmets strapping him into what looked like a dentist chair as a woman in a lab coat applied some sort of pads with wires to his forehead.

"What are you doing?" he shouted, trying to break free, but the straps held firm.

One of the black helmets tightened them even more, sending pain shooting through his arm. "Don't move," he said, his voice that same odd monotone. "Disobeying orders will cause you pain."

"Don't worry, this should only hurt when it's meant to," the woman in the lab coat said. She bent down over Owen, spread his eyes wide with her fingers, then stared into them one at a time. "We put any suspected fictional sympathizer through this mental test to determine where their loyalty actually lies. And if you *are* a traitor to your reality, well, you're not going to enjoy what comes next." She grinned maliciously.

"Traitor?" Owen said, his heart racing in a way that made him even more nervous. "This is all a huge mistake. I'm just a normal kid!"

The woman snorted. "I doubt that. But a little advice, just in case you *are* innocent: I'd try to relax. I'm told the process is slightly less painful if you don't fight it." She stood back up. "Now, please concentrate on the screen in front of you as long as you can. Most patients don't last more than a few minutes."

A few minutes?! What *was* this?

The woman and the black helmets all left the room, and for a moment nothing happened. Then a screen appeared in the air above him, just like when Charm used to write in midair using her robotic finger. A smiling man and woman flashed on the screen, both wearing lab coats as they walked through a park with children playing around them.

"Hello!" the man said. "My name is Dr. Anthony Root, and I'm real."

The woman waved. "My name is Dr. Emily St. James, and *I'm* real as well!"

Dr. Root gestured around himself. "That means we come from the real world, the *nonfictional* world. The nonfictional world is one where things make sense, and our children get to grow up safe from impossible things and ideas." He smiled and patted the head of a child who ran by, then put on a more serious look. "But our world is now threatened by one of the worst evils to ever exist: the fictional."

Owen bit his lip anxiously, not liking where this was going at all. What had happened here that everyone knew fictional people really existed? Could fictional people actually have invaded somehow in the last five years?

"These people, the fictionals, don't truly exist like we do," Dr. St. James said. "Because of that, they hate us. And that hatred compels them to do anything in their power to destroy us." She smiled at Dr. Root. "That's why we're all so thankful for the PFFIA, the Protection From Fictional Invasions Agency. As everyone knows, the PFFIA was created after the first invasion from the fictional world."

This had really happened? But how could fictional people invade the real world if Nobody had separated the two worlds?

As if the video heard his thoughts, the screen shifted and turned much darker. Images now showed evil-looking soldiers rising up out of the pages of books, wearing science fiction armor and shooting strange laser weapons at fleeing crowds of what had to be nonfictionals. At the bottom, a disclaimer stated that this was a reenactment of events, even as a fictional warrior laughed evilly on the screen.

"The problem is, fictionals often look just like you and me," Dr. Root said as the horrifying reenactment faded away. "So how can we tell the good, nonfictional people from the evil, reality-hating fictionals?"

The image shifted to scientists just like the ones who'd tested Owen and Kara. "The PFFIA has advanced technology that can determine if a person is fictional or not," said Dr. Root's voice over an image of a man being scanned. The video zoomed in on the scan, which showed a human shape; a large stamp then came down on the scan that read "NON-FICTIONAL" in big red letters.

Next, a second man was scanned, only this time, the machine showed the outline of a monstrous creature with huge, clawed hands and tentacles coming out of its back. The creature was stamped "FICTIONAL," and alarms began to ring.

"But sometimes, we can't tell a person's true nature just by scanning them," Dr. Root said, appearing back on the screen. "Sometimes, nonfictional people are brainwashed or tricked into helping the fictionals. And there are some who even hate the nonfictional world themselves, and so side with evil against their own people."

"To root these traitors out, Dr. Root and I came up with a series of questions that will help us determine if *you*, in fact, side with our enemy," Dr. St. James said, smiling at the camera.

"You're going to be given a series of questions to see where you, a supposed nonfictional, stand on fictionals," Dr. Root said as a boy skipped by him holding ice cream.

"Let's hope you show yourself to be a true nonfictional," Dr. St. James said as fireworks started exploding in the daytime sky behind them and music swelled. "After all, if you're siding with the fictionals, you're putting your entire world in danger." Black helmets filled in around both doctors, pointing their weapons directly at Owen. "And if there's one thing the PFFIA won't allow, it's for our people to ever live in danger."

Both doctors disappeared then, and words appeared line by line on the screen.

Question 1: When was the first fictional invasion of our world?

A. Four years ago, by a group of futuristic terrorists.

B. They've been invading our minds for centuries whenever we read a fictional book.

C. What invasion?

"Please answer each question verbally," Dr. St. James's voice said from off-screen.

Owen started to hyperventilate, the image of the black helmets aiming their ray gun rifles at him flashing through his mind. How was *he* supposed to know when the invasion happened? Should he pick *B*, since that seemed like a pretty safe choice considering how much these people hated fictionals?

But what if the buttons on his head could determine if he was lying, just like the interrogators had earlier? Maybe it'd be better to just answer honestly, so they'd give him points for not lying? "Uh, answer *C*," Owen said quietly.

"I'm sorry, that's incorrect," Dr. Root's voice said. "Obviously the invasion four years ago was the most notable time, but in actuality, the fictional world has been infecting us with its impossible ideas since the very first book was written."

Both doctors appeared back on-screen. "Realizing the true history and extent of fictionals' hatred of us is important," Dr. St. James said, stepping forward. "To help you learn, our scientists have determined that each wrong answer must be punished. That way your mind will internalize the correct responses quicker!"

"Don't worry, though," Dr. Root said. "This punishment will be nothing you haven't seen before. That's because our machines will take your own worst memories and make you relive them for each wrong answer. This way, you'll be on the right track to learning in no time!"

Owen's eyes widened. What did they—

A Tyrannosaurus rex ran at him, its mouth wide as it roared. Owen screamed in terror and tried to run, but he just wasn't fast enough. All around him the jungle was too dense to push through, and if he stayed on the path, he'd surely be eaten.

The T. rex lunged, its jaws dripping . . .

Owen let out a terrified scream, only to find himself back in the dentist chair, staring at the man and woman on-screen again. He screamed again, then again for good measure as his heart raced in his chest. That had felt so *real*, like he was actually being chased! But if that was a memory, when had it happened? He remembered the time prison, and dinosaurs roaring outside, but he and Kara had escaped out the exit door the very first day he'd woken up. He'd never been eaten by dinosaurs . . .

Had he?

What if he really was there for more than one day, and some part of his mind . . . remembered?

"That wasn't pleasant, I'm sure," Dr. St. James said.

"So for your sake, try to get this next question correct," Dr. Root said with a smile.

Question 2: Are all fictional people bad?

A. No, just the majority. There are probably some good ones, I assume.

B. Yes, every single one of them hates our reality and would destroy our world if they could.

C. Just the villains, like Dracula and Frankenstein's monster.

"Again, please respond verbally," Dr. St. James said.

Sweat ran down Owen's neck as he squirmed in his bindings. He couldn't deal with another wrong answer, not if it was anything like the first. But what did these people want to hear? Obviously they hated fictional people, apparently because of the invasion. Though Kara's idea that their lack of imagination made them selfish since they couldn't picture what it was like to live as someone else seemed to make more sense.

If that was the case, then it seemed like they'd think answer *B* was the right choice, then.

"Um, *B*?" Owen said, then winced.

"*B is* the correct answer," Dr. Root said happily, back on-screen, only to have the image shift, like it'd been edited, and Dr. Root jumped to a slightly different spot on the screen. "However, our sensors tell us that you are, in fact, lying. We can see that you actually believe that answer *C* was right. And for that, you must be punished once more."

Before Owen could even react, another memory filled his mind.

A boy in a question mark mask stood over Owen as his mom's library burned around him. "I'm taking your life, you pathetic failure," the boy said. "You never knew how good you had it, but I'll make the most of it."

"No!" Owen shouted, trying to stand up, but the boy used a stolen wand to cast a spell, paralyzing Owen. He struggled to move, but it was no use.

"You never deserved your life . . ."

"*Stop!*" Owen shouted, back in the chair.

"Isn't this fun?" the woman said, smiling widely. "Now, on to number three."

Question 3: Why do fictional people want to take over our world?

A. They hate us for not reading their books.

B. They hate our reality, because they're not truly real.

C. They're just evil.

"None of the above!" Owen screamed, not even caring anymore. He knew that something bad was coming, but what could he do? The machine knew if he lied, and none of those options *were* true! Fictional people *weren't* evil, not any more than nonfictionals were. Whoever had invaded might be, if that was really even what happened, but they didn't represent all fictional people. This whole thing was ridiculous, and he knew that even *without* his imagination.

Dr. St. James reappeared on the screen and shook her head. "Hmm, it does seem like you're doing rather poorly on this test. I think we might have a fictional sympathizer!"

"Let's try upping the punishment, and see if that makes a difference?" Dr. Root said.

Dr. Verity stood over Owen, a scalpel in his hand. "It's nothing personal, Kiel," the Quanterian villain said. "I just need your heart to open the Source of Magic. Well, that, and it's also very personal." He leaned over and touched the blade to Owen's chest. "I'm going to enjoy this quite a bit."

The scalpel pushed down . . .

And Owen's eyes flew open. He was barely able to breathe as terror filled his body. "No, please, Dr. Verity!" he screamed, flailing in the seat. *"Let me go!"*

Dr. Root and Dr. St. James smiled down at him on the screen for a moment, but before they could speak again, the video flickered, then, weirdly, disappeared into thin air.

Owen frantically breathed in deeply over and over, trying to calm himself down before whatever horror was coming next. The test couldn't just be three questions, could it? The original scientist had said something about it only lasting as long as he could take it, so maybe he'd had enough? He definitely didn't want to see any more of his own worst memories, that was for sure.

A door opened somewhere behind him, and he struggled to turn his head to see what was happening, but he couldn't move enough to look. Footsteps crossed the floor, getting closer, and Owen's heart began beating wildly once more.

"Well, I must say, this is a surprise," a familiar voice said. "I don't recognize *you*, but somehow you know my name. And that makes me curious!"

An older man in a lab coat wearing goggles leaned over him, eyes wild with a sort of dead interest.

Owen's entire body went cold. They were still punishing him. This had to be a dream, or a very, *very* bad memory.

"So, *have* we met?" the man asked. "Because I'm Dr. Verity, and trust me, I'm very interested in getting to know *you* better."

CHAPTER 16

From out of the darkness, several red laser sights shone down the hallway as the clanking intensified. Several robots passed the doorway, though none of them looked like the Science Police Bethany had seen before. Instead, one hovered with some sort of metal wings, looking like a human bird of prey. Another was almost bigger than the hallway, looking like a troll with a sinister robotic head. The one in the lead was tiny, like a gnome, and moved quicker than the rest, leaping from wall to wall with some sort of grappling gun, much like her Twilight launcher.

"HEAT SIGNATURES DETECTED," the smallest one announced in a monotone voice, crunching its metal feet into the wall. "VOICE RECOGNITION DOES NOT MATCH ANY KNOWN QUANTERIANS. DEFENSIVE MEASURES INITIATED."

Kiel winced and pulled out his wand-knives. "They must have been changed by the possibility weapons, and no one was left to turn them off," he whispered to Bethany. "I'll handle them. You just—"

Bethany rolled her eyes, then leaped up and whipped three Twilight throwing stars at the smallest robot. "Initiate that, you robotic jerks!" she shouted, only to cringe as the throwing stars bounced off the robot's metal chest.

"You can't just attack them head-on!" Kiel shouted, pulling her back farther into the lab. "They'll cut us apart with their lasers!"

"I've *got* this, okay?" she hissed, shoving him off of her. She shot her Twilight launcher out into the hallway, then clicked the retract button, holding on tightly. The launcher sent her soaring through the door just as she changed into a statue of herself made out of steel, which crashed into the gnomelike robot with a building-shaking crunch.

"NONSCIENTIFIC BEHAVIOR DETECTED," the second science soldier said. "POSSIBLE MAGIC DETECTED. ANTIMAGIC COUNTERMEASURES INITIATED."

The flying robot started emitting some sort of gas, so Bethany quickly changed into a giant fan, blowing it away from her and

Kiel. The former boy magician used the confusion to leap into her flow of air and throw himself into the gigantic robot, digging his wand-knives into its chest. Even weakened from lack of food and hiding for days, Kiel managed to hold on while the robot swept massive arms around, plowing through walls and other robots until its body began to sizzle with electrical sparks. The robot collapsed forward, and Kiel leaped off right before it hit the ground, grabbing its laser rifle as he moved.

"I'm not totally useless," he told Bethany with a wink as he aimed the laser rifle at the small robot. That robot fired its own laser right through Kiel's cape, and he swore as he threw himself back into the laboratory.

Bethany quickly morphed back, ready for more. "Just stay back, Kiel," she shouted, and started to turn into a tank, only to scream in pain as another laser grazed her shoulder. She fell to her knees, holding her shoulder as the robot shot through the spot she'd been standing.

"Beth!" Kiel shouted, and jumped toward her, but the flying robot slammed him in the chest. He crashed back into the lab, breaking the computer they'd been using earlier as well as plenty of glass beakers.

As Kiel collapsed in the lab, Bethany's entire being lit up

with rage. "Don't you touch him!" she shouted, mirrorlike armor growing out all over her as she stood. The remaining robots shot at her with their lasers, but the beams just reflected off in various directions as they hit.

"DETECTING FURTHER NONSCIENTIFIC BEHAV-IOR," the flying robot said as she strode toward it, her body growing larger with each step. "NOT DETECTING MAGI-CAL ENERGY. UNSURE OF—"

"Detect *this*!" Bethany roared, bringing a now-massive fist down on the robot's head. The force of her blow almost crushed it completely, and she turned to the rest of the robots, her arms spread wide. "Who's next?"

The robots looked up at her with confusion, or maybe even fear, as Bethany continued to grow, now taller than the massive troll-like robot had been. Her head pushed up against the hallway's ceiling, and she grunted in annoyance, shoving upward with her shoulders, crumbling the floor above her with a snarl. Rubble and lab equipment came tumbling down onto the robots. They tried to escape, but Bethany just reached out and gathered the rest of them in her giant hands.

"You do not attack my friends!" she shouted, her voice echoing through the collapsing building as she grew through more floors above them. She clapped her two hands together and enjoyed the satisfying crunch, then opened her hands and let the metal parts fall back to the ground, now at least thirty or forty feet below her.

Kiel slowly emerged from the laboratory, holding his hand over his head as light shone down from outside. "Beth?" he shouted up at her. "I'm okay! You can turn back to normal!"

She looked down at him and released a huge sigh of relief, which almost knocked him off his feet. "Looks like the great Kiel Gnomenfoot needed someone else to be the hero for a change, huh?"

He cringed at the force of her voice, then nodded. "I've got zero problems with that. Just come down here."

"Why?" she asked. "The view is great up here. And I can make sure there aren't any more Science Police."

But as she looked around, she realized there wasn't much of *anything* anymore. The white wall of nothingness had moved in closer, having now reached the gelatin-like city square. The rest of the city had been enveloped. The multiplex had basically collapsed around her, leaving just the space she was standing in free of rubble. She glanced back down at Kiel and wondered what she'd been thinking. He could have been hurt! She had to be more responsible! And all of this while the city was disappearing around them and her father was in danger!

Wait a second. No, that was how the *old* version of Bethany thought. This one had just saved Kiel, and everything had worked out okay. And why worry about her father when she'd obviously find a way to fix things? That way just made her crazy.

"I think you got them all!" Kiel yelled up to her, cupping his hands around his mouth. "But also, you seem to still be getting bigger. Can you at least stop growing?"

She smirked down at him, then leaned over and picked him up by his cape.

"Hey!" Kiel shouted, twisting around in the wind as more of the science center came down around them. "Are you sure this is safe?"

She shook him a few times. "Do you really think I don't know what I'm doing, Kiel Gnomenfoot?" She lifted him up to her eye level. "I can't believe you said *you'd* handle them. You must be so embarrassed right now."

He slowly spun around at the ends of her fingers, trying to turn himself by kicking or waving every so often. "You know, we *could* talk about this back down on the ground?"

"Oh, I'm very comfortable," she said, jiggling him again.

"That's not helping!" he shouted. "How are you doing this, anyway?"

"I told you, Charm gave me superpowers," she told him. "I've got the ability to turn into anything inanimate."

"Oh, really? Because you seem pretty animate to me!" he said, still twirling around.

She paused, staring at him. Yes, he was being annoying, but he did have a point. Just like the superstrength, she shouldn't have been able to grow to giant size or create the mirrored armor.

So how exactly *was* she doing this?

CHAPTER 17

D r. Verity leaned over and unlocked Owen's straps, an evil-looking ray gun in one hand. "Looks like we're going to need to talk, just you and me, up in my laboratory. I wouldn't try to escape if I were you. After all, I can vaporize you without a second thought." He paused, considering it as he tapped the ray gun against Owen's forehead. "Sometimes without even a *first* thought. Instinct, you know."

At the touch of the ray gun, Owen's imagination flooded back into his head. "But . . . but how did you get here?" Owen asked, not able to stop himself as a surge of curiosity filled him from out nowhere. "You shouldn't be here. How did you cross over to this world? I thought all the portals were gone. Did you find another way? I bet I can think of some . . ."

The questions seemed to confuse the scientist, and he stood back up. As soon as he did, Owen's imagination disappeared, and he started feeling much less curious and a lot more terrified. "You know my name but don't know how I got here?" Dr. Verity asked, frowning. "Now, that might be even *more* unexpected. How do you know me?" He peered at Owen, bending down so they were just inches apart. "I really haven't seen your face before." He stood back up, biting his lip. "Quite a mystery, my friend."

Owen glanced at the nearest door, trying to think of how serious Dr. Verity's threat of vaporization had been. He slowly lifted a hand, only to have the ray gun barrel pushed into his forehead hard enough to leave an imprint. "Ah-ah, you don't move until I say so," the scientist told him.

Again, a flurry of ideas filled Owen's brain at the touch of the fictional ray gun. "We've never met," Owen said quickly, his mind racing. "I just had nightmares of you after reading the Kiel Gnomenfoot books!"

Dr. Verity's eyes widened with rage at Kiel's name, and the ray gun pushed harder into Owen's skull. "I'd watch your language around me, child," he said. "Saying that name could give you quite a headache." He left the ray gun in place for another moment, then pulled it away, and Owen took in a deep breath in relief, only to immediately freeze as the ray gun abruptly pushed into his head again.

"Now, wait a minute," Dr. Verity told him, staring him right in the face from just inches away. The doctor was so close, Owen was almost overpowered by his breath, a mix of garlic and death. "The machine doesn't take nightmares. It only uses *memories* you've experienced, and dreams aren't stored in the same cortex in your brain. You couldn't have seen me in it if you'd never met me. *Try again.*"

Owen's mind raced with possibilities, and part of him was surprised by how clearly he was thinking with his imagination back. It wasn't just having more ideas. It was like he could think around problems and see them from multiple sides. Right now, he needed a story to tell Dr. Verity, but not just any story. It had to be something the fictional scientist would believe too.

"Um, I saw the movies about you and, um, he-who-must-not-be-named—"

"Now you're just insulting both of us," Dr. Verity said, his finger twitching on the ray gun. Owen scrunched his eyes closed, hoping getting vaporized didn't hurt as much as being eaten by a dinosaur. Then something beeped on Dr. Verity's wrist, and Owen's eyes flew open. The doctor glanced down in irritation, then looked curious for a moment. He ran his wrist over Owen's chest and paused.

"Interesting readings," the scientist said, putting his ear against Owen's ribs and tapping them with the ray gun. "See, most of you reads as a native to this reality. But not *all* of you. In fact, there's a specific part of you that shows as coming from *Quanterium*. Now, how is that possible?"

Owen opened his mouth without knowing what to say, hoping that something brilliant might fall out, but before he could speak, Dr. Verity pushed his head in close again. "You wouldn't be here as a spy for the Quanterians still out there, would you?" He tapped Owen's chest. "And what is this, some sort of tracer? A weapon that they'll use once I'm in range?" He gave Owen a disgusted look. "As if you or those idiots could ever harm *me*. Either way, it's a waste of good science. Still, I can use it. Come along, and we'll figure out this mystery together." He clapped his hands, then moved toward the door opposite the one Owen had come in.

His imagination disappearing left Owen feeling more drained than he remembered. Was this what life was like without it all the time, and he just never noticed? Through the haze, he did realize one thing: He needed to escape, and with Dr. Verity's back to him, this seemed like a pretty logical time to try.

While the scientist focused on a tablet for a moment, Owen counted to three, then leaped off the dentist chair, sprinting for the exit. His hand reached the door just as a ray bolt sliced through the air inches from his ear.

"Are you too backward to understand simple commands?" the scientist asked, not even turning around, in spite of the fact that the ray gun still pointed directly at his head. "I said *come along*. This is your last warning."

Owen swallowed hard, then turned and followed Dr. Verity out the other door. There, he gasped, realizing he recognized where he was for the first time. A long spiral staircase led both up and down, and solid wooden doors dotted either side of the hall in both directions. Many of them had intense-looking keypad locks on them now, which was new from the last time he'd been here.

This was the Magister's tower, the one in Jonathan Porterhouse's yard that he and Kara had seen before they were tested. That meant that all the guards and force fields were protecting Dr. Verity. But were they keeping him in . . . or others out?

"Chop-chop!" the doctor yelled, and started climbing the stairs two by two. Owen moved to follow, passing by rooms where magical creatures and deadly experiments had once been kept. Now, though, Owen could hear humming machinery, and odd bursts of light shone from beneath the cracks of many of the doorways.

"I wiped this place clean of all its filthy magic, of course," Dr. Verity was saying from a dozen stairs up, the ray gun still aimed right between Owen's eyes. "Truly disgusting. Why your world let it fester here for so long, I'll never know. But once I took over, I turned it into a sort of monument to all that is good and scientific." He glanced back down with an evil grin. "Plus, I know it'll just kill the Magister when he finds out."

When he finds out? That was an odd way to put it. Could Dr. Verity have a way back to the fictional world?

A thought hit Owen out of the blue, and he almost tripped on a step. Either his imagination wasn't fully gone, or his brain wasn't as far gone as he thought, because Owen realized that if Dr. Verity could get back to the fictional world . . . maybe he, Kara, and Bethany could get there too! If they could find more of their friends, they might actually have a chance to beat Nobody.

Except his older self had told him that was exactly what

would happen. Owen and his friends would fight their way to Nobody, but one by one, he'd lose his friends along the way, leaving Owen to face the fictional monster alone.

"Are you seriously just standing there?" Dr. Verity shouted down from the stairs above Owen, sounding deeply pained. "You're not making a great case for keeping you alive, you know. You'd be just as easy to carry up here as a corpse."

"Sorry!" Owen said, then quickly followed Dr. Verity the rest of the way up, making sure not to get lost in thought along the way. Knowing that the scientist knew of a way back to the fictional world changed everything. Now he couldn't just run away. First, he needed more information. And that meant keeping Dr. Verity as close as possible, just so he could think clearly with his imagination intact.

They reached the top of the tower, where a now-metal door was covered in keypads, handprint identifiers, and even retina scanners. As Dr. Verity typed in numbers on a variety of the pads, the scanners all covered him from head to toe, running laser beams over his face, eyes, and hands. Finally, a voice said, "Welcome, Your Eminence," and the door slid away, revealing what used to be the Magister's office.

Instead of a cozy library filled with magic, though, everything was now covered in shiny metal, with lab equipment buzzing and beeping all over the place. Science Police robots, the foot soldiers of Dr. Verity that had terrorized Magisteria during the war, stood at attention around the enormous room, while various experiments bubbled or made eerie noises on almost every available surface. Everything looked like it was about to explode or rupture or suck in all space and time at the slightest touch, so Owen made sure to keep his hands to himself as he followed Dr. Verity inside.

"All aboard," the scientist said, slapping the only empty spot in the lab, a long metal table covered in white paper.

Owen lay back on the table, trying to stay calm by taking deep breaths. Whatever the evil scientist had planned wasn't going to be good, so he was going to have to pick his moment incredibly carefully if he had any chance of escaping.

Dr. Verity began fiddling with various machines across the room, and several beams of light passed over Owen's chest. Dr. Verity frowned, then came closer to the table. Owen stopped breathing, wondering if he'd have a chance to attack, but the scientist passed right by him and knocked on the head of one of the robots.

"You, and your friend there!" Dr. Verity said to the Science

Police robot. "Come hold this kid down. We're going to do some surgery."

Owen's eyes widened. Did he say *surgery*? That wasn't part of the plan to get back to the fictional world!

The two Science Police stepped out of their lineup and grabbed Owen's arms. He struggled against them, but they barely seemed to notice as they strapped him down. A moment later, he was trapped once more.

Only this time, instead of his being interrogated or brainwashed, Dr. Verity planned to cut him open.

"What are you going to do?" Owen shouted, struggling with all of his strength, but the straps were too strong. Even so, the Science Police robots bent down to hold him in place, cutting off all movement.

Dr. Verity rolled his eyes. "Why do I even talk if no one listens? I told you, I'm going to pull out whatever technology is inside you, so I can figure out where it came from, which will probably be the Quanterians who haven't been rounded up. Sure, they're a great scapegoat for the nonfictionals, but I'm getting bored with controlling a population through fear. Gets old after a while, you know? I need the Quanterians for my brainwashed army anyway." He leaned in close. "Now hold still while I knock you out. Trust me, this is going to hurt. A *lot*."

The doctor pushed something against his arm, and Owen felt a strange, wet mist touch his skin. Immense pain flashed through his body from his arm outward, growing so intense that he quickly, mercifully passed out.

CHAPTER 18

Bethany gently set Kiel down on top of the science center rubble, then brought her newly enormous hands close to her face to stare at them.

How *could* she have done this? She'd definitely been getting better at using her inanimate superpowers during her training; her father had made sure of that, running her through drill after drill, changing out just her hands or feet for inanimate objects, switching on the fly. But changing between a bouncing ball or a statue was still incredibly different from turning herself into a giant or giving herself superstrength.

"Maybe it has something to do with Quanterium?" Kiel shouted up from below. "Maybe whatever Charm's machines did to the planet is changing your powers, too."

She considered this for a moment, then shook her head. "I was able to do something like this back in Jupiter City, too," she told him, poking her gigantic arms. "Maybe I should just turn back."

Kiel nodded and moved away to give her some room. Bethany closed her eyes and concentrated for a moment. It had all happened so fast during the battle against the robots, but whatever she'd done, it hadn't really felt like using her superpowers did . . . or jumping in and out of books, for that matter. This seemed *different* somehow.

"Are you changing yet?" Kiel asked. "Because nothing's happening."

She opened her eyes long enough to stick out her tongue at him. "Shh. I'm thinking."

"I have faith in you, Beth," he shouted. "You've got this!"

She smiled briefly, then turned away from him, not needing the distraction. This shouldn't be *that* hard, honestly. She'd done it once . . . but what had she actually done? She retraced the steps in her mind. Both times she'd used this new power, she'd been frustrated or in pain, and just sort of . . . changed. It was almost like a subconscious desire more than anything.

She tried picturing herself back as a normal-sized Twilight Girl, like she did when using her superpowers, then opened her eyes and cursed. Still a giant. Just to experiment, she next tried using her superpowers to turn into a tiny bouncing ball again, and that worked, sending her plunging down toward the science center. She switched herself back to human in midfall, only to find herself forty feet tall still.

"This is annoying!" she shouted, punching the ground in frustration. The entire science center shook at the impact, making Kiel almost fall over, though he still looked supportive. What *was* this new power? Admittedly, it was awesome, but the whole thing was useless if she couldn't control it!

This kind of thing had never happened before she'd been separated from her old self. Had her nonfictional self been holding her back with all of her rules and guilt and anxiety? If that was true, then this new power must be a good thing, because anything her nonfictional self was against, Bethany was definitely for.

For a moment, she brought to mind what things were like when she was half-fictional, when her whole life had been miserable because of one small part of her, the part that forced her to hide everything that she liked and made her special, just so she wouldn't get into trouble. And because of that, look how long it'd taken her to find her father. All those years he'd been held by Nobody, when she could have saved him, if only she hadn't let that horrible part of her hold her back for so long!

Almost without meaning to, she focused in on her normal, nonfictional self, hatred flooding her brain. Yes, Nobody separating the worlds was a bad thing, but every day without that part of her was a blessing—

"You did it!" Kiel said, clapping her on the shoulder. "See? I knew you could."

Bethany opened her eyes to discover she was a whole lot shorter. "I did?" she asked, looking around. "See? I knew I could!" She laughed, covering her confusion.

It didn't make sense. *None* of this did. She'd just been thinking about her nonfictional self, and suddenly she was back to normal.

So wait a second. What if this wasn't related to her superpowers or Quanterium or anything so much as Nobody separating her? What if now that she was completely fictional, she could rewrite herself, just like Nobody could? He'd mentioned that there was no way she could beat him without rewriting. A grin spread across her face.

Well, look who learned how to do it on her own, Nobody.

"Are you okay?" Kiel asked, his hand still on her shoulder. "You're smiling creepily."

She turned to him and laughed. "I think I figured it out. You might want to back up, 'cause I'm about to do something *awesome*."

He did, and Bethany concentrated on one part of herself, just her arm. She remembered how her old powers changed her body into words when jumping into books, so she imagined her arm as literal words instead of skin and bone.

And then, in her mind, she rewrote those words, changing them to become a long, superstrong arm.

As she watched, her arm grew out to twice its usual length, bulging with muscles.

"Um, didn't you just fix that?" Kiel asked.

"I've got it!" Bethany said, closing her eyes. She rewrote herself into being able to fly, and just like that, enormous butterfly wings sprouted on her back. With a joyful cry, she took to the air, her eyes wide with delight. "Are you seeing this? How amazing is it?"

"It's like magic without the spells," Kiel said, staring at her in awe. "But are you sure this is okay? This seems really similar to what happened here to Quanterium and the Science Police. Even your dad switched into different versions of himself, right? What if you disappear too? Maybe it's not safe."

Bethany laughed. "Not safe? That's hilarious coming from Kiel Gnomenfoot. Watch *this*." She landed back on the ground, and her wings disappeared, only for her head to rise into the air, pushing up from a long, green, scaly neck. Her arms moved forward on her body as they grew larger, and her hands transformed into enormous, scaly paws. A moment later, she snarled down at her friend as a dragon. "Now, little magician, think you've got what it takes to defeat me?" she growled, then winked at him.

Kiel didn't wink back, though. Instead, he looked worried. "Beth, this is fun, but it really does seem too coincidental, you discovering new powers as everything on Quanterium falls apart. We should get back to figuring this out instead of just playing around."

"You're the one who told me to be more fictional!" she growled through her dragon teeth. "There's nothing more fictional than rewriting yourself. Why don't you try it? Maybe you could learn magic again!"

"I'm fine without it," Kiel told her, smiling slightly as he shrugged. "I'm also fine with you as you are too, by the way. Now, why don't you turn back to yourself, and we'll go find Charm and find a way to fix Quanterium and save your father?"

She rolled her eyes, then tried to turn back to her normal self, only it wasn't easy, as a thousand more fun ideas passed through her mind. She frowned and concentrated harder, remembering her worrying, awful, nonfictional self and what it felt like to hate everything awesome.

Immediately her body morphed back into its normal shape. Apparently all it took was picturing herself as the worst, most boring version of herself, and she instantly became normal again. Disturbing, but at least it worked.

She turned back to Kiel, thrilled with her newfound knowledge. "You're not getting it. If we figure *this* out, we'll be able to do anything. Maybe *I'll* learn magic! If I can rewrite myself, we don't even need Charm. I'll be able to fix everything on my own. Watch!" She concentrated, rewriting herself into someone who knew magical spells, then held out a hand. "Fireball, LAUNCH!"

Nothing happened.

"Huh," she said, then rewrote herself into a lava monster that could shoot fireballs from her hand. Her feet began to burn through the rubble beneath her, but this time, she successfully launched a ball of magma from her hand. "Ah, there it is!"

"Beth, you're going to burn the science center down!" Kiel

shouted, leaping away from her and the heat she radiated. "What's left of it, anyway."

Reluctantly, she shifted into a water elemental and put out the fire, then sadly imagined her nonfictional self and reverted back to her lame normal body. "When did you get so *boring*?" she said, glaring at him. "You used to be the one jumping into danger without a second thought!"

"I'm still that person," Kiel said, looking relieved now. "But I also took a long time to figure out who I wanted to be, at least before Nobody captured me. There's no challenge to life if you can change into whatever you want, Beth. I learned that when I lost my magic. Suddenly everything was harder, but now things actually mean something when I succeed at them." He half grinned. "Which I do all the time, obviously."

She rolled her eyes. "So, what, you think rewriting yourself is cheating or something? That doesn't make any sense."

"Magic has consequences," Kiel said. "Even if you don't see them at first. Just because you *can* do something doesn't mean you should."

"If you tell me that with great power comes great responsibility, I'm going to punch you," Bethany told him. "And look, I'm fine. So what's the problem?"

He stared at her for a second. "What happened to your cape?"

Huh? Why was he changing the subject? "It's right here, what do you . . ." She felt around to her back, only to have a cold shiver go through her.

There was nothing there. Her cape was gone.

Kiel reached around and pulled a small bit of fabric off of her back, then held it out to her. "This is what I meant. Consequences."

Bethany couldn't think of a thing to say, staring at the few inches of what had once been her Twilight Girl cape as it slowly dissolved in front of her.

CHAPTER 19

*Y*ou thought you could trick me?!" a voice shouted in the darkness.

Owen opened his eyes slowly, feeling more *normal* than he had in months. Not only were ideas and questions pouring into his mind like a steady rain, but it was almost as if he could suddenly see again after being blind. The whole world seemed different, less horrible and more hopeful.

And it all came down to one thing: He could *imagine* again!

He almost shouted in joy, before realizing there was an enormous ray gun aimed right at his nose, humming with terrible power. The ray gun was easily half the size of Dr. Verity, who seemed to be having trouble holding it.

Owen swallowed hard, noticing for the first time a faint pain in his ribs. "Oh, um, hi. Sorry, I was distracted for a second. Can you repeat whatever you said?"

"How could you think I wouldn't recognize the heart *I gave you*?" Dr. Verity shouted, leaning closer until the ray gun's multiple barrels were just inches from Owen's face. "I implanted it in you! Of course I would know my own handiwork. You thought that I, the most brilliant scientist who ever lived, wouldn't know upon seeing your heart that you must be Kiel Gnomenfoot in disguise?!"

Owen blinked several times in a row. Um, *uh-oh*. Things seemed to have taken a bad turn while he was unconscious. He looked down and saw the faintest hint of a scar running down his sternum. "Wait, *you opened me up*?" he shouted. The doctor's threat to take his heart came rushing back, and he almost dry heaved.

Dr. Verity had been inside his chest? *Again?*

"You don't get to be indignant with *me*, magician!" Dr. Verity roared, then swept the ray gun over the table next to Owen, sending instruments of all kinds crashing to the floor. "It wasn't enough to leave me to die in the Source of Magic vault. No, you have to follow me to this pathetic, science-draining world too? I won't have it!"

Owen's mind raced with options, and he couldn't help but delight in it, even as he feared that Dr. Verity would disintegrate him at any moment. Denying he was Kiel Gnomenfoot, while ironically the truth, didn't sound like it'd accomplish much. Attacking the man wasn't going to do much with that ray gun so close. And if Owen tried using his time powers, they could kill him.

So what if he pretended to be Kiel again? *That* opened up some possibilities.

"You've found me out, you, um, evil scientist," Owen said, glaring at the man. "Yes, I *did* return here to defeat you. But now you've got me at your mercy, so you might as well tell me all your plans, like how you intend to get back to the fictional world!"

"I should have let your little robotic heart *die*, like everything from our world does here," Dr. Verity continued, his eyes filled with rage. "But then I wouldn't be able to turn you into a mindless zombie and force you to first kill the Magister, then take on my *real* enemy, the one who exiled me here. So I'm resisting killing you for now. But don't test me!" Abruptly, the anger seemed to disappear, and he grinned. "By the way, you're welcome for fixing your heart, *Kiel*. It should last another few years in this world, even though it'd tick on for a thousand years back on Quanterium."

Wait, that was a *lot* of new information. Verity had fixed his heart? Could that have brought back his imagination? It made sense, since the doctor must have used fictional parts to repair a fictional heart.

Except he'd already *had* a fictional heart, even before it broke using his powers. And he'd lost his imagination as soon as Nobody separated the worlds. Why had it stopped giving him his imagination, then? Did it have something to do with the last bit Dr. Verity had said? "My heart doesn't work as well here? Why not? What's wrong with it?"

"Nothing works correctly in this world!" Verity roared, the anger quickly resurfacing. He screamed loudly and shot his ray gun through a blinking machine to Owen's side, blowing it apart. "Nothing Quanterian, at least! It all slowly breaks apart, which should be impossible. But here, nothing's impossible, apparently!" He paused, raising a finger to his lips as the rage seemed to be replaced by an epiphany. "Maybe I *should* leave you here so it breaks again. Failed by the only science you've ever relied upon! That'd be poetic." He grinned widely, then spat in disgust, right on Owen's foot. "I can't believe a clone of *mine* would become so enamored with that foul *magic*. It's enough to make me want to just end this farce right here and now!"

If fictional things gradually broke down in the nonfictional world, then Owen might not have his imagination back for long. He'd have to use it as best he could while he had the chance. And that meant getting all the information he could from Dr. Verity at the moment.

"Magic just makes more sense," Owen said. "Besides, it defeated you, didn't it? That must have hurt a lot, considering you're trying to get back to the fictional world for revenge. How exactly are you doing that again?"

"Magic didn't defeat me!" Dr. Verity shouted, banging his ray gun on the now-empty table. "Kiel, you are my *clone*. Anything you did is all because of me! Everything that happened had to have been planned from the start. My genius allows for nothing less!"

His eye on the ray gun, Owen wondered if he was maybe playing with fire here. Maybe he should back it up a bit? "How did you get out of the Source of Magic? I thought the vault couldn't be teleported in or out of, and you set off that bomb. It must have been a pretty smart plan if I couldn't stop you, honestly."

"Because I foresee all, know all!" Dr. Verity roared, glaring at Owen. "I had my escape in place from the start!"

Owen gave him a disbelieving look. "I'm not sure I buy that. Even you couldn't have gotten out all on your own. You probably had help, right? From your Science Police or something?"

Dr. Verity blushed a bit, then turned away and whispered something Owen couldn't hear.

"What was that again?"

"I said that I, uh, *arranged* to be removed from the vault at the last moment by a faceless pile of human-shaped mush," Dr. Verity said, glaring back over his shoulder. "Obviously I knew that only one with powers like his could have saved me, or I'd never have allowed you to close the vault door with me in it. I must have foreseen it. There could be no other reason!"

Oh, *wow.* Nobody rescued Dr. Verity? Sure, he was probably the only one who could have. But why would he do that? "What did this, um, faceless pile of mush say?" Owen said, sitting up on the table. Nearby, a few Science Police robots whirred their heads around to face him and aimed their laser rifles at him, an unsubtle warning not to move any farther.

"He claimed some ridiculousness about me being *written* like this, to be some sort of villain," Dr. Verity said, sneering. "As if my all-encompassing intelligence could ever be constrained by such quaint ethical constraints as good or evil. No one could craft the perfection that is Dr. Verity. I am all-knowing, I am all-powerful, and I am *all-science!*"

"So he just . . . let you go?"

The mad scientist sighed dramatically. "*No*, he didn't just 'let me go,' you simpleton. When I proved his intellectual superior (and perhaps also threatened to tear him down to his component atoms), he sent me *here*." Dr. Verity made a disgusted face. "He pretended to want me to see proof of his impossible claim, that this was a nonfictional world to our fictional reality, and from here, so-called writers invented our clearly superior, fictional universes." He looked around with a haughty sniff. "The very *idea!*"

"Why did you stay here, then? I mean, you said you had a way back, didn't you?" This was going better than Owen could have expected. All he had to do was make sure he didn't anger Verity too much, or he'd be disintegrated.

"I don't have to answer your questions!" Dr. Verity shouted, bringing his ray gun back around again, and Owen winced, realizing he might have just crossed that line. But then Verity seemed to realize he couldn't continue his story if he didn't, and he relaxed a bit. "But if you *must* know, the featureless monster suggested to me that I *rewrite* myself into a quote better person unquote. Obviously I couldn't let that insult go unanswered, so I destroyed him!"

Owen's eyes shot wide open. "You did? But . . . but when?"

Dr. Verity rolled his eyes. "Well, mostly destroyed him. In that I blew him up, and then he reformed a moment later and suggested I stay here as a learning experience. As if Dr. Verity could learn anything from anyone, let alone a world such as this!" He leaned in closer, his eyes flashing with madness. "No, instead, I'd prove that Nobody wrong. If he thought he had been controlled by the nonfictional idiots around here, then I'd become *their* masters. I decided to take charge of this world and prove once and for all that Dr. Verity is superior to anyone, anywhere, in any reality!"

Owen flinched as spittle flicked on him. If what he said was true, Dr. Verity taking over things here explained some of what was going on. Certainly how fascist everything had gotten. But how could the world just let him do it? "I don't know," Owen said carefully. "The people here seem to hate all fictionals. Why would they have let you take charge?"

"Who do you think made them hate fictionals?" Dr. Verity shouted. "Shortly after I arrived, I set out to determine the psychological makeup of this planet's people, in order to most conveniently rule them. What I discovered was not only were they hideously behind in technology, but the reason for that seemed to be a complete lack of any creative imagination. With that knowledge, it was easy to use my overwhelming inventiveness to provide the old rulers with all the technology they could use in exchange for *power*."

"Like hover shuttles?"

Verity rolled his eyes. "Child's play. I'm referring to weapons, you clod! These nonfictionals live within arbitrary borders and fear anyone from the other side. They couldn't get enough of the weapons I provided. Soon I didn't even need to ask for authority . . . they freely gave it! And then, when fictional people began appearing, I was in a position to further stoke their fears and make sure that instead of seeing the fictionals as helpless refugees, they believed them to be an invasion force!"

Owen stared wide-eyed at the scientist. Kara had been right all along. Losing their imagination *had* made nonfictional people more selfish, even paranoid toward one another.

But that didn't explain where the fictional people came from. "So what was the invasion?" Owen asked. "Who invaded?"

"That was the best part!" Verity screamed. "It was my old people, the Quanterians. They managed to destroy their world somehow, and then sought refuge here!" He clapped his hands and danced around Owen gleefully. "Can you even imagine? A few months without me and their home planet gets destroyed, I'm told. It still makes me laugh!"

What? Quanterium was destroyed? "What happened to the planet?"

Dr. Verity looked left and right, like he wanted to be sure no one could overhear. "I'm not going to tell you exactly what they built," he said, then pulled a smaller ray gun out of his lab coat. "But let's just say that I . . . *improved* upon it." He patted the ray gun lovingly. "And now it's the perfect weapon for when I see that nebulous waste of a faceless space."

That was ominous. "But how could the Quanterians get here?"

Dr. Verity waved off the question. "They used *magic* of all things. Which of course backfired and trapped them within a bunch of those horrible books about Kiel's . . . about *your* adventures. Eventually, though, just like my science does in this infernal dimension, the magic gradually faded, the spell wore off, and BOOM, suddenly you've got people popping out of books left and right!" He cackled. "You should have seen it. Quanterians everywhere, confused and bewildered, begging for help, while I've got this world's people convinced they're being invaded by fictional monsters with incredible weaponry. The easiest time I've ever had taking over a planet, honestly." He winked.

Owen couldn't even find the words to respond. The Quanterians had escaped to his world as refugees, and the nonfictional people had thought they were invading and therefore evil? That couldn't have happened, it couldn't! Yet he'd seen the mobs burning books, and the PFFIA seemed pretty convinced it all took place. And then there were all the tests to determine if he and Kara were fictional.

"After the invasion, they gave me even more power," Dr. Verity continued. "Resources. Anything I asked for! And what I wanted was *this* place, a replicated tower of that Magister fool. It still reeked of dead magic when I arrived, even after so many years. But it had what I needed to return victoriously to my planet. That idiot magician has a portal that spans dimensions in each of his towers. This one would lead me right back to the original one in Magisteria, if only its magic still worked. But thanks to you, I've found a way around that too. All that was left was needing an invasion force."

Owen shook his head, not believing it.

"Oh, yes, my little clone!" Dr. Verity shouted. "I brainwashed all the Quanterian refugees and put them under my control. Those black helmets? They're filled with tech that keeps my old people docile and ready to obey my every command." He raised his hands toward the ceiling, thrilled at his own plan. "Soon I will get my revenge. Soon I will march my army back to my home reality, and use them to destroy Magisteria *once and for all*, before taking on the real enemy, that Nobody idiot!"

"No!" Owen shouted. "You can't do this. This is *beyond* wrong. You have to let your people go!"

"Aw, is someone feeling left out?" Dr. Verity said. "Don't worry, I told you, I'll bring you back to Magisteria with us. You can ride with me at the head of the army, in chains of course, so I can show the Magister his favorite apprentice one last time before he dies. He might even surrender!" He clapped his hands again. "Won't that be fun?"

"They're your people!" Owen shouted. "Don't you care about them? What if they get hurt?"

Dr. Verity rolled his eyes. "That's why it's called *war*. Anyway, I don't have much longer to chat. Too much to do! Let's get you ready to be brainwashed."

He picked up a black helmet and moved it toward Owen's head.

"Wait!" Owen shouted. "Are you sure you want to do this?"

Dr. Verity stared at him from behind the helmet. "Of course. It's not even a question. This is the perfect revenge, setting you on your old master."

"But I'll be brainwashed, so you won't get to see the look on my face as it's all happening," Owen said quickly, hoping to appeal to Verity's horrible nature. "Wouldn't it be more satisfying if you made me watch all the destruction at your side?"

Verity seemed to consider this, and Owen held his breath, hoping that the doctor would fall for the obvious trap. If Owen could just get back to the fictional world, then he'd have a lot more options. He could open pages to his friends' stories and bring them all together. Rescuing Kara at that point would be easy, and then all they'd have to do was face Nobody—

"Nah, this is a trap," Verity said, then grinned. "Nice try, but I've been fighting you too long to believe you don't have something up that stupid sleeve of yours. Still, you're right that brainwashing you might not be much better. You're bound to break the programming right at the worst possible moment." He tapped his chin for a moment, then brightened. "Wait, I've got it!"

"I don't think you do," Owen said, not liking where this was going. "Really, I'm sure I won't escape or anything—"

"I'll freeze you here in the dungeons!" Verity said. "I had them put stasis chambers in where the Magister's old cells were. Those things will keep you on ice for a thousand years, and by that time, you'll be all alone on a sad little planet, with no way back." He clapped his hands, definitely excited by the idea. "Oh, this is perfect! And by the way, before I forget?"

He snapped his fingers, and an image of Kara's time bracelet appeared in midair.

"Thank your little friend for me," Verity said. "I've been trying to make a time machine for *years*, but couldn't ever get the sad local technology to withstand the pressures of time distortion. Finally, I gave up and set up a tractor beam, just in case anyone traveled through the fourth dimension anywhere close by. Had just about given up on my whole invasion plan too, when your friend finally got sucked in by my tractor beam." He shook his head in disbelief. "Sometimes, I do wonder if that faceless guy wasn't all wrong. I mean, think about it: If someone *is* writing this stuff, the way things are going, they must *love* me!"

CHAPTER 20

What's *happening* to me?!" Bethany shouted as she grabbed the remains of her cape from Kiel and watched it slowly dissolve in her hands, only to gasp as her fingernails began to disappear as well. Horror filled her as the tips of her fingers soon followed, dissipating into nothingness.

Kiel grabbed her hands and squeezed them tightly, forcing her to look at him. "Concentrate on *who you are*," he said. "You can fix this! It's going to be okay. Just bring yourself back."

Bethany shook her head, barely able to think. *What was going on?* Why was she disappearing? Where were those parts going? "I can't—"

"You *can*." He squeezed her hands again. "Focus. You can do this."

She reluctantly closed her eyes, her heart racing as she began to breathe faster and faster. She tried to think about awful, nonfictional Bethany, but the image in her head kept fading away, even as she tried her best to hold on to it. Not only that, but now she couldn't feel her fingers at all anymore, and Kiel moved his hands to her wrists. Was the rest of her body dissolving too? Why was this happening?!

"*Kiel,*" she said, her eyes flying open as panic filled her. "I can't do it. I can't!"

He shook his head. "Nonsense. You're Bethany Sanderson, and right now, that's all you need to worry about. Just, you know, be less fictional." In spite of the situation, he grinned.

A short, almost hysterical laugh escaped her. She closed her eyes, trying to picture the whole Bethany she'd been before Nobody separated the worlds, Bethany Sanderson. The Bethany who had been filled with guilt over losing her father, but went looking for him every night. The Bethany who constantly worried that her mother would find out she'd been jumping into books against her wishes, but checked out new ones from the library every day. The Bethany who had been obsessed with rules, but broke them constantly.

The Bethany who somehow had held two very different

people in one body, even as she almost ripped herself apart with contradiction.

To turn back into her regular body before, she'd basically rewritten herself into her nonfictional self. But this time, she remembered what it felt like to be half-fictional once more, two halves that didn't quite line up, but still came together, fused together, becoming whole—

"See?" Kiel said, releasing her hands. "I told you!"

She opened her eyes, and almost cried in relief when she saw her that all ten fingers were back, nails and all. She reached behind her and felt for her cape . . . but it was still gone—not like it'd been cut, but more as if she'd never had it to begin with. "My cape didn't come back?" she asked, starting to panic again.

"Don't worry about that now," Kiel whispered to her, grabbing her hand and pulling it back around her. "You're okay, and that's what matters. But it definitely looks like there's a price to pay for . . . well, whatever that was, when you were changing everything."

"I really was rewriting myself," she said, shaking a bit. "My father told me Nobody taught himself how to do it, and I guess now that I'm one hundred percent fictional, I can do it too.

You could too, if you wanted to disappear." She laughed softly without humor. "But this can't have been this easy all along. If it had been, any fictional people wanting to be different could have just transformed like I did."

"I wanted to be different, and it took me months of trying," Kiel said, still holding her hands. "Trust me, it wasn't just a matter of wishing. I think you're right that something's changed."

"It must have to do with Nobody separating the worlds." She pulled her hands away, watching as they still shook a bit. "He warned me, when we first got here, remember? He said that I wouldn't be able to hold myself together."

"Looks like he might have been right," Kiel said. "But Nobody still does it without having this problem. What's his secret?"

"You know who might know?" Bethany said. "The Magister. He helped Nobody separate the worlds. And that gives us another reason for a visit."

"If nothing else, we can probably grab a location spell from his spell book and track down your man in the suit," Kiel told her. He held out his hand. "Not that this will be easy. He did try to kill us last time. Are you ready to face my old teacher again?"

She took his hand and snorted. "I beat him once, I can do it again. But how are we getting there?" She pointed at the wall of white nothing that had inched closer. "I hope you didn't park a spaceship on the other side of town."

"No, but I might know of one that's parked a little higher," Kiel said, and pulled out a small button from his pocket. "Let's hope it's still there, or we're not going to be getting off Quanterium anytime soon." He pushed the button, then grinned in triumph as a small light began buzzing around their midsections.

Bethany smiled too as she realized what was happening. The destroyed science center disappeared around them, replaced by what looked like the interior of a spaceship the size of a tour bus. Over Kiel's shoulder, an enormous view screen showed twin planets orbiting around each other: Magisteria and Quanterium.

"I've missed teleporting," she said, moving to the view screen to get a better look at the planets. "It'd make crime fighting so much easier." She glanced around. "This is Charm's ship?"

Kiel moved to the computer and began typing. "Yup. And if it's still here, then that means she hasn't gone far." He frowned as various information scrolled over the screens. "She went to Magisteria, but beyond that, I can't tell much. There are a *lot* of teleportation records of trips up to the ship, more than I can even count. But strangely, only one down to Magisteria. What do you think that means?"

"It means we've got another question for the Magister," Bethany told him.

He nodded. "Just don't underestimate him, Beth. He might be old, but he's been practicing magic for thousands of years."

"Um, I'm the one who stuck him in a textbook, and that was before I had superpowers," Bethany told him. "Besides, you're talking to Twilight Girl here. If saving my father means I have to punch out an old magician, then I'll just try not to enjoy it too much."

He grinned, shaking his head. "Fair enough. Let's go see if my old teacher is home." He took her hand and hit the button again. A moment later, the spaceship around them morphed into a cozy, bookshelf-filled magical study, one that was much too familiar to Bethany.

An old man with a long beard sat at a desk, his fingers steepled in front of him.

"My old apprentice? Is that really you?" the Magister said, his voice emotional like he was welcoming back an old friend. Then he noticed Bethany, and all the emotion dropped away, leaving behind a cold, threatening tone. "And look. You've brought an old friend too."

CHAPTER 21

A Science Police robot led Owen into the dungeon of the Magister's tower, which looked nothing like the one in Magisteria. Instead of bars and hay on the ground, Dr. Verity's cells were each gutted, then fitted with high-tech freezers designed to put a prisoner into stasis. Each cell was then enclosed by an enormous metal door with only a small frosted window for light. The entire dungeon was chilled to the point Owen could barely stop shivering, and he wondered if he'd freeze on his way to being frozen.

Only one of the cells seemed to be in use right now—a soft glow shone from within, while all the other windows were dark. Owen paused at this door and tried to look in, but the Science Police robot just dragged him past. "CONTINUE WALKING," it said, pulling him down the hallway toward an open cell door at the end.

In spite of the cold, a panicked sweat rolled down his face. If the robot put him in stasis, that'd be it: He'd be completely at Dr. Verity's mercy, and all his imagination would be good for would be dreaming (if you even dreamed in stasis). No, he needed a way to fight a robot, just without any weapons. Could he rewire the robot somehow? Or trip it through the open cell door and trap it inside before the robot could stop him? Maybe if adrenaline gave him superstrength, and he punched the robot in the head so hard he put a dent in it?

Or how about something really wild, like taking a long shot to see who was out there?

Readers, I don't suppose you're still out there, choosing the story? Owen thought. *Because now would be a really great time for a random ray gun to fall from the ceiling or something.*

He crossed his fingers, but sadly nothing awesome happened, and instead, they reached the open door. The robot pushed Owen inside a tiny cushioned room filled with little nozzles that probably produced whatever freezing gas it was that kept prisoners iced up, and he cursed his useless imagination.

The one time I need you, you completely let me down! he shouted at his brain.

"STEP INSIDE," the robot ordered, and gestured for Owen to go in.

Owen sullenly stepped in, reminded of just how useless he was against anyone fictional, imagination or not. He wasn't a hero and never would be. He was just too normal and regular a boy.

The Science Police robot began to close the door, and Owen frantically wracked his brain, taking any idea his imagination could come up with, no matter how ridiculous. Invisible gnomes? The robot breaks down from staying in the nonfictional world too much? Kiel Gnomenfoot shows up out of nowhere? *Argh*, none of these ideas were possible!

The robot seemed to slow down in front of him as it pushed the door closed, which was good, as it gave him more time to think. Inside his chest, his heart began to race, probably from fear, and . . .

The robot creaked to a halt, the door propped open just enough for Owen to slip through. He stared at it in shock, not sure what was happening. Had it just broken down? Could it be possible?

His heart beat so quickly that he started to worry about it breaking down again. He put a hand over it, wondering why it was working so hard, only for realization to slap him in the face.

He was using his time powers . . . and there wasn't any pain! His time powers weren't killing him anymore!

Owen gasped audibly, then slapped the robot before him, now frozen in time. Of course. Dr. Verity fixed his heart, so of course it'd work again!

But for how long?

That was a question for later, though. The powers worked now, which meant he had to escape while he could. Sticking out his tongue at the robot, Owen carefully pushed past the machine and stepped into the dungeon hallway. Not able to help himself, he shoved the stupid robot as hard as he could into the cell.

"Oh no, did you trip?" he shouted, doing a quick victory dance over his fallen enemy. Then, not wanting to waste any more time (or break his heart any more than he had to), Owen went to work.

It took several stopped minutes to get the robot into the tiny freezing chamber, considering the thing weighed half a ton. Once the robot was seated properly, Owen closed the door and hit the lock button, then slowed down his personal time to give his heart a break, and watched as jets of gas came pouring out, freezing the robot as it tried to reorient itself.

"Ice to *freeze* you!" Owen said, banging on the window as ice formed on the robot. Okay, it wasn't the *greatest* line, no, but he'd just gotten his imagination back, so he was a bit rusty. Besides, no one was around to hear it anyway. For once, things seemed to actually be going his way, and stupid pun or not, why shouldn't he enjoy it?

That's when alarms went off throughout the dungeon.

Owen slapped his forehead. The robot must have some sort of shutdown warning! Which meant Dr. Verity would know that Owen hadn't been frozen. And *that* meant more Science Police.

Or in other words, time to go.

As he ran down the hallway, the light in the other cell caught his attention, and Owen stopped short, even with the alarms blaring. Dr. Verity had someone else trapped here, and Owen couldn't just leave them in there. Besides, it might be Kara! She seemed like the most obvious choice.

He banged on the cell door's unlock button, but nothing happened. The alarms continued blaring, and he glanced around in rising panic at the other doors. Were they all locked down? That'd make sense, considering Verity wouldn't want anyone letting his prisoners escape. But how to open the doors, then? Did the robot have a key?

If it did, there was no way Owen was getting it back now.

From the direction of the exit, metallic footsteps clanked on the stairs. More robots, and they'd be here soon. Owen banged his hand against the door in frustration. If only there was some way to unlock it, or at least break it down. But the doors had to be pretty strong and durable to resist the freezing cold gas inside the cells. If that kind of cold couldn't break the metal, then what would?

You've got your imagination now, so maybe use it! his mind yelled at him. *What did the Countess's daughter teach you about your powers?*

Owen blinked, not really thrilled with his mind using that tone, but it did have a point. Dolores had copied his time powers, then evolved them to the point she could slow things down and speed them up just by touching them. Or at least that's what he half remembered from the time prison. Still, if he was right and she had done just that, then so could he . . . maybe?

Dr. Verity had claimed the chambers could keep you frozen

for a thousand years. What if Owen made those thousand years go by a bit . . . quicker?

He put his hands on the door and pushed his awareness out, trying to encompass the entire chamber. Fortunately, if Kara *was* in there, she'd remain frozen in time, no matter what he did, so she should be fine. He took a deep breath, then pushed his powers outward, away from his body and into the cell, willing time to speed up just in this one area.

The metallic footsteps grew closer as the gas in the cell door window began to swirl faster and faster, moving so quickly that it became an opaque cloud. A daze fell over his mind again as his chest tightened with pain, his imagination draining out of him as his heart slowly wore down, but that wasn't going to stop him now. Instead, he tightened his grip on the door and sped the chamber's time up *faster*, hoping that there'd be some sort of sign that it was almost done so he didn't end up aging whoever was inside into dust.

"BACK AWAY FROM THE CHAMBER," said a metallic voice, and a laser shot past Owen's shoulder. He yelped and quickly raised his hands before realizing he'd just released his hold on time in the cell. Argh! Had that been enough?

Owen stepped away from the cell, spots floating in front

of his eyes as the pain in his chest continued to throb. It was definitely harder to think now, though the headache wasn't helping. Speeding up something else's time this long was *not* something he should be doing if he wanted his heart to hold out for more than a few years.

"I'm not . . . supposed to be here," Owen said, unable to think of anything more clever to say. Speaking at all wasn't easy, actually, and he was finding it harder to breathe. "I—"

"SILENCE," the lead Science Police robot said, and four of them moved to surround him. "YOU HAVE BROKEN THE LAWS AND WILL BE DEALT WITH SUMMARILY. WE—"

The door to the cell exploded outward, crashing into two of the Science Police. One of them swept an arm out as it hit the wall, and knocked Owen to the ground as the robots' parts rained down around him. Smoke gushed out of the cell, obscuring everything as a third robot grabbed for Owen, then went flying down the hallway like a rocket.

"STOP," the fourth robot said to whoever it was in the cell. They didn't. Instead, the prisoner lifted the robot up, then slammed it down on the floor headfirst, crushing it into something no bigger than a garbage can.

Owen gasped at the carnage, trying to wave the smoke aside to see who it was.

"Hello?" he gasped. "I'm on your side. You don't need to hit me!"

The prisoner snorted, then stepped forward. "Look who's finally back," said a girl's voice, and a hand appeared out of the swirling mist in front of him.

". . . Kara?" Owen said, his mind swimming.

A robotic arm reached down and picked him up by his shirt with one hand. "Try again," Charm said, a half smile on her lips. "See? I *told* you I'd find you."

CHAPTER 22

"May I ask the meaning of this visit?" the Magister said slowly, not moving from his seat behind his desk.

Bethany slowly held up three Twilight throwing stars. "Pain, mostly," she growled in her best Twilight voice. "And *answers*."

"Whoa," Kiel said. "I realize we're not exactly friends here. Magi, you tried to kill the two of us, and we . . . well, we're pretty blameless, actually."

"She left me in a book of scientific facts!" the Magister said, strange energies beginning to swirl around him.

"It was a math book, genius," Bethany said. "Now you don't get to talk anymore. I'll ask the questions, and you'll only speak when I give you *permission* to do so."

"You *dare* try to control me?" the Magister roared, rising to his feet. Twin wands rose into the air behind him, swirling ominously. "You've lost none of your nonfictional arrogance, you—"

"Hey!" Kiel shouted, moving to stand between them. "First of all, she's entirely fictional now, so let's not start bringing up old, weird prejudices. Second, we need your help, Magi."

"What?" the Magister said.

"What?" Bethany said. "You're doing this all wrong. The good cop is supposed to give the perp donuts and stuff, but not until *after* I threaten him!"

"Nobody has destroyed Quanterium, Magi," Kiel said. "We learned from a message that Charm came here looking for help. Did you speak to her?"

The Magister narrowed his eyes. "I did. And I offered her the same mercy her people would have once offered me."

"Oh, *that* doesn't sound threatening at all," Bethany said. "Kiel, can we just fight him already? This talking stuff is really kind of boring, honestly."

"What did you do to her, Magi?" Kiel asked, and this time, he was the one sounding dangerous.

The Magister turned his gaze to his former apprentice and seemed to soften a bit. "I gave her refuge, as she asked. I sent her to a world I knew would accept those like her, where she might be safe. A world of scientists."

Kiel nodded slowly. "See, Beth? He helped the Quanterians. He can't be *that* bad—"

"Why are you sticking up for him?" Bethany hissed at Kiel, turning away from the Magister.

"Because I don't have any magic, and you might disappear if you try to fight him," Kiel whispered back. "I'm trying to avoid us getting turned into toads or something!"

"He was going to blow up Quanterium!" Bethany whispered. "You think he really is going to help them get to safety?"

The magical energy surrounding the Magister intensified for a moment, then seemed to dissipate. "I admit that in the past I was . . . not the most reasonable," he said, slowly sitting back down. "But I am a new man now. I have changed."

"Changed how?" Kiel asked.

"No one changes," Bethany whispered to him. "Don't fall for this."

"*I* just changed," Kiel told her out loud. "All you have to do is want it. So please, Magi, explain."

"I would like to . . . *apologize*, Bethany," the Magister said, looking a bit uncomfortable with his words. "The man you first met, the one who attacked you and Kiel . . . that was not *me*. At least, not the version of me that sits before you presently."

"Really?" Bethany said. "So who was that, a clone?"

"Oh, please, no," Kiel said. "Let's not start that whole thing up again."

The Magister gave Kiel the hint of a smile, then turned back to Bethany. "What I did, what I *tried* to do, back in the other world . . . those actions do not represent my true self. I cannot claim to fully know what pushed me to such a place." He paused, and his face darkened. "But I suspect that man, that *author* who presumed to control us . . . perhaps he had something to do with it."

Bethany gave Kiel a side look, putting every ounce of *Are you seeing this?* she could into the glance.

The Magister clenched his fists, then released them, and the darkness seemed to pass like a cloud over the sun. "However, Nobody showed me how to change, to fix any lasting damage that man might have caused. All it took was rewriting myself, changing into the human being I'd always wished to be. And now, ever since the worlds have separated, I've felt no hostility toward anyone, be they Quanterian or nonfictional. I would not even hold a grudge against Dr. Verity, if he were still around."

"Oh, well, that's *great*, then!" Bethany said, waving her arms.

"So just blame all your crazy behavior on an author, and now that things have gone your way, you're happy?"

The Magister glared at her, but slowly nodded. "I can see how it would look a bit suspicious. But I bear you no ill will, and if you do desire my aid, I will do what I can to help. You may trust me at my word."

A Twilight throwing star embedded itself in the wood just next to the Magister's head. Two more quickly followed, each one missing the man by mere inches, and Bethany crossed her arms as Kiel jumped back between them. "Trust?" she said. "If we're all just one big happy family here, why are you still using a protection spell? I never would have missed otherwise."

"Whoa!" Kiel said, spreading his arms wide, apparently not sure if she was going to throw any more weapons. "It's a good thing he had it on! Apparently he needed a Big Bubble of Safety spell!"

"Protectorate of Physicality, actually," the Magister murmured, staring at Bethany. "You really have changed quite a bit, now that you're fictional, haven't you?"

"Considering you were there when Nobody *pulled me in two*, that shouldn't surprise you," she said, glaring at him.

The Magister nodded, almost sadly. "Regrettable, indeed.

But Nobody surmised that your halves would in fact be more content in your separate worlds, that being forced into one whole was actually leading to unhappiness. He thought that was why you were so restless in your life."

"Restless?" Bethany said, her eyes widening. "I was searching for my father, who Nobody kidnapped!"

"Maybe it's time we asked some questions, before things get out of hand again," Kiel said, blocking Bethany's view of the Magister.

"It warms my heart to see you, Kiel," the old man said to his former apprentice. "If I can be of aid in any way, please ask. I owe you that, and so much more." His mouth seemed to quiver a bit, and Bethany rolled her eyes. Kiel, though, seemed to be entirely taken in by the old man's act.

"Are you serious?" she hissed at Kiel, but he gave her such a pathetic look that she sighed and let it go. "Fine. If Charm is safe, then we need to find out what Nobody's doing with the possibility machines she built. According to Kiel, he plans on starting the fictional universe over entirely by first turning all of the worlds into pure possibility. Do you know anything about this?"

The Magister stared at her for a moment, then shook his

head. "That would explain many puzzling bits and pieces I've seen in the last few months. How would he go about restarting our reality if we were but pure possibility?"

"He intends to do it himself, Magi," Kiel said. "He thinks he'll be the last one standing after we're all absorbed into possibility, and then he'll begin anew with himself in the role of author instead of nonfictionals. That way he'll be able to create a world without their interference. He's clearly missing some irony here."

The magic behind the Magister began to intensify again. "That . . . would not be advisable," the old man said quietly.

"I thought you were full of peace and love now?" Bethany said. "Don't tell me you'd be angry at Nobody for this?"

"We're also looking for someone, Magi," Kiel said quickly, glaring at Bethany. "Could you try a location spell, to see if you can locate him? He works for Nobody and has been distributing possibility machines to other worlds."

The Magister seemed lost in thought for a moment, then nodded. "I will need some sort of description of the man."

Kiel turned to Bethany, who sighed. "Tall guy, really muscular, wearing a suit and sunglasses. I chased him from Jupiter City to Quanterium. He knew who I was and that I was fully fictional now. He had a portal to Quanterium, but once I made it through, he'd disappeared. A moment later Nobody showed up, and we lost all track of my suspect."

The Magister nodded. "I will see what I can find." He began mumbling words beneath his breath, and his hands started to glow, forming a golden ball of light between them. Recognizing this as the same one they'd used to find her father back in Owen's library, Bethany watched the spell carefully, hoping it'd lead her to her missing suspect.

But after a moment, the light just faded away, and the Magister dropped his hands. "My magic cannot find him, either here or any fictional reality. As far as it can tell, he doesn't exist."

Bethany shoved Kiel out of the way and slammed her palms down hard on the Magister's desk. "Are you *kidding* me? I chased him here, to this reality. He's here somewhere!" She leaned in closer, giving the old man a death stare. "*Try it again*. Maybe you messed up when you described him to the magic spell."

"I didn't describe him, I used the image in your head."

"You read my *mind*?!" she shouted, Twilight throwing stars in hand again.

"Next question!" Kiel said, grabbing her hand and pulling it down to her side. "We're also hoping you could check Bethany out magically. She seems to be, how do I put this . . . dissolving."

Bethany glared at him, but he just shrugged apologetically. The Magister gazed at them curiously, then came out from behind the desk and waved his wand gently at Bethany. She put up her hands to defend herself, but just felt a gentle light wash over her, and she relaxed slightly. The light moved from her to the Magister, and he frowned. "I am seeing nothing more than a normal, healthy girl. There is no indication of anything wrong with her."

"Show him what happens if you rewrite yourself, Beth," Kiel said.

She pulled up her sleeve and concentrated on rewriting herself, pushing her arm out toward the Magister. As she reached, her arm grew longer and longer until her fingers brushed up against the invisible magical bubble around him.

"Ah, you've learned how to rewrite yourself as well!" The Magister actually seemed to enjoy this for some reason. "It really is the key to fixing all sorts of personality issues. If you want any suggestions on that—"

"Uh, Magi, there's more," Kiel said quickly, stepping

between them as Bethany's fingers clenched into a fist. "Watch what happens next."

The Magister leaned forward, peering down at her hand over the top of his glasses as her fingertips began to slowly dissolve, just as they'd done back on Quanterium. *"Extraordinary,"* he said quietly, running his own fingers through the space where hers had been. "And you can bring them back?"

"I hope," Bethany whispered, and rewrote her arm to normal. Three fingers and her thumb rematerialized, but her pinkie finger was completely gone.

"Hold on," Kiel said, grabbing her other hand as she began to panic, breathing faster and faster. "You can fix this. Concentrate just like last time."

Bethany nodded, trying hard not to hyperventilate. She pictured her old half-fictional self, with all of her anxieties, rule-breaking, and fictional friends and family (also *not* missing any fingers), and desperately tried to focus on what it felt like to be that girl again.

At first, nothing happened, but soon her pinkie finger slowly pushed up out of her palm. It stopped before the very tip of her nail grew back, but at least she had all of her fingers.

"Ah," the Magister said, replacing his glasses. "I've seen

something like this before. This, my child, is the same problem many apprentices have with magic, when first learning it. You are having trouble controlling the chaos within yourself! The power to rewrite one's very essence is great indeed, and can be extremely dangerous in the wrong hands. To conquer it, you first must defeat your own inner doubts, or you shall dissolve into chaos."

Kiel raised an eyebrow at this. "I've never heard of problems like this, Magi. Yes, magic asks a great price, but I never dissolved. Don't you think—"

"You weren't exactly lacking in self-confidence, Kiel," the Magister said. "Now, perhaps you might help your *friend* here with some lessons on controlling chaos within ourselves. I must look into your suggestion that Nobody means to restart the worlds. If that's true, I might have to take action."

Kiel flashed Bethany a smile. "See? This all worked out. Now we've found an ally against Nobody!"

"Perhaps," the Magister said, then looked up as if distracted. "Ah, my new apprentice approaches. I'll have to send him back to his lessons."

Kiel's smile slowly died, and he turned to the Magister with a hurt look. "Your new *what*, now?"

Someone knocked on the door behind them.

"Before you returned, I was sought out by one who wished to learn," the Magister said. "That would be him now."

"What's the matter, Kiel?" Bethany whispered, elbowing him playfully. "People change. You can't expect him to not ever take on another apprentice, right?"

The Magister waved his hand, and the door opened by itself. From behind it, a brown-haired boy in black clothes and a cape just like Kiel's poked his head in.

A very *familiar*-looking boy.

"Oh, hey, you two," Fowen Conners said. "Is this a good time, Magi? Because I'm really excited to show you how powerful my Penchant for Destruction spell has gotten!"

CHAPTER 23

 harm?" Owen said, not sure he wasn't dreaming.

The half-robotic girl yanked him to his feet, then hugged him so hard that some of his ribs felt like they cracked. He whimpered, and she let go, her smile actually growing.

"Leave it to you to rescue me, when I was trying to rescue *you*," she said, picking up one of the Science Police laser rifles and tossing it to him. She took two ray guns for herself, sticking one in a holster that popped out of her robotic leg. "How long was I here, a day or two?"

Owen winced. For all he knew, it could have been years. "Something like that. How did you get here?"

More metallic footsteps sounded from the stairs outside, and Charm nodded at the door. "One second," she said, and led the way down the hall, a ray gun in her human hand, her robotic one curled into a fist.

The first Science Police robot that came running into the dungeon got Charm's robotic fist right through its face. She yanked her arm free of the robot's head, then shot the next one in the chest, whirled past it, and punched a third one into the nearby tower wall hard enough to crumple it into pieces.

"Sorry about that," she said, brushing wires off of her robotic hand. "What were you saying?" She glanced over at Owen, whose mouth was hanging open.

"I, uh, wow," he stammered, having trouble thinking. For once, it wasn't just the fault of missing his imagination either, now that his heart wasn't working well again. Though with Charm here now, at least he had someone fictional to jump-start his imagination in emergencies.

"Hey," she said, glaring at him. "Don't look at me like that. I've got some pent-up hostility. Feels good to let it out."

"That was the coolest thing I've ever seen you do," Owen said, completely sincerely. "And I've seen you do a *lot* of cool things."

The slightest tinge of red bloomed in Charm's cheeks, and she rolled her eyes. "You don't have to say every single thought that pops into your head, you know. Some of them can just be for you."

Owen nodded a few times, then followed her out of the hallway. "Dr. Verity is at the top of the stairs," he said, pointing.

"Good," Charm said, starting up the stairs. "He's got my people somewhere, and I'm not going anywhere without them."

"He's got my friend up there somewhere too," Owen told her. "And something we're going to need if we ever want to get home."

Charm raised an eyebrow. "He's got Bethany? How did you turn her back from that ray of light?"

Owen blinked. "Um, long story. But no, different friend. Someone who helped me escape from Nobody, actually."

Charm narrowed her eyes at the name. "Was he the reason you went missing in Jupiter City? I *knew* it wasn't my fault. That's another thing I owe that faceless piece of garbage-ridden—"

"We should hurry," Owen said, looking up nervously as the alarm blared. "There'll be more Science Police on their way."

"Let them come," Charm said, giving him another half smile. "I could use some exercise." She began to climb the spiral staircase two by two, and Owen raced to catch up.

"How did you get here?" he asked again, just before she

shoved him backward against the wall. Lasers came sizzling past him, and she shot two more robots with her ray gun.

"The Magister wanted some revenge, so he took it out on my people at our lowest moment," she told him, eyeing the stairs for more Science Police. "I'd built an experimental machine to give myself powers just like Bethany's, only without any restrictions. I wanted the powers so I could go after Nobody, only the machine didn't work right, and then Nobody showed up anyway and used my invention against Quanterium." She gritted her teeth, and her robotic hand dug into the wall behind them with a crunch.

"What did the invention do?" Owen asked quietly.

"It was *supposed* to let me turn into whatever I wanted, just like Nobody does. But it wasn't controllable. When Nobody used it on us, it messed up the entire planet, making it too unstable to safely stay. I rounded up my people using our emergency measures, then went looking for help from the Magister." She swore a few times under her breath. "He put some kind of spell on me, and the next thing I knew, I was waking up in your stupid library again."

This time, she punched her fist into the wall just above

Owen's head, her arm shaking in rage. Owen waited as she calmed down enough to continue.

"The magician turned me into a *book*," she said finally. "Eventually the spell either wore off, or it was set to free me when someone opened my book, because the first thing I saw was some woman screaming. More of my people popped out in the same way, so I imagine they're all around here somewhere."

All of that fit with Dr. Verity's version of things. But it still didn't answer one important question. "How could you have gotten *here*, though? To this world?" Owen asked her, hoping she knew of a way that Dr. Verity didn't. Not having to fight the scientist to use the tower's portal to get to the fictional world would make things a *lot* easier.

"No idea," she said. "Once we started waking up, or whatever we were doing, the people here got terrified. Called us an invasion." She snorted. "Nice way to treat a bunch of people fleeing for their lives, by the way. They start rounding us up, bringing us here for 'reprogramming.'"

She dragged Owen up a few more stairs, then leaned out into the middle of the staircase, aimed her ray gun up, and took down two more Science Police a few floors above them. The robots tumbled down the middle of the stairwell, then exploded loudly as they hit the floor at the dungeon level.

"Didn't work on me, though," Charm continued. "Probably too many computer parts in my head. But they brainwashed my people. Now they do whatever Verity says. How *he* got here, I don't know either. But whoever sent him here instead of letting him die at the Source of Magic is going to talk to my fist."

"I bet," Owen said, scrunching even farther back against the wall as more lasers went sizzling past.

Charm went silent for a moment, holding up a finger for him to be quiet. She began to slowly climb the stairs, listening as well as watching for something, and then cursing under her breath. "Hear that?"

Owen paused, trying to listen as hard as he could, but whatever it was, he couldn't make it out. It probably helped to have robotic ears. "No, what—"

"More guards. But not robots this time. I think he's sending my people down after us."

And now Owen *could* hear it, footsteps from above them, but like Charm had said, not as heavy or metallic now. "We can't fight *them*," he whispered. "What do we do?"

She sighed. "I'd normally say run for now, and then figure out a way to free my people before going after Verity. But if your friend is up there, then we don't have a choice. We're not leaving anyone behind."

Owen nodded. Though part of him *did* want to run, there was no way he was leaving Kara now. Charm returned his nod, then put away her ray guns. "I guess we go hand to hand and try not to permanently damage any of them, then."

A black helmet appeared above them, armed with a laser rifle. He fired, and the shot grazed Charm's shoulder, in spite of the bit of shelter offered by the walls. She growled in pain as more appeared behind the first, and soon they were completely pinned down by all the blasts filling the air.

This wasn't going to work. Even if Charm could reach the black helmets through the laser beams, there'd be no way she could take them all down before one shot her. No, there was only one way through this.

"Don't let go," he told her, and grabbed her hand in his. Her eyes widened, and she looked at him in confusion. "Might as well use that power you gave me," he said, then sped up time.

His heart immediately started racing as the lasers around

them began to freeze in midair, shortening into smaller blasts of light now instead of a continuous laser beam. Considering the lasers were still moving at the speed of light, they weren't stopping altogether, even with time moving this quickly, but they had slowed enough for Owen and Charm to dodge through them.

Even if the lasers hadn't frozen, the black helmets *had*, so the number of blasts lessened considerably as soon as they passed the first volley.

"I knew I was good," Charm said as they climbed carefully past the black helmets, "but I didn't realize I was *this* good."

Owen tried to smile, but the pressure on his chest was getting worse. He looked up the stairs and groaned at the sight: There were black helmets all the way up to Dr. Verity's office now.

"Let's just hurry," he said, his voice breaking with pain.

Charm looked at him with concern. "You okay?"

"My heart . . . doesn't do so great when I use these powers now," he said, sliding past another black helmet while making sure not to touch the Quanterian.

Charm stared at him for a moment, then picked him up,

threw him over her shoulder, and began to run. Even moving quickly, she still was careful not to accidentally bump a black helmet off the stairs, though she did come close a few times, especially as they neared the top.

Finally, as the pain started turning unbearable, Charm reached Dr. Verity's office. She threw her weight against the metal door, knocking it open in spite of the security measures, then jumped inside and slammed it shut, locking it. Owen immediately slid off her shoulder to the ground and released his hold on time, barely able to even think through the pain.

"Oh, look!" said a familiar voice. "I love when unwanted guests just appear out of nowhere."

Owen looked up to find Dr. Verity standing over Kara, who was tied down on the same table he'd used when operating on Owen. Kara looked like she was frozen midscream, with wires attached to her head and monitors above them showing all kinds of different versions of her time bracelet. "I'd love to know how you did it," Dr. Verity continued. "But no time for that now. I've got what I need, so enjoy yourselves here. I really have to be going back to the past, before the tower's magic faded. The dimensional portal doesn't work here in the future, and how else am I going to get back home? Lots of Magisteria to destroy, after all!"

He touched the time bracelet on his hand, and everything in the lab, including the computers, the Science Police, and even Kara, all silently disappeared.

CHAPTER 24

"Kiel?" Bethany said, her voice just above a whisper. "Stay here. See if you can get anything else out of the Magister."

"Where are you going?" Kiel asked her.

"I just need a minute," she said, then grabbed Fowen by his shirt and threw him out of the Magister's office.

"Whoa!" Fowen said, throwing his hands up in surrender as she slammed the office door behind them. "I get it, we didn't leave things on the best of terms last time. But that's all behind us now!"

"How did you get out of the book I left you in?" Bethany demanded, bashing him against the wall. "How did you get *here*? Why is the Magister teaching you magic?"

Fowen grinned. "Well, he had an opening, since Kiel's not interested anymore—"

Bethany shook him over and over, then threw him against the wall a second time. "Who set you free? Tell me or I *will*—"

"You'll what?" Fowen asked, giving her an almost pitying look. "You're not exactly in a position to threaten me anymore." He held up a hand and sent sparks flying from finger to finger. "But we're getting off on the wrong foot here. I'm not your enemy, Bethany."

"*Really?* Because I remember you trying to drown me and steal my powers not too long ago!"

Fowen actually looked a bit embarrassed by that. "Okay, yes, but in my defense, they were really *awesome* powers. But that's all over now. I don't need them anymore. I have my own!"

Bethany glared at him. "Who. Let. You. Out."

Fowen sighed. "It was Nobody, okay? He came to get me not long after you left me there. I only got through, like, one Sherlock Holmes case as part of the Baker Street Irregulars." He rolled his eyes. "I barely had any time to show off my knowledge of modern science!"

Bethany let go of him and took a step back. "Nobody rescued you? Why would he bother?"

Fowen gave her a pained look. "*Ouch*, first of all. Second, I think he was just cleaning up your mess, actually. For a long time, he just left me in some weird plane of all white where nothing happened and time didn't exist. I just floated there, bored out of my mind." He shuddered. "The worst torture you could imagine. But eventually he came back and offered me a second chance. Said that's what the fictional world was all about—possibilities."

"Yeah, he definitely seems interested in starting things over," Bethany said, narrowing her eyes. "And that's when you, what, joined up with the Magister?"

Fowen blushed. "Actually, that's when I helped Nobody steal that light machine from your dad and his sidekick by pretending to be Nowen."

Rage flooded her mind, and Bethany grabbed for him again, but he quickly jumped out of the way. "Hey, we were rescuing you!" he said, backing away. "You *could* say thank you!"

"Oh, I'll be *happy* to thank you," Bethany said, running through images in her mind. She could turn into a steamroller and drive over him. Or morph into a giant anvil and drop on him from above? That might be fun.

"No worries," Fowen said, staying just out of reach. "Besides, aren't you happier now with the worlds the way they are? You've got your father back, and no one cares about your secret anymore."

"That's not the point," Bethany said angrily, though he wasn't wrong.

"I'd be mad too, I get it," Fowen said. "But because I'm a nice guy, I'm going to do you a favor—"

"A *favor*?! You tried to drown—"

"Fine!" Fowen said, shaking his head. "I'm going to pay you back, okay? Is that better? Think of it as a peace offering."

"What could you possibly do for me?"

He smiled. "I *might* have been listening at the door. And before you hit me again, I can help you. I know a way for you to not only rescue the Quanterians, but also gain the power to beat *Nobody* once and for all."

Bethany froze midgrab for him. If she could track down the Quanterians, maybe she'd find Charm. And if anyone could figure out how to fix the effect of the possibility rays, it'd be Charm and her scientists. She could cure her father *and* stop this insane plan of Nobody's, assuming Fowen wasn't lying about a new power.

Wait a second. This was Fowen. Of course he was lying! "No deal," she said. "I've got no reason to believe you."

"See, that's where you're wrong," he told her. "You think I want to get turned into pure possibility and get erased? There's no way Nobody would be bringing *me* back. I want to take him down the same as you do!"

"Fine," Bethany said. "But if this is a trap, one of us won't be walking away from it."

"That'd be more threatening if what you said wasn't the exact definition of a trap," Fowen said, then ducked as Bethany punched right where his head had been. "Okay, I'm sorry! Follow me."

He led her down the stairs in the tower, passing door after door with weird lights and odd noises coming from within. Bethany recognized a lot of it from her time in the nonfictional version of the Magister's tower, back when he'd been trying to unleash fictional monsters on nonfictional people.

Wait. She never used to call it the nonfictional world. It'd always been the real world to her. When had that changed? Was the fictional world the real one now? The idea both startled and thrilled her.

They continued downward in silence, Bethany watching Fowen for the slightest hint of betrayal, while he seemed to be counting doors as they descended. Finally, he stopped in front of one close to the bottom and murmured some words that Bethany couldn't hear as he shook his finger at the lock. "I decided I didn't want to learn using wands," he said, looking back up at her as he pushed the door open. "They get lost too easily."

"Or someone steals them and erases your memory," Bethany said, glaring at him.

Fowen coughed. "Yeah, that too. Anyway, it's in here." He entered the dark room and murmured another spell. One by one, his fingers began to glow. The small lights then rose off his fingertips toward the ceiling, illuminating what looked like a storage area.

"Charm and Kiel used this room back when they were look-ing for the keys to the Source of Magic," Fowen said. "There's a special item in here that's going to solve all of our problems. Come on."

He led her farther into the still-dim room, past several objects covered by large cloths. One of the objects moved as they approached, but Fowen just shushed it, and whatever it was seemed to calm down.

"At one point in their adventures, Kiel and Charm had to travel to other dimensions in order to find one of the keys,"

Fowen said, stopping in front of a large mirror on the wall. "And this is what they used to travel between those alternate dimensions."

"A mirror?" Bethany frowned. "Kind of . . . ordinary."

"No way, mirrors are *classic* portals," Fowen said, touching a hand to the glass, then pushing through it as if the mirror were no more solid than the surface of a swimming pool. "This one's special, too. It needs a twin on the opposite end to work, so you can only go where there's another mirror just like this one. The mirrors aren't connected like the nonfictional and fictional portals used to be, but think of it like needing an airport to land at the end of a flight. Without one, you're probably going to crash."

"But you said they traveled to other dimensions to find a key."

"Maybe 'alternate dimensions' is the wrong way to put it," Fowen said. "Think of them as parallel dimensions, other realities where another Magister built another tower with a mirror just like this one. The key was hidden in one of them, so Charm and Kiel had to search through a bunch." He shrugged. "At least that's the understanding I got from the Magister. Not like I ever read the books."

"So what are you saying? I should use this mirror to travel to a parallel dimension? What good does that do me?"

"You're not seeing the possibilities," Fowen said. "Think about where you could go."

"Fowen," Bethany said, getting angry again.

"That's not my name," Fowen hissed, before catching himself and forcing a smile. "Let's back up a second. Do you know what the Quanterians planned in case of a planet-wide emergency? They were at war for years, so had to prepare. Any ideas?"

She just stared at him.

"Right, moving on," Fowen said. "Well, you've teleported before, obviously. The fun thing about teleporting is that basically it beams you up into a computer by turning you into pure information, then sends that information wherever you're teleporting to and reverses the process. Now, if your whole planet was disappearing, what do you think would be the fastest way to get everyone to safety?"

"Teleport them somewhere."

"What if you didn't know where to take them yet?"

Bethany growled. "Just tell me—"

"Charm arrived here with the information of her entire

people, Bethany," Fowen told her. "She teleported them all up to her ship, but never sent them anywhere. That much information takes up a lot of gigabytes, or whatever they call them here, but it still takes up a lot less room than millions of people. And Quanterians have some pretty big memory drives."

Bethany furrowed her brow. "You're saying Charm showed up here with the entire population of the planet in, what, her pocket?"

"Who knows where she keeps stuff with all those robot parts," Fowen said. "Maybe in her arm. But yup, she showed up here and asked the Magister for help."

"He told Kiel and me that he sent them to a world where they believe in science," Bethany said.

"Well, that part is true, I suppose," Fowen said. "But he had to get one last dig in, so he came up with something that was pretty cruel, all things considered. And that says something coming from *me*."

Bethany stepped closer, not willing to wait anymore. "Tell me what he did, Fowen. Tell me *now*."

Anger flashed over his face at the name, but he forced himself to calm down, then nodded. "You know how the Magister hates the idea of an author controlling his life? Well, he hates Quanterians just a little more. I guess he wanted to make them both miserable, so he used magic to turn Charm and all of her Quanterian people into books." He shrugged. "It wasn't that hard, actually, considering all but Charm were already made of information."

"Books?" Bethany said, shaking her head. "I don't see—"

"Think about it. He floated all the books down here and sent them through a portal to another world, with another tower." Fowen gestured at the mirror. "Don't you get it? Remember what happened in *Story Thieves*? The Magister built a tower in the *nonfictional* world, Bethany. That tower has a mirror, which means this one connects to it. All of those Quanterians just got sent into your nonfictional world as books. And if anyone opens them, BAM, the spell is broken, and all of a sudden, Quanterians everywhere."

Bethany fell back against the nearest wall, unable to believe any of this. Even the Magister wouldn't do such a thing. "That *can't* be true."

"It is. Oh, and there's one more secret I should admit before we go any further," Fowen said, then started murmuring under his breath. As she watched, he began to glow, slowly growing in height and muscle. His black outfit and cape morphed into a suit, and sunglasses appeared on his face.

"What?!" Bethany shouted. *"You?"*

"Pretty handsome, huh?" said the man who'd been smuggling possibility ray guns into Jupiter City, flexing his enormous muscles.

CHAPTER 25

No!" Owen screamed, lurching forward into the now-empty laboratory, then falling to his knees as the pain in his chest erupted. He breathed in deeply over and over, trying his best not to faint. "Verity took her, Charm. He took Kara!"

Charm reached around beneath his arms and lifted him back to his feet. "Don't worry, we'll find him. Do you know where he went?" She tilted her head, like she was listening for something. "Wherever it was, he took all of my people with him. Science Police, too. I'm not hearing anyone or anything outside on the stairs now."

Owen just shook his head. "Back in time. That thing on his wrist was a time bracelet, a time machine. He went back in the past, to use some portal in this tower to jump back to your world and invade Magisteria using the brainwashed Quanterians. After that, he planned on fighting Nobody, though I don't know how even an army would help him with that."

Charm's eyes narrowed thoughtfully. "Okay, that's a lot. But this is nothing we haven't handled before. Remember when we went to the future and found out you didn't survive the fight against Dr. Verity? This is basically no different. We beat him then, and we'll beat him *now*."

Owen sighed, and suddenly his older self's words came back to him. *Tell her it was you. Not Kiel, you.*

He glanced at Charm, who was smiling at him of all things, trying to make him feel better. He couldn't tell her now, he couldn't. They were right in the middle of an army invading a fictional world and Kara being kidnapped by a madman. If he told her the truth, she'd know he'd been lying to her from the very beginning. That everything they'd done together, everything they'd faced was based on a falsehood.

He couldn't tell her, it just wasn't the time.

But then again, it never really would be the time, would it?

"Charm, I have to tell you something," he said quietly, not looking at her. "I'm not . . . I'm not Kiel Gnomenfoot."

Her smile faded, and she groaned. "Not this again. I don't know why you insist on pretending, but you've got the heart I gave to Kiel Gnomenfoot, the one that Dr. Verity put into you. Why you're in disguise, I don't know, but—"

Feeling weak from more than his heart problems, Owen moved to stand against the nearest wall, using it for support. "I should have told you all of this earlier, but I didn't know how. That was me then, when we went to find the last key and crashed on Quanterium, but I'm not really Kiel. *This* is the real me. When you knew me as Kiel, I was in disguise. The real Kiel was here, on this world."

Charm rolled her eyes, looking more irritated now. "That doesn't make any sense. I tested you. My sensors did a complete analysis, and you checked out. Why are you doing this? What is this game you're playing? We don't have time for it, whatever it is!"

Owen shrugged halfheartedly. "The disguise spell fooled your sensors. And it's no game. I'm serious. This is the real me."

Charm just stared at him, looking more confused than he'd ever seen her. "You're not Kiel? But . . . why? And who are you?" She slowly reached for the ray gun at her hip.

"I'm the same person you knew," Owen said, holding out a hand for her to stop. "You can trust me. I mean, I know I lied and all, but that was before I knew you, really knew you. And I honestly was trying to do what was best for Magisteria. I was going to give up my heart to open the Source of Magic."

She took another step forward, her hand still on her ray gun. "Who *are* you?" she said again.

Owen slid down the wall, not able to hold himself up. "My name really is Owen. Owen Conners. I'm from this world. In the past, years ago, we were able to see into your world through books. Remember how Bethany jumped us in and out of them? That's her power, but the rest of us just read them and followed your stories. I read about you and Kiel both, so many times. And after reading about your adventures, everything you went through, it just felt like I knew you." He winced, knowing how this all sounded. "I get that it's weird, but thousands of people have read about you in this world. You have a lot of fans, a lot of people rooting for you."

Charm didn't speak, she just kept giving him the same confused look.

"When I found out about Bethany's powers, I asked her to take us into Kiel's story, while you and he were in the end of everything. We went in, and I rescued the Magister from Dr. Verity. Verity was supposed to kill him, but I stopped it. Unfortunately, the Magister figured out where we came from, and he and Kiel traveled to this world, leaving me behind in the tower.

I couldn't just let Dr. Verity win, so . . ." He stopped, shaking his head. "No, let me be completely honest. I wanted to know what it was like to be Kiel, to be a *hero*. I'm no one, a regular kid, nobody important. So I thought it'd be amazing to be a hero for once. To cast spells, fight Science Police—"

"And lie to me?" Charm said, staring at the floor. "I wondered why you were so different after the sixth key. I thought it was because you were mourning the Magister, but it didn't fit. Now I understand." She glanced up, and her eyes were red. "So, what, you thought this was all fun? My life? Kiel's life? You just wanted to play along with us like we were toys?"

Owen sighed. "I know I was beyond stupid, trust me. I had no idea what I was doing. But when I found out that I had to give up my heart, I wanted to quit. To leave. I didn't want to be the hero anymore. But you came to me, in the Magister's tower, to convince me that I should do what was right, for people I'd never met and didn't know. And you *did*." He looked up at her, trying to show her how much that had meant to him. "You made me believe I could do it, Charm, and didn't have to be just some . . . nobody."

"Except you let me keep thinking you were Kiel after that, even when we went to Jupiter City."

"I didn't want to, but I didn't know the right way to tell you!" Owen hit the floor now, not even able to look at her. "I was just so happy to see you. I'd really missed you, especially when Kiel, Bethany, and I would go on adventures. Those two would—"

"Kiel *knew* you'd done this?" Charm said.

Oh, whoops. "Uh, not at first," Owen said quickly. "But he found out later and came in to take my place before the final fight against Dr. Verity. He didn't want me to die for him. You know what he's like. I know where he is now, by the way. I found out while you were all in Jupiter City that Nobody captured him. Just one more thing he took from us."

Charm nodded, her eyes on the wall above Owen. "Everyone is taken from me. Why would Kiel be any different?" She rubbed her human arm against her eyes. "So what now, then?"

What now? "I can't even begin to apologize—"

"*Don't,*" Charm said, turning her back on him. "Just don't. I don't care. You lied to me, you tricked me, and you made me think you were my closest friend while doing it. There's *nothing* you can say that will make me trust you again or let me look at you without wanting to throw up." Her hands curled into fists. "All I want is to save my people from Dr. Verity, then stop

Nobody. You are going to help me do that, and then I will never, *ever* see you again. Is that clear?"

Owen's insides curled up into a little ball, and he wanted to groan in pain, everything hurt so much. But for once, it wasn't so much about the physical pain in his heart. "Okay," he said finally. "I'm not sure how we can do it, but I'll help you as best I can."

"Yes, you will," Charm said. "Try to be *useful* in some way."

The words hit him like a punch to the gut. "I . . . I will." He pushed himself up the wall again, knowing she wasn't going to help. "We need to find a way back in time. There's a portal here in the tower that should be able to get us back to your world, but it doesn't work here in the future. It's been in this world too long, and the magic won't work anymore. We need to get back to the past and use it there. Hopefully we can get there before Dr. Verity does and warn Magisteria what's coming. Maybe they can use their magic to unbrainwash the Quanterians?"

"So we just need something to get us back in time, then," Charm said. "*That* should be easy."

"Dr. Verity said he was making a time machine, but I assume he took all of his plans with him," Owen said, shaking his head. "Maybe they have technology we can use in this time period.

Or maybe Dr. Verity did leave something behind that we can fix up somehow—"

"Oh, he had all the plans on the monitors, and whatever I see gets saved in the robotic half of my brain," Charm said, tapping her forehead. "I can recreate the bracelet, or at least a close approximation, if we can find a few Science Police to steal parts from. But it'll only work once, if that."

"Once should be enough," Owen said, limping over to her.

"Then let's get started," she said. "The sooner I never have to look at your face again, the better." With that, she strode over to the door, threw it open, and left him standing alone in the remains of Dr. Verity's empty laboratory.

CHAPTER 26

Turn into a train and run Fowen over, Bethany thought. *Morph into gravity a thousand times worse than normal. Become a poison and inject yourself into him!*

She grabbed her head, almost in pain from too many ideas coming at once. "You . . . you brought those possibility ray guns to Jupiter City," she said quietly, her mind racing. "Do you understand what you've done?"

"Yeah, I got *you* here," Fowen said, sounding proud. "Like I said, Nobody wanted to leave Jupiter City alone, but I needed you here if we had any chance of fighting him. You'd never have come if I just showed up as myself, you know that. You'd have attacked me, I'd have won, and we'd both be in trouble, because you're the only one who's going to be able to stop Nobod—"

She grabbed him by the neck, her muscles growing super-strong as she grew in height, towering over Fowen's disguised

244

self. "*My father* was hit by one of those rays," she said quietly as Fowen's eyes widened in surprise. "He's going to *disappear* unless I can find a way to save him. And you did this . . . just to get my attention?"

"I'm sorry, I didn't know!" Fowen squeaked, turning back into his regular self so that he now hung several feet off the floor. "You have to believe me. I was trying to help! I thought you'd find me before anything bad happened, I swear!"

She roared in anger and tossed him against one of the nearest walls. He slammed into it hard enough to knock the air from his lungs with a whoosh, then slumped to the floor. "This is all your fault!" she screamed, stomping over to him, the tower shaking with every step. "And you thought you'd get my *help* this way?"

Fowen quickly scrambled to his feet, mumbling a spell under his breath. Lightning exploded from his fingers, but Bethany just let it hit her, shrugging off the pain. "*Whoa,*" he said, backing away from her with his hands raised in surrender. "Listen to me! I really am trying to help. I did the same thing to your nonfictional version. I left her and Nowen a note in one of the Quanterium books and told them to open it. Right now, they're probably freeing Charm and all of her people and they'll be on their way back any minute. I'm on your side, trust me!"

She grabbed him by his shirt and held him over her head. "You're on no one's side but your own!" she roared. "Tell me what your real plan is!"

"To stop Nobody, really!" he said, flinching before giving her an odd look. "Um, did you know you're disappearing?"

She glanced down and saw that her free hand had lost its fingers. She screamed in frustration and tossed Fowen aside, turning herself back to normal as quickly as she could. Thinking about her old self wasn't comfortable, but the process seemed to go more smoothly this time. Unfortunately, when she regained her original form, it took far longer to get her fingers back. She struggled with it, getting more and more frustrated until finally they emerged, and she let out a huge sigh of relief.

"You shouldn't do that, you know," Fowen told her. "That's what Nobody *wants*, for us all to disappear like that. You're turning into possibility. That's what happens without the non-fictional world anchoring ours. There's nothing keeping us from rewriting ourselves into pure ideas."

Bethany took a deep breath, just trying not to punch him again. "Now is *not* the best time to tell me what to do."

He nodded. "Fair enough. But this is what's going to happen to every fictional person, world, everything, if no one stops Nobody. This was his plan even before he discovered Charm's invention. Have you been getting swamped with too many ideas anytime you're trying to decide something? It's happening to some extent to all of us, and it's only going to get worse the more worlds are absorbed by Nobody's possibility waves. The whole thing is speeding up, and we've run out of time."

She frowned, thinking about how she couldn't just think of one thing to turn into when using her superpowers the last few times. "Fine. Let's pretend you're actually doing this to help people. How do we fix it?"

"That's why I brought you down here," Fowen said, rubbing his neck where she'd grabbed it. "*Not* to get into a fight, I might add. Like I said, this portal can connect with the non-fictional version of the Magister's tower. All you need to do is go through and rejoin with your nonfictional self. Then you'll have the power to face Nobody, because your nonfictional self will give you an anchor again. You'll be able to rewrite yourself all you want without dissolving away. Which means you'll be able to fight Nobody on his own terms. Winning, though, is something else." He shook his head. "This isn't a sure thing, by the way. Not even likely. But you, the *whole* you, are maybe the only one anywhere who even has a chance to save us all."

Bethany stared at the portal, almost getting light-headed before she realized she'd stopped breathing. "No," she said softly. "I don't need her. She'd just hold me back. I'll fight him myself."

Fowen blinked. "Are you kidding? He'll destroy you! You can't rewrite yourself without fading away. He *can*, Bethany. I don't know how, but he's not disappearing like everything else. Plus, the more you rewrite yourself, the more you add possibilities into the world, and everything falls apart even faster. You need your anchor. You need your nonfictional self back!"

"No, I *don't*!" she shouted at him. "All of this is her fault. I would have found my father years ago if she hadn't kept me home, afraid of my mom, of getting discovered, of *everything in life*. I didn't need her then, and I don't need her now. All she does is feel guilty and worry about things. I'm a thousand times happier without her!"

"Yeah, you sound *so* happy," Fowen said, giving her an odd look. "And you're telling me you're not worried about your father and our worlds? Maybe you're not really seeing things clearly—"

Bethany reached out and grabbed his shirt again. "You want me to fight Nobody, and I will. I bet there are spells you can use to keep me together. If you can't, then the Magister can."

Fowen's eyes widened. "There's no way that'd work. Magic *is* pure possibility already. Without the nonfictional world anchoring us, magic is maybe the least reliable tool we have right now!"

"The Magister seems to be doing fine," Bethany said, releasing him. "I guess I'll go see what spells he's got. Maybe it's not magic that's the problem, *Fowen*. Maybe you're just not very good at it."

He clenched his fist, looking away. "My *name* is *Owen*."

"Someone better than you already owns that name."

"*I* am Owen!" he shouted, rage flashing across his face. "I'm the only Owen who matters! Your version has been tossed around by Nobody, thrown in a time prison, and kicked back home, useless to anyone. *I'm* the one saving the world, the one being a hero, fighting the big villain. And if that's a problem for you, then I suggest you take it up with your pathetic friend, because I don't see him doing *anything*."

She glared at him for another moment as he took a deep breath, calming down. "He might not know magic or be a hero," Bethany said finally. "But he's a better person than you'll *ever* be."

"Guess we'll have to agree to disagree," he said, narrowing his eyes.

Bethany nodded, then moved to leave the room. Fowen swore behind her, then raced to stop her. "You can't do this!" he said. "Magic or not, you don't have a chance without your other self."

She threw a look back at him over her shoulder. "Stay out of my way. I don't like you, and I definitely don't trust you. If you're telling the truth, we're on the same side . . . for now. But the moment that's not the case, you're *mine*."

CHAPTER 27

As Owen and Charm made their way down the spiral staircase and out of the tower, they didn't run into a single person, let alone a black helmet soldier. However Dr. Verity had modified Kara's time bracelet, it now seemed to work on large groups of people without needing any physical contact, because he'd taken his entire brainwashed army with him.

As they exited, Charm looked over the barren grounds of what used to be Jonathan Porterhouse's mansion, searching for more technology to make a time machine. A few scientists nervously peeked out of their tent buildings, probably as thrown by the disappearance of the black helmets as Owen was.

"They might have some useful stuff," Owen said, pointing at the tent where he'd been tested for being fictional.

Charm didn't respond, but instead moved purposefully toward the building, sending the few scientists glancing outside scurrying back into the tent. As she entered, Owen heard raised voices, then shouts of surprise and terror. Something hit the side of the tent hard, then slid down the wall as a loud crash sounded from within.

A moment later, each of the scientists who'd tested him went running out the back of the building in terror.

Owen entered the front of the tent to find Charm silently tearing apart computers and lab equipment. "That was quick," he said, hoping a little humor would lighten the mood. "Did you have a good talk?"

She pointed at the ground, where the scientist who'd taken his blood lay unconscious. "That one annoyed me. The rest were smart enough to leave before I was done with him."

Right. Humor wasn't helping. "Any luck here?"

Charm shrugged, then roughly pushed past him, dragging wires and computer chips behind her.

As they entered the next building, there weren't even screams; the scientists rushed toward the exit as soon as they saw her coming. This one had no testing equipment, but did have quite a few laser rifles and some empty black helmets. Owen briefly eyed one of the helmets, wondering if it might be useful, especially since he was basically powerless with his heart not working. He picked it up and stared inside, trying to see what it did.

"I wouldn't," Charm said, and knocked the helmet out of his hand, sending it crashing to the floor. "Those reinforce a hypnotic suggestion directly into the brain after an initial persuasion session. Might brainwash you even without that." She abruptly seemed to notice that she'd protected him and clenched her fists, turning away. "Or do whatever you want, I don't care."

He sighed. "I should have told you, back when I first saw you."

"I probably would have ray-gunned you."

Owen winced. "You still might."

"Fair point." She walked out, carrying a much larger assortment of tech this time.

It took ransacking three more labs (and scaring off a barracks full of nonfictional soldiers after Charm bent one of their guns in half using just her robotic hand) before she finally stopped in the middle of the yard to assemble all the parts.

"Is there anything I can do to help?" Owen asked, nervously watching over her as she worked, having no idea what she was doing. Even if his imagination had been fully intact—and by now, it was barely holding on to what was left of his heart—he was pretty sure he couldn't have thought up anything as complicated as what Charm was building.

"Are you good for anything other than lying?" Charm asked. "If not, then I'm thinking no, you can't."

He sighed, and she turned away, wiring chips together as she projected various holographic screens in midair that showed the schematics that they'd seen back in Verity's office. One of her robotic fingers popped open, revealing a tiny welding torch, and she used it to carefully meld some of the chips together.

None of what Charm was doing resembled the time bracelet in any way. Still, that didn't matter as long as it worked. While she assembled her machine, Owen paced around her anxiously. He knew that with time travel, it didn't actually matter how long it took to build the machine, since they could pick the time they were traveling to. But Verity had an army of black helmets already in the past, ready to go to war. And more importantly, he had *Kara*.

He couldn't really blame her for tricking him into coming now, not after everything he'd seen. His older self had been right. There was no way he could just let all of this happen. Maybe it was his heart being fixed up a bit, or maybe he'd just snapped out of whatever funk he'd been in, but right now, people needed him, and he wasn't going to let them down.

Did it have to take *so long* to build a time machine?

"You sure I can't help in any way?" Owen asked after Charm had been working for what felt like a thousand years, but might have been ten minutes.

One look made him go silent again, as well as take a few steps backward for safety.

"I'm done anyway, I think," she said, then stood up, holding a huge mess of wires, diodes, glowing blue electrical laser things, and a bunch of technology that Owen had no words for. Whatever it was, it didn't look pretty.

"You think?" he asked.

"No way to know without testing it," she told him.

"How does it work?"

"It's time travel," she said, glaring at him. "It's not difficult. I put in a time and place, and we show up there. Do you really want to know more than that? About what's actually happening to your physical form as we travel through the seventh dimension to shortcut the fourth? Do you want me to describe how close to obliteration you'll come if I made even the slightest miscalculation? Because I can go over all of that, in minute detail."

He shook his head over and over. She nodded. "Good. Now,

this isn't my choice, but the plans Verity had on his screens required us to be touching. He must have changed something after, to take his army. Anyway, give me your elbow or something."

Owen slowly moved his arm toward her as she watched him with irritation. "We need to go back, like, five years," he said, as she roughly grabbed him and yanked him closer. "The portal in the tower will hopefully still be working at that point. But we're going to need—"

Before he finished, she slammed a button, and everything immediately turned upside down and very, *very* wrong.

Kara's time bracelet had been a bit disorienting, especially when they'd traveled slowly through time in either direction. But Charm's version seemed to stretch their bodies out from the present to the past, pulling them apart until their very atoms felt like they were going to snap, if that's how atoms worked.

And then something twanged like an elastic band, and Owen thankfully found himself in the very same spot in Jonathan Porterhouse's yard, now empty of buildings other than the tower and the author's mansion.

"Aaaaaaaaaah!" Owen shouted, releasing the terror he'd felt

during the trip as he collapsed to his knees, trying not to puke.

"We're here," Charm told him calmly, like their bodies hadn't just been pulled apart. The time machine in her hand began to sizzle, and she dropped it as smoke started pouring out of it. "Like I said, one-time use. So what now?"

Owen stared at the machine as it caught fire, having seconds ago been the only thing between them and apparent obliteration. "Uh, right," he said, trying not to let his voice shake. "First, we need to figure out if we arrived before Dr. Verity. Hopefully we can be ready and waiting for him."

The front lights of the mansion flipped on, and one of the double doors opened. Jonathan Porterhouse appeared in a robe and pajamas, peeking out carefully. "More of you?" he shouted, then flipped a switch, and the enormous yard lit up with spotlights. "I've called the police, whoever you are! You better leave now if you don't want to be arrested!"

More of them? Owen sighed. That answered the question of whether they'd beaten Dr. Verity to the past. They were too late! He looked around at the now-lit lawn and saw that all the grass was trampled down, most likely by Verity's soldiers. "So much for setting a trap," he said quietly.

"So we catch up to him," Charm told him, striding forward

toward the author with one of her ray guns raised. "But that means we have no time to waste, especially with people yelling at me in their nightclothes."

Even from a distance, Owen could see the author's eyes widen to the size of dinner plates. *"No!"* the man shouted. "Didn't I suffer enough with Kiel and the Magister? Now *she's* here too?"

"Wait!" Owen yelled, stepping between the half-robotic girl and her creator. "He's . . . actually, let's not even get into that. It's not important. He owns this house. Let me go talk to him while you get the portal ready in the Magister's tower to send us to Magisteria."

Charm rolled her eyes, but set off toward the tower without ray-gunning anyone, so that was a victory. Owen jogged over to the terrified author. "Mr. Porterhouse, sorry to do this to you again," he said, raising his hands to show he came in peace. "I'm guessing a whole army of people showed up earlier?"

"Just . . . just a few minutes ago," he said. "But they disappeared as quickly as they appeared. I don't know where they went. The police aren't really coming . . . they didn't believe me. Said it was impossible."

"They're a bit lacking in imagination right now," Owen said, frowning. "But we won't stay long either. We're just going to need to use the tower real quick." He paused, feeling bad about the next thing. "Also, I could use another favor. If you don't mind, can I make a quick phone call? Remember my friend Bethany? She lives just a little ways away in town. We're going to need her for this too."

If anything, Mr. Porterhouse's eyes grew even wider in terror. "The . . . the one who—"

"Don't worry!" Owen said, raising his hands up to calm the man down. "She's coming with us. I *promise* you won't be stuck in any horror stories tonight!"

CHAPTER 28

"Hey, Kiel?" Bethany said, reentering the Magister's office, with Fowen just behind her. "Can I talk to you for a minute?"

Kiel nodded, walking over to her from where he'd been chatting quietly at the Magister's desk with the old magician. "Let me guess," he said, pointing at Fowen. "Did he try to steal your memories?"

Fowen snorted, and Bethany faked a smile. "Funny you should bring that up. I need you to do something for me."

"If it involves pushing this version of Owen down the stairs, I'm on it," Kiel whispered to her, then winked at Fowen, who glared back.

She led him out into the hall and filled him in on the situation. "So now I'm going to have a little chat with the Magister. After what he did to Charm and her people, I think it's safe to say he won't enjoy it." She grinned evilly.

Kiel just stared at her. "If he really did that, there's no forgiving him. But I don't understand why you didn't return to your world and rejoin your other self. If Fowen's telling the truth, you could have kept yourself from disappearing!"

"Don't you start too," she said, glaring at him. "She was everything wrong with me, okay? Maybe I don't have her anchoring me anymore. Well, guess what, that just means I can fly free now."

"Bethany, this seems like a bad idea," Kiel said. "It's not too late. Let's go down to the portal and find your other self. At least talk to her. I'm sure she'll want to help too."

Bethany sighed, dropping her head into her hands. "No! No more talking, to her or anyone. I'm going to *do* something for once, because that's the only way things happen. If you want to go talk to her, be my guest. I'm gonna go make the Magister fix me with magic."

She turned back toward the door, but stopped as Kiel grabbed her shoulder. "Are you sure—"

Without looking, she stuck her hand in his face and morphed it into sleeping gas, using her superpowers. "Yes, I'm sure," she said as he fell unconscious. She caught him before he could collapse, and gently laid him down on the ground. "It's better that you stay out of this anyway. Without your magic, you could get hurt. And I'm not going to let that happen, not after what happened to my father."

Bethany touched his cheek gently, then stood back up and went into the office, closing the door behind her.

"He's just going to get something from Charm's ship," she told the Magister. "Can we talk while he's gone, though? Alone, maybe?" She glanced at Fowen.

"As his apprentice, I should probably stay," Fowen said, glaring at her.

"That isn't necessary, my apprentice," the Magister told him, gesturing for Fowen to leave them, which he did, though he did shut the door pretty hard. "Was the boy of any assistance to you?"

"More than you'd think," she said, slowly walking over to the magician's desk. "I just think we should be honest with each other while Kiel's not here. See, I don't think you've changed quite as much as you say you have."

He smiled sadly at her. "And why would you think that?"

"Maybe because you turned the entire population of Quanterium into books and stuck them in the nonfictional world?"

His smile faded, and a shadow passed over his face. "I have nothing to apologize for. Those science-worshippers deserved whatever they got."

Bethany grinned. "Oh, see, thank you for saying so."

"And why is that?"

"Because that's really the only excuse I needed to do *this*," she told him, and morphed into sleeping gas again. Before he could move, she surrounded the man and floated her way toward his nose and mouth. His eyes widened with surprise and he quickly covered his mouth, mumbling something behind his hand as Bethany oozed in around his fingers and up his nostrils.

Before she could get into his lungs, though, something pulled at her from behind, and abruptly she went spinning away from the Magister, caught in an invisible whirlwind in the middle of the office. Papers and books swirled up and around with her as the Magister coughed at his desk. *"You dare?"* he shouted, his voice thunderous and threatening.

A few dozen ideas filled her head, but Bethany just picked the first one that made sense and morphed into a whirlwind herself, one large enough to engulf the Magister's magical version. Now twice the size, she increased her pull, reaching for the old man, but he disappeared before she could reach him.

Instead, the force of her whirlwind sent his desk crashing into several bookshelves around her as the rest of the small office got caught up in her winds.

She switched back to normal, but the Magister hadn't reappeared, and she started worrying that he'd teleported away. Ignoring the hundreds of ideas in her head, she instead rewrote herself to be able to see heat signatures, and searched the room in case he was invisible. Yes, she was taking a chance with that, but it wasn't a *big* rewrite, and hopefully wouldn't be enough to make her dissolve again.

She made a circle, but didn't see anyone else in the room. Was his invisibility spell powerful enough to mask his heat, too? Or had he completely escaped? She rewrote her vision back to normal, wanting to punch something for not managing to catch him by surprise. Why hadn't she been *faster*? She needed the Magister at her mercy if she had any chance of getting him to fix her with his magic!

Something passed over her like a wave, and she found herself frozen, only able to move her eyes and jaw. The Magister appeared in front of her, growing from a microscopic size into his regular height, his wand aimed right at her. He murmured another spell, and a muddy fog filled Bethany's mind. "Now I have used a truth spell on you, girl. What is the purpose of this attack?"

Bethany gritted her teeth, wanting to unleash a horde of awful insults and profanity, but instead, her mouth betrayed her. "I wanted to force you to fix me using magic. Fowen said I should rejoin my other self to fight Nobody, but I'm afraid to see her."

Wait, *what*? What had she just said?

The Magister stared at her for a moment. "His plan would have merit, if there was any chance of hiding it from Nobody. But I don't believe that would be possible." He moved in closer. "You fear the person you were?"

Of course not! she screamed in her head, but again, her mouth had other ideas. "A lot of horrible things happened in my life, and I always blamed myself for not thinking ahead enough. But this is my chance to prove that wrong. I can show her, can show *myself*, that even if things go wrong, they're not always my fault. That sometimes you just need to take action, take risks. If I go back now and tell her that I need her help, then I'd be admitting I was wrong all along, and that I'm useless without her. The idea terrifies me."

Stop lying! Where were these words even coming from? This

was *not* how she thought of herself. Being afraid of her nonfictional self? The idea was insane!

"Ah," the Magister said, and turned around. "Unfortunately, even if my apprentice's idea were to work, you'd still lose. Nobody is far too powerful. Indeed, I believe the only chance to save myself might be to flee, though I know not where."

Don't say another word, Bethany told herself, struggling as hard as she could against whatever spell held her, but it was no use. She frantically tried to think of something she could morph into, but her head flooded with images, just like Fowen had said, from airplanes to toy trucks to dust to skeletons to doorknobs to picture frames to Jet Skis to sheet music, and a million other things.

"Does . . . Kiel know what I did?" the Magister asked, his voice sadder now. "I would spare him that knowledge, if it's not too late. I care for the boy and would not wish him to think of me that way."

"He knows," Bethany said immediately. "Now please stop asking me questions, I'm trying to think."

Argh! This truth thing was *way* too revealing!

The Magister turned and gave her an odd look, and she silently cursed the truth spell. There was no other choice now:

She'd have to rewrite herself before she came out and *admitted* she was thinking of ways to escape.

Holding her breath, she quickly rewrote herself to be free of the Magister's paralyzing spell. As soon as she did, the mystical powers loosened their hold, and she slumped just a bit. Catching herself, she stayed as still as possible, so as not to alert the Magister she was free. This way, she at least had a second chance at surprising him.

"Thinking about what?" the Magister asked. "If you have any idea of how we should go forward, I'm willing to entertain it."

"I do have one, and I think it's good," Bethany said. "My idea is, I'm going to attack you again, because I rewrote myself out of your spell." Immediately she clapped her hand over her mouth, but it was too late, and she screamed into her palm in frustration. The stupid truth spell—she'd forgotten to rewrite herself out of that, too!

As the Magister stared at her in surprise, she shot her arm out like a rocket, straight at his face, and rammed her fist into his chin.

The force of the hit sent the old man to the floor in a daze. Ideas of what she could morph into began exploding in her head, but she immediately shut them down. Instead, she went with a much more nonfictional approach: She leaped on the Magister, then punched him in the face. His eyes rolled back into his head, and he fell unconscious.

Sometimes doing things the nonfictional way really could be satisfying.

She took a deep breath, then slowly stood up, looking around for something to tie him up with, maybe even gag him so he couldn't use his magic. Maybe she could find his spell book too, and not even need him. She'd found the location spell easily enough the last time. How hard could a Don't Dissolve When Rewriting Yourself spell be to cast?

As she turned around, she found a horrified Kiel Gnomenfoot standing in the doorway.

"You knocked me out?" he said, almost in a daze as he surveyed the room. "Fowen woke me up using magic. Bethany . . . *why* would you do that?"

Bethany winced. But before she could say anything, the door to the Magister's office exploded open, slamming Kiel against the overturned bookcases. From the other side, a bunch of men and women in strange, reflective black helmets stormed in, all holding what looked like Science Police laser rifles.

"See, here's the thing," said a voice from outside, a moment before Fowen came flying in the door as well, landing hard on the floor. "I swear I thought I just left you in the nonfictional world, like, five years in the future. Am I going crazy?"

And then a man wearing a white lab coat and huge goggles stepped inside the Magister's office, someone Bethany hadn't seen since she'd first met Kiel.

"*This* place looks familiar," Dr. Verity said, holding a nasty-looking ray gun. "I haven't been here since I tried to kill the Magister the first time, back when Kiel found the sixth key. Why don't we see if this second try goes a bit better than the first one did?"

CHAPTER 29

Bethany!" Owen shouted in relief as his nonfictional friend appeared in the doorway of the portal room in Jonathan Porterhouse's version of the Magister's tower. It'd taken a lot of convincing to bring her here, and he half believed she still wouldn't come.

"Owen? *Charm?!*" Bethany stopped short as she noticed the half-robotic girl standing before a large glowing mirror. "What is going *on* here?"

Owen blushed as Charm hugged Bethany. "Glad to see you turned back from a beam of light," the half-robot girl said. "I was planning on helping with that, but my planet ended up getting destroyed before I could really focus on that part."

"Thanks," Bethany said. "And it's good to see you, Charm. But how did you get here? Owen, what happened to that other girl? And what is *that* thing doing?" She pointed at the portal behind them, the mirrorlike surface whirling with some kind of weird, magical energy.

"How about I just leave you to it, then?" Jonathan Porterhouse said, looking like he was about to vomit. Owen nodded, and the author quickly pushed past Bethany to sprint out the door of the tower. They all waited a moment until they heard the door to the mansion slam shut, then Bethany whirled on Owen. He thought she'd be mad, but instead, she almost looked like she was pleading with him.

"Owen, we're going to be in *so much trouble*," she said, grabbing his shoulders, her eyes wide. "Look at this. We're breaking every single rule ever, and it's all going to get worse. Is Kara okay? Did you at least send her back to wherever she came from?"

"Dr. Verity has her," Owen said quietly.

"DR. VERITY?!" Bethany took a step back in shock, then grabbed her forehead like she had a headache. "This is so bad. So bad!" She glanced at Charm. "And now you've pulled Charm into this too? Owen, we said we weren't getting involved in this stuff anymore. It always leads to bad things!"

Charm's eyes narrowed, but Owen didn't wait for her to start in. "Bethany, Dr. Verity was *already* here, in our world. In the future. Well, and in the recent past now too, I think. And maybe the present?" With his imagination barely intact, he had a hard time following his own logic, and Bethany didn't seem to be having it any easier. "It's a little confusing, but that's not important right now. We're not entirely sure where he went, but Charm thinks he used this portal just a few minutes before we got here, based on the fact it was already up and running, and—"

"Owen, listen to yourself!" Bethany said, giving Owen an amazed look. "We left this all behind to be normal, to not have to worry about this kind of thing. The fictional world doesn't need two ordinary people to save it. It has all the heroes it could ever need, and we couldn't do anything anyway!" She took his hand and looked at him earnestly. "But it's not too late. Whatever's going on, we can just leave it all behind, and *go back home*. We'll tell our moms what happened, and they'll punish us, probably, but that's okay, and we'll get back to our regular lives—"

"Everything *won't* be okay," Owen interrupted. "Things are bad in the future, Bethany. I've seen it. It all happens because we're missing our imaginations, and some Kiel Gnomenfoot books turn into . . ." He trailed off as a memory of a man in a suit flashed into his head, back before Kara showed up. The man had given them a box of Kiel Gnomenfoot books and seemed to know who they were, but they hadn't recognized him. The man said he came from Jonathan Porterhouse, too. Was he involved with all of this? And if so, who *was* he?

"I don't even understand what you're saying," Bethany told him, shaking her head as she derailed his train of thought.

"That's because you don't have your imagination anymore," Owen told her. "I got mine back just by touching someone or something fictional. It should work with you, too, and you'll realize that we need to save both worlds! Did you feel anything when you hugged Charm?"

Bethany just stared at him. "You mean like happiness to see my friend?"

"Not exactly." Owen turned to Charm. "Um, would you mind touching her again, just for a moment?"

Charm groaned loudly at him, but placed her hand on Bethany's shoulder. Both girls turned to stare at Owen.

"I don't feel any different," Bethany said.

Owen frowned. "That's weird. It works instantly with me. Maybe Charm is less fictional than Kara?"

"I don't know if that's insulting, but I'm *taking* it that way," Charm said to him in a threatening voice.

"Here, touch my shoulder," Owen said to her. "Let's do a test."

"If I do, you're going to lose it."

"Maybe my fictional self got all of my imagination," Bethany said. "But that doesn't make any difference. I'm still able to think logically, and common sense tells me we shouldn't get in the way of people who actually can fix things, not when we're just two regular kids!"

Charm groaned loudly. "I don't care *who* comes, but we don't have time for this. Bethany, *listen*. I made a machine to help me fight Nobody, so I could rescue you and the boy I *thought* was Kiel but turned out to be a liar."

Bethany's eyebrows shot up at that, but she didn't interrupt Charm. "But Nobody found out about my invention, and used it to basically destroy Quanterium. I had to rescue my people, so I teleported them all into my ship, then took their stored information with me to the Magister and asked for his help." Her hands clenched into fists as she spoke. "He then did what the Magister always does to Quanterians: made our lives much worse. He turned all of us into books and sent us here."

"That happened *already*, Bethany," Owen told her. "The Quanterians are here, as we speak, in book form. At some time in our future, that book spell will wear off, leaving our world to believe there's been an invasion from the fictional world. Things get *dark* a few years from now. Trust me, we have to do something. There's no way you'd let that happen if you just saw it for yourself!"

Bethany seemed to struggle with this for a moment, but her shoulders drooped, and she shook her head. "I'm not sure I understand everything, but even so, I really don't imagine things could change that much, Owen. Look around—life is so normal here! Do you really think Quanterians are just hiding in books?"

"They're *trapped* in them. And later Dr. Verity brainwashes them to use them to invade Magisteria!" Owen said.

Bethany rubbed her forehead again. "Ugh, this is so complicated it gives me a headache," she said. "But I give up. Charm, what do you need to do to get back to your world?"

Charm pointed at the portal, still whirling with magical energy. "It's already set. Supposedly magic doesn't last very long in this world, which is why the portal wasn't working in the future, but whatever. Right now, this is set to take us to the Magister's tower on Magisteria." She glanced around. "I really don't want to know why there's a tower here, too, do I?"

"Kiel knows, he can tell you," Bethany said, looking at her sadly. "Anyway, I think it'd be best if you go home and leave us out of this. Please tell Kiel that I miss him, will you?" She patted Charm on the shoulder while the half-robotic girl stared at her oddly.

"Bethany, we have to go *too*," Owen said, grabbing Bethany's arm.

She just looked at him with that strange, sad gaze. "Charm, would you mind going through first? I have to talk to Owen for a minute."

Charm rolled her eyes, and with one half glance at Owen, stepped through the portal.

"Bethany, we *have* to go," Owen repeated, but she didn't seem to be paying attention to him. Instead, she moved around the dusty room like she was searching for something. She picked up a sheet covering something large and dusty, only for whatever it was to rumble threateningly, causing her to drop the covering immediately.

"Keep talking," she said to him. "I just need to find something real quick."

"Dr. Verity has *Kara*, Bethany," Owen said, following her around on her search. "We need to rescue her, among other things. She came here to help me. I can't just leave her in danger!"

"Charm will save her," Bethany said. She picked up an elaborate candelabra and hefted it, then frowned and set it back down. "That's what she does. She's a hero."

"She probably will, but I'm going anyway," he said. "You need to come too! This involves you as much as it does me. Things are going crazy in our future *and* over there, and it sounds like it's all because Nobody separated the worlds. We can fix this. We can reunite you with your other half!"

"Hmm," Bethany said, and tried to pull down a sconce holding a burnt-out torch on the wall. It didn't give way, and she growled in frustration.

"What are you *looking* for?" Owen finally asked.

"Aha!" she said, and grabbed a long, heavy-looking gold hammer from behind some boxes. "I hope this isn't magical."

"I'd say it one hundred percent is," Owen told her as she approached the portal. "What are you doing with that?"

"What do you think?" she said, hefting it and taking a practice swing.

His eyes widened, and he moved to grab for her, but she turned the hammer toward him, and he backed away. "You can't do this, Bethany!"

"You've lost your mind, Owen!" she shouted, swinging the hammer between them. "Think about it! If you go over there, you might get hurt, or even killed. You just talked about Dr. Verity's *army*. You're not a magician or half-robotic, you're just a normal kid. So am I! If I let you go over there, I wouldn't be your friend. I'm doing this because you're confused about what matters, and I'm not going to let you get yourself killed, running off on another adventure, especially after what Nobody did to you last time!"

Owen put his hands up in surrender, but slowly moved closer to the portal. "Bethany, think about what you're saying. The fictionals are already *here*. They're trapped in books right now, as we speak! Things are going to be just as dangerous here as they are there, soon enough."

"Unless your imagination ran away with you," she said, thrusting the hammer headfirst at him, pushing him backward. "I'm not letting you get hurt. I might have had to leave my dad behind, and not be able to see my fictional friends anymore, but I'm *not* going to let you just run off into danger, not when I can stop it!"

"Please, Bethany! They *need* me over there!"

"No, they *don't*, Owen!" she shouted. "You're *not* a hero.

You're my best friend, but you're just a nonfictional kid. They don't need either of us!"

"I can't let you do this," Owen said, hoping his voice wasn't shaking as he said it.

"You don't have a choice," she said, and pulled the hammer back.

As she swung it forward, Owen jumped for it, knocking her off-balance. She shouted in surprise as the hammer went slipping from her fingers and plowed into the mirror frame with a large cracking noise.

"Bethany, what did you do?" Owen whispered as glass began to fall out of the portal, breaking into shards as it hit the ground.

"The right thing, I hope," Bethany said, looking at him sadly.

CHAPTER 30

O h, look, someone's already been playing with the Magister," Dr. Verity said, striding past Bethany as the black-helmeted guards surrounded her, their lasers all aimed at her chest. The mad scientist stopped right next to the unconscious Magister, kneeled down, lifted his head, then let it drop back to the floor. He frowned. "Not exactly sporting this way," he said, then shrugged. "Not that I'll let it stop me. Good-bye, you doddering old wretch!" He raised his ray gun at the Magister.

"No!" Kiel shouted, leaping up from the floor to plow into two of the black helmets. All three ended up back on the ground, and Kiel wrenched one of their lasers away, knocked the butt of it into both of their helmets, then aimed it at Dr. Verity, slowly rising to his feet.

"Hold on a minute," the doctor said, standing up too. He waved his ray gun at Fowen. "I thought *that* one was Kiel

Gnomenfoot. How are there two of you now? If you tell me you cloned yourself, I'm going to be *extremely* upset. That's my genetics too, you ungrateful little—"

"How are you *alive*?" Kiel shouted as more black helmets came pouring in the door. "I left you in the Source of Magic with your own bomb about to explode!"

"I already went through the whole story with *that* Kiel," Dr. Verity said, nodding at Fowen. "Though if I'm being honest, I do prefer the classic look. It just feels *right*, you know? Like old times."

"What do you want?" Kiel said, his laser not wavering as black helmets surrounded him.

"Kiel, my boy, what do I *always* want?" Dr. Verity said, looking frustrated. "How many times have we covered this? I want to wipe every Magisterian from existence. And now I've got an army of brainwashed Quanterians to help me." He gave Kiel an apologetic look. "Honestly, I thought you weren't even here, so your death would have to wait until later. But look at you, obliging me by showing up anyway! And killing two of you will hopefully be twice as nice."

"Drop the weapon," one of the black helmets said to Kiel in its strange monotone voice. Bethany sidled along the wall, moving slowly so no one would notice her, getting ready to attack when the moment was right. But could these soldiers really be the missing Quanterians? How had Dr. Verity brainwashed his own people?

And if they were just innocents, how much would she have to pull her punches?

"Kiel, you might want to do what he says," Dr. Verity said. "There do seem to be more of them than you."

"Maybe, but I bet I can still laser *you* before they can stop me," Kiel said. "Want to test that?"

Dr. Verity laughed, an evil, cackling sort of thing. "Oh, I've missed you, Kiel, I really have. That other Kiel wasn't nearly so much fun. This you is so grown-up, and acting all tough!" He sighed deeply. "Remember when we first started all of this, and you could barely even cast a spell, let alone stop a war between two worlds? You didn't even know you were my clone back then!" He shook his head, still chuckling. "Memories, am I right?"

Then he aimed his ray gun back at the Magister.

"Put it down!" Kiel shouted at him as more black helmets moved in around him.

"Wait, I thought you said to test you?" Dr. Verity said, looking confused. "That's what I'm doing. Now, depending on where you hit me, my finger might pull the trigger reflexively. So be careful when you aim. Ready?"

"Don't do this!" Kiel shouted.

"On the count of three," Dr. Verity said. "One . . ."

"*Three,*" Bethany growled in her best Twilight Girl voice, kicking two of the black helmets into each other. She dodged a third's laser blast, then swept his legs out from under him, tumbling him into the fourth. The fifth moved to grab for her, but Kiel kicked him backward straight into the door, slamming it shut as more black helmets tried to enter the room.

Bethany stood back up and moved to Kiel's side, hoping she'd looked as awesome as she thought she did. "The Magister definitely deserves punishment, but that's not your call," she growled. "So step away from the old man unless you want this to end badly for you."

Dr. Verity just blinked at her. "I'm sorry, do I know you? I like the colorful outfit, but you don't even have a weapon. Also, you didn't let me get to the count of two. What's *that* about?"

The door burst open behind them, and black helmets leaped inside, firing their lasers. Bethany pulled Kiel down to the floor, using the unconscious bodies of the soldiers she'd already taken out as cover. "You take the doctor," she told Kiel. "I'll get the rest of these guys."

"You can't handle them all," Kiel said, firing over the heads of the oncoming soldiers, purposely not hitting them. "If they're Quanterians, we can't hurt them. Beth, we need a *plan*."

"Trust me," she said, and winked at him. Before he could respond, she closed her eyes, ready to use her superpowers. The first thing that came to mind was a bulldozer, so she started to push herself into that image. But as she did, more ideas flooded over her, just like during her fight with the Magister: She could become sleeping gas, a tank, some sort of robotic dinosaur, a tornado, a large broom—

Gritting her teeth, she shook off the other ideas, and through sheer force of will, pushed herself into the image of the bulldozer, trying desperately to hold it steady in her head. Her body morphed into the construction machine, and she revved her engine, causing several of the brainwashed Quanterians to actually take a few steps back. She stepped on the gas and went racing toward them, planning on bulldozing them right out the door . . . only to shift into a giant broom at the last moment, crashing into the assembled black helmets with all the force of a stern sweeping. Her momentum carried them back out the door, and she slammed it shut again, wondering how she could get it to *stay* closed for once.

"Beth!" Kiel shouted, ducking behind the Magister's over-turned desk. "You're losing control!"

But she could barely hear him as ideas completely filled her head, and she changed from a fiery sword to a baby bonnet to a guitar, not able to control it anymore. Each time something new popped into her mind, her powers pushed her into it, and she began to panic. This had to stop!

"Well, I can't say I saw *that* coming," Dr. Verity said, watching her changes with interest. "Who did you say she is?"

"I didn't," Kiel said, aiming his laser at the scientist again after one more concerned look at Bethany. "Put the weapon down now, Verity. I'm not going to ask again!"

"C'mon, really?" Dr. Verity said. "Where do you think I got all the Quanterians to brainwash, Kiel? *The Magister* sent them to the nonfictional world. He turned them into books, too, so that the nonfictionals would think they were being invaded by the fictional world." He paused. "I mean, they might have had some help with that theory, but still. *He* did this!"

Kiel pulled the trigger, and a laser beam blasted the wall just inches to Dr. Verity's right. "See, that right there is your problem," Kiel said. "You can't stay focused. I told you to put the ray gun *down*."

Dr. Verity growled at him. "Focus? Wait till you're my age, kid. You're a clone, remember? *This* is what you've got to look forward to." He sighed. "I take back what I said before. You used to be more fun when you were younger. Oh well. Be seeing you."

Then he tossed something to the ground, and thick black smoke filled the chamber.

As Bethany continued morphing uncontrollably, she concentrated as hard as she could, just trying to aim changes toward something useful. Various ideas popped into her brain that might help, and she gratefully pushed herself into each one as they arrived, morphing into a whirlwind, then a giant fan, followed by a huge straw, and finally a vacuum cleaner, using each form to collect the smoke as quickly as she could. Finally, she'd removed it all and turned herself toward the door, blowing it open to expel the smoke right out of the room.

The effort seemed to have tired her brain out a bit, as the ideas came less quickly now, so she seized her moment and concentrated on turning back into a human. Even though this launched her brain into another wave of ideas (*a human painting, or a human statue!)*, she ignored them and returned to her normal self, never more thankful to be flesh and blood in her life.

"They're gone," Kiel said, waving his hand around the room.

That caught her attention, and she quickly saw he was right. Both Dr. Verity and the Magister had disappeared. Most of the black helmets were still around, though they were unconscious, so they had a good excuse. "How did they escape?" she asked, wearily pushing herself to her feet.

"Here," Kiel said, and ran to a hole in the floor right where the Magister had been. "Verity must have cut it," he said, glancing down inside it, only to immediately pull his head back as a ray gun beam ripped through the spot he'd just been in.

"You're not invited!" Dr. Verity shouted from below. "The Magister and I have some adult matters to discuss!"

"The stairs," Kiel whispered, and quickly raced to the door, with Bethany right behind him. They surprised several of the black helmets, who'd just emerged from the black smoke Bethany had blown outside. Kiel knocked them back to the ground and pulled Bethany through the doorway to the stairs, which they now saw were covered with troops. One flight down, Dr. Verity emerged with the Magister floating behind him on some sort of metal platform, bright lights glowing on the bottom.

"For some reason, I've changed my mind!" he shouted. "Instead of killing him outright, I think I'm going to find a parallel dimension that's deadly to humans and send the Magister through, just so he can suffer before he dies. Or maybe one where there's only science, and magic has died out." He laughed evilly. "Where did all of these ideas come from all of a sudden? So many options!"

Lasers began pounding into the stone above them, and Bethany pulled Kiel back into the relative safety of a doorway. "Are there really dimensions like that?" she said, ducking as a beam of light sizzled past.

"I don't know," Kiel said. "There are an infinite number of realities out there, though, so probably. Where did Fowen go? I don't like him running around without supervision."

"Dr. Verity brought him into the office," Bethany said, then realized that he hadn't been there when the smoke cleared.

Uh-oh. Where *was* Fowen? Had he escaped? Or more importantly, was he going for reinforcements?

If so, whose side would they be on?

CHAPTER 31

The portal to Magisteria sparkled in the light of the storage room as Owen stared at Bethany in horror. "Why would you do that?" he shouted at her.

"To protect you!" she said. "I couldn't let you go. I couldn't let either of us go, even if I wanted to. I'm not losing any more of my friends or family. I've given up too much for the fictional world, and I'm done with it. It just takes everything you have!"

Owen watched as a shard of the mirror fell to the ground, shattering. Around half the glass had remained in the broken mirror's pane, but what did that matter, when the portal wasn't working anymore?

Then some movement caught his eye in the glass, and he realized it wasn't a reflection. Leaning closer, he gasped.

The glass still in the mirror was swirling with mystical energy.

Instead of a gentle breeze, it now looked a lot more like a thunderstorm, wild and unpredictable.

But that didn't mean it wouldn't still get him where he needed to go.

Without a word, Owen took a step back from the mirror and prepared himself. There wasn't enough glass left to walk through, so the easiest thing would be to dive into the remaining mirror and hope he made it.

"What are you doing?" Bethany asked. "Owen, you can't be serious."

"I talked to my future self, Bethany," he said quietly, not looking at her. "He told me that if I don't face Nobody, then the future I saw is going to come true, and even worse things will happen in the fictional world. I can't just let that happen."

"You're talking about future selves *again*?" she said, gritting her teeth in frustration. "Didn't Kara say he was dying? Is that because *he* faced Nobody?"

"Yes!" Owen shouted. "He lost, okay? Just like I have, just like a thousand Owens have, apparently. But it's the only way. He told me himself. He and I and the rest of us need to keep trying until we figure out some way to defeat Nobody, or—"

"Or *what*? A bad future might happen that you said already

has? Then what use is it to fight someone if you know you're going to lose?"

Owen clenched his fists at his side and turned to look at her. "I know I'm no hero, Bethany. I know that. I learned that lesson back when I almost died fighting Dr. Verity. You and Kiel rescued me, because you two, both of you, *are* heroes. You're people who do what you have to do, no matter what. Kiel still is. I don't know which part of you has that bravery now. But even if I can't make a difference, I'm going to *try*. I'm going to go face Nobody and do my best. If it's not good enough, the next me can try again, over and over until one of us finally succeeds."

"Do you hear how ridiculous and impossible you sound?" she said, her voice cracking with what sounded like sadness. "Just let it go. Stay here, and we'll figure out how to make the future better in *normal* ways. But we'll stay safe while we do it."

"And how would we do that without an imagination?" he asked. "How will we ever change anything if we can't even imagine a better future? No, we're stuck in this time line, and I'm *not* just letting it go."

"Owen," she said, but he shook his head as another piece of glass fell from the mirror.

"Good-bye, Bethany." Without another word, Owen started a run toward the portal.

"No!" she screamed, and he heard her footsteps just behind him. He doubled his speed, then just before he reached the mirror, he dove forward, aiming for the only bit of glass still big enough for his body. His foot struck something as he passed through the mirror, slowing him down, but he made it through . . .

And found himself falling.

Owen screamed, and around him, a line of Owens extending into infinity screamed too. Before he knew what was happening, the mystical energy storm swept him away, buffeting him around like a tornado, swirling and tossing him until he had no idea which way was up.

"Owen!" someone screamed, and he looked down to find Bethany holding tightly to his ankle. His eyes widened, and he realized it wasn't him hitting something on the way through, it'd been her grabbing him. "We're going to die!" she said, looking terrified. "Where is the other side?"

"I don't know!" he shouted back, looking around in every direction as the magic threw them around. And then a light shone up through the mystical storm, and he realized that down in the eye of the whirlwind, there were people moving.

Another portal, in another tower. And that entrance was still open.

"We have to get down there!" he shouted to Bethany, trying his best to point in the same direction as they swirled around.

"How?" she shouted.

"I have no idea!" he said.

"You're the one with the imagination. Can't you use it?"

Weirdly, here surrounded by magical forces and intense winds, he did feel like his imagination was back, as strong as ever. But what could it do to get them out of the wind and safely to the other side?

Control it, his mind said. *This is magic, right? So make it do what* you *want it to. That's all casting spells does.*

Owen flinched, not really liking the odds of this working. But his imagination wasn't coming up with much else.

"Magic!" he shouted to everything around him. "I don't know the right words, or even if you'll listen to my commands, but if I have any power over you whatsoever, carry me and Bethany down to the portal below, safely and calmly!"

"You're just going to yell at it?" Bethany said. "That's what your imagination came up with?"

"I don't think it had a whole lot of options!" Owen shouted back at her. But when he looked down, he noticed something odd. The light from the portal below them seemed closer.

The whirlwind around them slowly lessened in speed and intensity, gently dropping them toward the portal as it did.

Wait a second. Had his horrible idea actually worked? "Look, Bethany!" he shouted, laughing crazily. "See what an imagination can do! I'm controlling the magic and the storm. We're going to be fine!"

"No, you're not!" Bethany shouted up at him. "Look above you!"

Not liking her tone, Owen followed her instructions and winced. The portal they'd jumped through had just one, narrow pane of glass left. It had been the broken mirror falling apart that was ending the whirlwind, not his pathetic attempt at talking to the storm.

And as he stared in horror, even that last bit of glass fell to the ground, shattering. Instantly, the portal back to the nonfictional world closed off forever, and the magical storm disappeared completely, sending them plummeting straight toward the Magisterian portal, screaming at the tops of their lungs.

CHAPTER 32

As lasers sizzled through the air around them, Bethany took a deep breath, wondering if she could count on her superpowers anymore. "Don't worry, I can take care of them," she told Kiel, not sure she was telling the truth. Still, she had to try.

The stairs were covered in Quanterians, so she needed something quick, painless, and immune to lasers. A thousand images began flashing through her mind, and her head began to ache like someone was hammering her skull. She groaned and dropped her head into her hands, only to feel Kiel's tap on her shoulder.

"I think I have a way around this," he said, then hit a button in his hand.

The Magister's tower disappeared around them, replaced by Charm's ship, the *Scientific Method*.

"What are you doing?" Bethany shouted, barely able to

think with all the possibilities still running through her mind. "We can't run away!"

Kiel glared at her. "We're not. And don't think that I've forgotten that you knocked me out while you fought the Magister, Bethany. Whether or not you agreed with what I was saying, that wasn't okay."

She sighed, her head still throbbing, but the images at least had started to fade. Even with the pain, though, she noted he used her full name. That wasn't a good sign. "I know, I get that," she said, gritting her teeth against the pounding. "But can we save the guilt for . . . I don't know, my nonfictional self? I'd already decided not to join back with my other self, so I didn't want to have a whole argument about it."

"Sometimes there are arguments worth having," he said, shaking his head as he looked at her with disappointment. Anger, sadness, and guilt blossomed inside her chest, and for a moment, she remembered very clearly what it'd been like before Nobody had separated her.

It wasn't a feeling she enjoyed.

"Can we save everyone first and *then* talk about this?" she asked, hoping he would forget about it if everything ended up okay.

Kiel paused, then nodded and clicked the button again. The spaceship transformed into the same dusty, cloth-covered room with the magical portal that Fowen had shown her earlier.

Unfortunately, they appeared at the same time as Dr. Verity reached the doorway, with too many black helmets to count just behind him.

"Wait!" Dr. Verity shouted as his brainwashed troops all raised their lasers to fire. "You can't just kill them without letting me gloat for a bit. Do you people not understand how this is *done*?"

"See, *this* kind of thing makes me think we really *are* being written," Kiel said to Bethany. "Who takes the time to brag instead of just doing away with us? We're definitely going to find an opportunity to beat him now."

Bethany grinned in spite of herself, her head feeling slightly better now that she wasn't trying to use her superpowers. She readied some Twilight throwing stars and prepared for a fight.

"You think I can't hear you, you little monster?" Dr. Verity snarled. "No one wrote *me* this way. No one could ever sculpt the purity and greatness that is me! I am *Verity*, the genius and the truth, and there is no one in the infinite universes that could contain me in their mind!"

"You know I'm a clone of you, right? So aren't you just insulting yourself when you call me a monster?" Kiel threw Bethany a quick wink, a sign that he would distract Dr. Verity while she got the drop on him. It was a solid plan, one her father would approve of, for sure.

Except Kiel didn't know what a mess her powers were right now. She bit her lip to keep from crying out, then opened her mind.

A thousand objects slammed into her with the force of a flood, and she took a step back in shock. Feeling like she was drowning in her own head, her thoughts disappearing beneath the weight of the possibilities, she grabbed for something, anything that could stabilize her mind, and came up with sleeping gas.

Before it could wash away in the river of ideas, she focused all her attention on it and started to turn. But as soon as she did, she realized that Dr. Verity's Quanterian soldiers all probably had breathing devices inside those black helmets, and sleeping gas would be useless.

Silently groaning, she released the image and dove back in.

Giantmirrortorelfectthelasersmightsendthemrichocetinginto-KielorevenoneoftheQuanteriansMaybeshecouldbecomealaserrifle-

herselfandshootalloftheirweaponsbutnosheuwouldn'tbefastenough-
Whataboutouhowaboutwhatabout—

As if from an enormous distance, a small part of her could hear Kiel still trying to distract Dr. Verity. "Why don't you let the Magister wake up, and see if you can take him in a fair fight?"

"Why would I ever do that?" Dr. Verity asked. "Fair fights are the worst kind. Only a fool doesn't prepare ahead of time, which makes the fight unfair in his favor. Now enough of this! It's past time that I doomed the Magister to some parallel death hole. Or maybe a world full of magician-eating fish. Or one where humans are made of fire, and for the rest of his life anyone he ever tries to touch will burn him!" He frowned. "Why can't I just make up my mind? This is unusual for me."

"Sounds like you're getting old," Kiel said, throwing Bethany a look that she barely noticed through the barrage of ideas.

Dr. Verity sneered. "You seem anxious to cut in line for your own fatal trip through the portal. If that's the case, I'm happy to oblige. I'll even grant you a swift death, if you bow before me and admit my superiority."

"Nah," Kiel said, stepping forward. "That'll never happen.

Because I'll beat you. I *always* beat you. We've fought each other for seven books—"

"Don't *you* start!"

"Everywhere and every *when*," Kiel continued, "from the future to the lairs of the snow giants, from alternate realities to beyond the end of everything. And the one thing you've *never* been able to do is stop me."

Dr. Verity pointed the smaller ray gun he had in his lab coat at Kiel. "I'll take this as you volunteering, then."

"Bethany?" Kiel whispered back at her. "I'm ready when you are!"

She stared at him, her mouth hanging open, not sure what to even do.

Icouldbecomeatruckoranaircraftcarrierexceptthatwoulddestroy-thetowerHowaboutagiantcannonoranotherbulldozerNothatwouldn't-workAnelectricfenceamirrorawashingmachineadollwithcreepyeyes-acastleapileofdeadleavesaswimmingpoolarocktworocksthreerocks—

Dr. Verity strode forward and placed the tip of his ray gun up against Kiel's forehead. "There you go, boy. I'm giving you your moment. Now, tell your jokes. Give me some more of that arrogance. Be the hero. Show me how brave you are, so much braver than me, the man you'll someday become."

"Never," Kiel said, practically spitting with disgust. "You think I'd wear a lab coat out in public? Look at me. I'm *rocking* this cape!"

Bethany clenched her fists, desperate to just pick something, *anything* at this point, but separating the possibilities was like trying to stop a gushing faucet.

AlightrayoraTwilightthrowingstaroranowlstatueorabookof-poemsorapenciloraspaceshuttle—

Dr. Verity slowly smiled. "You do know exactly how to push my buttons, don't you?"

Kiel shrugged, throwing a quick look back at Bethany. "You just make it so easy. If you're such a genius, how have you managed to never pick up any fashion pointers?"

"I know what you're doing here, Kiel," Dr. Verity said quietly, his smile fading. "I know that you're all too ready to throw down your worthless life for what you believe in. I have no idea where you got *that* from, since I'd certainly never be that gullible. But I also know your weakness."

Kiel abruptly froze and flashed another look at Bethany. "No," he whispered.

Dr. Verity smiled and nodded at Kiel. Five of his Quanterian black helmets surged forward and grabbed the boy, holding him tightly as Dr. Verity advanced toward Bethany, his ray gun now aimed at her.

Her eyes widened as he neared, but the ideas in her head only increased, just images now of everything and anything she could think of flashing through her mind.

Cowsfencesbarnshighwaysmotorcyclesbicyclesshovelsvaultsdoors-bathtubsrocketshipscreditcardscellphones—

"It's never about your own personal safety, is it, Kiel?" said the scientist. "It's always been about the Magister, or Mentum's daughter, or *this* girl, hasn't it? You have to be noble. To be good. To be protecting someone."

"Don't, *please*!" Kiel shouted as he struggled against the black helmets holding him down.

"I guess you weren't doing as great a job distracting me as you thought, were you?" Dr. Verity asked. To Bethany, he leaned in, the tip of his ray gun now on *her* forehead. "Give me a show, will you, girl? I want this to really get to him."

A tear slowly slipped down her face as she realized she couldn't stop, couldn't focus, couldn't do anything. Too many options, she was paralyzed, she couldn't move, couldn't think, couldn't become anything, she had to *rewrite* herself into something that—

And then Dr. Verity pulled the trigger.

CHAPTER 33

The ray passed right through Bethany and hit the wall behind her, which immediately began to warp from wood to brick to cement.

Dr. Verity frowned. "Now that's unexpected." He fired several more times, but the beams traveled right through her just like the first.

Bethany, as surprised as anyone, brought her hands up to touch her face . . . only to have them pass through her head as well. She looked down and saw that not only were her hands transparent and fading fast, but so was the rest of her body.

She'd rewritten herself at the last possible moment, turning into a cloud. But it'd been too much. She couldn't hold herself together anymore.

"No!" she tried to shout, but no sound came out. Her legs began to separate, floating away like fog in a slight breeze. She grabbed for them, but her hands left too, slowly fading as they went.

"Beth!" Kiel shouted, struggling against the black helmets.

"I'm so sorry, my boy!" Dr. Verity said, looking genuinely sad. "I really thought I could kill her in front of you. I don't know what's going on!"

Scattered memories seemed to pass through her mind like a swiftly flowing river through her brain. She grabbed for the ones she could, holding on to them tightly, no matter how unimportant: eating lunch with Owen in the cafeteria at school, hiding books beneath her bed, helping Kiel set up his magically created house down the street so he could go to school with them.

But this time, the memories didn't fix anything. This time, it was too late.

Dr. Verity lowered his goggles over his face and stepped in close, examining her transparent hand as it wandered away from her. "Fascinating," he said, the goggles whirling and lighting up. "The things we learn while on murderous rampages!"

She screamed silently, doubling down on her memories in an attempt to pull herself back together. There was her mother, crying over the news of a Doc Twilight comic book selling for some crazy amount on television. Here was Kiel, hugging her good-bye when he left for Magisteria, telling her he'd see her again in a year. And then Gwen, amazing Gwen, showing her the fortress of friendship she'd built for the two of them on the moon.

She closed her eyes, concentrating as hard as she was still able. *Remember what it was like to be half-fictional. Remember your nonfictional self. Remember what it was like to be whole—*

Suddenly she felt something pass through her body, sending even more parts of herself floating away. Her eyes flew open, only to find an even bigger shock awaiting her.

"You?" said a Bethany in a normal, everyday school outfit, her eyes widening as she looked up from where she'd apparently landed on the floor. "You're . . . you're disappearing!"

"Bethany?" Kiel said, still held down by the black helmets. "Where did you—"

"Owen brought me," nonfictional Bethany said, still staring at herself in wonder and horror.

Cloud Bethany glanced over and found Owen also on the floor, a few feet away from the portal, as if he'd come flying out of it somehow.

"Bethany?" Owen whispered, looking at her with horror. "What *happened* to you?"

"Are you kidding me?" Dr. Verity roared. "How many of you people *are* there? Two of the girl, and three Kiel Gnomenfoots? All we're missing is—"

"Me," someone said from behind him. Verity whirled around and found a very angry Charm standing behind him. She reared back, then drove her robotic fist into his stomach so hard he went flying across the room.

Bethany just stared as she continued to disappear, not believing what she was seeing. Where had Charm and Owen come from? And why was her nonfictional self here, of all places? Had she come to judge Bethany one last time?

"Charm?" Kiel said, watching in wonder as the half-robotic girl laid out the remaining black helmets holding him down.

"Are you really you?" she growled, grabbing Kiel by the shirt and looking him right in the face.

"As much as any of us are, I guess."

"Vague answer checks out," she said, dropping him to the floor. "But trust me, we'll be having a *very* long talk later." She spun around toward the mad scientist. "Verity! Free my people, or I'm going to shove that ray gun somewhere you won't like."

The doctor held up a hand for them to wait a moment as he wheezed in and out, trying to recover his breath. Finally, he opened his mouth to speak, but instead, he aimed his ray gun at Charm and pulled the trigger.

The blast shot out far too fast for anyone to completely dodge. Instead, it hit the lower half of Charm's robotic arm as she brought it up to protect herself, the arm immediately morphing into a short, straight sword extending from her elbow to what used to be her hand.

"Could you please just stand still?" Dr. Verity snapped as Charm stared down at her former arm with disbelief. Verity aimed again, but this time, Kiel was ready and threw one of his wand-knives straight into the scientist's shoulder. Dr. Verity screamed, dropping the ray gun, and Owen grabbed it, then aimed it at the scientist.

"Don't move!" he shouted. "Unless it's to fix Bethany. Then you can move all you want." He paused, glancing at Bethany with concern. "What did you do to her, anyway?"

"It wasn't him," Kiel said, moving over to Bethany and staring at her sadly. "She rewrote herself too many times, just like Nobody does. Only now that the worlds are separated, there's nothing anchoring her, nothing holding her back from just . . . becoming pure possibility. This happened a bit before, but she was able to pull herself back from it."

Owen stepped in closer to Bethany, but it was getting hard for her to see him. The entire room seemed to be getting fuzzier by the minute. "Bethany, can you come back to us?" he asked quietly. "We'll help. *You'll* help—your nonfictional self, I mean!"

Everyone turned to look at nonfictional Bethany, who took a step back. "Wait . . . I don't . . . if we go back—"

"She needs you," Kiel said softly, and fictional Bethany felt like she'd been punched in the heart.

"Look at her, Bethany," Owen said to her nonfictional self. "She's going to disappear. It's like Kiel said, she needs an anchor. And that's you."

Her nonfictional self cringed, but she nodded and stepped closer, raising a hand toward Bethany. "Look at you," she said. "You messed up again, and now I have to fix things. Just like *always*. Thanks so much for that."

Bethany tried to say something, shouting about how her nonfictional self was really to blame, but even if she could speak, she knew it was pointless. She really had done this to herself, and without her other self, she'd disappear.

Maybe she really *had* been the side of Bethany messing everything up all along.

Her nonfictional self took a deep breath, then let it out.

"I'm . . . I'm sorry. I can't keep blaming you." She looked around for a moment. "Of all the people to not show up here, I could have really used Gwen right now. She'd be the first to forgive us both. Wouldn't even matter what we'd done."

Bethany nodded her agreement as her nonfictional self's hand drew closer, brushing against Bethany's arm. As the two touched, Bethany screamed out in silence as her other self did the same much more loudly, incredible pain coursing through them both. The agony was so intense that they each pulled away, staring at the other.

The floor began to shake, first gently, then harder until her friends all almost lost their footing. Bethany tried to find the source of the rumbling, but she couldn't move anymore, could barely even think. What was happening?

"You should have listened to me," a familiar voice whispered from behind her, then moved around to face her. "But now it's too late," Fowen said so softly that only she could hear. "I had to tell him what was happening. If I hadn't, he'd have known I betrayed him. This is on *you*."

Owen groaned loudly. "Are you *kidding* me? Him? Again?"

"Oh, stop it, *Nowen*," Fowen said. "Like I'm not sick of you too." He looked back at Bethany and lowered his voice again.

"I told you to go over to her world. If you merged there, he'd never had known. But here, he was going to find out. And he'd know I was involved. You didn't give me a choice."

Bethany felt a chill run through her noncorporeal body. Did he mean . . . ?

The floor above them—no, the entire *tower* above them disappeared. In its place, a featureless giant peered down at them, empty eye sockets glowing with dark purpose. Behind the creature, the sky glowed from a white void of nothingness surrounding everything.

"I warned you what would happen if you didn't stay in Jupiter City, Bethany," Nobody said. "If you can't follow my very simple rules, then I'll have to deal with you permanently."

CHAPTER 34

Nobody pushed a hand inside the room, then sent a finger snaking toward the portal, smashing the glass into pieces.

"No!" nonfictional Bethany screamed. "That's the only way back!"

"You're all to blame for this," Nobody said, sliding his other hand to the floor. As it touched down, his body seemed to flow from outside the tower, down his arm, and reform in a normal, human size where his giant hand had been. "I tried to give you a chance to live your lives, but you couldn't let things go."

"You monster!" Kiel shouted, leaping at Nobody with his wand-knife in hand. He stabbed toward Nobody's stomach, but a hole opened where the knife hit, then closed around the wand, ripping it from Kiel's hand. Nobody absently threw his arm out, smacking Kiel into the wall, where he slid down to the floor, barely conscious.

Charm roared in anger and swept her new sword arm down at Nobody's nearest leg, and this time, it cut right through him. Only the leg immediately reconnected, and Nobody just shook his head sadly. "You really are disappointing me, all of you," he said, holding out his hand toward Charm. His fingers shot out and grabbed her robot leg, then retracted back into his hand, throwing her across the room easier than he might swat a fly.

Owen looked down at the ray gun in his hand, then aimed it at Nobody. "Don't move," he said, hoping he sounded more intimidating than he thought. "I don't know what this thing does, but I'm sure it's not good."

Nobody turned his faceless head in Owen's direction, and a chill went down his back. His older self's words flashed through his head. *One by one, you'll lose your friends along the way, until finally it's just you against Nobody. And that's a fight that no Owen Conners has ever won yet.*

But wait a second. His older self had said that Nobody would be in a castle, somewhere within the story Owen had written about Bethany's father. Was this not the right time?

Or better yet, maybe he had a chance *now*, instead of when all his other selves failed?

"How is your heart, Owen?" Nobody asked him almost casually as he reached out and slammed Kiel back against the wall. "Have you figured out by now that fictional inventions won't last very long in your world?"

"They would if the worlds were still connected," Owen said. "Now back off or I ray-gun you."

Nobody spread his arms wide, and a smile appeared on his face. "You think you can hurt me with that? Oh, Owen. You've never been able to stand against me. You played the hero, but that's all it was: a game. Now please, step aside, if you want me to save your friend."

Owen dropped the ray gun slightly in surprise. "Save . . . what, now?"

Nobody pointed past him, to where fictional Bethany was barely still visible, just bits of her at a time, and even those were fading. "You're not relevant here, Owen. Go back to your world and live your normal life. You have no place in this story anymore."

Owen blushed hard but lowered the ray gun, unsure if Nobody was telling the truth, but not willing to let Bethany suffer if he was. Nobody nodded, then moved past him toward where both Bethanys waited, each staring at Nobody with pure hatred.

"You two obviously can't be left to your own devices," he said, approaching the twins. "I gave you both the gift of freedom that we fictionals never had, and you betrayed that gift. You betrayed *me*."

He stopped before fictional Bethany and extended a hand. As it grew out toward her, it slowly formed into a long, transparent sort of cylinder.

"You can't be trusted, I'm afraid," Nobody said to her. "And for that, I have just one last solution."

"Oh, it's you!" said a voice from right behind Owen. As Owen whirled around, something hit his hand holding the ray gun, and he dropped it, groaning. A wrinkled hand caught the ray gun, then brought it up to point at Nobody.

Dr. Verity grinned. "Guess what? I'm so glad you showed up today! After I took out the old magician, I'd planned on tracking you down and paying you back for leaving me in that world of science toddlers. You coming to me just makes this all much easier."

"You cannot harm me, Verity," Nobody said, eye sockets

growing in the back of his head as he kept his cylinder hand near Bethany. "Don't make me teach you another lesson."

"No one teaches Dr. Verity *anything*!" the mad scientist yelled, then sighed. "Trust me, I did *not* do very well in school. But that may be because I'm a better teacher than student. Here's a lesson for you—a simple one, in fact: Never turn your back on me!"

"I *have* no back—" Nobody started to say, then jerked as a blast from the ray gun hit him in the shoulder. He turned to look at the spot as it bubbled and hissed, then slowly began to grow something . . . odd. Something featureless. Something with eye sockets.

A duplicate head turned to look at Nobody from his shoulder.

"What did you *do*?" both heads said, turning to Dr. Verity in unison.

"The way I hear it, Charm and my fellow Quanterians developed a possibility machine," Dr. Verity said, shooting Nobody in the stomach, which sent him doubling over. "Then someone turned it into a weapon. Good idea. But it wasn't fully formed yet."

A small locomotive engine grew from Nobody's stomach as he groaned in pain. He pushed both his hands on the emerging engine and pushed it backward into his stomach, reabsorbing it into himself. Dr. Verity laughed, then shot three more times, and Nobody collapsed to the floor.

"See, the version the Quanterians had just added pure possibility into something. But I made some modifications. Now it shoots both possibility *and* specificity. Not only does it make it possible that you can change, but it will up the likelihood to about a hundred percent that you will change into whatever *I* want. Because why leave things to chance?"

Three more shots, and now Owen could barely even recognize Nobody in the midst of all the things growing out of his body. His left leg resembled the arm of a troll, while his right arm looked like a blackboard filled with math equations. A barking dog poked out from underneath his arm, and tiny Nobodies ran in circles over his body, still attached by their feet.

"Not that I wanted to think of something new for each shot," Verity said. "That part wasn't so important to me, so there's a randomizing setting too. What *is* important, though, is watching you *suffer*." He patted the ray gun fondly. "Seems like it's working pretty well, wouldn't you say?"

Nobody roared and tried to push to his feet, but Dr. Verity

just shot him again, and the featureless man began turning a variety of colors, like a kaleidoscope.

"Does it hurt?" Verity asked, leaning in close to the writhing Nobody. "I'm guessing you haven't felt anything like this, have you? For the sake of science, maybe you could share what you're experiencing, just so we can get some solid data out of our little testing here." He frowned. "Unfortunately, I foresee this experiment not ending well for you, but that's how science goes sometimes. Can't make nuclear elevators without breaking some eggs, I always say."

Nobody tried to reach for him, but Verity just shot his palm, and it began to split into smaller hands, then split again, over and over until there were too many to count.

"No interrupting!" Dr. Verity shouted, shaking his head. He glanced over at Bethany. "And then there's this poor girl. You claim that fictional people are better off with control of their own possibilities? Look at what this annoying girl has done with hers! You think I'm going to let that happen to *me* if I start daydreaming about becoming a little less chubby or something? It's a sad day when I have to save all of reality, just to protect myself." He glanced at Kiel and grinned. "Guess I'm the hero now, huh, boy?"

"You are *not*—" Nobody said, but Verity just unleashed the gun on him over and over continuously.

"What did I just say?!" the mad scientist screamed, the sizzling of the gun almost overpowering his voice. "You don't get to talk. This is *my* time to monologue! This is about *me*, not you, you idiotic fool! Don't—"

The gun began to smoke and started making a strange buzzing noise. "Whoops!" the doctor said. "Almost used up the entire charge in one go. Just two shots left. Where would you like it?" He moved the gun over Nobody's body slowly, then finally stopped at what Owen thought was his head. "How about the face? Maybe it'll grow you some eyes."

Owen couldn't believe this was happening. Was Dr. Verity actually defeating Nobody? But why hadn't Owen's older self seen any of this? That was a good sign, right? Anything different had to be good, since all of the other Owens had failed.

"Say good-bye, you creepy, faceless pretender," Verity said quietly. "You presumed to think yourself better than me? NO ONE—"

A massive hand pushed up out of Nobody's chest, grabbing Dr. Verity around his torso and head, then poured around him, covering his entire face. The hand lifted the scientist up off the ground, while another arm grew out of one of the hand's massive fingers and plucked the possibility gun from Verity's grasp. And then the hand squeezed, and a muffled scream sounded through the room, making Owen shudder in horror.

A moment passed before Nobody dropped Dr. Verity to the ground, and the scientist hit with a groan. Nobody slowly rose to his feet, the various different possibility growths all absorbing back into him. As he rose, he seemed to grow several feet taller now, like the possibilities he'd absorbed had added to his mass somehow.

"What you'll never understand, my good doctor," Nobody said as he aimed the possibility gun at Dr. Verity, "is that you, like me, are made of infinite possibilities *already*. Adding more just makes us stronger . . . *if* we have taken control of ourselves."

Dr. Verity shoved himself away on the ground, shaking in fear. "That's impossible! You should have dissolved like that girl did. There were too many possibilities for you to handle!"

A smile split Nobody's face like a crack in an egg.

"There's no such thing as impossible," he said, and shot Dr. Verity with the ray gun.

The doctor screamed in pain and collapsed back to the floor. His wild mad scientist hair slowly drooped down, and he slowly picked himself up, the insanity now gone from his eyes as he gazed clearly at Nobody. "What did you do to me?" he asked, his voice much calmer than it had been a moment before. "I feel . . . more peaceful."

"I gave you the least likely possibility you'd have ever chosen for yourself," Nobody told him. "I made you *decent*."

Owen gasped. Of all the things they needed right now, a non-evil Dr. Verity was *last* on the list. Nobody lowered the possibility gun, and for a moment, Owen thought he might be able to grab it, if he were quick . . . but then Nobody tossed it against the wall, breaking it into several pieces.

Owen's shoulders went limp, and he dropped his head into his hands. Nonfictional Bethany had been right. He had no business being here. What could normal human beings do against . . . this? Fictional people who could rewrite themselves into anything?

"And now, we were discussing what to do with *you*," Nobody said, turning back to the Bethanys. Reforming the transparent cylinder, he closed it around fictional Bethany, encompassing her on all sides. She began to scream noiselessly, but Nobody just put a finger to his nonexistent lips, asking for silence. He slowly lowered her cylinder to the ground, where it separated from his wrist, becoming a glass container.

"This will keep you in one piece for now," he said, using his other hand to rip open a page in midair next to her. "As for the future, there are no promises." He picked the cylinder back up and started to walk through the page.

"Where are you taking her?" nonfictional Bethany asked, her face a mixture of uncertainty and fear.

"Don't worry," Nobody told her as an arm pushed out of his back. "You're coming too."

Before Bethany could move, the arm wrapped around her and dragged her into the ripped page as well, and she screamed for help.

"No!" Owen shouted, running toward them, hoping he could at least jump through to wherever they were going.

"You know you cannot beat me, Owen," Nobody said as nonfictional Bethany struggled in his grasp. "I endeavored to show you the truth of things, but you refuse to learn. Come after me, and the lessons shall be over. You will be my enemy, and I will deal with you in the harshest possible way. You won't receive another warning."

Owen started to respond, then went silent, and he looked away, his face bright red.

"Good," Nobody said, then looked around the room. "The rest of you, go back to your stories while they still exist. And when the end comes, and you are absorbed, have faith. I shall build a new world with no taint from the nonfictionals. If you happen to not be brought back, I apologize, but we must have standards."

With that, he stepped through the ripped page and disappeared, the page closing behind him.

CHAPTER 35

A moment went by where no one spoke.

Footsteps came rocketing down the hall outside, and Kara Dox burst into the room, handcuffs on her wrists. "The whole world is disappearing out there!" she shouted, then skidded to a halt. "Owen?!"

"Kara!" he shouted, breaking into a grin in spite of everything. She was safe!

She came running straight at him, beaming, then leaped at him, and he had to hug her to keep them both from toppling over. "You're okay!" she shouted.

"Well, mostly," he told her, not wanting to get into it all just yet. "How about you? Did Dr. Verity hurt you? Where did you come from?"

"Those black helmet soldiers were holding me outside, thousands of them," she said. "But then something happened, and every one of them just dropped to the ground, like someone turned them off."

Charm stood up, leaning from the weight of her sword arm. "Verity probably controlled them with some sort of receiver. Whatever Nobody did to him must have shut them all down at once."

"Yeah, I saw him break the tower and was so worried," Kara said as Owen grabbed one of the lasers and carefully burned through her handcuffs. "But that doctor creep kept bragging about a way to kill him, so I hoped maybe he'd actually have a chance."

"Nope," Owen said, shaking his head. "He didn't. Not even filling Nobody with possibilities stopped him. I'm not sure *anything* can." He pulled the now-cut handcuffs off of Kara's wrists and looked her in the eye. "What did Dr. Verity do to you? Are *you* okay?"

"Interrogated me, mostly," she said, shuddering at the memory. "When I wouldn't talk, he just hooked me up to some kind of machine that could pull my memories out of my head, so he could get a visual of what the time bracelet looked like inside."

"And from there, he upgraded it," Owen said, giving the

scientist a death look. The now-rewritten Dr. Verity just waved back with a pleasant smile.

Ugh, it was going to be hard to hate the guy in his new state of not being evil.

"And after he used it, he destroyed it, before we came through the portal to this world," Kara continued, shaking her head. "Without my time bracelet, I'm not sure how much I can help."

Join the club, Owen thought. Not that he'd let that stop him. Bethany, both Bethanys, were in trouble, and Owen wasn't just going to leave them there. Besides, he knew from his older self that he'd be facing Nobody eventually one way or another, and that he'd do it alone.

But that raised a good question: If he was going to be alone anyway, maybe he could save his friends by leaving them behind from the start? Then they wouldn't get hurt along the way.

He cleared his throat, then purposely made his voice sound as pessimistic as possible. "Nobody just took us all down without even trying, Kara. I think we're doomed. Dr. Verity's weapon didn't stop him. At best, it slowed him down for a moment, but even that's broken now. I'm not sure what chance we have against him at this point."

"Are you kidding me?" Charm said, running wires from her remaining robotic arm down over the sword half, either to control it better or to add some sort of electric field to the sword. "Stay here if you're too afraid, Owen. But I'm going after him. He has my possibility machine and destroyed my planet. For that, he's going to *pay*."

"He can become *anything*," Owen told her. "And look at us. Kiel doesn't know magic—"

"Though I'm still amazing in other ways," Kiel pointed out.

"Kara has no powers—"

"Unless we come across any paradoxes, I guess?" she said, trying to sound hopeful.

Owen couldn't help but smile at that, but it faded quickly. "And I can't use my superpowers again without my heart literally breaking. And you might be superstrong and a genius and all, Charm, but Nobody can match those things, even surpass them. He just has to rewrite himself."

For a moment, they were all silent.

Then Charm snorted. "So?"

"*So?*" Owen said. "Did you not hear anything I just said?"

"I heard it," she said, sending electricity crackling down her sword forearm. She swung it around, then gave it a satisfied nod. Turning to Owen, though, her face melted into a disgusted look. "You're thinking small, which shouldn't surprise me. He can handle any of us individually, maybe, though I still think I can take him. But if we all come at him at once, he won't be able to compensate. He can't rewrite a different defense against every one of us at the same time. All we have to do is attack as a unified force. It's not rocket science."

"He's not going to need much to compensate against me, unfortunately," Kara said.

"And honestly, I probably work better without others getting in the way," Kiel said.

"Oh, I think you're *all* completely worthless, but that doesn't make the strategy less sound," Charm said, glaring at them. "How are you not getting this? If *I'm* saying we need to work together, you know things are about as bad as they can get. So maybe just do what I say and stop with all the pointless objections."

Kiel and Kara exchanged glances.

"That doesn't really seem fair," Kara said.

"She's always saying my objections are pointless. It's really insulting," Kiel agreed.

"Owen told me you two had been working together for years, though."

"Well, I'm very understanding of other people's flaws."

Charm's ray guns buzzed to life. "One more word from either of you, and I shoot you both."

Owen quickly stepped between them all and pushed her weapons down. "Those were on stun, right?" he whispered.

She gave him a long look, but didn't say anything.

He sighed and backed away before Charm decided to turn her ray guns on him. Why did all of his friends have to be so brave and selfless? He was trying to save them here. But if he came out and told them what his older self said, they'd be even more likely to come along, because they wouldn't believe it could be true.

Still, he had to give it one last try.

"Even if we do all attack as a team," Owen said, "it's not going to be easy to reach him."

"I was his unwilling guest for a while, but I'm not sure I could tell you where that was," Kiel said. "Not to mention we can't travel between worlds anyway, unless we take the Magister with us."

"Um, are you *kidding*—" Charm said, but Owen quickly interrupted.

"I can travel between worlds," he said. "I learned how a few months ago, before Nobody sent me home. But I know where Nobody is, and it's a really dangerous place."

"Who cares where he is?" Charm said. "I've been to the end of the universe. There's nothing I haven't seen."

"Try a time prison in the Mesozoic Era that resets your time line every day," Kara told her. "Owen's right. Nobody's not going to just make it easy for us."

"So back out if you're so scared," Charm said, glaring at her.

"Am I missing something?" Kara asked. "What is your problem with me?"

Charm glanced at Owen, then turned away angrily. "I don't have a problem with *you*. I have a problem with all of this!"

As Kiel joined in the argument, Dr. Verity stood up and walked over to Owen. Owen automatically put his fists up, ready for a fight, but the doctor just gave him a friendly smile. "I might be able to help, if you don't mind?" he said, moving to take something out of his pocket.

"Slowly!" Owen said, not sure what he'd do if Verity pulled some kind of science fiction weapon on him. His heart began to beat even faster when the scientist produced his possibility ray gun, now looking good as new, "But I thought Nobody broke it. How did you—"

"Oh, it didn't take much to fix," Dr. Verity said. "Unfortunately, it's just got one charge left. But maybe that'll be of some use?"

Owen took it, just to get it out of the doctor's hands, in case he turned evil again. "I don't know, it didn't seem to do much but slow Nobody down."

Dr. Verity shrugged, still smiling, which weirdly made Owen more nervous. "You never know! It contains literally any possibility you can think of, so just use your imagination. You might be able to come up with something good in the moment."

Right, because Owen's imagination had been so much use in getting him this far. At least now that he was back in the fictional world, it seemed to have entirely returned. "Thanks," he said, turning away from Dr. Verity.

"All you have to do is concentrate on the effect you want it to have, and the ray gun will do the rest," the doctor continued, coming around to face Owen. "It's tuned in to the brain waves of whoever's holding it. Little something I added to Charm's design. But that's not *all* I've got to offer."

Owen had to fight the impulse to just punch him. "Oh, great, there's more?" he asked through clenched teeth.

"Well," he said, and started gesturing in the air, leaving

holographic marks behind, just like Charm. "From the way I understand our two realities, the nonfictional world was once connected to this one, correct?"

"Through our imaginations," Owen said. He realized the others had quieted down, and saw they were all watching Dr. Verity just as nervously as he was. At least he had backup.

Dr. Verity nodded. "Perfect," he said as he drew a stick figure human. "That fits in exactly with what I'm thinking. Nobody claims that the fictional world is made up entirely of possibilities, right?"

"A bunch of magicians made it using magic from all of humanity," Kara pointed out.

Charm snorted, rolling her eyes.

"She's not big on magic," Kiel told Kara.

"Call it magic, call it words, call it ideas, but what it all comes down to is possibilities," Dr. Verity said. "Words are just words, spells are just spells without someone using them. What's an idea if someone's not thinking it?" He drew a thought balloon above the stick figure's head, then drew another human inside it, reminding Owen uncomfortably of his time with the comic book pages while his friends were in Jupiter City.

"Is this like if a tree falls on Quanterium but everyone's in the Nalwork, does it make a sound?" Kiel asked.

"He's talking about quantum physics," Charm said, sounding annoyed. "When you get down to the building blocks of atoms and such, the smallest building blocks we can conceive of all are in a state of flux between two separate possibilities. Think of it like a computer that's either on or off, but you don't know which until you type something on the keyboard."

"Exactly," Dr. Verity said, now drawing lines out from the thought balloon above the stick figure's head out into a circle he labeled "The Fictional World." "Science has determined that those tiny particles actually are *both* off and on at the same time, to use Charm's delightful metaphor, until someone looks at them. And then they become either one thing or the other. And that is what's happening here, in the fictional reality!"

He looked around at a sea of uncomprehending faces.

"Don't you get it?" Dr. Verity asked. "If the nonfictional world has been creating this one all this time, that gives Owen here a power the rest of us don't have. And all it takes is his imagination!"

CHAPTER 36

Owen just blinked. "I think you lost me." *A few miles back,* he thought.

"Imagine the fictional world as a blank piece of paper," Dr. Verity said, drawing one around the circle labeled "The Fictional World." "The paper is blank when you start, but you could fill it with any story, any thought, any idea you had. The paper has infinite possibilities before you start writing. But once you do, just like with quantum physics, you've chosen one of those possibilities to become real. Now, there's a story." He tapped Owen on the chest. "And that's what you people do!"

"With our imaginations?"

"Yes!" Dr. Verity said, getting happier as he mistakenly thought Owen was following. "Your imaginations are the pencil on the paper. You create worlds out of the infinite possibilities, and off they go! But just like a scientist observing a tiny particle, you're not affecting it after you channel it into being. You don't control this world any more than you control a rocket after you set it off from the ground. That rocket's going to go where you aim it for a moment or two, but after that, who knows!"

"So nonfictional people *do* create things here with their imaginations?" Owen asked.

"I think that's what your authors do," Dr. Verity said. "Or really anyone with a strong will. Their will influences our worlds, shapes them, creates them. Then we're let loose to do as we choose." He started drawing all kinds of crazy things in the Fictional World circle. "But your imagination is still in place, so you can picture it all in your head as it's happening. And somehow that connection keeps our reality anchored in place, so that the possibilities don't overwhelm what little foundation is here."

"That's what's been happening to Bethany," Kiel said. "She didn't have her nonfictional self as an anchor anymore."

"From what I could tell by examining her for a few seconds, yes," Dr. Verity said with zero hint of irony. "Without an anchor to the nonfictional world . . . in her case, her twin, if I'm following correctly . . . she took on too many possibilities and lost what made her *her*." He drew another blank sheet of paper. "After all, it's hard to hold up against this much blank possibility."

"Hey, Owen," Kara said, frowning. "Didn't we see something like that in the future? I can't remember it exactly, which is weird for me, but I've got a vague memory of finding ourselves in just nothing but whiteness in every direction."

Owen frowned. "Did we?" He didn't even have a half memory of this one.

"That's what the place Nobody trapped me in looked like too," Kiel said.

While Owen couldn't remember what Kara was talking about, he did recall he'd been trapped in a place of nothing but white in every direction, back when he'd first met the Magister. And then again when Nobody brought him out of the comic book world to the place between stories.

"Nobody should be careful," Dr. Verity said. "If he's playing around with possibilities like this, it could unleash them into the fictional world. He could end up erasing every single one of us, and every world that ever existed in our reality, if he's not careful."

Kiel coughed. "Yeah, um, unfortunately that's his plan."

"Oh, well, that's not good news," Dr. Verity said, his eyes widening. "But what puzzles me is how he's rewriting himself. He *should* be disappearing, just like your friend. But if he's not, then he must have some kind of anchor, holding him in place."

"Would he need something nonfictional for that?" Kara asked.

"Most likely a person," Dr. Verity replied. "An object wouldn't be enough."

A person? But who would Nobody . . .

Owen gasped. "Mason Black!"

They all just stared at him.

"Mr. Black is Nobody's creator, the guy who wrote him first," Owen explained. "I saw Nobody take Mr. Black somewhere, but I couldn't tell where. He must be using him as an anchor!" He cringed. "It'd fit. He *hates* that guy."

"See? There's our plan," Charm said. "We take out this Mason guy—"

"*Rescue* him, you mean," Owen interrupted.

Charm just shrugged. "Whatever. Then Nobody can't rewrite himself, and we melt him into a huge pile of mush. Problem solved."

"And Owen, you said you know where he will be," Kiel said. "So let's go rescue Bethany!"

"One more thing," Dr. Verity said, and tapped Owen's head. "It might be wise to look in on him, just to confirm he's where you think he is. I'd suggest using your imagination to make sure before you run into what could be a trap."

"My imagination? How would that work?"

Verity seemed confused by this. "Just use it for what it was intended for."

Owen raised an eyebrow. "To . . . daydream?"

Kara looked at Owen in excitement. "No, it's like that old magician said when he created the world. Use your imagination to see what possibilities are!"

"Which you do by seeing what *we* do," Verity said. "Now, if you were to look for, say, *Nobody* . . ."

Owen's eyes widened. "You think I could see him in my head, just by imagining where he is? But wouldn't I just be putting him into whatever story I imagine him into?"

"You can't control him, like I said earlier," Verity said. "He's the rocket that was launched long ago. But if you let your imagination guide you, and let it take you to him on its own, you should be able to see where he is and what he's doing right now."

Charm groaned. "I thought this was about science. Let me know when you all come to your senses."

Owen half agreed with her, but Verity seemed pretty sure of himself. And if they could see what Nobody was up to, that might help them make plans. "I guess it's worth a shot," he said, closing his eyes.

He tried to let himself just daydream, which wasn't easy, considering his older self had already told him that Nobody would be in the story he himself had written. But if it helped to see what they'd be up against ahead of time, it didn't hurt to try. So deliberately ignoring that knowledge, Owen just let his imagination run wild.

Immediately his mind went to Charm, and he pictured her forgiving him for lying to her. Not the most positive start, considering there was no way *that* was going to happen. But from there, he imagined what it must have been like for Charm to lose her family, and then to find out that her best friend wasn't who she'd thought he was. Not to mention later having her planet destroyed.

This all must have been so hard on her, losing everything. Of course she'd be upset. And now all she wanted was a chance to get justice for her people and for her planet.

His mind drifted to Quanterium, picturing what it had been like when Nobody unleashed Charm's possibility machine.

Everything would be different, from weird loops in the roads to, well, something as ridiculous as the city square being made of gelatin. Houses could have their gravity reversed inside. It'd be chaos.

Then Nobody would use her invention on other worlds too, reabsorbing them all back into the possibility. He imagined Nobody setting off Charm's machine in a fairy-tale world, in Kara's future, in Fowen's hometown, as well as worlds completely unfamiliar to him.

And then, Owen thought, satisfied with what he'd started, Nobody would come back to the one place no one could reach him, a place he didn't believe ever should have existed, so was okay to change however he wished.

He'd be in a castle. A castle made out of storybooks. Owen could see him there in the castle's throne room now. Nonfictional Bethany and her fictional, ghostly self were both there, in the castle of the King of All Stories in the story Owen had written, and Nobody was talking to them.

He took a deep breath and opened his eyes. His older self had been right.

You'll have to fight your way to the Storybook Castle at the end of the story, but one by one, you'll lose your friends along the way, until finally it's just you against Nobody. And that's a fight that no Owen Conners has ever won yet.

Owen looked down at the ray gun that Dr. Verity had given him. One shot left. What good would that even do? He'd have one chance to change something about Nobody, and that was—

His eyes widened as an idea occurred to him. One shot might be all he needed.

Maybe his imagination wasn't so useless after all!

"I can see Nobody," he said, turning to the others. "And I think I have a plan."

CHAPTER 37

Nonfictional Bethany watched her fictional self float in a large glass cylinder in the middle of what looked like a castle throne room. Instead of bricks or stone, though, the walls looked like they were made out of giant storybooks. One cover said *Nursery Rhymes*, another *Mother Goose*. Beneath her feet, an enormous drawing of Humpty Dumpty stared up at her with a terrified expression as he fell off a wall. She scuffed her shoe on Humpty's nose, and it felt smooth and plastic-y, just like a book cover.

"This is my fault," she said to her fictional self. "From the very beginning, I didn't protect us enough. I let us do things I knew would lead to bad consequences, and that's on me. None of this would have happened if I'd just protected us better. I'm . . . I'm sorry."

"She's losing herself," said a voice from all around her.

Nobody's voice. "Even contained, she won't last more than another day or two."

Bethany turned around in a complete circle, but couldn't find the featureless man anywhere. "What do you want from us?" she shouted out into the otherwise empty room. "Why did you bring us here? Can you fix her, keep her from disappearing?"

"You care so much for your fictional self?" Nobody asked from behind her, and again, Bethany whirled around, but he was nowhere to be seen.

"She's a part of me," she said. "Of course I care about her. Just because I don't agree with her, or even like her, doesn't mean I don't want her to be safe. She has to be there for our father! Otherwise, all of this was for nothing."

"I thought nonfictionals missing their imagination would be without empathy. And yet, you still care for her, and Owen, too."

Bethany glared at the air around her. "Well, maybe I'm just special."

"You are definitely that. You have no imagination, even in this reality. Your fictional version took all of that from you."

"Good, she can have it," Bethany said. "Maybe she'll use it

to think of ways to follow the rules when she's better."

"I imagine it's more of a curse than a blessing," Nobody said, still all around her. "While other fictionals have more ideas than usual, with that much imagination, she's probably inundated with thoughts she can't control. That may be why she's falling apart even faster than the rest of us."

"What do you want from me?" Bethany shouted. "Can you fix her or not?"

"Would you like to know why I had to separate the worlds?"

Bethany ground her teeth in frustration. "No? All I want is for you to fix *her*, then send me and Owen back to our world, where he's safe. And put her back with my dad, so at least one of us has him!"

A moment passed. "You were truly happy in the nonfictional world, then?"

Bethany sighed. "Of course not! I had to give up my father to the worst part of myself. And as much as I want to blame her for all of this, I know I could have stopped it, but I didn't. I *let* her run wild, and this is where we've ended up. But at least I'm not lying to my mother all the time or getting my friends hurt. Owen is safe in that world, and so is my mom. Safe from *me*."

There was a pause. "Bethany, tell me this: If I order you to not merge with yourself again, will you disobey me? And yes, I know you won't be able to lie, not without an imagination."

She slowly looked down at the floor. "Yes, I will. I'll try to save her no matter what you say."

Another pause. "Do you miss your father?"

Bethany felt a cold chill go down her spine. Why would he ask that? "More than anything," she said quietly. "But if she gets to have him, I could live with it. And I knew she'd do everything in her power to protect him."

"Did she?"

Bethany froze. "What do you mean?"

But Nobody went silent.

"What are you talking about?" she screamed. "What happened to my father?"

A page ripped open in midair, and a mass of shadows with red eyes floated into the room. Bethany's heart almost stopped, and behind her, she could hear her fictional self banging on the glass cylinder.

"The Dark?" she whispered.

"For now," Nobody said. As she watched, the shadows whirled around, then transformed back into her father in his Doc Twilight costume. "But I want you to see him as he should be, here at the end. Your fictional self failed him, and he was struck by a possibility ray. He is but moments from disappearing entirely."

"Dad?" she said, her voice barely audible even to herself. But her father didn't move, didn't even breathe. It was like he was frozen in time.

"If I were to release him from my power, he would be gone," Nobody said. "And I shall do so, if you disobey me."

Her eyes widened. "You can't do that! Please!"

"I won't, if you refuse to merge back with your former self. I assume that your friends are on their way to rescue you, and I cannot keep an eye on all of you at once. Your fictional self especially is quite resourceful when she needs to be. So I leave it to you, the rational one, the practical one. The protective one. If you stay separated, I promise to return you and Owen to the nonfictional world. And perhaps your father can join you too."

"You'd . . . you'd give me back my father?" she said, her voice cracking.

"I can be merciful as easily as I can be cruel, Bethany."

Bethany turned to look at the version of her trapped in the

glass cylinder. They stared at each other for a moment, and then her fictional self nodded.

"What . . . what will happen to her?" Bethany whispered.

"The same that will happen to every fictional being. She will be reabsorbed into pure possibility, and then I shall create new fictional worlds, all without the influence of the nonfictional. She will reach heights she never dreamed possible, if you allow her to."

Bethany swallowed hard. Her fictional self nodded more urgently, encouraging her to take the deal. But was she trying to sacrifice herself for their father . . . or did she have a plan?

"What happens if you break your end of the deal?" Bethany asked.

"I wouldn't. I have no reason to."

"What if you're lying?"

"What would I gain from that? I could destroy you right now, along with your fictional self and your father. But I choose to be merciful and allow you a life you otherwise wouldn't have. Now make your choice, or I shall release both your fictional self and your father, and we can watch them disappear together."

"NO!" she shouted, then dropped her head into her hands. "I . . . I'll do it. I won't merge with her again. I promise you. But if you don't live up to your end of the bargain—"

"You have my word," Nobody said, and then said nothing more.

CHAPTER 38

Owen concentrated, remembering the trick to ripping open portals between worlds that had been taught to him either by his older self in Kara's future or by a magician at the beginning of time, he wasn't honestly sure which. Either way, the method was the same. He envisioned the world they wanted to travel to, reached up into the air, and slowly pulled downward.

A page ripped open in midair as he did, creating an opening that led to another world.

"Everyone ready?" he said to his friends.

Kiel and Kara nodded. Charm just glared at him, lifting her ray gun in her nonsword hand. Dr. Verity, however, shook his head. "I'm going to stay here with the Magister, my boy," he said. "Together, the two of us might be able to reverse this field of possibility that's enveloping Magisteria." He pointed up through the hole in the tower at the field of white above them. "If he's willing to help, I can't imagine there's anything science and magic together can't fix!"

"It's a worthy goal," Kiel said, having a hard time looking at him. "And I just, um, wanted to tell you that if I *am* ever going to turn into you, I hope it's this version."

Dr. Verity beamed. "Come here, son!" He held his arms wide for a hug, and Kiel gave Owen a terrified look.

"We probably don't have time for long good-byes," Owen said quickly, and Kiel let out a huge sigh of relief. "We should get going. I'll go through first and yell if there's anything dangerous."

"Or I could go, since you're basically useless and would instantly die if there was danger," Charm said, glaring at him.

"I'm sure she meant that in the nicest possible way," Kiel added.

Owen forced a smile. "Oh, she didn't. But no, I'm the only one who knows how to rip a page back if something happens, so it makes sense for me to go. Trust me, I won't stay long if there's something waiting to kill me."

Not waiting to argue any further, he stepped through the ripped page onto some bright green grass as a pleasant, warm breeze blew through his hair. He inhaled the fragrant air deeply, looking around for whatever trap Nobody might have waiting.

A paved path outlined with black borders started next to a small farm and led toward a walled city. Beyond the city, a castle rose into the sky as majestic as it was imposing. The walls of the castle looked like they were painted various colors, but it was hard to see what the design was meant to be from a distance.

All in all, it looked exactly like the story he'd written months ago about Bethany's father, and therefore not at all what he had expected. What was Nobody hiding? Where were the security forces or the death traps? It couldn't be as easy as it'd been in his story, could it?

He turned around to face the ripped page opening, then felt a chill as he saw what lay beyond. The same white nothingness that was inching toward Magisteria was here as well, just a few yards away.

Apparently Nobody meant to turn this world into pure possibility along with the others.

"I think it's okay," he called back through the open rift. "You can come through now."

The others slowly passed through, all but Charm seeming to relax as they saw the peaceful scene before them. The half-robotic girl seemed even more on edge than she had been, which was odd.

"Something's wrong here," she said. "What is this place?"

"Let's get moving, and I'll explain on the way," Owen said. He pointed at the road that began just past the farm. "That's the way to the city, and beyond that is a castle where Nobody has Bethany. But, um, don't look behind us."

Instantly, they all turned around.

"It's happening here too, then," Kara said softly.

"Looks like we don't have much time," Kiel said. "Maybe we should hurry?"

"Catch up or I'm leaving you all behind," Charm said, striding toward the path.

The rest followed and started down the road toward the castle, with Owen watching their every step carefully. Kara stopped for a moment to stare at the scenery on their right, and Owen had to grab her before she accidentally stepped over the black border on the edge of the path. "Um, let's all stay on the actual road, okay?" he said, his hands shaking with worry. "It's sort of a rule around here."

Charm snorted in front of him. "Or what, we get arrested?"

"Something like that," Owen said nervously. "Here's the thing. I may have kind of sort of *written* this story."

That stopped them all in place, including Charm. Three pairs of eyes turned to stare at him.

"And that means *what* exactly?" Kiel asked finally.

"I thought I was just messing around, you know?" Owen said, pulling them farther into the middle of the road. "I just started typing on my computer, telling a story with Bethany, Kiel, Charm, and me. I didn't know that what I wrote would actually exist!"

"You did *not* make up stories about me," Charm said, looking disgusted.

"More people should make them up about *me*," Kiel said with a smile, but even he seemed uncomfortable with the situation. "So you think you created this world, Owen?"

"No. Maybe? I guess," Owen said, feeling miserable about it all. "It's like Dr. Verity was saying. I must have pushed this place into existence with my imagination."

"So you know how everything works, then?" Charm asked. "Don't you think you might have wanted to *share* that?"

Owen winced. "It's all pretty embarrassing, honestly. I

thought it'd be fun to do all kinds of writing references, and, um, let me start over." He gestured toward the castle before them. "This is the Kingdom of Story, where the evil king lives. Me, Bethany, Kiel, and Charm all had to fight our way to the castle to defeat the king, who turned out to be Bethany's father." He gave Kara an apologetic look. "I hadn't met you yet, or I would have included you, too."

She shrugged, giving him a tiny smile. "We'll edit me in later."

"But then Nobody appeared in the words I was writing," Owen continued. "He said I was controlling the lives of real people, the people here in the kingdom. He told me I had to stop, which I *did*, right away!" He looked down at the road, not wanting to see the judgment in their eyes. "I think he decided to come here because he didn't see these people as real, so he could do whatever he wanted in this place."

"Or he's still trying to teach you a lesson," Kara said quietly.

"None of this matters," Charm said. "Give me *facts*. What are we going to be facing here?"

Owen nodded. "Well, the people here are all based on word-play, writing concepts, and, you know, puns."

Charm revved up her ray gun.

"So I'll start here," Owen continued quickly, pointing back at the farm a few yards behind them. "When you begin writing, you need an idea first. That farm is the place where ideas grow. It looks like Nobody got rid of the man who I had living there, the Idea Man. Probably didn't want anyone having ideas he didn't like."

"If one of the ideas is a fruit-related supervillain, Owen, there's going to be trouble," Charm said, her voice low and dangerous.

"So next comes this road," Owen said, ignoring the sweat running down his forehead. "This is the Outliner's path. He's the one who dictates where a story goes, and he hates it when characters step outside his lines." He gave Kara an apologetic look. "That's why I wanted everyone to stay in the middle of the road."

Kara's eyes widened. "Good advice. So Nobody's in the castle, then?"

Owen nodded. "See that town just before the Molehill Mountains? We're going to have to make our way through Grammar City in order to make it to the Storybook Castle. And that's where the really powerful challenges are, like the Grammar Police and the bookwyrms."

"Bookworms?" Kiel asked. "Worms who read?"

"Wyrms with a *y*," Owen said. "Which is an old name for dragons. These dragons are made of books, and they guard the castle courtyard." Even as he watched Kiel's interest rise, Owen shook his head. "Don't get excited—they're invincible. You can't kill them any more than you could kill a book."

"Challenge accepted," Kiel said. "Anything else?"

Owen thought for a moment, looking around. "Oh, see those potholes on the road?" he asked. "Those are plot holes. Watch out for them. I used them in my story as a joke, but who knows if Nobody changed them."

Kara stepped over and peered into one, then pulled back, looking dazed. "*Wow*. It's filled with illogic. It hurts my brain just to think about it all. And I thought I was immune to that sort of thing."

Owen helped steady her. "I think that's it for now, but just keep an eye out for anything. And whatever you do, don't step outside the line in the road."

They all nodded, and Charm led the way down the road, being careful to stay right in the middle. As they walked, Owen noticed little notes every few feet, much like an outline would have when writing a story. He paused at one, looking down at the words to see if they maybe held a clue as to what would be coming next.

The closest note mentioned Kara falling into a plot hole, and his eyes widened. But that was crossed out, and the words *Let them continue on their way toward Grammar City for now* were written over them.

He shuddered at what had almost happened, not liking this at all. The next note was just ahead, so he walked over to it carefully and leaned down to read it.

And then Owen steps off the path, and the Outliner shows up.

His eyes widened, and he stood back up quickly, backing away from the edge of the road. That couldn't be true, could it? He was being so careful—

The heel of his foot caught in another plot hole, and he windmilled his arms, stumbling backward. He desperately tried to catch himself, but his momentum sent him too far, and one of his feet touched down outside the borders of the road.

Uh-oh.

Catching his balance, Owen carefully, quietly picked up his foot and moved it back onto the road, not even daring to breathe. He turned around in a circle, not sure where the Outliner would be coming from, but knowing it was only a matter of time.

"Owen?" Kara said from farther up the road. "What's wrong?"

Charm groaned. "Don't tell me you stepped over the line?"

He raised his hands up for silence and waited another moment. When nothing happened, he let out his held breath and smiled. "I think it's okay!"

The black borders on the sides of the road rose up from the ground, twisting and tying around themselves to form a vaguely human-looking shape.

"You would *dare* deviate from Nobody's prescribed path?" the creature made of black lines shouted. "I will not allow it! Nobody has conceived carefully laid out plans, and you will *pay* for not following them. So declares the Outliner!"

Owen quickly ran to catch up to the others as Charm snorted. "Really? A bunch of string is going to hurt us?"

The Outliner sneered in her direction, then leaped at her, its strings unraveling as it struck. She sliced at it with her sword arm, but the cut lines just reattached themselves, forming up around her arms, legs, and head. She shouted in surprise as the strings attached themselves to her, wrapping around her, holding her still. Then the ones around her head seemed to pulse, and the light left her eyes.

"Now," Charm said in the Outliner's voice as she struck the same pose it had a moment before, "if you refuse to follow Nobody's plan, I will erase you from the story myself!"

CHAPTER 39

The Outliner pulled Charm's hands up, aiming her ray gun at Kara and Owen. "How *dare* you make your own decisions!" the creature's voice shouted through Charm's mouth. "Nobody has planned out everything for the good of us all, and given me the task of ensuring his plot is followed line by line!"

A Twilight throwing star zipped past Charm's arm, slicing through one of the strings. "Nobody tells *me* what to do," Kiel Gnomenfoot said, three more throwing stars in his hand. "Um, you know what I mean. No one tells . . . you get it."

The Outliner recoiled as pain flashed across Charm's face. The cut string snaked off of her arm and headed for Kiel. He threw the rest of his throwing stars, then stabbed at the strings with his wand-knives, but the Outliner was too quick, and soon strings wrapped around *his* body too.

"That's two of you back in line," the Outliner said from both

Kiel and Charm's mouths simultaneously. Both of his friends flung out their hands, and more strings snaked their way toward Owen and Kara.

"How did you beat this in your story, Owen?" Kara shouted as she backpedaled away from the quickly approaching strings.

"We never left the road!" he said, trying to stomp on his own string, but nothing was working.

"It's far too late for that now!" Kiel and Charm shouted in the Outliner's voice. "I will walk you right into oblivion, in order to keep his story in line!"

Owen growled in frustration. Why had he written this story to begin with? If Nobody was trying to teach him a lesson, he got the point. There had to be a way out of this! In another moment, he and Kara would both be mind-controlled too. And then the Outliner would throw them into the white wall of nothingness, and they'd just . . . disappear.

"But you made this guy up, right?" Kara asked. "Do you remember if there was any way to beat him?"

Owen swore softly as he dodged strings from each direction. He tried to think back to writing this horrible story about finding out Bethany's father was the king of a land of stories, and how the Outliner made sure everyone followed the plot. Had he given the Outliner any weaknesses?

No, because he was just messing around, so hadn't actually thought it through that much!

A string grabbed Owen from behind, wrapping itself around his chest. Another snaked around his neck and slowly squeezed, cutting off his air supply. He started to choke, flailing around, trying to get a hand on the string, but soon both his legs were captured too.

Finally, one last string wrapped itself around his head, and Owen seemed to sink back into his own mind, still able to watch what was happening, but completely out of control of his own body.

"Owen!" Kara shouted, staring at him in horror.

"There is no Owen anymore," the Outliner said from his mouth, as well as from Kiel's and Charm's. "There is only Nobody's plan, and your disobedience. Come, girl. Join your friends, and suffer together."

Kara just stared at him for a moment, then looked down. "I think I know what I have to do, Owen. I have no idea if it will work, but it's all I've got. I hope you can forgive me for this."

"There will be no forgiveness!" the Outliner shouted, and now Owen's strings shot out after Kara too.

She grabbed some of Kiel's throwing stars and sliced the strings closest to her. Giving Owen one last look, she jumped over the line and into the grass on the side of the road.

Rage reverberated through Owen's mind as the Outliner screamed in horror. He, Charm, and Kiel all stared at Kara, daring to commit the worst crime of all, standing outside of the outline. "You would flout Nobody's story even *now*?" they all said in one voice.

"What are you going to do about it?" Kara yelled, turning back toward them but still moving away from the road. "I *dare* you to come after me. Cross your line, if you can!" She backed farther into the grass, her arms spread wide.

Kiel, Charm, and Owen's bodies all moved toward the side of the road, only to freeze as they reached the edge. The Outliner's strings pulled up and off their bodies, reaching out toward Kara over the grass, but not daring to touch the ground. "If you do not come back, I will punish your friends for your actions!" the Outliner said through their voices, though they didn't sound as in sync anymore.

"And yet, I'm still out here, ruining your carefully laid plans," Kara said with a shrug. "And you can't do anything about it, can you?"

The strings surged forward, each one almost pulling itself off of Owen and his friends. "You have no idea what you're doing!" the Outliner yelled. "Nobody knows all, and he has decreed how this story must go! If you stray from his path, you will ruin *everything*!"

"Maybe I have a better plan?" Kara said, taking a few steps back toward the road, but staying just out of the strings' reach. "Maybe Nobody's plan was terrible all along, and mine will get us where we're going quicker, and with much cooler action scenes."

"*NO!*" the Outliner shouted, and Owen, Charm, and Kiel all screamed in pain as the strings ripped off of their bodies, reforming into the original creature's shape as it leaped onto the grass. It seemed to shudder as its feet touched the land outside the path, but it quickly lurched toward Kara. "No one's plan is better than Nobody's!"

With his body back under his control, Owen collapsed to the ground, almost too weak to hold himself up. He pushed himself dizzily to his feet, slowly understanding what Kara was doing. "No," he croaked, his throat dry from the Outliner using it to scream. "Kara, no!"

"Go!" Kara shouted at Owen as she backed away farther

363

from the path. "Without my time machine, this is all I can do to help! Get to Nobody and save the world. I know you can do it!"

"You can't do this!" Owen shouted. He stumbled to the side of the road, but Kiel and Charm both grabbed his arms, holding him back.

"If you go out there, he'll just take control of you again," Kiel said. "You have to trust her."

"It's okay, Owen," Kara said quietly as the creature drew closer to her. She backed up closer to the wall of possibility. "If you don't get to Nobody, all of us are going to disappear anyway." She forced a smile, still staying out of range of the Outliner's strings. "Besides, my older selves are still alive, so that means I get out of this somehow. I think, anyway. You know me . . . immune to paradox. What could go wrong?"

Owen struggled against Kiel and Charm, but they held him fast. "Let me go!" he screamed, trying desperately to pull them along with him. "You can't go, Kara. This is insane!"

"I'll see you again," she said as the Outliner's strings began circling her legs. As they attached, she yanked herself backward, dragging the Outliner along with her toward the wall of nothingness. "Maybe it'll be in the future," she grunted, "or maybe just the past me . . . but I'll see you again, somewhere in time. I *promise*."

"Kara, we don't know what will happen to you if you go out there!" Owen pleaded, his eyes wet. "*Please*, don't do this! There has to be some other way!"

"What are you doing?" the Outliner shouted as it just now seemed to catch on to Kara's plan. "You would erase us both? I have no plan for this!"

"That's the problem with plans," Kara said, giving Owen one last look. "They never quite go the way you hope."

And with that, she grabbed the Outliner with both arms and yanked him backward. He toppled into her, and the two fell into the nothingness, disappearing completely.

As they did, the wall of possibility seemed to glow brighter and surged forward several yards. It stopped just a few feet away from them, then resumed its normal, creeping speed, enveloping the entire world as it went.

Kiel and Charm released their hold on Owen, and he dropped to his knees, his mouth hanging open. Kara had . . . she didn't . . . this couldn't be *happening*.

"She saved us," Kiel said quietly to him. "She was every bit the hero we needed."

"She was my *friend*," Owen whispered bitterly. "I needed that more than I needed a hero."

Kiel went silent, while Charm crouched down beside him. "We shouldn't let her sacrifice be in vain," she said. "Hold on to that feeling, her being taken from you. Use that against your enemy. Sometimes . . . that's all you have left."

Owen turned to look at her, ready to yell at her, to scream, *anything* . . . but Charm just stared at him with sorrowful eyes, and he realized she knew exactly what he was feeling.

He clenched his fists, then pushed himself to his feet. "You're right," he said, turning to face the city walls. "I'm done with this." He cupped his hands over his mouth and shouted as loudly as he could. "Nobody! *Come out and face us!* We're done with your games!"

There was no reaction, not even an echo. Instead, the wall of nothingness seemed to absorb his voice, leaving nothing but silence behind.

"Are you a coward?" Owen screamed. "Kara was fictional, and you just *destroyed* her. She was one of your people!"

Still no response.

"We'll win our way through to him," Kiel said, laying a hand on Owen's shoulder. Owen shook it off, though, not wanting to hear anything positive right now. Kara was gone, and there was nothing he could do about it!

"I'm not waiting," he said. "There's something I wrote into this horrible place, another stupid book reference. It was something I tried, back when the Magister stuck me outside of your story, and it didn't work then. But I'm going to *make* it work now."

Charm and Kiel both looked at him with confusion, but it didn't matter. Nobody was going to face them, *right now*, even if Owen had to jump forward in time to make it happen.

One by one, you'll lose your friends along the way, until finally it's just you against Nobody.

That was *not* going to happen. He wasn't going to lose another friend, no matter how much the story or Nobody tried to force him to.

"I'm coming for you, Nobody," Owen said, his heart racing with anger. He held his hands aloft, and just like his characters had done in his story, he clapped loudly and declared, "CHAPTER!"

CHAPTER 41

Instantly, everything changed. Instead of the road toward Grammar City, now Owen, Kiel, and Charm were surrounded by a dirty dungeon cell, their feet bound to the wall by long metal chains.

"Whoa," Kiel said. "Um, can I ask what just happened?"

"Who locked me up?" Charm shouted, pulling as hard as she could at her chains. Unfortunately, they seemed to be reinforced against her robotic strength. Even her sword arm just set off sparks as it bit into the chains, unable to slice through them. "Owen, what did you do?"

"This place works just like books do," Owen said, his anger losing a bit of its edge as he realized he may have made a mistake. "You know how books have chapters? Well, I jumped us ahead to the next one, figuring we'd have reached Nobody. But it looks like things didn't go so well between then and now."

"Didn't *go* well?" Charm shouted. "We're in a dungeon!"

"That's okay, I'll just try again," Owen said, pulling his hands together for a second try.

"No, *wait*—" Kiel shouted, but it was too late. Owen clapped his hands again.

"CHAPTER!"

CHAPTER 42

"Order!" a judge shouted, slamming his gavel down on a large desk in front of the three of them. "I will have *order* in Nobody's court!"

Owen looked around, not liking this much better than the dungeon. Now they were apparently being tried and sentenced for crimes, it looked like? Someone wearing a uniform with GRAMMAR POLICE printed across the chest sat in the witness stand, and a host of odd-looking citizens were screaming for their heads in the audience section.

"This doesn't seem like an improvement," Kiel whispered to him.

"I don't get it," he whispered back. "I know we make it to Nobody. My older self told me we do. How did we get captured?"

"Well, when would we have escaped if we keep jumping forward?" Kiel asked, raising an eyebrow.

"The story continues on, but we skip ahead," Owen said. "It's just like how chapters in a book will—"

"Could you *please* stop saying that?" Charm demanded, not looking at him as she instead stared down the judge.

"You stand accused of breaking grammatical rules," the judge said, reading from a long list of crimes, "fighting a legion of Grammar Police, breaking out of jail using plot holes, destroying the globes of several world builders, and attacking our head grammarian with a story sword stolen from a wordsmith."

"What?" Kiel shouted. "We did all of that, and I missed it?" He gave Owen an annoyed look. "Don't keep jumping us forward like that. That story sword stuff sounded exciting!"

"Not to mention forging unlawful vocabulary at the wordsmith," the judge continued, and Kiel groaned loudly.

"Just once more," Owen said, shaking his head. "I can't deal with any of this ridiculousness. We need to face Nobody *now*."

Charm slapped her forehead as Owen shouted, "CHAPTER!"

CHAPTER 43

"I've never seen such blatant disregard for words in my life!" the judge shouted, his wig askew on his head. The entire courtroom looked like it'd been destroyed, with chairs broken and Grammar Police unconscious everywhere.

"We missed the exciting stuff again!" Kiel said, pushing the remnants of a desk off of himself.

Why wasn't this working? Eventually things had to stop getting worse, didn't they?

"CHAPTER!" Owen shouted again.

CHAPTER 44

A cold wind hit Owen in his face, and he shivered violently as he found himself hanging from a deflating hot air balloon as it sank back toward Grammar City in a zigzag path with the words WHETHER BALLOON written on the side.

Right. It couldn't decide *whether* to go right or left. Ugh.

Below, Grammar Police shot word arrows up at them from the streets.

"Owen, this isn't helping!" Charm shouted from below, where his friends were now hanging from his feet.

"CHAPTER!" he shouted.

CHAPTER 45

I finally found you!" Dr. Verity shouted, reaching out toward him before Owen even knew where he was. "I think I have a way to defeat Nobody—"

Owen leaped back, startled by the scientist's sudden appearance. "CHAPTER!"

CHAPTER 46

Owen looked up to find Kiel tied to a large wooden beam, hanging over an enormous pot of boiling alphabet soup. "Are you *kidding* me?" Kiel shouted.

"Don't worry, I'll jump us forward again!" Owen shouted back.

"NO!" Charm and Kiel yelled at the same time.

Meanwhile, Dr. Verity was nowhere to be found, if that really had been him in the last chapter. Had he really had a plan for taking down Nobody? Owen groaned, wanting to pull out all of his hair. Why did he have to keep making mistakes? Couldn't he just for *once* do the right thing?

"Let me get out of this myself!" Kiel said. "Are you two free?"

Wait, *were* they? Owen glanced around, and just then realized he and Charm were alone on a rooftop above the crowds cheering for Kiel's . . . cooking. Not only that, but they were at the edge of Grammar City, right by the Storybook Castle, a large, imposing structure made entirely of giant hardcover picture books. "Um, I actually think we *are?*" he shouted back to Kiel.

"Get away, then!" the former magician shouted, quickly untying himself, then swinging his body around to grab ahold of the top of the beam. Below, the crowd started screaming in anger at his escape, but Kiel just winked at them. "I've got this. I'll distract them while you two go find Bethany. Tell her I said hello, okay?"

No! Not another friend! This was going just like his older self had said, no matter what Owen did. Now he was losing Kiel, too, not just Kara?

For a moment, he considered jumping one more chapter ahead. After all, they were bound to save Kiel at some point . . . right?

Unless things just kept getting worse, and Charm would disappear next.

"We'll find her, Kiel," he said quietly. "We'll rescue her, then come back for you. Stay safe, okay?"

Kiel saluted them, then ran down the beam, leaped off it, and tackled a group of Grammar Police. "This is for making me miss all of the fun!" he shouted, grabbing what looked like a nightstick made of dangling participles and knocking it against another Grammar Policeman's head.

And then the crowd blocked Owen's view, and one more friend was left behind.

CHAPTER 47

Enough time had passed while they were skipping chapters for the wall of nothingness to reach the edge of Grammar City. Owen nervously watched it inch forward, knowing they didn't have much time left. They'd have to figure out a way to restore everything it had already absorbed before it took over this world too.

That was assuming they could beat Nobody to begin with, which, in spite of Owen's plan, still seemed pretty far-fetched.

"Look at these shoddily made walls," Charm said, pointing at the city walls between them and the castle with distaste.

Owen glanced over and made a face. The walls looked like someone had just sketched them in with a pencil. "That was probably my fault for not describing them enough," he said. "But at least it should make getting past them easier."

Charm nodded. "*Much* easier." She leaped down off the roof

and sliced her sword arm right through the city wall like it was paper. Her cut seemed to reverberate through the rest of the wall, and soon the entire thing was wobbling. She pushed her nonrobotic hand against it, and the wall came tumbling down.

Beyond the now-destroyed wall, Storybook Castle rose majestically, its storybook ramparts shining in the setting sun. The castle gate lay straight ahead, beyond which lay the most dangerous of the challenges on the way to Nobody: the two bookwyrms.

A drawbridge led across a moat filled with alligator-like creatures that Owen remembered as allegories, another dumb pun he'd made. They wouldn't be a danger from a distance, given that their only power was to declare whatever hidden meaning something had as they ate it.

Next to the drawbridge, a sign read ABRIDGED/UNABRIDGED, and the first word was circled. As Charm noticed it, she immediately pulled out her ray guns and blew it to splinters. She threw Owen a half-apologetic look, then shrugged and led him across the drawbridge.

Before she reached the other side, Owen grabbed her arm and pulled her to a stop. "There are two bookwyrms in the courtyard," he whispered, pointing ahead of them. "Like I said earlier, they're dragons, just made out of books. These two have read every single novel ever written, so to get by them, we have to answer three questions. Miss even one, and they eat us."

Charm gave him a confused look. "So why don't we just fight them instead of wasting time with riddles?"

Owen blinked. "Because they're dragons? You know, huge monsters with teeth and claws who breathe fire? Well, these ones breathe pages on fire, but same thing."

She snorted. "I've been killing dragons with Kiel for years. I'll handle them."

Owen shook his head. "Let's just try it my way first, okay? The last thing we need is you . . . I mean, for either of us to get hurt here and not be able to go on."

She glared at him, then gestured for him to lead the way. He did, not entirely thrilled to be going first, and found himself in a courtyard tiled with smiling fairy-tale book covers. In the middle of the courtyard, two enormous dragons with books for scales lay waiting, their eyes on Owen the moment he entered.

"Look, Gutenberg," one of the dragons said to the other. "Another human infestation. I hate these things. Shall I destroy them with fire?"

"Please do, Alexandria," the other said, waving a clawed

paw lazily. "Can't stand the little monsters. Fire away."

The bookwyrm named Alexandria rose up on her haunches, her long neck reaching up into the sky as she opened her mouth, revealing a glowing orange light.

"See?" Charm said, readying her sword arm. "Let's take them!"

"No, wait!" Owen shouted, rushing into the courtyard with his hands up in surrender. "We're here to accept your challenge!"

Alexandria paused, her mouth snapping shut in confusion as smoke began to rise from her nostrils. "Gutenberg, it appears these insects can speak. How interesting."

"It claims it's here for a challenge," Gutenberg responded. "Are you aware of any such thing?"

"Can't say that I am," Alexandria replied.

"Yes, you are!" Owen shouted, sweat trickling down his neck. "You know, the challenge where you test us to see if we can correctly identify lines from three books. You offer that challenge because you've read every book ever written and want to make sure we're worthy of entering the Storybook Castle!"

The two bookwyrms looked at each other. "What a ridiculous concept," Alexandria said.

"Why would we care if humans have read a book?" Gutenberg replied.

"It seems to me that maybe the creature is simply stalling, to prolong its life," Alexandria said. "And if we let that happen, then we'd clearly be failing at our job to protect the inner keep from visitors."

"And that would make Nobody upset," Gutenberg said, shuddering. "I wouldn't want to see him angry, would you?"

"Not me," Alexandria said. "Now, little human creatures, I'm afraid it's time to burn you up. We'd eat you, but, well—"

"You smell disgusting," Gutenberg said. "And probably taste worse."

"Exactly," Alexandria agreed, opening her mouth again.

"Owen, when I say go, you run between them to the castle," Charm hissed, stepping in front of him. "I'm going to distract them while you get past, then catch up to you."

As terrified of the bookwyrms as he was, the idea of leaving Charm behind and going on alone almost scared him more. "I'm *not* leaving you," he said.

"All that matters is taking Nobody down," she said. "And if you tried to distract these things, they'd set you on fire in seconds. This is our only choice." She stepped forward, raising her sword arm toward Alexandria. "Dragons!" she shouted. "I'm Charm Mentum of Quanterium. I think dragons are ridiculous and magic is dumb, so I'm going to stab you until you stop moving. Now *come at me!*"

The two bookwyrms turned to look at each other, then back at Charm. "Um, no?" Gutenberg said.

Instead of responding, Alexandria unleashed a torrent of fire directly at the half-robotic girl.

As Owen dodged to the side to avoid being burned, Charm leaped straight up, using her superstrong robotic leg to boost her. Flipping in midair, she pulled a ray gun out of her leg holster and began firing toward Alexandria's mouth.

The beams struck the bookwyrm in the throat, and she yanked her head backward in pain and alarm. "That *hurt*, you little monster!" she screamed. "Gutenberg, destroy her!"

"Owen, now!" Charm shouted as she landed, then used her robotic leg to launch herself right at Gutenberg, her sword arm locked at the elbow and aimed at the bookwyrm's eye.

Owen ran straight forward, right between the bookwyrms. To his left, he heard Gutenberg shriek in pain, only to duck beneath one of Alexandria's claws as she swiped at him. Another beam struck her leg from a distance, and Owen looked up to find Charm climbing around to Gutenberg's neck, her ray gun still glowing from the shot she'd just taken. Gutenberg, meanwhile, had a gash down the side of his face where she must have sliced him.

Both bookwyrms were now definitely focused on Charm, and the way was clear. On the other side of the courtyard, a double set of heavy wooden doors led farther into the castle, and they were close enough that Owen could reach them now, even if the wyrms turned on him.

"Don't mess this up, Owen!" Charm shouted. "You have to beat him for all of us!"

He glanced back at her, realizing she knew that she wouldn't be catching up after all. Distracting the dragons wasn't going to end well for her, and she knew that. As Owen watched, Gutenberg bit down on Charm's sword arm and ripped it off at the elbow. The sword clattered to the courtyard floor between the bookwyrms while Alexandria shot another blast of fire toward Charm.

This time, Charm was too slow with the ray gun, and her blast went wide as the searing flame struck her human shoulder. She gasped and fell from the bookwyrm's back, crashing hard to the ground.

"Go!" she shouted at Owen, crawling with one arm toward her sword. "Get out of here! I've got this!"

Gutenberg slowly pushed one of his paws down on top of her back. "Oh, do you now?"

"GO!" she shouted again, then screamed in pain as the bookwyrm's claws dug into her.

His older self had predicted this. Owen would face Nobody, but he'd do it alone. To even reach the man, he'd have to abandon all of his friends, leave them behind, sacrifice them for the greater good.

Except he couldn't, not this time. Not *her*.

"Shall I roast her for you?" Alexandria asked Gutenberg. "If you *do* have to eat such a foul thing, it might taste better cooked."

"Please do," Gutenberg said, then let out an enormous shriek as a metal sword sliced into his paw. He reared back in pain and searched the courtyard for the cause.

"If you're not going to challenge me," Owen said, Charm's sword arm in his hand, "then I guess I'm going to have to challenge *you*. Now, like my friend said, *come at me*."

CHAPTER 48

Alexandria reached down and grabbed the sword from Owen's hand and flung it away so hard it embedded itself in the storybook wall. "Was this what you meant?" she asked him, bringing her enormous head within inches of his. "Or was there some other challenge you were referring to?"

Owen swallowed hard. That had gone about as well as he should have expected. But now he was left with only one option.

"Hold on," he whispered to Charm, who was slowly crawling toward him. "I've got this."

"I thought not," Alexandria said as Gutenberg brought his head in too. "Since he hurt you, my dear, would you like to be the one to roast him alive?"

"I would indeed," Gutenberg said, and inhaled deeply, the glow in his stomach promising to be the largest eruption of fire yet.

"This all could have gone a lot easier if you'd just asked me to identify book quotes," Owen said, then watched as flames began to rise slowly up from Gutenberg's throat. The fire slowly passed through the bookwyrm's jaws, then froze in place. As they did, Owen doubled over in pain, the pain in his chest almost too intense to bear.

His heart racing, he wiped sweat off his forehead, then collapsed toward Charm, too weak to grab her hand.

As they touched, Charm began to move, and stared up in surprise at the frozen fire emerging from the bookwyrm's mouth. "You're using your powers? But you shouldn't—"

"No choice," Owen said, trying not to faint. "Not leaving you. But can you . . . can you carry me maybe?"

She nodded and pushed to her feet, a bit unstable as well. She picked Owen up using both her regular human arm and the remaining half of her robotic one, letting the latter hold most of his weight as she limped forward, moving carefully between the bookwryms' heads. "You came back for me," she said, sounding more curious than anything. "You didn't need to. I had them distracted. Why did you come back?"

"I've left . . . too many friends behind. Not . . . not leaving you. Not you."

She kept facing forward, but her human arm tightened around him at his words. "You *might* not be the absolute worst person in the world," she whispered.

Owen almost smiled at such high praise, but his vision began to get blurry, and he wondered if he was even going to make it out of the courtyard. "Hurry," he groaned.

Charm nodded and leaned forward on her robotic leg, then pushed off, leaping them both all the way across the courtyard. She landed just in front of the double doors, shoved the right one open with the side of her robotic arm, then slid them through. A moment later, she slammed the door behind them, and Owen released his hold on time.

"Can they break through these?" Charm asked, dropping a large metal bar across the doors to lock them.

Owen tried to speak, but the pressure on his chest hadn't gone away for some reason. He shook his head, then gasped as another intense spike of pain shot through him. "I think I might . . . have made a mistake," he said, his face contorted with agony.

Charm dropped to his side as they heard the bookwyrms begin to rage outside in the courtyard, realizing their prey was gone. "Stop it," she told him, trying to sound meaner than her face suggested. "You're going to be fine. It's just a little pain."

"Oh, really?" Owen hissed, clenching his eyes shut through the throbbing torture in his chest. "Feels . . . like a *lot*, actually."

She pulled his hand from his chest as the bookwyrms began to beat against the double doors. Flames licked through the gap beneath them, only to stop within inches of entering the room as if they hit some sort of invisible wall. Whatever magic held the bookwyrms in the courtyard appeared to be keeping their fire out too.

"You should have just gone on without me," Charm told him, holding his hand tightly in hers. "That was really dumb, Owen. I would have been fine."

"You would have . . . been eaten," he said, trying to take in a deep breath, but the pain was too intense.

"But you didn't leave me," she whispered, staring at him. "Everyone leaves me, but not you. I don't . . . I don't know what to say to that."

Something wet hit his cheek, and he looked up to see another tear fall from her human eye. He reached a trembling hand up to wipe it away, only to have her fade into darkness as he fell into unconsciousness.

Distantly, he could hear a voice screaming his name, but

that didn't matter anymore. Instead, he watched as memories floated past him, images of his friends, his family, his life. Bethany was there, and Kara, Kiel . . . Charm smiled at him, and he knew that this couldn't be real, but it didn't matter, everything was so peaceful . . .

Everything except the screams. And the pounding. What was this pounding—

"Aaaaaah!" he shouted, bolting awake as Charm slammed the side of her robotic arm down onto his chest. "Ow!"

"You're alive!" she shouted, then grabbed him and hugged him tightly. "*Never* do that again! I thought you were gone!"

"I'm fine," Owen said, not sure that was true. "But . . . thank you for . . . for that."

She grinned at him, then hugged him again. "Come on," she said finally, rolling up to a crouch. "Let me help you up."

Between the two of them, they got Owen to his feet. But even with Charm's support, he found he felt much weaker than normal. He'd gone too far with his powers, clearly. His heart wasn't able to take anything else, even back here in the fictional world. It might not be degrading any further now, but the damage had been done. One more use of his time powers, and that would be it.

"So where is Nobody?" Charm asked, walking them down the hallway away from the double doors, which the bookwyrms hadn't stopped trying to break through.

"You can't handle him on your own," Owen whispered. "We need to figure out another way."

"I'm not alone," she told him, giving him the slightest smile. "I've got you. Even if you're not much help in a fight right now. Or ever, really."

He laughed at this, then immediately regretted it as the motion sent pain radiating through him. "I do have a plan," he whispered as they neared the end of the hallway leading to the throne room. "If you can just get us to Nobody, I might have a way to defeat him once and for all."

"Deal," she said. "I'll get you there, no matter what. You've got my word on—"

A ray gun beam sizzled through the air, striking Charm in the chest.

She screamed, and a bright light emanated from her, blinding Owen.

"Charm!" he screamed, trying to hold on to her through the light, but she seemed to be disappearing from his grasp. He reached out blindly, hoping to find her, but soon there was nothing there within the light, nothing left of her.

Finally, the light dimmed.

Charm was gone.

Owen dropped to his knees in the spot where a moment before, she'd been standing. His mouth dropped in shock as tears rolled down his cheeks.

"You really messed this all up, didn't you," said a voice from inside the throne room.

Owen couldn't move, couldn't speak, couldn't even think. Charm . . . she was just *gone*.

Someone stepped in front of him and aimed a ray gun at his face. "Really?" the person said, and the familiarity of the voice pulled Owen back to reality. "Not even a hello for your favorite fictional character?"

Owen slowly looked up to find Fowen standing over him, the crown of stories from Owen's fan fiction sitting on his head as he aimed a possibility ray gun right between Owen's eyes.

"Guess not," Fowen said, then pulled the trigger.

CHAPTER 49

Owen flinched as the beam hit him in the forehead, expecting to explode in a flash of light or turn into an alternate version of himself.

Nothing happened.

"Yeah, that's what I thought," Fowen said, shooting a few more possibility rays at him. "These don't work on nonfictional people. That makes sense, though. What else could you people ever be in your lives, other than the boring old regular version of yourselves?"

Owen just stared at him, rage fighting with grief over Charm. He pushed to his feet, his weak muscles barely able to hold him up, but the desire to *destroy* his fictional twin gave him the strength he needed.

"Oh, stop it," Fowen said, and waved his fingers. Immediately Owen's body froze, and he slowly floated into the air. "I'm not here to fight you."

"You killed Charm!" Owen roared, his mouth the only thing he could still move. His muscles clenched as he fought back against the magic paralyzing him, but it was too powerful, even if he hadn't been weakened by using his powers. "Do you even understand what you've done?!"

"I do," Fowen said, strangely calm as he dropped the possibility ray gun to the ground. "I don't think *you* do. I didn't kill her, you pathetic, sad, basic version of me." He shook his head. "Wow, I hate admitting that we're related in any way. You're so useless, it hurts to even think that we could have anything in common."

The insults flew by him as Owen latched on to four of Fowen's words. "You *didn't* kill her? But she . . . she's gone, she disappeared—"

"I mean, to be fair, it's not like she's alive, either," his fictional twin said. "She's just pure possibility now. You can't destroy energy, Nowen. Haven't you learned that by now?" He clenched his fists and stepped in close, just inches away from Owen. "And *you* were supposed to be helping *me* defeat him!"

"What?" Owen said, still trying to work out what happened to Charm. "I didn't—"

"Exactly!" Fowen shouted. "You *didn't*! I handed you all

the information you needed, you and the boring version of Bethany. But you two didn't do anything with it!"

"You what?" Owen said. "I haven't seen you since Nobody split the worlds."

"Not *this* me!" Fowen said. "The me in disguise!" He waved his fingers again and transformed into a tall, muscular man in a business suit. He tore the sunglasses from his face and glared at Owen. "How could you not follow one simple instruction? I told you to open the book. I even handed it to you! It explained the whole plan: how the books were actually Quanterians, how Bethany needed to rejoin with her fictional self, how I would get that version of Bethany to you through the Magister's portal, *everything*. But you messed it all up!"

Owen glared right back. "We never even opened it."

"Oh, well, that's just great!" Fowen shouted, turning around and slapping his thigh. He waggled his fingers again, turning back into his usual self. "Here I am, trying to save the world, and I can't even count on you people to do one simple thing. And I had to deal with two Bethanys, too! While you were accomplishing nothing, I had released Kiel from Nobody's prison, so he'd be free to help too, while also tricking Bethany into coming to Quanterium. Don't you get it? She's the only one who could have beaten Nobody. Now he has her, and that's it. We're all gonna get erased into possibilities. And it's *your* fault!"

"*I* brought Bethany here!" Owen shouted. "*And you killed Charm!* You don't get to judge me. You don't get to even *speak* to me! Now let me go!"

Fowen stared at him for a moment, then strode back over and punched him in the face.

In spite of the impact, Owen's head didn't move, as the magic held him in place, but he could feel a bruise rising on his cheek.

"You still don't get it, Nowen," Fowen said. "I'm superior to you in every single way. *I* convinced Nobody to let me join him, to help him, all to find out what he was doing. *I* learned his plans to restart the fictional universe by turning us all back into pure possibility. And *I* came up with a plan to stop him!"

"And here you are, still working for him," Owen said. "You must be so proud."

"I have no choice now!" Fowen shouted. "You and Bethany messed it all up, so I'm left picking up the pieces. You know, I'm *glad* I brought those possibility ray guns to Jupiter City. Nobody ordered me to leave Jupiter City until the end, because he wanted to be merciful on Bethany, now that she actually had her father back. But I knew we needed her, so I went behind his back and smuggled the weapons in." He smirked. "I told her I didn't know Doc Twilight had gotten hit, but that was a lie. I'd hoped that would happen. Even if I needed Bethany, I still owed her for what she did to me. And what better revenge than making her father disappear?"

Owen screamed in rage, pushing with all of his might against the magical bonds. "I'm going to erase you, Fowen!" he shouted. "I promise you that. I will use that possibility ray gun on you as soon as I get free!"

Fowen laughed. "Here's the thing. Nobody's expecting you to show up in a few minutes. I used a couple of spells to make sure he couldn't see or hear what happens, but he's going to get impatient if an Owen doesn't show up soon. You have no chance, obviously. But I might have a way to fix all your mistakes still." He wiggled his fingers, and suddenly his black pants, shirt, and cape all morphed into clothes that matched Owen's exactly. "Maybe it's not too late to save the universe. Maybe it's just going to take a *real* hero to do it."

"You can't win against him, Fowen!" Owen shouted. "None of us can! A thousand Owens tried, and they all failed. Some of them even tried using magic, but it didn't matter. He defeated them all!"

"Those were all *nonfictional* Owens," Fowen said, looking disgusted. "All versions of useless old you. Of course they failed." He grinned, then waved his fingers, and the floor below Owen split in half. "Before I seal you up in the castle and go save the universe, I want to hear you say one thing. If you do, I might even remember to come back for you when this is all over."

Owen screamed incoherently, trying one last time to break his bonds. This effort exhausted him, though, and he gave up, breathing hard as he stared at the floor.

"That was incredibly sad to have to watch, Nowen," Fowen said. "Anyway, all you have to do is say the words 'Fictional Owen is the greatest Owen of all.' That's it. Do that, and I'll come back for you. Don't and, well, maybe the wall of nothingness outside the castle right now will free you. Or maybe it'll erase you, too, nonfictional or not."

Owen slowly looked up at him, his mouth dropping open. He began to laugh, softly at first, then louder and harder until Fowen's eyes hardened and he held up his hand, ready to cast another spell.

"Shut up!" Fowen shouted. "Why are you laughing?"

"Because . . . ," Owen said, trying to catch his breath.

"Because you actually care that you're the best Owen. You really do! That's *so humiliating* for you!"

"Right," Fowen said, and waved his fingers. "Enjoy your time in the castle."

And with that, Owen slowly lowered into the floor of the castle, now potentially his tomb.

CHAPTER 50

"You can't beat him!" Owen shouted at his fictional twin as he slowly descended into the mouthlike chasm in the floor. His mind raced, trying to think of a way out, but all he could come up with through his terror was a bargain. "I've got the only thing that might have a chance!"

"What, your little time powers?" Fowen said, snorting. "I know he can match those. Nice try."

Time powers? That wasn't what he'd meant. But wait a second . . .

Time powers.

"That's before I learned how to stop other people's time!" he shouted as Fowen moved farther away. "I learned it with Kara, while in the time prison."

Fowen took another step, then stopped and turned around

to stare at him as Owen's entire lower half now passed into the floor. "It *could* work," Fowen said, tapping his finger against his chin. "He never mentioned that power, so it's possible he has no idea. And if I could get in close enough . . ."

There it was. Fighting back a smile, Owen pretended to be freaking out as he proceeded to reel Fowen in like a fish. "*You?*" he said. "I'm the only one with the power, Fowen. Magic can't recreate it. Charm made it. She modified my DNA. You have to let me go, or Nobody will win."

Fowen slowly grinned, and Owen knew he'd fallen for it. "Maybe I can't give myself your powers," Fowen said. "But if I used magic to put *my* mind in *your* body . . . I'd still remember all my magic, but have your time powers too. I'd be unstoppable!"

Owen was now up to his neck in the floor, and he winced, wishing Fowen would just get on with it. "No, please, don't," he said, trying to act as scared of that idea as he was of being entombed in a castle made from picture books.

Fowen grinned even wider. "Oh, this is brilliant, Nowen. I'm actually a little impressed that you thought of it. Granted, you knew about it and I didn't, but for you, that's still saying something." He gestured, and Owen flew up out of the castle floor.

He let out a huge sigh of relief, but made sure to still look scared. "You can't take my body!" he shouted. "Please, Fowen! I'll say you're the best. You *are* the best! You're the best Owen of all Owens!"

"That's right," Fowen said, closing his eyes to take in Owen's praise. "I *am*. And you're easily the worst. But that's all about to change. Because from here on out, I *am* you."

"NO!" Owen shouted, but Fowen wiggled his fingers, and both of their heads began to glow.

The light grew brighter and soon blinded Owen as the spell holding him in midair released, dropping him to the floor. That made sense . . . Fowen wouldn't want to be trapped when he switched into Owen's body. For a moment Owen considered attacking while he had the chance, but he was far too weak to do much at this point.

Besides, waiting would lead to something *much* more satisfying.

The light became more intense, and suddenly Owen was floating again. He still couldn't see or feel anything either, but at least he did have a sense of movement this time.

And then he felt his feet hit the floor, and the light started to fade. As the room grew darker, Owen waited for his eyes to adjust. Finally, he could see enough to watch his own body rubbing its eyes from across the room.

"You switched us?" he shouted, needing Fowen to do one more thing.

"I sure did," his fictional self said, now in Owen's nonfictional body. "I've been a little jealous of these powers, I'll admit it. Why not? Now that you've admitted I'm the best Owen, what do I care what you think anymore?"

"You've outwitted me again," Owen said sadly, wishing Fowen would hurry up and get on with it.

"I'd ask you how to use the powers, but I know you'd just lie," Fowen said. "Besides, I'm pretty sure I can figure it out. Why don't I test them by speeding up my time, then seeing how many times I can punch you before I get tired?"

"No, please, don't," Owen said again in a monotone voice, covering his smile with his hand.

"Too late!" Fowen said, and laughed joyfully as his body began to vibrate. Faster and faster it moved, and various parts of him started disappearing as his powers kicked in.

And then Fowen doubled over in pain and gasped loudly.

"What did you do?" Fowen rasped, collapsing in a heap.

His body continued vibrating as Fowen convulsed with pain, then stopped abruptly as he lost consciousness.

Owen moved quickly to his side and felt for a heartbeat. The robotic heart now in Fowen's body had stopped, and for a moment, Owen knew he could stand up and walk away, and no one would judge him for it.

Instead, he fell to his knees and started pounding on his old chest using the CPR lessons he'd been taught in school, just as Charm had done for him.

A minute passed, and he started to worry. Yes, he hated his fictional self, and Fowen had erased Charm from existence! But he couldn't just let him die, either. Even someone as terrible as Fowen didn't deserve that.

Another minute, and Owen began to panic. "Wake up, you jerk!" he shouted, rhythmically pumping Fowen's chest over and over. What if this didn't work? Could he maybe use the last shot in Dr. Verity's possibility ray gun to make Fowen's heart work again? But no, the heart was trapped in a nonfictional body, and the possibility weapons didn't work on nonfictionals.

Just as he was about to give up, Fowen sat up with a start,

sending Owen tumbling backward. Fowen sucked in a huge breath, his eyes flying open. "What . . . what . . . huh?" he said, his voice almost too soft to hear.

Owen wiped the sweat off of his forehead, exhausted but relieved. "I saved you," he said simply.

"You . . . you *tricked* me," Fowen said. "You tricked me *again*!"

"Sure seems like it," Owen said, throwing Fowen's smirk back at him. "Guess that means you're not the best Owen after all, are you?"

"What . . . what's wrong with me?" Fowen asked, still gasping for air.

"That'd be your fictional robotic heart," Owen told him. "It's just barely hanging on. But it should be okay as long as you don't do anything strenuous, like use your time powers, or probably cast any magic spells. But don't worry, I know of a place that will take good care of you. And if you do happen to die, you'll be good as new the very next morning."

"What do you mean?" Fowen said as Owen stood up and ripped a page in the air, revealing a small cot in a dark, humid jail cell.

"Welcome to the Jules Verne Memorial Time Prison,"

Owen said. He took Dr. Verity's possibility ray gun from his fictional self's pocket, picked Fowen up, and shoved him through to the Time Security Agency's prison for time offenders in Kara's story. "Watch out for the dinosaurs. I feel like I remember them biting."

"You . . . you can't leave me here," Fowen said. "I'm *you*! You can't do this to yourself. You have to be better than this. Be better than me!"

"Oh, Fowen," Owen said, shaking his head. "Didn't I already explain this? I don't *care* if I'm better than you."

And then he slammed the page closed, cutting off anything else his fictional self had to say.

For a moment, Owen just stood there, a shudder running through his body. Then he fell to his knees and dry heaved as the past few moments all crashed in on him at once.

Charm and Kara were gone (he couldn't even think it without almost breaking down), he had no idea how Kiel was doing, and now his mind was in Fowen's body, which meant . . . what? At least his heart was working again, but now he couldn't speed up time if he needed to, much less anything else.

He was now completely and utterly *normal*, just as he was

about to face Nobody. And if he lost here, the fictional universe got erased. Everyone he knew here, everyone he'd ever read about, gone completely. Not to mention that he'd get sent back to the nonfictional world to be operated on, and—

Wait a second. His heart wasn't robotic anymore. What did that mean? Had he broken the cycle of all the Owens failing to beat Nobody? Did that mean he actually had a chance?

Or did it mean that this was all going to be over, once and for all, even if Owen lost?

There was no way to know, so he had to assume it was all down to him. Him, and the one shot he had to take down Nobody, literally.

Owen shuddered and tried to push back to his feet. He failed at first, as his hands were shaking too hard, but finally he got his feet under him and stood up, though the shaking didn't stop. He shoved his hands into his pockets and touched Dr. Verity's ray gun, feeling the tiniest bit of hope.

"Nobody!" he shouted as he entered the throne room, trying to sound confident. "I'm here! I beat all your challenges. Now give me Bethany back!"

"You did indeed defeat my challenges," said a familiar voice, and the wall behind the throne at the end of the room disappeared, revealing the featureless man, Bethany next to her fictional ghostly self in a glass cylinder, and what looked like Doc Twilight hanging motionless in the air. "And now, it appears, we have finally arrived at the end of your story, Owen. Let's try to at least make it a good one, shall we?"

CHAPTER 51

It all came down to this. Owen tightened his fingers around the possibility ray gun in his pocket. He'd only get one shot before Nobody would destroy the weapon. But that was okay, considering it only had one charge left anyway.

"Owen, he'll send us back to our world if you just give up," nonfictional Bethany said. "It's going to be okay. He'll even send my dad with us!"

He looked at her for a moment, at both Bethanys watching him nervously. Had Nobody really agreed to that? Even if he had, there was no reason to believe him, not anymore.

"Was it worth it?" he asked Nobody softly, waiting for the perfect moment. If he could get Nobody talking, and therefore distracted, he might have a chance. "Everything I went through to get here, everything you put me and my friends through . . . was it just to get revenge? Or did you have fun watching us suffer?"

"I could ask you the same question anytime you read a book," Nobody said. "I don't see a difference."

"The difference is you *made* this happen! This is all on you!"

"*You* created this world, Owen," Nobody said, shaking his head. "Don't blame me for your mistakes. Speaking of that, in your original story, I seem to recall you rewriting many of the city's inhabitants while making your way here, and even the King of All Stories at the end. Why didn't you try that today?"

Owen ground his teeth together, not liking where this was going. "Because . . . because they're *real*. They exist. I didn't know, I didn't realize when I was writing—"

"And yet, your ignorance has resulted in a city filled with real people," Nobody said. "People you've limited with your wordplay and writing metaphors. Did you enjoy meeting your creations?"

This was a mistake. Debating wasn't going to distract Nobody. This is what he lived for. "I might have written this place into existence, but Dr. Verity said nonfictionals just create these worlds, and then the fictional people take it from there. Whatever these people choose to do—"

Nobody cracked a grin in his otherwise featureless face. "The good doctor *guesses* at things he has no experience with. But that's neither here nor there. The only question I have now is this: What should I do about you?"

Owen blinked, a little surprised by this. "Um, are you taking suggestions? How about you reconnect the worlds, join Bethany back together, and then put everyone back where you found us?"

Nobody laughed. "Ah, no, I'm afraid that won't happen. Besides, I have been quite merciful with you so far, and you haven't seemed to appreciate it."

"Mercy?" Owen said, his eyes widening. "When exactly was that? You trapped me in a time prison with dinosaurs. I think one might have *eaten* me at least once! Not to mention—"

"And yet, you still didn't learn anything."

"What was I supposed to learn? How much of a crazy, evil villain you've turned out to—"

"You were supposed to learn how wrong you are!" Nobody roared, his body growing larger in his rage. "I have shown you many times over that your people are a pestilence upon mine, that your control over our possibilities imprisons us, holds us back. But you refuse to see!" He clenched his fists for a moment, then abruptly released them and slowly began to shrink again. "I have been merciful until now because I hoped

that you would come around, that you would learn. But that's clearly not going to happen. So if reason won't reach you, then you leave me with no other choice."

Owen took a step backward nervously, throwing a look at both Bethanys. Only the fictional version would look at him, though. Nonfictional Bethany just stared at the floor instead.

If his stupidly ridiculous long-shot chance at beating Nobody was going to work, he'd need Nobody to get closer to him. But doing that meant he'd be in range of Nobody's horrible, stretchable arms. Granted, it wasn't like he was really out of Nobody's reach even now, so what was he going to lose? Might as well jump in with both feet.

"So, what, you're just going to kill me?" Owen said, trying to sound tough. "You don't have the *guts*."

Nobody stepped closer, and he brought his hands together in front of him like he was asking for forgiveness. "Of course not, Owen. I'm no monster, no matter what you might think of me. I would never hurt you, not if it can be avoided. But I can't allow you your freedom, either."

"Oh, so you're going to control me like you think nonfictionals control you? *That* makes sense," he said, taking another step closer to Nobody.

"If you had learned your lessons, you'd have lived free for the rest of your days," Nobody said, stretching out his arms. "This is on you, not me."

"Sounds like you're trying to convince yourself of that," Owen said, taking one more step closer. If Nobody did the same . . .

He did. The featureless man took another step, shaking his head. "No, I know I am in the right here. Now, I'm afraid I have no choice but to—"

Owen grabbed the possibility gun from his pocket and quickly aimed it at Nobody. "No choice?" he said quietly. "Don't worry, I've got one more possibility for you."

Nobody cracked another smile. "You think you'll have more luck than Dr. Verity did? I can absorb any possibility you could inflict upon me, Owen. Not to mention that ray gun only has one charge left."

"That's all I need," Owen said. He took a deep breath, steadied his hands, and pictured the possibility he wanted Nobody to experience. Then he pulled the ray gun's trigger.

A beam shot out, striking Nobody right in the chest. He stumbled forward, an awkward expression on his featureless face.

"What did you . . . do?" he said, then grabbed for his chest as a hole began to open within him.

Mason Black, writer of the Doc Twilight comics and sort-of grandfather to Bethany, slowly pushed out of Nobody, then fell to the ground in front of him.

"No!" Nobody shouted.

"Oh, yes!" Owen said. "Go ahead, Nobody! Rewrite yourself now. You've lost your nonfictional anchor, so you'll disappear if you try!"

As the hole closed in his chest, Nobody stood up straight, then launched his hands out toward Mr. Black. Owen just stared in shock. How was he still rewriting himself without fading away like Bethany?

"No, please!" Mr. Black shouted. "You can't put me back in there. Haven't I suffered enough?"

Nobody picked the writer up and brought him back toward his chest, where the hole reopened. "No amount of suffering will ever be enough," he said quietly, then reabsorbed the old man back into himself.

Owen fell to his knees, unable to believe he'd failed *again*. Just like a thousand other Owens, just like the last two times he'd faced Nobody, Owen had been completely useless. The one plan he'd had, to inflict the possibility that Mr. Black would escape from Nobody, hadn't even worked. Which meant that everything he'd gone through to get here, the friends he'd lost, was all for nothing.

"So that's it?" he whispered to Nobody. "You're just going to erase the entire fictional universe, and that's that?"

"Owen, I'm not erasing anything," Nobody told him, almost gently. "I'm starting it over from the beginning, the way it should have happened. Everyone who exists today will have every possibility of returning, and if they do, they'll be free to become whatever they wish. And this time, whoever they become will be entirely their own choice, not that of some author in a distant universe."

"Who decides who comes back, Nobody? You? So now you're the author of everything?"

"I will be nothing like an author," he said, staring down at Owen sadly. "I do it for *their* sake, not for anyone's entertainment. I am saving this reality from a terrible burden that's been inflicted upon it since its beginning: the imagination of non-fictionals."

"You're saving it all by destroying it! Do you even hear yourself?"

"I'm done arguing, Owen," Nobody said. "I made a promise to Bethany that I would send you and her home, with her father. But that was before you . . . changed." He reached out a hand and set it on Owen's shoulder. "You are fictional now. Traded bodies with your fictional self, I take it? Unfortunately, I can't send you back to the nonfictional world, then. You wouldn't belong there anymore. You, along with *all* of my people, must once again become possibility."

"That's not what you promised!" nonfictional Bethany shouted, but Nobody ignored her. He slowly reached a hand to his chest, and Owen went cold all the way down to his toes as the man pulled open another hole in his body.

"No!" Owen shouted, scrambling backward, but Nobody grabbed him with newly formed third and fourth arms, holding him tightly.

"You have forced me to do this," Nobody said, opening the hole within himself wider, now big enough to fit Owen in. As Owen stared into the darkness within the monster, he could make out a tiny Mason Black, somehow shrunken within Nobody's body. There had to be magic involved.

But he wasn't alone, either.

Owen looked closer, then gasped, pulling away.

"Say hello to James Riley," Nobody said as a second tiny person—a red-haired man Owen didn't recognize—peered around from behind Mr. Black. "Once upon a time, when Mr. Black refused to teach me to write, I sought out another non-fictional author instead. Mr. Riley wasn't much, but I gleaned enough information from absorbing him that I was able to follow your story, and Bethany's, too."

"His name was on that *Story Thieves* book," Owen said, things starting to fall into place.

"Seemed only fair to give him the credit," Nobody said. "Since I absorbed him, he and Mr. Black have helped anchor me whenever I've rewritten myself, enabling me to reach heights I'd previously never even dreamed of, even after the worlds split." He smiled. "If *you* had anything to offer, I would absorb that, too. But I can't imagine what that could be. I've already absorbed everything I could from your fictional self, and Kiel Gnomenfoot." His featureless face seemed to frown. "I once thought I might learn magic that way, but apparently knowledge can't be absorbed like talent and ability. Shame. But the Magister provided what I needed in that department anyway."

"You had Fowen in here?" Owen asked, swallowing to keep from throwing up.

Nobody nodded. "When I absorbed him, I thought at first that he didn't have much to offer either. But soon I realized I was being far too lenient on my fellow fictionals, and began to conceive of the plan to erase everything to restart it all. Perhaps some of that was your fictional self's influence. Or perhaps I've had that side of me somewhere all along."

"This wasn't the deal!" Bethany shouted from behind them. "You said you'd return me, Owen, and my father to the non-fictional world."

"Circumstances have changed," Nobody told her as his two extra arms pulled Owen toward the hole in his chest. "If you defy me on this, Bethany, our deal will be off. Would you give up your life with your parents for one friend?"

"No!" Owen shouted, kicking at Nobody's arms, but every blow just disappeared into his flesh without a mark. "You can't do this! *Please!*"

"Good-bye, Owen," Nobody said, as his body enveloped Owen, closing around him. "You've always been a disappointment."

"Bethany, it's not too late!" Owen shouted as the light began to fade. "You have the power to—"

And then Nobody closed his chest, and Owen was gone.

Nobody turned to Bethany, who was staring at him with wide eyes. "If you'll excuse me for just one moment, I need to make sure all three of these gentlemen are secured. Wouldn't do for them to have any chance to escape in these last moments. I shouldn't be long, and I promise to be back before the world disappears. Wouldn't want to miss that, after all."

Before she could say a word, his head melted down into his body, as did his arms and legs, and soon there was just a large block of featureless torso left.

CHAPTER 52

Let him out!" Bethany shouted, then ran over to Nobody and began punching what remained of him as hard as she could. Her fists pushed into Nobody's body like it was a beanbag, and she howled in frustration, but she didn't stop.

It took a moment before she even realized Nobody hadn't reacted, let alone moved. Even worse, she was getting tired and couldn't even tell if her punches were accomplishing anything. Had he even felt them?

She stopped hitting the monster and stepped away from him. "Hello?" she said, waving her hand in front of him, but again, she got no response. Was he really in his own body, helping Owen get absorbed?

Or was she just so inconsequential that he didn't need to even bother with her?

Behind her, she heard a sound of breaking glass, and she

whirled around to find her fictional self smacking her cylinder with mostly solid hands, as the rest of her grew even more translucent. "What are you doing?" Bethany yelled, running over to her. "If you break that, you're going to dissolve away into nothing!"

"What choice do we have?" her fictional self said, her voice muffled by the glass. She kept hitting it as it cracked further, but didn't shatter. "He's got Owen!"

"If you come out of there, you're going to disappear," Bethany said quietly. "Unless we rejoin, I mean. And if we do that . . . we'll lose Dad."

Her fictional self shook her head violently. "Nobody already broke the deal. We can save both Dad and Owen if we *fight*. We just have to stand up to him!"

"But what if we lose? We'd be losing Dad forever, not to mention Owen!"

"We've already lost Owen! I'm not going to just let Nobody have him, deal or not. Dad would want us to fight."

"Dad would want us to think things *through* and figure out what makes the most sense!" Bethany shouted back.

"Stop being such a coward!"

"I'm trying to protect Dad!"

"He doesn't need your help!"

"But *you* obviously do! Look at you, you're barely there. And whose fault is that?"

Fictional Bethany glared angrily at her, then slowly floated back to the bottom of the glass cylinder. "You're right," she whispered, so softly Bethany could barely make it out. "This *is* my fault. If I hadn't rewritten myself so much, I'd still be able to do something here and wouldn't need you. So get your I-told-you-sos out of the way. I deserve them."

Bethany opened her mouth to do just that, then took a deep breath instead. As she released it, she brought Gwen to mind again, remembering how amazing it felt to have a friend who just liked you for who you were, no matter what mistakes you made.

"I'm just as much to blame," she said finally. "If I'd let us take more risks, we maybe could have stopped all of this before it started. I was so afraid of getting in trouble that I held us back, even when it made sense to jump in."

"You just wanted to protect us."

"And you just wanted to save our friends and Dad." She shook her head. "But it doesn't matter what got us here, not anymore. We need to decide what to do *now*."

"I'm not leaving Owen inside Nobody," fictional Bethany said. "Even if it kills me, I'm going to try to rescue him."

Bethany stared at her for a moment, then looked up at her father, floating motionless in midair. *Is that really what you'd want us to do?* Her eyes fell on the Twilight symbol on his chest, and she knew the answer to her question.

Fictional Bethany was right. Their father would never want his own safety to come before anyone else's.

"Okay," she said to her fictional self. "Let's get you out. We can't join back together with you stuck in there."

Her fictional self stared up at her in surprise, then smiled and began banging on the glass even more enthusiastically. Bethany looked around for something to help her and spied the possibility ray gun Owen had used on Nobody. "Hopefully this will be good for *something*," she said, then ran it back to her trapped fictional self and used the ray gun's handle to smash the glass from the outside.

With them both working on it, the glass shattered quickly, and fictional Bethany poured out of the container and onto the floor like a misty fog. She lifted one semisolid hand toward Bethany, who bit her lip, then pushed her own hand toward her twin's.

"This is going to hurt," Bethany said, wincing. Her twin winked at her and grabbed her hand.

As their fingers touched, an uncomfortable pressure filled her hand, like her skin was too small to contain all of her. As their fingers slowly merged, the pressure grew worse, and without even realizing it, Bethany started to pull her hand away. But strong fingers grabbed her wrist, holding on.

"We can do this!" her fictional self said, now much more solid as she held Bethany's arm with her nonmerged hand. "Don't let go, or we'll lose Owen!"

"I know that!" Bethany shouted as their hands and wrists came together, and she bit her lip to keep from groaning at the pain. "I just want it . . . to hurry up!"

Their arms slowly pushed together, and now pain started shooting up to her shoulder. Bethany growled and stamped her feet, just trying to distract herself. "When we're . . . back together," her fictional self said, sounding just as uncomfortable, "what's the plan?"

"You're asking *me*?" Bethany said. "That's . . . new!"

"I can't keep . . . jumping without looking first," fictional Bethany said. "You need to hold me back for both of our sakes!"

"Right now," Bethany told her, gritting her teeth, "I think

it's time . . . for you to go *wild*. Give Nobody . . . everything you've got!"

Her fictional self looked at her almost gratefully, only to be yanked away by an enormous hand.

"Oh, Bethany," Nobody said, shaking his head, holding her fictional twin off the ground. "Should you really be out of your cage?" He squeezed his fingers together, and her fictional self let out a scream of pain. "You've broken our deal. And you know what that means."

"No!" both Bethanys screamed at once, but Nobody had already turned to their father.

"Once more, you've let him down," he said to them, gesturing with a free hand. Doc Twilight dropped to the ground in a heap, then slowly looked up at the scene before him.

"Girls?" he said in shock, then turned to Nobody. "Let them go!"

"You have but a moment left before you disappear, Christian," Nobody said to him. "Do you really want vague threats to be your last words to your daughters?"

Their father looked down at himself, then raised a translucent hand and watched as it disappeared. *"No,"* he whispered, then turned to his daughters. "Bethany, both of you, I love you more than you could possibly imagin—"

His mouth faded away, but his eyes still stared at them, filled with both fear and love as tears slowly passed through what remained of his body.

And then even those disappeared, and their father was gone.

CHAPTER 53

"YOU MONSTER!" fictional Bethany shouted, rewriting her arm into a huge sword. She swung it right through the arm holding her, but the sword just passed through him, his body opening and closing as it passed, never completely separating.

"You knew the rules," he told her. "I thought of all things, your father would be able to keep you under control. But not even his life was enough. This is entirely upon *you*."

She cried out incoherently and stabbed at him again and again as her body started fading away, just like their father's.

"Bethany, stop!" nonfictional Bethany shouted up at her twin. "You're going to disappear too!"

"I don't care, as long as I take him with me!" she shouted, finally freeing herself as she stabbed through the hand holding her in the air. It disappeared as the sword passed through it, and she fell to the ground hard.

"I cannot allow that, I'm afraid," Nobody said, letting fictional Bethany's strikes pass right through him as he spoke. "I must be left to restart our world, to build it anew. But I don't believe you have long left before becoming potential. Perhaps I won't bring you back in our new world. I can't have you constantly trying to change things back, after all."

Nonfictional Bethany stared at the spot her father had just been, and tears rolled down her cheeks. She'd lost him, and this time, it *was* her fault. Both Bethanys were to blame, and now she was going to lose her fictional self too, not to mention Owen.

She had to do something. But as she turned to watch her other self fight against Nobody, she realized she had no idea what.

Fictional Bethany had all of the imagination, and that left nonfictional Bethany with no ideas of where to even begin.

"Fight me, you coward!" fictional Bethany shouted, launching herself straight at Nobody in the shape of a rocket. He caught her right before she hit him, though, and slammed her into the floor so hard the castle shook.

"There's nothing you can do to stop me," Nobody told her calmly, holding her down. "Even if you were whole, you'd have no hope of defeating me. Not when I can match any rewriting you do myself."

Fictional Bethany struggled against his grip, morphing into several things and growing fainter by the minute. She shouted in frustration, and her eyes locked on Bethany's, pleading for help.

Be more fictional, she heard Kiel say in her mind. But that was the last thing she could do now! She literally didn't have it in her.

But maybe she could take a lesson from someone who did?

"I'm afraid this is the end, Bethany," Nobody was saying to her fictional self. "I truly intended to bring you back into my new world and give you the family you were always meant to have, just with a few changes. I could never allow your father to return. He would never consent to live under my new order. But now you shall join him in whatever lies beyond possibility. Say good-bye to your nonfictional self."

"How can I?" Bethany whispered. "She's gone."

"What?" Nobody turned his head to look, just as a rocket ship slammed into his head, this one identical to the one fictional Bethany had made a moment earlier. The impact sent him crashing through the castle wall, collapsing it around him.

Fictional Bethany, now free, slowly stood up and looked through the hole in the wall with surprise. "Bethany?" she said quietly.

A moment passed, and then nonfictional Bethany stumbled through the rubble, shaking her head. "Sorry I couldn't think of anything original," she said, limping toward her fictional twin. "Without an imagination, I had to steal from yours."

"But how did you do that?" her fictional self said as she continued fading away.

Bethany grinned. "Hey, I still have my superpowers. Charm changed our DNA, so we both got them when we split. I just never had a good reason to use them before."

Fictional Bethany laughed, then hugged her twin with what was left of her arms. Bethany hugged back for a moment, then separated. "Ready?" she asked.

Fictional Bethany nodded. "I'm so sorry for everything I did. I promise to listen to you from now on."

"Don't," nonfictional Bethany said. "We need us both. Look at us separately. Neither of us is working right. Maybe we don't need to live in harmony so much as just try to be happy with each other." She smiled. "I'm trying to be more like Gwen and just think the best of everyone."

"Solid role model there," fictional Bethany said, and pushed herself into her twin.

"No!" Nobody shouted from the hole in the wall. An enormous hand grabbed the rubble and pulled him back into the throne room. But this time, he was too late.

The pain was still there as they merged, like their skin was too small to hold all of them. But somehow, Bethany found it more bearable as their bodies and minds merged, becoming one again, becoming half-fictional again.

This feels . . . better, one version of her said in her mind, though she could no longer tell which one.

This feels right, thought the other version. *I had no idea how much I was missing without you.*

And then there was just Bethany Sanderson, complete and whole. The pain disappeared as quickly as it had come, and she turned to face Nobody, a smile on her face.

"Well, well, well," she said quietly, cracking her knuckles. "Look who's back."

A sneer appeared on his face. "It doesn't matter!" he shouted. "There's nothing you can do to stop me!"

"Let's test that out," she whispered, then rewrote herself into a giant fist and punched him through the wall again. As he went crashing through, she gave herself Owen's time powers and sped up time so that she appeared right next to him as he flew, then rewrote herself into a giant anvil, dropping on him as he landed. The force of the impact sent a quake running through the remaining walls of the castle, tumbling them to the ground.

Nobody roared in anger as Bethany rewrote herself back to normal, completely whole this time, thanks to her nonfictional half. He shoved one hand at her face, only for it to disappear inches from her, turning into a mist of some sort. His other hand punched her in her stomach, and she doubled over, inhaling the mist automatically as she sucked in air. "I just infected you with the most dangerous viruses to ever exist," he said as she quickly covered her mouth. "You'll be dead within seconds if I don't cure you. Now *stop* this!"

Bethany's eyes widened, and she rewrote her entire body into pure flame. The intense fire scorched the viruses out of her system, and she rewrote herself back to normal. "It's not too late to end this," she told him. "We can bring the worlds and everyone back. Together I'm sure we can find a way to turn back the possibility wave, and—"

A thousand fists exploded out of his chest, flying at her head.

She put up as many arms as she could create to block them, but a few got through, and she cried out in pain. "I never wanted this, Bethany," he shouted as more of his fists got through her defenses. "I thought you would see reason and go back to the nonfictional world. I never wanted to see you harmed!"

"Enough lies," she snarled, rewriting her new arms into a solid metal shield and pushing back to her feet. "You think you're such a hero? You're erasing everyone in this reality just because you're annoyed that someone might have thought you up. Oh, no, *join the club*. We're *all* created by someone else. They're called parents."

"I want to do what is *right* for my people!" Nobody shouted, and slammed his hands into her shield, splitting it in half. As she rewrote it back into her body, Nobody brought his hands down, right at her head.

This time, she saw it coming and rewrote her upper half to separate around his hands, then join back together, trapping him. Another rewrite, and she cut his arms off completely, then threw them as far from them as she could. "Fine," she said, rage filling her. "Then I guess I'll just cut you into pieces until I find Owen!"

Nobody shook his head. "You have no idea what I can

become, child. It doesn't matter how little or how much of me remains. That's the beauty of possibility!" He pointed up at the wave of nothingness that had now reached the top of the castle. "I will survive this wave, Bethany. The possibility will overwhelm your nonfictional heritage. The two nonfictionals within me will anchor me while you are washed away, like a fire razing a forest to allow for new growth. Surrender now, and I promise I will bring you and your friends back in my new world!"

Bethany glanced up at the wave above her head and the nothingness it left behind, then turned back to Nobody. "Here's my answer," she said, and grew a mix of magical and science-fictiony armor out of her skin, then rewrote her right hand to grow a massive glowing sword.

"Very well," Nobody said, matching her with a sword of his own and growing a similar suit of armor. "Then I shall destroy you utterly!"

He reared back to attack, only to pause, a strange look on his face.

Then, out of nowhere, thirteen separate hats grew out of his head.

CHAPTER 54

Owen opened his eyes to find himself in a familiar-looking white space of nothingness and immediately panicked. "Hello?" he shouted, circling around, searching for someone, anyone who might be able to help. "Mr. Black? Other guy? Can you hear me?"

No one answered, and his heart began to race. Was he stuck in here, inside Nobody? But how was there this much room? Nobody wasn't that big, not usually. Had Nobody rewritten himself to be bigger on the inside than the out? Was that even possible?

The nothingness extended in every direction, as far as he could see, so he tried running to his right. Only no matter how far he went, nothing changed. It was just like when he'd been behind the scenes in Jupiter City . . . or in the nothingness that the Magister had stuck him in, back when Bethany had first taken him into the Kiel Gnomenfoot series.

That raised some terrifying questions too. Had he been inside Nobody those other times as well? Nobody had shown up both times in person, yes, but for someone who could rewrite their body, it wouldn't be difficult to make a smaller version inside himself.

"Let me out!" he shouted finally, more for his own sanity than anything. The idea that he'd be stuck here while Nobody did whatever he wanted to Bethany and everyone else made him want to punch something. But there wasn't even a wall of Nobody to hit anywhere. He tried stomping as hard as he could on the ground, but the ground didn't seem to mind, and it hurt his foot, so he quickly gave up on that, too.

So what, this was it? He'd failed against Nobody for the last time, and now he was just going to be another nonfictional that Nobody had absorbed? Just like all the other Owens . . .

Except the other Owens had been sent back to the nonfictional world, where their hearts didn't work. But he hadn't been because he'd switched bodies with Fowen. Did that mean he *wasn't* destined to lose, like all of his other selves?

Except he'd *already* lost. Just because he'd found a new and exciting way to do it didn't all of a sudden give any reason for hope. So great, he'd become fictional and now wouldn't even get another five years to live, not with the possibility wave coming.

All in all, being fictional was really not all it was cracked up to be.

Some small part of his mind seemed to object to that. Something about being fictional was . . . important, somehow? Owen furrowed his brow, trying to think of why it'd matter. Now he could be erased by the possibility wave, so that wasn't exactly a great thing. And if he went back to the nonfictional world, he'd probably slowly stop working, just like his heart. No, being fictional didn't give you anything good except . . .

Except being able to rewrite yourself.

Owen gasped so loudly it echoed. Without waiting another moment, he concentrated as hard as he could on his hand, just as he'd seen Nobody do, both in comic panels and in real life. He clenched his jaw, willing whatever words made up his hand to rewrite, to change into describing a cat's paw instead.

And as he watched, fur began to grow up from his skin. His fingers merged together to form a paw, and claws extended out from where his fingernails had been.

"WHOA!" he shouted, swiping at the air in front of him with his new, awesome, if not terribly inspired cat claws. It hadn't been the *coolest* rewriting he could have done, but this was his first time, and more importantly, it worked! *That* was what mattered. He quickly rewrote his hand back to normal, ready to try again, only to realize something was missing.

One of his fingernails was gone.

This must be what had happened to the fictional Bethany. And that meant if Owen continued rewriting himself, even a bit, he might disappear too. A chill went down his spine as he imagined turning translucent, then gradually fading away into nothingness. Would he still know what was happening if he was just pure potential? Or would that basically be . . . it? The end?

Owen dropped his head into his hands, not sure what to do. If he stayed his normal self, he could be safe and whole, at least until Nobody was erased by the possibility wave. And that could be anytime now. On the other hand, if he rewrote himself, there was a chance he might help his friends and actually stop Nobody once and for all, just at the cost of disappearing completely.

An image sprang into his mind: sitting with Charm in the Magister's tower before facing Dr. Verity at the Source of Magic. The moment he'd found out that Kiel Gnomenfoot had to sacrifice his own heart to save everything, Owen had just wanted to go home, to forget about being a hero like Kiel. But Charm had talked him through it, made him realize that he couldn't just abandon people who needed him, whether they were fictional or nonfictional.

And really, how were things any different now?

"Maybe I'll get to see you again when we're both possibilities, Charm," he whispered, then sighed. That didn't seem likely, but at this point, it was the only thing he had to hold on to.

Owen squeezed his eyes shut, picturing Charm in his mind for one last time, then began to concentrate. There was only one thing he could think of that might stop Nobody at this point. Whether it would work or not was still pretty debatable, but there weren't any other options.

"I am now an *author*," he said as quietly as he could.

In his mind, he imagined himself as a writer, coming up with plots, characters, settings, everything. He imagined having the power to write a story and make it real. He imagined creating characters, and a plot for them to live out. He imagined a setting, an entire world for them to live in. Heroes, friends, villains . . . especially villains.

And then he imagined he could rewrite them. All of them. Especially the villains.

In his mind, he became an author. But more importantly, he became *Nobody's* author in particular. Not Mr. Black, but someone who could change Nobody just like Nobody believed authors could.

He slowly cracked one eye open and looked down at himself. He looked exactly the same as he had before, only now there was a laptop in his hand. That made sense, he supposed. Maybe that was how his imagination had decided he was going to rewrite things?

Weirdly, he was also missing a shoe. Odd, but maybe that was a normal author thing, to always forget one shoe. Either that, or his imagination had some strange ideas.

The important question was, had it worked? Owen dropped to the ground and opened the laptop. The screen brightened, revealing an empty page.

Nobody, he wrote, *suddenly is able to be rewritten by Owen Conners, author.*

He paused, then hit enter and waited. Nothing happened, but that made sense too, because he hadn't really changed anything yet. First, he'd have to experiment a bit.

Nobody loves wearing thirteen hats all at once and does it all the time.

Okay, that was a bizarre place to start, but why not? Owen hit enter, only to brace himself as the ground shook all around him. Had it worked? The nothingness still looked like, well, nothing. But something had happened. Maybe Nobody now wore thirteen hats. If not, it couldn't hurt to try his big gun:

Nobody releases the two nonfictional men from his body.

CHAPTER 55

The hats absorbed back into Nobody's body almost as quickly as they'd appeared, but he seemed just as confused as Bethany did. "What are you doing?" she said, ready to attack again in case this was a trap.

"Owen," Nobody whispered, then gasped as two adult men started to push out of his body. One of them saw Bethany and reached for her desperately, but before she could even move, Nobody pushed them back inside his chest.

Joy filled her as she realized Owen was not only still okay, but attacking Nobody from inside the monster's body. "Owen!" Bethany shouted as loudly as she could. "Whatever you're doing, try it again! He's scared!"

Nobody snarled at her and attacked her with his enormous sword. She blocked it with hers, then sent a wave of electricity through her arm and into his sword. The energy exploded into him, sending him stumbling backward. He quickly morphed into wood, a nonconductive material, which canceled out the electric shock. She leaped forward, slicing at his vulnerable wooden arm, only to have her sword bounce off metallic armor once more.

"You can fight *me*," she said, slowly grinning, "or you can stop Owen. But I'm guessing you can't do both at once."

"I can do *anything*!" Nobody shouted, right before fur sprouted out from his empty eye sockets.

Nobody has fur for eyes, Owen wrote.

Nobody only eats roses while thinking about the ocean.

Nobody loves to wear blue on odd-numbered days.

The shaking grew worse with each possibility, and suddenly a body rose out of the nothingness beside him, forming into Nobody. Before he could speak, Owen quickly typed:

Nobody can't see Owen inside of him.

"Owen!" Nobody shouted, his voice echoing within his body as his featureless face turned toward Owen, then past him. "Where are you? I imprisoned you here, and you shouldn't have been able to leave. What are you doing to me? Why can't I find you?"

Owen quickly typed more rewrites.

444

Nobody lived on the moon and drank from the sun.

Nobody walked backward and wore mushrooms for shoes.

Nobody got chicken pox three times as bad as anyone, ever.

The smaller version of Nobody screamed as various possibilities bubbled out of him, only to get absorbed back into his body. All around Owen, the shaking grew more intense, and now he could actually see *shapes* through the nothingness, as if Nobody's body was fading away around him.

A huge hand appeared within the body, big enough to crush Owen. It reared back, then crashed down toward Owen as he quickly wrote: *Nobody's hand is intangible to Owen.*

The hand passed right through him, and Owen grinned, wondering what else he could do. This was kind of fun!

That's when he noticed that he could see through the entire lower half of his body.

Bethany swung her now-dual swords at the mushrooms on Nobody's feet, trying to keep him off-balance. He leaped backward to avoid the blows, but he wasn't quick enough, and her swords cut through both of his ankles. He shouted in pain and started to topple over, only for new legs to grow out of his back, catching him before he hit the ground.

Bethany grinned. "You know, you're starting to look a bit transparent around the edges. You really should be more careful with all of this rewriting."

Nobody glanced down and growled at the sight of his see-through hands. "It won't matter!" he screamed. "None of this will. You can't defeat me, Bethany. I will save the fictional world no matter *what* it costs me!"

He drove his sword forward, and it cut into her side, right through her armor. She gasped, quickly knocking his weapon away, but the blow left her off-balance, and Nobody seized his moment, growing multiple arms and swords to strike her again and again.

The force of his attacks sent her reeling backward, and she could barely keep up with his swords, trying to match every newly appearing sword with one of hers.

"*I* am the hero here," Nobody whispered to her, driving all of his blades down toward her head as his body shifted and morphed with Owen's rewrites. "Don't you see, Bethany? You were always the villain in this story!"

"Pretty sure that's what every villain thinks," she grunted, then dropped backward, using her momentum to fling Nobody over her and into the floor a few yards away. Instantly, she rolled to her feet and tossed three flaming Twilight stars at him. "Recognize that move? It's one of my dad's favorites!"

The throwing stars struck Nobody right in his face, and he started to absorb them, only to stumble forward as one of his legs completely disappeared. "Owen!" he screamed. "You will suffer like *no* nonfictional ever has!"

Nonfictional? Owen looked down at his missing lower torso. Not anymore.

With all of this rewriting, he didn't have much time left. And now there'd be no Kiel Gnomenfoot to switch places with him, to save him before the end. But he couldn't stop, not if he wanted his friends to make it out of this.

This was for Bethany. For Kiel. For Kara.

For Charm.

Nobody's pants never fit.

Nobody dreamed of being a dentist for clouds.

Nobody learned real magic just to be a stage magician and wondered why no one believed him.

The smaller Nobody had disappeared at some point when Owen looked up from his laptop. Now that he could see through the nothingness, though, he watched in amazement as each of his ideas pulsed out over the larger Nobody.

Entire heads pushed out of Nobody's body, each one of them a different version of the Nobody Owen was writing. Various hands and feet tried to move the central Nobody in their own directions, all their own characters, as other limbs slowly disappeared, the rewriting overpowering even Nobody's nonfictional anchors.

Just beyond Nobody, Owen could barely make out Bethany dressed in some kind of amazing magical armor, striking with, like, fourteen swords at the monster. He grinned in spite of himself. Between the two of them, they actually had a shot at this.

Nobody can't stop his nonfictional prisoners from escaping.

"Yes!" Bethany shouted from outside, and leaped forward toward Nobody. Her hands grabbed for something out of Owen's vision, then returned with two tiny arms: Mr. Black and the red-haired guy, both incredibly small for some reason. She yanked them backward as Nobody screamed, and the men abruptly expanded to normal size as Bethany stepped in to block Nobody from retrieving them.

Had . . . had they done it? Nobody wouldn't have his anchors anymore, which meant he couldn't protect himself against the rewriting. Had they won?

Owen turned back to the laptop, but now saw that the ground he was sitting on was as transparent as glass, and felt just as fragile. Below him, he could see straight down to the ground, what looked like hundreds of feet below.

Uh-oh.

Had Nobody shrunk him, or had the monster grown in size at some point? What would happen if Owen fell? He might be able to rewrite himself into having wings, but there was no guarantee he'd even stay together long enough for that to work.

But none of that mattered. He couldn't stop, no matter what! If he let up for just a moment, Nobody might still find a way to reabsorb his nonfictional prisoners and pull himself back together. No. Owen had to stop Nobody completely, once and for all.

And he had to do so before he disappeared himself.

All right, imagination, Owen thought to himself. *Let's do one last huge burst of weirdness. Give it all you've got. Everything depends on this, right now. So . . . write!*

For a moment, his fingers paused over the keys, and he felt panic fill his chest. Had he just now run out of ideas? Really, right now, this had to be when writer's block hit? What if that dentist-for-clouds thing had been the high point, and Owen would never come up with anything like that ever again? What if he could never even *write* again? The whole fictional universe would be erased, and so would all of his friends!

Owen took a deep breath, then put his fingers back on the keyboard.

Owen starts having confidence in himself, he wrote.

And just like that, he did.

Nobody secretly hates Christmas because he never got the pony he wanted.

Nobody is a potato.

Owen's right hand disappeared, but he didn't slow down, just switched to typing with his left.

Nobody lived to be ten thousand years old, but he always had a bad back.

His entire right side was gone now, leaving just his left hand, arm, and head.

Nobody loves broccoli so much he gives up everything else in life just to build a home out of it, where he lives happily ever after, just the broccoli and him.

Now his left fingers began to disappear too, and Owen realized he only had seconds left. But Nobody was still absorbing the ideas! He needed something better, something that would stop the monster from ever hurting anyone again.

And then he realized what he had to do, and he quickly typed it out.

Nobody loses, *and turns into pure possibility.*

Outside, Nobody's heads and potatoes and poems all roared in terror as more and more possibilities pushed out of his body. "You can't do this!" the heads and such all shouted. "I will *not* just fade away!"

"I don't think you have a choice," Owen heard Bethany say quietly.

"You will pay for this!" Nobody shouted. "Whatever happens to me, I will ensure that you and those you love will get what you deserve!"

Owen's left index finger paused on the keyboard, the last part of him that hadn't turned ghostly. Then he typed the individual letters of one last line:

Nobody gets what he *deserves.*

As soon as he hit the enter key, Nobody's body disappeared. So did Owen's.

CHAPTER 56

"No more!" Nobody shouted, changing in too many ways to count before Bethany's eyes. "Please, Owen, stop! I only wanted to help my people!"

Bethany couldn't even speak as she watched the featureless man in front of her try to absorb the vast possibilities erupting all over him. Had Owen really done all of this? But how?

Nobody shrieked in terror one last time, then dissolved away, his gaze locked on Bethany as he disappeared.

As soon as she realized what was happening, Bethany leaped forward, hoping to catch Owen as he appeared. But there was nothing left, not a sign of either Nobody or Owen.

"Owen?" she shouted as the possibility wave above her seemed to jump closer, as if Nobody's disappearance had added to its power. "Owen!"

He *had* to have escaped. There was no way he could have

done all of that to Nobody and not made it out himself. It just couldn't be possible!

"Bethany!" said a voice, and for a moment, she felt hope as she whirled around, hoping to see her friend. A mixture of disappointment and relief flooded through her when she saw Kiel picking his way over the blocks of storybooks, making his way toward her.

And with him, of all people, was Dr. Verity.

"Beth, you defeated Nobody!" Kiel shouted as they got closer. For some reason, he was helping Dr. Verity, his shoulder under the old man's arm. Apparently a lot had changed while she was gone.

"It wasn't me," she whispered, but he couldn't hear her. As she started to raise her voice, she noticed something lurking behind Kiel and readied herself for another fight. "Kiel, watch out!"

Two bookwyrms stood up on their hind legs, their giant clawed hands in the air. "We have no wish to fight you," one of them said.

"You defeated the master, freeing us," the other said. "For that, you have our thanks."

Kiel glanced back at them with disappointment, then sighed deeply as they flew off low to the ground, avoiding the possibility wave above them. "Maybe another time," he said.

"What is going *on* here?" one of the nonfictional men said, the older of the two. "Where are we?"

Bethany just looked at them sadly, not sure at all how to explain any of this. "We'll get you home," she said, not sure if she was lying or not. "Don't worry. Just maybe find a place to hide for right now."

The two men looked at each other, then took shelter behind some of the rubble from Bethany's fight against Nobody.

"Beth, Verity has an idea of how to keep everything from being erased," Kiel said. "It might be our only shot at surviving this."

"That I do," the scientist said. "The Magister and I tried it on our home worlds, but we were too late. He disappeared into possibility right as he sent me here in order to warn you, and maybe offer you a bit of hope." He looked around. "Though we might not have what we need here."

"We'll figure it out, just tell me the plan," she said, shaking her head. To have come this far and defeat Nobody, only to lose Owen and then still fail . . . it'd be too much to take.

Dr. Verity's goggles spun and clicked as he focused on her. "Ah, wait a minute!" he said. "I take that back. It looks like *you* are just what we need. I'd thought my plan would require

Nobody, but it seems that you'll do just fine. Do you remember when I shot him with my ray gun? How he absorbed all of the possibilities I gave him?"

Bethany nodded, weirdly remembering it from two different spots in the room. Being whole again was apparently going to take a little getting used to.

Dr. Verity pointed up at the sky. "Well, that up there is just more of the same. If you can absorb it into yourself—"

"If she can *what*?" Kiel shouted. "You didn't tell me that was the plan. Absorbing that much would be impossible. It'll destroy her!"

"I'd hoped we'd be able to either convince or compel Nobody to do it, honestly," Dr. Verity told him, actually looking sad. "But perhaps with your nonfictional anchor, you'll be able to control it."

Bethany just stared at the scientist, not sure what to say. She could absorb the possibility wave . . . into herself? Yes, that's what Nobody had done against both Dr. Verity and Owen. But this was different. The wave in the sky above them was *everywhere*, and on all worlds. It'd already erased entire planets! She'd *definitely* lose herself in the possibilities. There was no way she could do this!

Kiel ran over to her and grabbed her shoulders. "Beth, you *can't* do this," he said, more serious than she'd ever seen him. "There has to be another way."

"I'm open to suggestions," she told him as the wave began to slice into the remnants of the castle above their heads.

Kiel took her hands and held them tightly. "What if you don't come back? I can't let you do this. Let me go instead."

She stared at him for a moment, then broke out laughing. Kiel looked confused at this, and a little hurt, but this just made Bethany laugh harder. "Oh, Kiel," Bethany told him. "That's sweet, but you can't do this. I'm the only one who can."

Kiel slowly nodded, pointing down at the symbol on her superhero costume, which she hadn't even realized she'd kept when she merged. "Your father would be proud," he whispered. "He trained you well."

She glanced down at the symbol and smiled. "He did, didn't he? But he wasn't the only one." She ran a finger over the Twilight icon, and quickly rewrote the costume to now include a picture of the planet Earth next to the moon and stars. "Sometimes you have to learn how to look past your own mistakes and forgive yourself."

Kiel furrowed his brow, probably having no idea who she

was talking about, but there wasn't much time to explain. Bethany raised her head toward the wave of nothingness above them and clenched her fists to keep from screaming.

This was going to end her, erase her entirely. There was no way she'd come back from it.

But if she didn't do it, the entire fictional world would suffer the same fate. And there was no one else who could.

So that just left her. Twilight Girl. The half-fictional girl.

Bethany Sanderson.

"Find Owen for me," she told the others as she began to rise up off the ground, having rewritten herself the power to fly. "I . . . I don't know if he made it. But if he did, make sure he's safe. I couldn't stand it if . . . if neither of us got back."

Kiel nodded, and Dr. Verity did too. "You're saving us all," the scientist said quietly. "Thank you."

She didn't know how to respond. "Just trying to be me," she said, then gave Kiel one final look.

Then she soared up into the possibility wave.

From below, Kiel and Dr. Verity watched as Bethany hit the wave and immediately disappeared, dissolving into the same nothingness as everything else it touched. "No!" Kiel shouted. "It was too much for her!"

"Maybe," Dr. Verity whispered. "Maybe not. We have to have faith, my boy."

The wave grew closer, now just a few yards over their heads. There'd be no escaping it now, even if there was somewhere to go. As it drew closer, Dr. Verity sighed and lowered his head.

"I must have been wrong," he said. "I'm so sorry, Kiel. For you and her. I thought she could handle it. But maybe she never had a chance after all."

"If she didn't, none of us did," Kiel said, still watching the sky as it pushed forward, now just a foot over his head. "Goodbye, Dr. Verity. I've enjoyed the new you much more than the old version."

"Me too, my boy," Verity said, crouching to avoid the nothingness. "Me too."

As they both shut their eyes, waiting to be erased, something strange began to happen in the sky above them. The wave, invisible except for where they could see it dissolving the world around them, started glowing bright white and getting brighter by the moment. The light was blinding, but both of them looked up from behind raised arms.

"What's happening?" Kiel shouted at Dr. Verity.

The scientist slowly smiled. "Well, I don't have all the data, but my best guess is: She did it."

The sky continued to brighten, now too much for even their covered eyes. Both Kiel and Dr. Verity turned away, unable to watch, but even that didn't block out the light.

"Bethany!" Kiel shouted into the nothingness. "Come back to us!"

But there was no response.

Just as he thought the light was going to sear right through his eyelids, it abruptly cut out entirely, and everything went dark.

Kiel blinked hard, waiting for his eyes to adjust, but all he could see was a bright streak wherever he looked. "Is it gone?" he asked. "Beth? Are you here?"

Dr. Verity clicked his goggles a few times and scanned around. "The wave is gone, my boy!" he said happily, then sighed deeply. "But so is Bethany."

CHAPTER 57

Nothing existed.

Everything was possible.

Anything she could possibly want . . . was she a she? . . . was up to her. She could become whatever. She could control all things. All she had to do was decide, and everything and anything could be hers.

But how did one decide things? Where did you even begin? She could decide to know how to decide, but that involved a decision. And without deciding, there was still endless potential, so there was no hurry. Besides, deciding things just felt so . . . permanent. Why bother when anything could be . . . anything? She'd have to think about it to be sure, at least. A few million years could pass, and she could decide at that point.

Maybe by then she'd know who she had once been?

Except why did she have to be whoever she'd been? She

could change everything. She could be anyone, or anything. There was nothing beyond her, and no possibility out of her power. Why be dragged down by the past? Here, there wasn't any past, just potential.

Bethany. You can fix this. You've got the power to make it right!

She heard the words, but she wasn't sure who or what had said them. Make things right? What did that even mean? Here, everything was right and everything was wrong, all at the same time. How could someone make anything right? Why would you take away the possibility of it being wrong? What if right actually *was* wrong, and she made a mistake?

Worlds were erased. You can bring them back. The nonfictional part of you gives you that power. I believe in you!

Worlds erased? But what about the worlds that had never been? None of that mattered. The only important thing was what *could* have happened, what *could* happen now, or later. What actually happened was the boring part.

This isn't reality, not the one you know. You can beat this, I know it.

Reality? Who cared about reality? She had the power to make any reality. All reality was formed from chosen possibilities, and she had the power to choose whichever one she wanted.

But when she could have infinite realities, why pick one? Why not just enjoy the idea of them all instead?

They need you. And you need help, someone who knows them, as much as anyone can. Bring him back.

Him who? Him . . . that could be an infinite number of possibilities as well. She started to sort through them, but a name kept appearing over and over, from wherever the voice was coming from.

. . . Owen? That was the name. Owen.

A flood of images appeared before her. A normal-looking boy, with brown hair and a goofy smile. A friend. Someone she'd been on . . . adventures with. What adventures? She wasn't sure. She looked back through the possibilities and felt something like joy. There were so many of them! And all of them would be so entertaining to explore.

He knows stories, so many stories. Use his knowledge to restore the worlds. Bring him back!

Back? Where had he gone? But it didn't matter. This Owen brought her joy, so it was an easy choice for once. She wanted an Owen, and so, an Owen would now exist, just like the one that seemed the most likely in her mind. Flying through possibilities, she quickly found one that said Owen had lived through his fight with someone named Nobody, and she chose that.

Owen appeared just like the images, floating in nothingness. "Whoa!" he shouted. "Where am I?"

She looked at Owen and knew that had been the right decision. Within his head, she could feel . . . ideas. They were possibilities, yes, but possibilities with direction, with focus. And this focus . . . it was intriguing.

But who was the other voice? She decided that she needed to see that person too, to better know why they were speaking. So she decided to make that person known.

A middle-aged man in a purple cape and red costume appeared in the air right next to Owen, who jumped, though he couldn't really go far, given that he was floating. "Gah!" he said, then seemed to realize something. "You're . . . Doc Twilight?!"

The caped man smiled. "We've never officially met, have we?" he said. "My daughter's told me all about you, though. And I couldn't be more proud of you than if you were my own son."

Owen turned a deep red color, which seemed odd. What other colors might he turn? So many possibilities. "But what are we doing here?" Owen asked. "Where *is* here?"

The man's face fell. "Bethany managed to save the entire fictional world, Owen. But to do that, she absorbed an infinite number of possibilities and is having some trouble making up her mind about what to do with them." He looked around in all directions, as if he were searching for someone. "She has the power to restore all the stories that were erased by Nobody's wave of infinite possibility. And I suggested she bring you back because you've read so many of them."

"Wait. Bethany's here?" Owen said, looking all around him.

She watched and listened and understood, or didn't. That wasn't entirely clear. This caped man seemed . . . special to her. But partly unknown, as well. Who was he?

The man looked up from Owen, and she heard his voice in spite of his lips not moving. *I am a memory you created, Bethany Sanderson. You needed a trusted voice to help guide you, and so you brought me here. But you can recreate the true version of your father. You can bring us both back to where we belong.*

Where she belonged? She could literally belong anywhere she wanted!

The man smiled. *You're right about that. But you weren't always what you are now. Once, a version of you saved an entire universe, kept it from dissolving into what you are now. That ver-*

sion of you still exists, somewhere in here. You can bring it back and fix things. You can even reconnect two realities that desperately need each other.

"What's happening?" Owen whispered.

"Bethany's trying to figure out if she should rebuild the fictional universe and reconnect it to the nonfictional one."

"I don't hear anything," Owen said, giving the man an odd look. "How can you know what she's thinking?"

"Because I'm not really me," Doc Twilight said. "I'm just the memory of her father, not the true thing. She needed someone to guide her, and she subconsciously brought me here to help talk her through this."

Owen slowly nodded. "I have no idea what that means," he said, but he turned around. "Bethany?" he shouted. "You should listen to him! He knows what he's talking about, even if he is just a memory! Also, um, thank you for bringing me back?"

This Owen made her want to laugh, whatever that was. And this memory raised interesting possibilities. But why stop at connecting the two realities? Why not rejoin them completely? There could be *one* reality, united, just like she was. It'd be easy to do with the power she had now. And that felt right, like a good decision.

Whoa, uh, we might not be quite ready for that, the man said without moving his lips. *Maybe someday, but for now, we still have a ways to go. But if you come back, there'd be no one more suited to helping them get where they need to be. And then you could fully join the worlds.*

This caped man seemed intent on her returning somewhere. But why would she return? She was perfectly happy here.

"Bethany?" Owen said. "You should come back to us! Whatever you have to do to fix things, that's great, but come back, okay? I want you to. So does Kiel and EarthGirl and—"

The names immediately filled Bethany with strange feelings, and she instantly knew that they represented correct decisions, both of them. Even with an infinite number of other possibilities, she knew that there could be no two more important than whoever this Kiel and EarthGirl were. . . . Gwen? Yes, that seemed right.

They would have to come back, she decided. And to do that, they would need worlds.

And those worlds would need more worlds, if just to stay in their proper place. She reached out without hands and pulled image after image from Owen's mind, using his knowledge of stories to rebuild world after world, fictional after fictional, moving more and more quickly so she could get back to the magical boy and the superhero girl.

If you don't anchor them, these worlds will disappear once more, the caped man told her. *You'll need to build portals between them and the nonfictional world.*

Portals. Those felt like good decisions as well. She passed through each possibility, liking what she saw, then found hundreds more just like them and decided to go with all of them.

Wait, you can't create so many—

She ignored the caped man as joy filled her. The portals were too much fun, and now she knew what she wanted to do.

I will send you, the real *you, back,* she told the caped man in his mind. *Back where you belong. But do not worry. I will come too, when I'm done here.*

The caped man grinned, and she saw that his face was wet. "That sounds perfect," he whispered out loud, then disappeared as she returned him to his proper story.

"Where did he go?" Owen asked, looking all around. "Bethany? Are you still there?"

She *was* Bethany, that was clear. And if she wished to see those other humans again, to once more be friends with this

Owen, she would have to return to being Bethany again, just as she'd promised the caped man.

But what about all of the possibilities she'd be leaving behind?

Of course, even as a human girl, she would still have possibilities, wouldn't she? She followed that idea, what she would become if she returned to being human and found a string of possibilities that stretched out even farther than she could see. That made her feel joyful, so it was correct.

So yes, she would become this Bethany again. And she would bring this Owen back to his friends.

But first, she decided on one last possibility, one last choice she had to make before she left.

She decided that this, of all possible endings, would be a happy one.

THE END

UNCHAPTERED

"U gh," Bethany said, reading the last line of *Story Thieves: Worlds Apart*. "I never said that! I never even *thought* it. I even told this James Riley guy exactly how it went, and he made me sound all corny!" She groaned. "I never should have let him finish the series and publish it over here in the nonfictional world."

"Oh, I love it!" Gwen said at her side, wiping her eyes with the back of her hand. "It was the perfect way to end things. I was so worried about Owen, too!"

"You love everything," Bethany said, hugging her with one arm. "That's my favorite thing about you."

"Did I really help you forgive yourself?" Gwen asked her, blushing slightly.

"More than I even told Mr. Riley," Bethany said.

"I'd like to know why I was out of the story for so much of it?" Kid Twilight said from the roof of her house, where he was keeping watch over her quiet, nonfictional neighborhood. "And why do you always call me Kid Twilight? Use my real name."

Bethany slowly blushed. "Um, I'm not sure I know it?"

"What?!"

"You *want* me to know your secret identity?" Bethany asked. "And would you come down from there? There's no crime happening around here, at least not until Kiel shows up."

Kid Twilight snorted. "That's what the criminals want you to think. That's how they get you."

Someone opened the door behind them, and Bethany and Gwen both turned around to find Bethany's father and mother standing there, her father's arm around her mother's waist. "Did you finish the book?" her father asked.

"Yes, and I loved how it all ended!" Gwen said.

"It was kinda clichéd, I thought," Bethany told him with a shrug. "That guy needs to work on his writing if he's ever going to get anywhere."

"Did you know she doesn't know my real name?" Kid Twilight said from the roof above them.

Doc Twilight grinned. "Oh, come down from there, Orion. The city can take care of itself for a bit."

"Hey!" Kid Twilight shouted as Bethany and Gwen both started laughing. "You can't just give away my secret identity!"

"Like the constellation?" Bethany asked as soon as she could breathe.

"My parents were astronomers, okay?" Kid Twilight said. "They told me I'd shine as brightly as the stars!"

"And so you have," Bethany's dad said as now even her mom joined in on the laughter. "But come down. We're going to make s'mores."

"Nice!" Kid Twilight said, and landed on the ground right beside Bethany, then pushed past her parents into the house.

Gwen stood up and held her hand out to Bethany to help her up. "You were so nice to read the story to us!" she said. "Are you coming in?"

"In a minute," Bethany said, staring at the cover of *Worlds Apart*. "You go. I'll be right behind you."

Gwen patted her on the shoulder, then left with Bethany's mom as her father sat down beside her.

"I'm really impressed that you let that author release Nobody's books in the nonfictional world too," he said, tapping the cover. "You didn't need to."

She shrugged. "I was just so tired of hiding. Besides, there are so many portals now into the fictional world, it'll be nice for people to know why. Not that any of them will believe it's true anyway, unless they happen to find one."

"Is Owen coming over later?" he asked.

Bethany shook her head. "Now that we've freed all the Quanterians from their books and returned them to the fictional world, he, Kara, and Charm are back in the library, trying to restore all the worlds I missed. He thinks that reading their books will recreate the worlds. He might be right . . . it's worth trying, at least."

"Charm is reading . . . fiction?" her father asked.

Bethany grinned. "I think she might be there more for the company, honestly. She won't admit it yet, but she forgave Owen, and now she barely lets him out of her sight."

Her dad laughed, then patted her shoulder. "I haven't said this enough, but Bethany, I'm so very proud of you. Everything you've done, saving me, saving the fictional world, all of it . . . it's all down to you and Owen."

"Mostly me," she said, winking.

He snorted. "And there are thousands of portals now into the fictional world. People will find their way across in both directions, just like I did. Maybe you won't be the only half-fictional person in a few years, even."

She gasped. "Don't even joke. Could you imagine the destruction another me could cause?"

He grinned. "There have already *been* two of you, but I prefer the whole you best. I think you made the right call on that one." He stood up and offered his hand. "Ready for s'mores?"

"Just another second," she said. "I just want to look at the stars. Tell Orion I can see his belt."

Her dad chuckled and walked back into the house. Bethany heard the door into the house close behind him, then waited for another minute before glancing around, making sure she was alone.

"Did you bring it?" she whispered into the darkness.

"You're going to get us both in trouble, you know," Kiel Gnomenfoot said, stepping out of the shadows. "I want your dad to like me!"

"What he doesn't know won't kill him," Bethany said. "Now give."

"First, I want you to look at something," he said, and handed her a copy of *Kiel Gnomenfoot and the Source of Magic*. "Turn to the epilogue."

"You know I've read this one," she said, then paused, looking over the pages. Her eyes widened in surprise, and she read more quickly, then slammed the book shut. "Are you kidding me? Do you think Owen knows about this?"

"I doubt it," Kiel said, shrugging. "It's a new printing of the book. Jonathan Porterhouse sent me a copy to show me the change. Should we tell Owen?"

"I think he'll find out in his own time," Bethany said, then held out her hand again. "Now give me what I asked you to bring."

Kiel broke into a grin and handed over a new wand-knife, one that had been formed from two others: a simple, straightforward black wand-knife wrapped with a spiral wand that had tiny stars glowing from within it. "Now, magic isn't for everyone. Some people take a little while to get the hang of it—"

Bethany swung the wand around and concentrated, sending a huge spray of fireworks up into the sky. She shrieked in joy and embarrassment, then ran down the street to avoid her father, who was already on his way out.

"And some just come to it naturally," Kiel said, watching the fireworks, then turning and running off after her.

KIEL GNOMENFOOT
AND THE SOURCE OF MAGIC

EPILOGUE

Five Years Later

As you know, the tyrant Dr. Verity caused an accident six years ago that almost killed my parents and sisters," Charm told the crowd before her. "That accident took my eye, arm, and leg. Science saved me, giving me robotic parts to take the place of flesh and bone. But it took a friend with a time machine to save my family, and magic to truly make me whole."

She pointed at her now-human eye and held up both non-robotic arms. "This is what magic and science accomplished together," Charm said. "But it won't stop there. Together, Quanterium and Magisteria will become one and whole, like science and magic healed me. We shall move forward together as one planet once more, with one people of both science *and* magic!" The assembled Magisterians and Quanterians below her broke into cheers. She grinned and waved as she started to step offstage.

For just a moment someone in the crowd caught her eye. While most of the assembled people were cheering or clapping, one boy just stood silently, wearing what looked like an orange jumpsuit with some kind of writing on it. He flashed her a strangely satisfied grin, then waved mockingly and disappeared right in front of her eyes.

"Oh, come *on*," she whispered to herself, shaking her head, then rushed offstage.

"That seemed to go well!" her assistant said, a Magisterian boy just a couple of years younger than her.

"You'd be surprised," she told him. "Where's my minister of magic and science integration?"

"Here," said a voice, and Charm turned around to find Owen smiling at her. "It really *was* a good speech."

"You know I hate talking," she told him, grinning back.

"To crowds?" he asked.

"Or anyone else," she said. "Present company excepted. But I need to tell you something in private."

Her assistant quickly got the point and backed out of the room, bowing hastily.

"You don't need to do that!" she shouted at him, then turned back to Owen with a sigh. "You have no idea how many times I've told him not to bow."

"I actually do," he told her. "What's wrong?"

She looked him right in the eye. "I think I saw Fowen in the crowd."

Owen's eyebrows shot up. "Fowen? After all this time? Are you sure?"

She rolled her eyes. "You think I'd forget what you looked like five years ago? Even an alternate evil twin version?"

He started to blush, which she loved. "Um, right," he said. "But what does he want? What . . ." He trailed off, then looked at her strangely. "Was he wearing something odd?"

"Yeah, an orange jumpsuit. Not exactly a great look for blending in here."

"He doesn't want to blend in," Owen said. "He's sending a message. That's the TSA prison uniform. He came to tell us he broke out." He paused. "Was there anyone standing near him?"

Charm replayed the crowd scene in her mind, trying not to think about how much easier it'd be if she still had her robotic eye to record things. "I don't think so. There was a bald woman next to him, and a woman with white hair?"

Owen broke into a grin. "Oh, this is going to be fun. We're going to need Kara, though. If we can drag her away from Jupiter City."

Charm sighed. "I really hate Orion, and we'll never get Kara without him following her like some puppy. Do we really need her help?"

"Trust me," Owen said. "She's sort of the expert on this stuff."

"You haven't told me what the problem is yet," Charm said, glaring at him.

"I wouldn't call it a problem," Owen said, glancing down at his hand as he rewrote it into holding a ray gun. "More of . . . an adventure." He grinned at her, ripped open a page right there in midair, then held out his hand to her. "Ready, President Mentum?"

She sighed, thinking about her list of upcoming meetings. It wasn't easy, bringing the entire population of Magisteria back to Quanterium where they belonged, then convincing two planets full of people who hated one another that they needed one another, that one side had grown complacent and unimaginative, while the other was nothing but imagination.

Two sides of a whole, and neither complete without the other.

But all of that could wait.

"I suppose I've earned a few days off," she said, and winked at him, then took his hand, and together they leaped through the portal to another reality, the page closing behind them.

ACKNOWLEDGMENTS

So let me see if I'm following," Liesa Mignogna said, staring across her Batman-covered desk at James Riley. "You're telling me that you were . . . absorbed—"

"He basically swallowed me whole!" James said.

"By this faceless monster you call Nobody, which isn't the *least* confusing name I've ever heard—"

"I'm with you there."

"And then he, what, siphoned your writing ability out of you?"

"YES!" James shouted, leaping to his feet. "Like the Parasite in Superman comics!"

Liesa's look turned cold. "Don't mention that kind of blasphemy in *this* office. Batman or get out."

"Fair," James said, slowly sitting back down. "He used my author-y skills to write this series of books about these kids, right? Except they really happened! And I met the kids, when they freed me, and they said I could publish those books here, in the nonfictional world, 'cause Nobody only put them out in the fictional one."

"You know, there's no reason to pretend this really happened," Liesa said, frowning. "It doesn't really add anything to the books." She flipped through the copies James had brought from the fictional world. "I like the covers, though!"

"Those were by a fictional artist named Vivienne To," James pointed out. "Look! A dinosaur on that one!"

"Yes, I see," Liesa said, rolling her eyes. "Well, let me take a look at the books, and I'll let you know. I'll have to run them by a bunch of people first. Sarah McCabe would be editing these with me, so we can start with her. We can't go any further without senior managing editor Katherine Devendorf or copy editor Adam Smith. Mara Anastas and Chriscynethia Floyd, the publishers; Caitlin Sweeny, Catherine Hayden, Amy Hendricks, and Lauren Hoffman in marketing; Faye Bi and Jodie Hockensmith, who'd be your publicists; Sara Berko in production and Laura Lyn DiSiena, our book designer; Michelle Leo and the education/library team; Stephanie Voros and the subrights group, and Gary Urda, Jerry Jensen, Christina Pecorale, Victor Iannone,

Christine Foye, and everyone else in sales. They'd all need to get behind it or there's no point."

"That's a lot of people," James said, standing up. "Hopefully, they'll go for it. I mean, my agent, Michael Bourret, liked it okay, and he's impossible to please."

"He does have good taste," Liesa said, standing up as well. "Well, I liked those Half Upon a Time books you wrote, so I'll give these a shot too."

"Right," James said, looking at the ceiling. "Those books that . . . I wrote."

Liesa sighed. "Just . . . just go. And next time I hear from you, come up with your own, original series!"

"I will!" James said, walking quickly to the door before she could change her mind. "I've got this idea for a seven-book series, and—"

"Bye!" Liesa waved, then slowly sat down as he finally left. *"Story Thieves,"* she said, touching the cover of the first book. "Well, as long as they don't get too meta, maybe they'll be fine."

Turn the page for a glimpse
at the first book in a new
epic series from James Riley!

- ONE -

JUST MINUTES BEFORE THE ATTACK IN Washington, D.C., Fort's father was embarrassing him at the Lincoln Memorial.

"President Forsythe Fitzgerald," his dad said, pointing at the spot each word would go above the giant seated statue of Abraham Lincoln. "I feel like we're going to need a larger statue, though. These ceilings are high enough to fit that head of yours, but you're definitely going to need a bigger chair."

Fort rolled his eyes, but a grin popped out anyway. "I'm pretty sure that they don't let twelve-year-olds run for president," he said. "I think I have to be an adult, and that's when you said I was going to be leading a mission to Jupiter. And curing cancer, I think? The version of me in your head really needs to make up his mind."

"You'll do all of that and more!" his father shouted. Other

visitors to the Lincoln Memorial began to look at them, making Fort blush. "There's no time to be lazy, not with all the amazing things you're going to accomplish! And don't forget that I still want a flying car, so I'll need you to invent that too."

Fort tried to pull his father to a less crowded area, but his dad wouldn't move. "I will, if you just talk *less loudly*," he murmured as two girls slightly older than Fort stared at them, whispering. Fantastic.

"Um, I'm pretty sure as an adult, I can talk as loudly as I want," his father said. "But stop pushing us off topic, Fort. This is your future we're talking about! You're going to be a great man someday, and I for one can't wait to take pictures in front of your statue as children gaze up at it adoringly!" He waved at the two girls. "See? We've already got two volunteers!"

The girls both broke into wide smiles, and Fort felt his face burn with the heat of a volcano. "I'm sorry about this," he told them. "He thinks it's funny to embarrass me wherever he can."

"It's not *not* funny," one of the girls said.

"Intelligent youths around here!" his father shouted in response. "Listen to them, Fort. I hear that children are our future."

"*I'm* your future," Fort hissed at him. "Because once you're old, I get to decide which nursing home to put you in."

"Low blow, young man," his dad said, then pointed at Lincoln. "Do you think our beloved sixteenth president would have spoken to his father that way? And he's your personal hero!" He leaned closer to the girls conspiratorially. "When my boy here was in diapers, he'd stroll around in a top hat and make us all call him Fort Lincoln."

One of the girls snorted, while the other turned away to hide her laughter. Fort wondered how easy it'd be to spontaneously combust. "He's making that up," he told the girls, his face getting even hotter. "And we really need to be going."

"Oh, we have plenty of time," his father said, taking out his phone. "Besides, I think I have pictures of that in here. Girls, do you want to see?"

"I'm just getting really tired," Fort said, yanking his father by his arm toward the steps of the memorial. "Maybe we should head back to the hotel?"

"Nonsense!" Fort's father shouted. "Why, we haven't seen Einstein yet. Did you know there's a statue of Einstein right off the National Mall, Fort? And the Gettysburg Address!" He pointed at the speech carved into the wall of the Lincoln

Memorial to the left of the president. "Look at this. Two hundred and seventy-two words. Short and to the point!"

A slight tremble shook the memorial, like a heavy truck was driving by. Fort looked around nervously, but the tremor only lasted a few seconds, and no one else really seemed bothered by it.

"I think President Lincoln is waking up," his father whispered to him with a grin. "Did you know a second man gave a *two-hour* speech before Lincoln at Gettysburg?" He handed Fort a brochure with the Gettysburg Address written out in multiple languages. "I don't see that speech carved in marble, do you? If that's not proof that shorter is better, I don't—"

A second tremor hit, this one more violent. Several people shouted in surprise around the memorial, and Fort almost lost his balance, barely avoiding dropping to his knees on the marble. He looked up at his father in alarm. Was this an earthquake? What was happening?

His father reached over to steady Fort as the trembling stopped again. "Ladies, maybe you should go find your parents," he said to the two girls they'd been talking to, then turned to Fort. "Are you okay, kiddo?"

"Totally fine," Fort said, pretending his heart wasn't still racing. "It was nothing."

"That's the spirit," his father said, though he looked a bit shaken too. "But maybe we *should* head back to the hotel and grab some dinner. Einstein can wait. After all, time is his relative, I think. Probably a cousin."

Fort couldn't even bring himself to roll his eyes. Instead, he shoved the Gettysburg Address brochure in his pocket, and started to make his way through the now-unsettled crowd toward the stairs. As he reached the top of the steps, something strange caught his eye in the distance.

The Lincoln Memorial was surrounded by a circle of roadway, with the Reflecting Pool stretching out from the memorial to the Washington Monument almost a mile away.

But even from that distance, Fort could see lines of people quickly leaving the monument in every direction.

That wasn't a great sign. But the strangest thing about it was that as far as Fort could tell from this distance, all the tourists were running from the monument in single-file lines, each person moving at the exact same speed.

"Dad, do you see that?" Fort asked, turning around just as a third tremor struck, this time much worse than the last two. The stone of the memorial leaped straight up, throwing Fort a foot in the air. He landed hard as the stone cracked beneath him in a jagged lightning shape all the way down the steps.

"Out!" Fort's father shouted, pushing the girls toward the exit before grabbing Fort's hand and yanking him down the stairs.

They made it down to the street circling the memorial, with horrifying noises coming from behind them. The shaking grew more intense, and now people by the Reflecting Pool were running off, again in single file, one behind the other, not even looking as they crossed the street. Fortunately the cars had all stopped and the passengers had exited their vehicles, merging smoothly into the lines of fleeing tourists.

As odd as all of that was, even stranger was that no one was screaming in fear, yelling for a friend, or even saying a word. Instead, they were all deathly quiet, moving in unison like some sort of flash mob they'd been choreographing for months. The sheer silence of those fleeing sent a chill down Fort's spine.

A horrible new cracking noise erupted across the Reflecting Pool, like rock scraping against rock, and Fort's father shouted something, but the grinding stone overpowered his words. Fort turned to find people near him pointing at the Washington Monument, and *they* were all screaming. That at least felt more normal to Fort than the eerie silence closer to the monument and Reflecting Pool.

"Look out!" someone yelled as a car came speeding around the circle, right toward a large group of tourists. One of the two girls from above had just stepped in the path of the car, but the other yanked her out of its way as the car roared past.

"Off the road!" his father shouted, and pushed both Fort and the girls onto the lawn to the side of the crumbling Lincoln Memorial. "We have to get out of here!"

"My mom's still in there!" one of the girls shouted. "I need to go find her!"

"I'm coming—" the other girl started to say, then abruptly stopped, turned, and ran off toward the side streets.

"Megan?" the first girl called after her. "Where are you going?!"

Fort's father looked back up into the Lincoln Memorial, then down at Fort. "Wait here," he said. "Don't move until I get back! I'm going to go find their mother."

His father took the cracked steps two by two, pushing up against the crowd like he was swimming up a waterfall. Fort waited for a moment, then ran after him, followed by the remaining girl.

"Look!" someone shouted behind him.

"It *can't* be real," someone else said, filming with his phone.

Fort threw a look over his shoulder for a moment, then froze in place, halfway up the steps.

Next to the Washington Monument, something was pushing up out of the ground.

Something that looked like . . . claws.

Claws that were ten feet tall.

TWO

WHAT IS *THAT*?!" THE GIRL NEXT TO Fort shouted, her voice cracking with terror.

Fort couldn't respond, could barely breathe. This wasn't happening. This type of thing only happened in movies, not in real life. Definitely not in the middle of Washington, D.C.

Enormous black-scaled fingers pushed up through the ground, sending grass, rock, and dirt flying in every direction. A muffled roar sounded from somewhere beneath them, and Fort felt it even through the ground shaking.

"You get him, I'll grab her!" Fort heard his father shout from somewhere in the memorial, but Fort couldn't move. Fear pulsated through his body with every racing heartbeat, freezing his feet to the marble steps like he'd been sculpted there.

TV helicopters flew overhead toward the monument, only

to suddenly reverse course as they approached, flying back over the city. Sirens played in the distance too, but somehow never made it any closer. And now the crowds on the monument steps below Fort began to run off in silent waves, as if a command to escape was passing up through them one at a time. But even with the insanely ordered evacuation, the shaking ground made it hard to move, let alone run, and many of them lost their footing as they escaped.

"This can't be *real*!" the girl next to Fort said as one of the clawed hands reached up to the Washington Monument and grabbed it with its hundred-foot-long fingers. The obelisk began to tilt, then topple toward the ground.

When it hit, the ground jumped beneath Fort's feet, and he found himself flying in the air, only to slam into the steps a few feet up.

"Lauren, where is Megan?!" a woman shouted from above him. Fort looked up to find the girls' mother carrying an old man, one Fort had seen earlier in an electric scooter. "Where did she go?"

Lauren started to answer, only to go silent as her eyes glazed over. Without another word, she turned around and ran down the steps, away from her mother.

"Lauren!" the woman shouted, stumbling against the trembling ground.

"Dad?" Fort shouted up.

"Fort, get out of here!" his father shouted from somewhere inside. "I'll be right behind you!"

Fort looked back at the devastation across the National Mall, then turned back toward the memorial and forced his feet to move up the stairs, one after the other. *Don't look at it,* he thought, gritting his teeth to fight through the fear. *You can do this. Dad needs your help!*

He took a step, then another, fighting to keep his balance while trying not to think about the horrific creature emerging from the ground behind him. His father *needed* him, and there was no way he was going to let him down. He had to—

RUN.

The thought hit his mind like a hammer, and Fort instantly straightened up, his mind blank, then turned and ran down the stairs. In the distance, he could see the remnants of the Washington Monument, but that didn't matter. Nothing seemed to mean anything beyond leaving in an orderly fashion.

RUN.

He hit the bottom of the steps and ran toward the line of people escaping—

"Fort!" his father shouted, and somehow, it cut through the fog in Fort's head. He slowed to a stop, then froze in place, one foot hanging in midair.

RUN!

The power of the command crashed over him like an ocean wave, drowning out all his other thoughts, and he started jogging, merging in line with the other runners. But as he reached the side of the Lincoln Memorial, he slowed again, then stopped, shaking his head.

What was he doing? His father was still up there!

A young woman plowed into him from behind, knocking him off his feet. She stumbled a bit, then continued running like nothing had happened. Fort stared after her for a moment in confusion, then looked back up the stairs to find his father carrying an older woman who'd been with the man on the scooter.

Fort pushed himself up and made his way back to the steps. "Dad!" he shouted. "Are you okay? I can help!"

"No, just go!" his father shouted, waving with one hand as he slowly tried to maneuver down the shaking stairs.

Fort ignored him and started crawling up the steps on all fours. As he reached the halfway point, though, the marble beneath him exploded, throwing him off into the grass to the side of the memorial. For a moment, everything went blurry and he couldn't breathe, the air knocked right out of his lungs.

And then two ten-foot tall claws pushed up through the steps where Fort had been standing, and a roar shook the ground, a sound so powerful Fort could feel it in his chest.

A noise like torrents of rushing water thundered behind him, and he turned to find a nightmare rising from the middle of the Reflecting Pool, a giant black-scaled head covered in horns like some sort of crown. The water drained down into the hole it created, and the creature roared again, revealing what looked like row upon row of massive razor-sharp teeth. Its red glowing eyes stared down in fury, and the sheer impossibility and terror of it froze Fort in place. He couldn't even think, let alone comprehend what he was looking at.

More helicopters flew in, this time painted black, and these actually made it close to the creature. A missile rocketed out of one, slamming into its head, but the monster didn't even seem to notice.

"Fort!" his father yelled from above. Fort looked up to find his father on his knees on the steps just below the creature's fingers. The roof was crumbling down all around him, sending huge chunks of marble crashing into the steps.

"Dad!" Fort shouted, and tried to get to his feet, but the shaking was too intense.

The creature's hand pushed the rest of the way out of the stairs, closing around his father and the woman he'd been carrying. Fort's heart stopped as he watched his father disappear behind those scaly fingers.

But then the old woman came tumbling out from between the creature's fingers, crashing to the grass next to Fort, with his father pushing through right after her.

"DAD!" Fort shouted as the creature roared behind him. Something else hissed out of the helicopter and exploded against the creature, but it didn't matter, nothing mattered but his father getting free. He was almost there, half his body had already made it out of the creature's grasp—

But then the hand started pulling back below ground.

"Fort!" his father shouted. The creature's hand curled around him, rupturing the remains of the memorial as it descended back into the ground. "FORT—"

The creature's massive hand disappeared within the earth, and his father went silent.

"NO!" Fort shrieked, and he crawled toward the wreckage, trying to make his way to the hole his father had been pulled into.

NO. LEAVE NOW. *RUN.*

"I won't!" he shouted, not sure who he was talking to, but determined to find his father. "Dad! Can you hear me? Dad!"

He clambered up over the jagged stones, half climbing, half pulling himself toward the hole. A wave of heat swept out of the crack, almost too hot to bear, but Fort pushed himself onward and stared down into the abyss.

"DAD!" he shouted again. . . .

And then something took over, and Fort lost control of his body.

His hands pushed him away from the hole, and his feet climbed him down the rocks. Inside his mind, Fort watched his actions helplessly, almost from a distance, like he was staring down at himself from the wrong end of a telescope.

Inwardly, he screamed over and over, but no sound escaped his lips as his body continued on, jogging him away from danger and into a line with the rest of the silent, fleeing tourists.

NO! he shouted into the void, pushing back with all his strength against whatever force was taking him from his father. He fought and struggled and resisted, his efforts growing in intensity until pain filled his mind and he could barely think, the image of the creature taking his father propelling him to keep battling to free himself, to regain control over his mind, to make it *LET GO*—

And then, abruptly, his body was his own again. From an impossibly long distance, he heard a scream, and it echoed through his brain. It sounded like a girl's voice, and she was in pain, but that didn't matter, nothing mattered except that he was free and could go back to his father. . . .

But a wave of pain washed over Fort, drowning his mind in agony, and everything went dark as he collapsed to the ground.

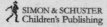